Some Wounds Never Heal

Some Wounds Never Heal

Rhonda M. Lawson

www.urbanbooks.net

Urban Books, LLC
78 East Industry Court
Deer Park, NY 11729

ISBN 13: 978-1-60162-358-4
ISBN 10: 1-60162-358-5

First Trade Paperback Printing August 2012
Printed in the United States of America

10 9 8 7 6 5 4 3 2 1

Distributed by Kensington Publishing Corp.
Submit Wholesale Orders to:
Kensington Publishing Corp.
C/O Penguin Group (USA) Inc.
Attention: Order Processing
405 Murray Hill Parkway
East Rutherford, NJ 07073-2316
Phone: 1-800-526-0275
Fax: 1-800-227-9604

Some Wounds Never Heal

by

Rhonda M. Lawson

Reviews for
Some Wounds Never Heal

Can a person ever heal and move on with her life, without ever forgiving the person who has caused them to be broken and hurt inside? Alexis White would say it is possible to keep on living, but Andrea Lee would beg to differ with her on this subject matter. For these two ladies, their lives changed fifteen years ago due to an affair that rocked the foundation of a marriage. Aside from both ladies having a close relationship with Brenda, the ladies had one other thing in common; both their lives were forever tainted due to the things that took place. The hurricane brewing in New Orleans is nothing compared to what will happen once Alexis and Andrea are in the same state and sharing friends, in Rhonda M. Lawson's *Some Wounds Never Heal.*

When Alexis and her fiancé, Jamar, left New Orleans in an attempt to get away from the impending danger of Hurricane Gustav, Alexis had a sense of foreboding of the things that were to come once they were in Virginia. She wanted to go to a place where she knew no one, but Jamar was not having it. He promised her that no drama would pop off while they were in Virginia. However, he made a promise that was as good as a blank check.

Brenda, Alexis's cousin, and Andrea's best friend, tried to fix the issues between the two people she cared about, but nothing she did worked. Brenda had come to the conclusion that it was best for everyone involved if she left well enough alone. How far would both ladies push each other before the other one lost it?

While Jamar is trying to keep Alexis from dealing with demons from her past, he realizes that something crazy is going on. Something he is too ashamed of to allow Alexis to ever get wind of. Unfortunately, the more he tried to keep her from finding out the more on edge he became. His behavior towards her caused some tension, all because he was trying to keep a secret that could possibly change the way she viewed him. What would upset her more; the secret or the fact that he even felt the need to keep a secret in the first place?

I love a book that is drama-filled, but not over-the-top; character driven but not so many characters that I cannot keep one straight from the next. *Some Wounds Never Heal* by Rhonda M. Lawson is an example of these two wonderful traits of high quality writing. There was a little mystery adding to the already tense storyline, which was an added bonus. The message of admitting and accepting, apologizing and forgiving, and understanding that we all make mistakes could be found throughout Ms. Lawson's writing. I understand that this book was the sequel to *Putting it Back To-gether*, however, I do not feel as though I have missed anything within the story since I did not read the first book. I know that I will go back and read the first book, only because the characters pulled me in and kept my attention from the first page. By going back and reading the first one, I get a little more time with these characters that kept me entertained. I recommend this book to Rhonda M. Lawson's fans and to readers looking for drama and mystery stories with a message.

Words Mosaic: 5 Mosaic Stones

—Jennifer Coissiere Words Mosaic Reviews

Reviews

In the novel *Some Wounds Never Heal,* author Rhonda M. Lawson continues the saga of Dr. Alexis White, a headstrong pediatrician with a less-than-angelic past. Fleeing from another potentially traumatic hurricane, Alexis and her fiancé, Jamar, leave their beloved New Orleans to wait the storm out in Virginia Beach. However, when they arrive there, Alexis's old stomping grounds prove to be more chaotic than Hurricane Gustav when she is forced to face all the demons from her past. From the bitterness of Andrea, the wife of the man she had an affair with during college, to the coincidental run-ins with Nikki, the ex-wife of the man she has never completely gotten over, Alexis can't seem to escape the mistakes of her youth.

Lawson delivers a page-turner with the third installment to the Alexis White series. From catfights to malicious plots, every moment is filled with dramatic highs and emotional lows. Well written, the book contains unpredictable twists and turns that should keep readers on their toes and begging for more. The title prompts the question, do old wounds ever heal? Or will an unwillingness to forgive, resentment, and lies tear friendships and lovers apart? Read the book to find out!

—A'ndrea J. Wilson, Ph.D.
Author of *Kiss & Tell, Ready & ABLE Teens,* and *The Things We Said We Would Never Do*
www.andreawilsononline.com

Chapter 1

"Déjà damn vu," Alexis mumbled, laying her head against the car window.

She and Jamar, her fiancé, had been traveling up Interstate 85 for the past hour, and the trip had grown old quickly. Her head hurt, she was tired of hearing the music on her iPod, and the constant view of the passing scenery would soon make her sick to her stomach, but not from being carsick. She just couldn't bear the thought of fleeing yet another hurricane.

"Why couldn't we have just stopped in Atlanta?" she mumbled.

Jamar cut his eyes at her, not knowing whether to laugh or get angry. She'd been in this mood ever since they left New Orleans seven hours ago. With more than twelve hours left in the trip, he wasn't sure how much longer he could put up with it.

"Woman, how long are you going to pout?"

"Until you explain to me why we have to drive all the way to Virginia Beach, when we would be perfectly safe in Atlanta or even South Carolina," she snapped without looking his way.

Jamar held back a laugh. "How many people do you know in South Carolina?"

"Nobody, but it would be a hell of a lot better than going to fuckin' Virginia Beach."

"I thought you said you were going to stop cursing?"

"Shut up!" she snapped, staring angrily out the window.

Jamar sighed and ran his fingers through Alexis's long black hair. "I know you have some bad memories there, but that was back when you were in college. I told you I'm not gonna let you dwell on that. We're going because my boy is letting us use his time-share so we can make this a vacation. On top of that, your cousin will be there. So, you won't be on your own."

Alexis continued staring out the window, digesting everything her fiancé said. They'd been through all of this before. She understood why they were going, but she couldn't bear facing the memory of her affair with Christopher fifteen years ago. She hadn't laid eyes on him or his wife, Andrea, since she left Virginia Beach, and she wasn't looking forward to seeing them again. What if they took one look at her and tried to go to war?

The fact that her cousin Brenda was also headed to Virginia Beach didn't lend her much solace. After all, Brenda was still Andrea's best friend. Even though Brenda had vowed not to let the past rule their present, the drama would be there no matter what. She'd try hard to keep them from fighting, but even Saint Brenda couldn't rule everyone's thoughts.

Alexis really hoped everyone had gotten over the affair. She certainly had. Although she'd had her own losses due to the affair, she'd grown in many other ways. Her private practice was booming, she was well known throughout the city, and her fiancé was a successful attorney. A couple weeks of sex when she was in college couldn't outweigh any of that, could it? It shouldn't, but who was to say that Christopher and Andrea felt that way?

She wasn't so worried about Christopher. After all, it takes two to tango, and he made the choice to sleep with her behind his wife's back. He'd be a fool to try to blame everything on Alexis. However, Andrea was a different story. She wisely blamed them both for the affair, but she'd never had the opportunity to give Alexis a piece of her mind. Brenda wouldn't allow it. Now that Alexis was coming back, would Andrea take that opportunity? There was little chance that she wasn't thinking about it. Andrea was from New Orleans, and Alexis knew better than most that a New Orleanian woman never forgets.

She watched a luxury car with Louisiana license plates coast past them. It was filled with boxes and suitcases, yet the driver was the only passenger. She guessed he didn't plan on returning to her beloved city.

It just didn't seem fair. Just when she thought she had gotten her life together, it had taken an ugly turn. Only three years earlier, she'd fled New Orleans with Tony, whom she was supposed to marry, before Hurricane Katrina killed that dream. Instead of living the American dream, the man she loved decided to stay in Houston and unceremoniously ended the relationship.

Now here she was, engaged to Jamar and fleeing the city again, because Hurricane Gustav decided to show its face. She knew Jamar loved the ground she walked on, but she couldn't help wondering if this would be the beginning of the end. The similarities were too coincidental. Was history doomed to repeat itself?

"Off in outer space again, huh?"

"What?" Alexis asked, shaken from her thoughts. She finally turned her head to face her fiancé. "Oh, yeah. Still thinkin' about this drama you're driving me into."

"You want me to turn around?" Jamar asked. "We can always go to Houston with your mom and them."

She made a face and tapped him on the back of the head. As much as she loved her mother, stepfather, and twenty-year-old stepbrother, there was no way she would return to Houston after what she had gone through with Tony. She would take her chances in Virginia.

"Very funny."

"I told you that you have nothing to worry about," he assured her while taking the exit for I-285. "We're going straight to the hotel when we get there. Then, after we get some rest, you're going to put your fine self into your bikini and walk down the boardwalk with me. I bet you didn't do that when you were there last."

Alexis smiled for the first time. "No, it was too damn—I mean darn—cold then."

"All right, then. Just relax. We don't even need to see old boy and his wife."

"I hope not."

"I don't know what you're worried about. You're not the same woman you were back then. You're older and smarter now, and I would hope they are, too. People do grow up."

Alexis shrugged. "If you say so, but I'll do what you said. I'm not going to worry about it."

"Good, because what you need to concentrate on is our wedding in March."

"That's if the city makes it to March," she mumbled, looking down. She kicked off her sandals and placed her right foot on the dashboard.

"Why would you say that?"

"Because as much as I love New Orleans, this will be the third major hurricane in three years," she explained. "Let's be real. Do you really think the city can handle that? The levees aren't even done yet. People aren't finished rebuilding their houses. Some of the businesses haven't even returned to the city. And the ones that did, many closed up way before Gustav came on the scene."

"Baby, New Orleans has come a long way since Katrina," Jamar said. "Besides, Gustav is only supposed to be a Category Three, and the levees can handle that. Mayor Nagin has the city ready for this one. We're not gonna get caught out there like we did last time."

"You always think you have the answers, don't you?" Alexis asked, shooting him a sideways smile.

"I know I do," he replied, popping the top of his T-shirt. "I didn't get to where I am today by playing patty-cake."

Their laughter lifted Alexis's spirits a little. A bit of worry still took residence in the back of her mind, but she did feel better knowing Jamar was with her. Any man who could put up with her attitude had to be strong.

"You can also look at it this way," he continued. "You and Brenda can go shopping for your wedding dress. I'm sure Virginia Beach has some different stuff than New Orleans."

"Yeah, I can do that," she agreed, "but what are you going to do? Your boy Kevin's not coming up, is he?"

"No, he and his wife went to Arizona."

"Are they coming back to New Orleans?"

"Yeah, they're coming back. Just about everybody I talked to said they were coming back."

"Well, that's good," Alexis said, leaning over and laying her head on Jamar's shoulder. "Maybe we *will* have a city to come back to."

"Of course we will," he replied, wrapping his arm around her. "Just have some faith." He glanced down at his fiancée and smiled. "And just so you know . . ."

She looked up. "What?"

"I don't care what New Orleans looks like when we get back. I'm marrying you there, even if it's in a rowboat floating down the middle of Canal Street."

Alexis smiled, closed her eyes, then buried her head deeper into Jamar's shoulder. Thinking of how she'd almost blown this relationship off, she could kick herself. When she had met him nearly two years ago, she was still struggling with her residual feelings for Tony and her rising feelings for her ex-boyfriend Reggie, whom she'd dated back in college. Neither of those relationships had ended well. So, in her eyes, agape love didn't lie in her future.

For the life of her, she didn't know why Jamar had hung in there. If she were him, she would have run for the hills long ago. How could a man who could have any woman he wanted put up with an attitude like hers? She wasn't sure, but she was glad he did.

"Now that's just nasty!" Jamar exclaimed.

"What?" Alexis asked, jumping from her position.

He looked at her and shook his head, his face still wearing a grimace. "I just looked out the window and saw a fat, hairy foot starin' at me."

Alexis looked past him at the car pulling ahead of them and caught a glimpse of the foot resting on the dashboard. She was disgusted but couldn't help laughing.

"At least she's comfortable."

"Yeah, but I'm not," Jamar responded, shaking his head.

She laughed again. "Now, don't act like you always look perfect. I've seen you in the morning."

"Yeah, and I've seen you when you sleep, but I would never let you go out in public like that."

"Excuse me? I don't know what you're talkin' about. I always look good."

Jamar sucked his teeth and pursed his lips. "Let *you* tell it."

Before Alexis could reply, her cell phone rang. She picked it up from the armrest on the door and checked the number.

"That's Roman," she said, then pressed TALK. "What's goin' on, li'l bro?"

"Nothin'," he replied. "Momma told me to call and see how y'all were doin'."

"We're good. We should be hittin' South Carolina in about an hour or so. Y'all in Houston yet?"

"Shit, the way this traffic is, we won't be there for another couple hours," Roman replied. "Seems like everybody and their damn daddy is headin' into Houston."

"I done told you 'bout your mouth, boy," Alexis heard her mother, Mary, snap.

Roman sighed. "One of these days I'ma be a grown man."

Alexis laughed. "Hang in there. Tell Momma and Frank we're all right and we'll call them when we get to Virginia Beach."

"A'ight, cool," Roman said. "Y'all be careful."

"How they doin'?" Jamar asked as Alexis ended the call.

"Still truckin'. Traffic's heavy."

"We'll check on them again in a few."

Alexis nodded and laid her head back on Jamar's shoulder. In turn, he wrapped his right arm around her while keeping his eyes on the road. He knew this wouldn't be an easy trip for his fiancée, but he was determined to make the best of it. He had worked too hard to get this woman to let her down now.

Chapter 2

Brenda and Darnell swayed back and forth in unison to Zapp and Roger's classic "Doo Wa Ditty." The fast beat and the funky sounds of the harmonica had the car rocking, while poor nine-year-old Elizabeth sat in the back, shaking her head and cringing in embarrassment.

"Do I . . . let me know . . . do I did it!" Brenda sang loudly, getting caught up in the music.

The sound of his wife being loud, wrong, and excited all at the same time nearly made Darnell swerve off the road in laughter.

"All these years and you still don't know the song," he said, tears filling his eyes.

"What?" Brenda asked, looking at her husband in confusion. "That's how the song goes."

"Baby, the words are 'Said I wanna blow . . . doo wa . . . just let me blow . . . doo wa ditty,'" he sang slowly, moving his finger like a conductor's staff. "'Blow my thing, baby. . . . Blow my thing . . . doo wa ditty.'"

"Blow my thing?" Brenda asked, in shock, eliciting screams of laughter from Elizabeth. "That's nasty. Stop lying!"

Darnell laughed again and shrugged his shoulders. "That's the words of the song. You know Roger was never known for being shy. Besides, I think he was talking about his harmonica."

"I would hope so," Brenda said, turning the radio down. "But I will say I love my old-school music. There's just nothing like real live instruments making music."

"You ain't lying about that," Darnell agreed. "I'll bet most people think Snoop Dogg's sample from that is the original."

"I thought it was," Elizabeth chimed in.

Brenda snapped around and stared at her daughter. "What do you know about Snoop Dogg?"

"I heard it on Q Ninety-three," the child explained.

"You did, huh?" Brenda said, squinting at her. "Just make sure you're learning those books like you're learning those songs."

"Aw, Mommy, you know I make good grades."

"Yeah, and I'ma make sure it stays that way."

"Brenda, get off that girl," Darnell said with a chuckle. "You know she's nine going on twenty."

"That's what I'm afraid of," Brenda replied, turning her attention to her husband.

"You don't have anything to be afraid of, because she knows I'ma get in that tail if she even thinks of gettin' in some kinda trouble," Darnell said, while glancing at Elizabeth through the rearview mirror.

"Mom! Dad!" the poor child protested. "It was just a song on the radio. You know I'm not getting in no trouble."

Darnell and Brenda looked back, then looked at each other and laughed.

"We know, baby," Brenda said. "We just gotta keep the fear of God in you, that's all."

"Huh?"

"It means we're watching you," Darnell clarified.

Knowing she would never win, Elizabeth sighed, folded her arms, and looked out the window.

"I wonder how Jamar and Alexis are doing on the road," Brenda said as Darnell pulled into Christopher and Andrea's driveway.

"When is the last time you heard from them?" he asked.

"Not since earlier this afternoon. She was all depressed."

"I don't blame her, but I'm not going back down that road with you," Darnell said, stepping out of their black SUV.

Brenda followed suit as Elizabeth jumped out and ran up to the town house. "I don't wanna hear it, Darnell. Everything's going to work out."

"I didn't say anything," he replied, holding his hands up in resignation. "I just don't want you to start fixing things again. Don't you think life is much easier when you worry about yourself from time to time?"

"I'm not fixing anything. I just want my sister-cousin to be here with me while we wait this hurricane out. We just started hanging out again, and I was hoping to keep it that way for a while."

"I feel you. Just keep your girl out of it."

"I'm not even trying to go there," Brenda stated as she rang the doorbell. "Andrea and Alexis will probably never get along. I accept and understand that."

"Good," Darnell said.

The door opened, unveiling a tall, muscular man with a mocha complexion. He wore a wife beater and jeans adorned with an oversize belt buckle, but his mustache and haircut were neatly shaven. Some might have grown nervous, thinking a gangster had broken into the Lees' home, but Darnell and Brenda knew better.

"What's up, son?" Byron greeted, running out the door. He shook his old friend's hand and then pulled him into a bear hug. "It's been too long!"

"You ain't never lied," Darnell agreed. "You look good!"

"I know, huh?" Byron said, showing all his teeth with a bright smile. "You ain't too bad yourself. Married life must be treatin' you right."

"Speaking of married life, you two remember us?" Brenda asked as she and Elizabeth leaned impatiently against the side of the house.

"Oh, my fault, Bren," Byron said with a laugh. He moved away from Darnell and gave her a hug. "You know it's all love with you."

"Can't tell," she replied with a smile.

"Aw, don't be like that," he pleaded. "Y'all come on in. Chris and Dee will be here soon. They went to pick up Latrise from some birthday party."

"They left you here by yourself?" Brenda asked.

"Girl, this is my brother's house," Byron proclaimed, tapping his chest lightly with his fist. "I practically live here."

The group entered the house and headed straight for the living room. Darnell, Brenda, and Elizabeth sat on the sofa, while Byron took a seat on the love seat across from them.

"And who is this queen?" Byron asked.

"Elizabeth," the little girl replied with a giggle. Bashful, she hid her face in her mother's side.

"Nice to meet you, Elizabeth," he replied. "I'm Uncle Byron, but I shoulda been your daddy."

"Boy, don't be tellin' my child no mess like that!" Brenda exclaimed as the men howled in laughter.

"Yeah, you'd rather tongue kiss a rattlesnake than try to live that fantasy," Darnell said once his laughter subsided.

"Boy, please," Byron replied. "I love Brenda like my sister. You lucky you came correct, or you woulda never came close to having her."

"Is that right?" Brenda asked with a smile. "If I remember correctly, when Darnell and I met, you were too busy running after those little chickenhead girls to be worried about what we were doing."

"Mommy, what's a chickenhead?" Elizabeth asked.

"On that note," Brenda said, nearly shocked that she'd forgotten her daughter was in the room, "on to the next subject."

The adults laughed, while Elizabeth looked at them in confusion, seeming to wonder what was so funny.

"Hey, Elizabeth," Byron said, clapping his hands together. "I think Latrise has some toys in her room you can play with. Want me to take you up there?"

"Okay," Elizabeth replied, jumping from the sofa. She grabbed Byron's hand and let him lead her upstairs.

"Looks like he's about ready for kids," Brenda whispered to Darnell once Byron was out of earshot.

"Don't even start," he warned. "The boy ain't even got married yet, and you're already tryin' to make him a daddy."

She smiled, trying to hold back a laugh. "No, I'm not! Why would you say that?"

He cut his eyes at her and shook his head before jumping up and heading to the door. "Anyway, you wanna go ahead and bring in the luggage?"

"So, you're just gonna change the subject, huh?" she called after him.

"I leave y'all for five minutes and you're already fightin'?" Byron asked, trotting down the steps.

"Boy, shut up," Brenda said, walking toward the door. "Ain't nobody fightin'."

"If you say so," Byron replied as he followed her outside. "What y'all doing?"

"He decided to bring in the luggage."

"Anything to get Miss Fix-It to be quiet for a little while," Darnell explained. He pulled a large suitcase from the back of the truck and glared at his wife.

"Aw, Lord, what's she tryin'a fix now?"

"Nothing!" Brenda snapped, folding her arms. She leaned against the house, refusing to help either of them. *How dare they try to gang up on me? If it weren't for me, they'd all be lost!* she thought to herself.

"It's nothing," Darnell said. He pulled out another suitcase and shut the hatch. "She just saw how you were with Elizabeth, and all of a sudden, she thinks you're ready to be a daddy."

"A daddy?" Byron asked, scrunching his face. He grabbed the suitcase from Darnell and walked slowly into the house.

"A daddy," Darnell confirmed, following close behind him.

Brenda rolled her eyes and trudged into the house, closing the door behind her. She loved her husband dearly, but she hated when he made fun of her. "It wasn't like that, Byron."

"Then how was it?" Darnell asked, leading the group upstairs.

"All I meant was that you were good with kids," she tried to explain. "I figured you'd be ready when you had them."

Byron nodded. "Uh-huh. Sounds like you said I'm ready to be a daddy."

"What I tell you, son?" Darnell said with a laugh.

"Shut up, Darnell!" she snapped. She turned back to Byron. "So you plan on having kids one day?"

He shot her a sheepish smile. "Actually, ole girl is pregnant now."

"What!" Darnell and Brenda exclaimed in a chorus.

Byron laughed. "Yeah, we just found out last week."

"She's not going to have a big stomach for the wedding, is she?" Brenda asked.

"Naw, we moved the wedding date up to next month."

"You sure you're ready for all that?" Darnell asked, taking a seat on the bed.

"Hell, yeah," Byron replied. "I've been with this girl for the last year and a half, and you know that's saying something right there."

Darnell and Brenda looked at each other and nodded. The Byron they knew when they left Virginia Beach ten years ago was anything but virtuous. Three or four dates in one weekend was the norm. And, most times, sex accompanied each of them. Girlfriends just weren't in Byron's vocabulary. However, Brenda could respect him because he was honest. All the women in his life knew where they stood, and those who thought they could go further were let down so smoothly, they wound up sleeping with him again without expecting a phone call later.

Only one woman had ever had the potential of making Byron walk the straight and narrow. Andrea. Her Southern charm and beauty, along with her Halle Berry–esque body, had him at hello. At first, his attraction to her was nothing more than a small crush and a fantasy on how he would get her into bed. But, when Christopher began dating her, he stepped back and relegated his crush to a "what-if." When they were married, however, Byron did his best to turn his "what-if" into a "never could have been."

Truthfully, it was Christopher's affair with Alexis that awakened Byron's love for Andrea. He saw the way she nearly fell apart when she found out her husband had strayed. She found out about the affair and Alexis's aborted pregnancy all at once, and it tore her apart. It hurt her even more to know that he had risked their marriage for a few rounds of meaningless sex. When she learned of the abortion, she began questioning herself, because up to that point, she'd never had a child. Christopher would always say they weren't ready, but since they never used protection, Andrea wondered if she could get pregnant. The fact that a two-week fling accomplished what she couldn't do in three years nearly did her in.

"So when do we get to meet this superwoman?" Brenda asked, taking a seat on the bed, next to her husband.

"She's coming by tonight to meet y'all," Byron replied. "You're gonna like her. The girl is bad."

"What's her name?" Brenda inquired.

"Rayna."

"Interesting name," Darnell said, nodding his head. "She from around here?"

"No. Actually, she's from the Midwest."

"Midwest?" Darnell and Brenda replied in unison.

"Is she black?" Brenda asked.

Byron doubled over in laughter, barely noticing that Darnell and Brenda sat erect on the edge of the bed, awaiting his answer.

"Yes, she's black," he finally responded, wiping the tears from his eyes. "There really are black people who live in the Midwest. She's from Detroit."

"Oh," Darnell said, relaxing a bit. "Just wondering."

"Hey!" a feminine-sounding voice called out from downstairs. "Where's everybody at?"

Brenda jumped up in excitement and ran to the top of the steps. "Dee!"

"Aw, here we go," Darnell told Byron as more screams filled the hallway.

The noise drew Elizabeth to the doorway, but when she saw her mother standing at the top of the steps, hugging her friend, she simply shrugged. "Where's Latrise?"

"Lizzy!" Latrise exclaimed from the bottom of the steps.

Seconds later, the two girls raced into the bedroom and closed the door.

"When did you get in?" Andrea asked.

"About an hour ago," Brenda replied. "What took you so long?"

"Him," Andrea replied, pointing at Christopher.

While passing the stairwell, Christopher looked up and smiled as he carried two plastic bags of groceries into the kitchen. "Can you please tell my boy and my brother to come down here so I can have some company while y'all talk about me?"

"On the way, Chris," Byron said as the two of them passed the women on the steps.

"We're not talking about you," Andrea told Christopher with a smile. "I was just telling Brenda how you *insisted* on stopping to buy groceries, even though you knew she and Darnell would be pulling up soon. We coulda done that later."

"You two ain't changed," Brenda said with a laugh.

"You're right. No miracles," Andrea agreed, leading her friend to the living room. "Come on and sit down."

"Girl, I done had enough of sitting down," Brenda replied. "Between that long trip and waiting on you two to come back, my butt's gettin' tired."

"You're not tired?"

"I'm sure I will be later, but right now I'm too spun up to sleep."

"If that's the case, you can help me cook dinner."

With that, they kicked the men out of the kitchen so they could prepare the meal.

"So whatcha want me to do?" Brenda asked, leaning against the counter.

"There are some steaks thawing in the refrigerator," Andrea said while pulling a large baking pan and a pot from the bottom cabinet and placing them on the stove.

"Steaks, huh? I feel honored."

"Well, I haven't cooked for my best friend in a long time. I think it counts as a special occasion."

"Awww, you're so sweet," Brenda said, flashing her friend a dimple-adorned grin.

The two women hugged each other once more and then got to work. Andrea began cleaning the collard greens, while Brenda seasoned the steaks. To add to the festivities, Andrea poured them each a glass of Riesling.

"So, um, is Alexis coming over tonight?" Andrea asked quickly before taking a sip of her wine.

Brenda's eyes bugged. She wondered if she'd heard her friend correctly. Temporarily turning from the steaks, she replied, "No. Do you want her to?"

Andrea swallowed and diverted her eyes to the wall. "Not really. I, uh, just figured she might be coming since she's in town."

"Now, Dee, you know I wouldn't do that to you," Brenda replied, turning back to her task. "I accepted a long time ago that you and Alexis will never get along, so I don't know why you think I would invite her here without talking to you first."

"I know, but I just had to be sure," Andrea said, relaxing a bit and turning back to the pot. "I know how close you two are, but I'd be lying if I didn't tell you the thought of seeing her makes me want to smack her."

Brenda placed the steaks into a marinade and then turned to her friend. "You mean to tell me after all these years, you still haven't gotten over that?"

"Okay, Bren, let's see how fast you would get over some woman sleeping with Darnell."

"I know what you're saying, but too much time has passed. You've forgiven Chris, so why can't you forgive Alexis?"

Again, Andrea turned away from the pot and faced Brenda. She finished the rest of her wine before replying, "It took a lot for me and Chris to get to this point. We went through counseling, a river of tears, and a mountain of anger before we could even get to the point where we could be in the same room with each other. We made vows to each other, and I was determined to stand by those vows. Then, when Latrise came along, it was like the first three years of our marriage came back and got even better.

"Now, with your cousin, I don't share any of that. I don't know her, and the only memory I have of her is her being in my house, sexing my husband. We never talked or went through anything together. So how do you think we're supposed to just forgive and be friends?"

"No one is saying you two have to be friends," Brenda said. "But if you let this anger eat away at you, you're just hurting yourself."

Andrea shrugged and poured herself some more wine. "I'm fine. Just don't be expecting me to welcome your cousin back here with open arms."

"I'm optimistic, not deluded," Brenda said. "I'm not even trying to make that happen, baby."

"Well, good, because I know how you are, Miss Fix-It."

"You know, that's the second time today somebody's called me that," Brenda pointed out. "I've got my own problems. I'm not trying to fix everybody else's."

Andrea smiled. "I hear you, and don't worry. I won't be stressing you all week about this. I just wanted to put that out there quickly while it was on my mind."

"It's fine. Like I said, you don't have to worry about that."

"You sound like you're getting upset with me."

"Hey, Dee!" Chris called from the backyard. "You ready for me to put those steaks on the grill?"

"Yeah," she replied, turning her head slowly toward the patio door. The faint smell of charcoal filled the kitchen. "Come get them off the counter when you're ready."

"I'm not getting mad, but I need you to remember the primary reason I came here, Dee," Brenda said once she had her friend's attention again. She took a deep breath before continuing. "There's a chance that my house could be flooded out. My family is spread out all over the South, trying to flee yet another hurricane. I'm still looking for a job. I just finished a twenty-hour drive with my husband and daughter, and I haven't rested yet. I didn't come here to fix things between you and my cousin. She's in town, yes, but this is not about you."

Andrea bit her lip. "I'm sorry, Bren. In all the excitement, it's easy to forget you have real issues going on."

"It's fine," Brenda mumbled, then took a long sip of her wine to calm her nerves.

She wasn't sure why the anger churned in her stomach. She'd had this same conversation earlier with Darnell. It wasn't Andrea's fault. She really couldn't blame her friend for not wanting to forgive Alexis. That would have been a tall order for anyone. Yet, at the same time, she really didn't want to spend her entire visit listening to everyone harp on the issue. In fact, it was time to change the subject altogether.

"What else needs to be done?"

"Let's see," Andrea replied, seeming to relax a bit. "Chris is cooking the steaks, and the collard greens are cooking here. You wanna start on the rice? I'll start peeling the potatoes for the salad."

"Okay, and if I remember correctly, you keep the rice in here," Brenda said, pointing at a cabinet next to the refrigerator.

Andrea laughed. "Good memory. Pass me the potatoes while you're in there."

Chapter 3

It was nearly 6:00 P.M. when Jamar and Alexis pulled into the Ocean Key Resort parking garage, but the sun still shone brightly. Alexis sat outside, marveling at the beauty of the boardwalk, while Jamar checked them in. She could even see sailboats in the distance. Families and couples were everywhere. The August wind allowed some to fly kites, but it didn't impede those who sought a late-summer tan. This definitely wasn't what she remembered about Virginia Beach.

Her legs shook impatiently as she waited for Jamar to return with their room keys. She couldn't wait to change into her bathing suit and stroll along the boardwalk with her husband-to-be. She smiled triumphantly at a couple of bad-bodied women walking past. *I know my thirty-three-year-old tail looks better than that,* she thought, stretching her well-toned legs out in front of her. *I'ma put these young girls to shame.*

The scene kind of reminded her of Sundays at Lake Pontchartrain in New Orleans. Just like the beach, the lake had its regular share of visitors. On Sundays the entire scene looked like an urban car show. Only here, instead of being surrounded by trees and grass, sand and an expansive boardwalk framed the scene.

The more she saw of this beautiful oasis, the more she was glad she had let Jamar talk her into coming back. It would be an excellent escape from the possible reality that awaited her back home. As much as it pained her to think of it, she needed to be prepared for the possibility that her home and her office wouldn't be there when she returned.

However, this wasn't the time to think about that. She was sure she'd get enough reminders of the state of her city each time she turned on the television. So there was no sense in crowding her mind with such thoughts if she didn't need to. Right now she would do just as Jamar had told her—turn this trip into an early honeymoon.

She looked over her shoulder to try to get a glimpse of her fiancé. There didn't seem to be a line. *What could be taking him so long?*

"I'm sorry, sir," the desk attendant whispered. The stressed lines in her forehead told Jamar that she was more embarrassed about the situation than he was. "Do you have a different card you can use? This one doesn't seem to work."

"It doesn't?" he asked, scrunching his eyebrows. "Can you run it again?"

"I ran it twice, sir," the attendant said, running her hand nervously over her blond ponytail.

Jamar sighed and glanced around, wondering if everyone in the lobby could hear their conversation. He knew he'd checked all his credit cards and accounts before leaving New Orleans, and they were all fine. He had even double-checked with his friend to ensure the time-share had been reserved for them. What could have possibly happened in the eighteen hours since he'd left home?

"Sir?" the attendant asked, tapping her bloodred nails on the counter. "The card?"

Guess breaking the news gets easier with time, Jamar thought while fishing out his American Express card. He glanced at the woman as he handed over the card. The look of distress she had when she first came over to break the news slowly disappeared as she took the card from him. How could she know he was a partner in one of the most distinguished law firms in New Orleans? To her, that rejected credit card represented just another person who couldn't manage his finances. He wasn't any different than anyone else.

That thought alone made Jamar want to hurry and get to the bottom of this. As soon as he got to the room, he would call the bank and reprimand them for this mistake. He was not one to be played with.

"You about ready?" asked a feminine voice from behind.

When Jamar looked up to find Alexis standing there, he grew nervous. There was no way he could let her find out he wasn't handling his business. This trip would be stressful enough without her worrying about whether or not they could even afford to be on the trip in the first place.

"Yeah, baby, we're, uh, good," he replied, glancing toward the attendant. If he could get rid of Alexis before that damn attendant came back, he could avoid the risk of even more embarrassment. No such luck, though. She was on the way back.

"Looks like we're good to go, Mr. Duplessis," she said, smiling.

It wasn't until he exhaled that he realized he'd been holding his breath. At least not *all* his credit cards were tripping. "Um, thanks."

"Will you be needing one or two keys?"

"Two," Alexis answered for him. "Do you have a room facing the beach?"

"Well, unfortunately, ma'am, because this is a time-share unit, the owner has a specific room assignment," the attendant explained. "But I can see exactly which unit it is to see if you have a water view."

"Thanks, um"—Alexis glanced at the attendant's name tag—"Brandi."

"You're so welcome," Brandi replied without looking up. She typed a few things into the computer and then looked up with a smile. "You're in luck. This does happen to be a room with a view."

"All right, now!" Alexis exclaimed.

"Uh, yeah, I knew my boy did it up big," Jamar finally chimed in.

"You okay, baby?" Alexis asked. "You look worried about something."

Jamar looked at Brandi, as if daring her to say something. She looked back like she didn't have a care in the world.

"I'm good, babe. Let's take these bags up before it gets too late."

"Here are your keys, and the elevators are to your right," Brandi said.

"Thanks," he mumbled, grabbing their suitcases and quickly shuffling Alexis toward the elevators.

"Enjoy your stay!" Brandi called after them.

"Are you sure you're okay?" Alexis asked once they reached the suite.

"I'm good," Jamar replied without facing her. He set down the suitcases and unlocked the door. "Why you keep asking me that?"

"Because you didn't say anything all the way up to the room."

"After you," Jamar said, presenting his arm in true doorman fashion.

Alexis looked at him curiously but decided not to push the issue. Instead, she took one look at the suite and fell in love. It was actually bigger than some apartments she'd seen! Besides having two bedrooms, it also had a kitchen and a living room.

"Oh, yes," she said, standing in the middle of the living room with her hands on her hips. "I could get used to this."

Jamar walked up behind her and wrapped his arms around her waist. He kissed her behind the ear and whispered, "I told you that you'd like it."

She smiled and kissed him back. "You love me?"

"Of course, Mrs. Duplessis."

"How much?"

"Enough to drive your ass eighteen hours without making you drive. That's how much!"

She laughed. "That was *your* fault."

"Uh-huh," he said, nodding. "See if you don't help me drive back."

"Hey, I got you."

"I'ma remember that."

"Speaking of that, let's turn on the TV so we can get an update," Alexis suggested, opening the cabinet that housed the thirty-two-inch television. They sat next to each other on the sofa and turned to CNN just in time to catch coverage of New Orleans's mayor, Ray Nagin, explaining that the city had already begun voluntary evacuations. They each took a collective sigh of relief that they hadn't waited for the mandatory evacuation order, which was sure to follow.

"I'm glad we left when we did," Jamar said. "Had we waited until Saturday to leave, who knows how bad traffic would have been."

"I know," Alexis agreed. "It was bad enough as it was. It took my momma and them almost as long as us to get to Houston."

"Yeah, my parents insisted on going to Houston, too, but at least they left Wednesday."

"That was smart. I wish we had done the same thing."

"We couldn't have done that. You had patients all the way up to the day we left!"

Alexis chuckled. "Yeah, all those parents wanting to get that last-minute medication before they left. I just hope we don't have to go through that ordeal again with those trailers. I can't take any more kids getting sick behind that."

It still shook her when she thought of all the patients she had as a result of the formaldehyde in those trailers. At the time, the trailers that the Federal Emergency Management Agency had given the Gulf residents while they rebuilt their homes seemed like a good idea. They could still live on their property while reconstructing their lives. But little by little, more and more people began complaining of sore throats, difficulty breathing, burning eyes, and even rashes. The symptoms were soon traced to mold and formaldehyde in the trailers. As a pediatrician, Alexis was struck by how many children suffered from the symptoms. She was glad many of them had gotten better, but there was a number whose condition still hadn't improved, and even more whom she couldn't help, because their symptoms were too far gone.

"But, on the real, I just don't understand why all those people keep running to Houston," Alexis said. "I went to Houston during Katrina, and if I had heard one more person blame us for their crime rate going up, I was gonna go off."

"You gotta admit, a lot of our criminals did go to Houston after Katrina," Jamar said.

"Yeah, but it wasn't like Houston was a country club before they got there," she shot back. "I had been to

Houston before. I felt safer in the Lower Ninth Ward in New Orleans than I did in some of Houston's areas. Yeah, we might have brought some crime to the city, but we didn't bring all of it. Between that and the way Tony treated me, I'll be damned if I ever set foot in that city again."

"All right, all right," Jamar said, holding his hands up in surrender. "I'm not the one who said it."

"Shut up, Jamar," Alexis snapped, smiling in spite of herself.

"Anyway, you gotta give it to Mayor Nagin," Jamar continued, turning back to the television. "He definitely learned a lot from Katrina, and he's doing his thing now. He even got buses to take people out of the city."

"That's good," Alexis replied absently, watching the images of the evacuation. "You heard from your momma and them?"

"Yeah, I called her right before I checked in. She's good. You tell Brenda you were here yet?"

"No, lemme call her now," she replied, digging her cell phone out of her purse.

"Okay, tell her I said hi," Jamar said while quickly rising from the sofa. "I'ma go lay down for a bit."

He walked into the master bedroom and closed the door behind him. Alexis looked puzzled but shrugged it off and called her cousin.

"Yeah, no offense, Rayna, but we did think you were white," Darnell said. "I'm from Cali, and my wife is from down South. We just don't know too many black folks from the Midwest."

"You ain't heard?" Rayna asked, wrapping her arm around Byron's neck. "We're just like Martin Luther King Jr. Boulevard. Every city's got one."

The group cackled with laughter.

"Girl, you're crazy," Brenda said, wiping a tear from her right eye.

Rayna definitely wasn't white, but she was very fair-skinned. She also didn't seem to be the type of woman Byron was known to date. Instead of chemically straightened curly hair, she proudly wore waist-length honey-blond locks reminiscent of the actress Kim Fields's earthy look. She also didn't don herself in the shortest outfits possible. Instead, she dressed in conservative jeans and high heels. Even her size seemed different. Although a size ten was hardly overweight, Rayna would look heavy standing next to the size sixes Byron usually dated.

Brenda wondered how the two of them got together. Rayna was gorgeous, but she seemed a bit removed from Byron's personality. Byron was definitely friendly, but Rayna seemed to take social to a new level. She seemed to love to talk and laugh. She was charming, but Brenda wondered if her charm could quickly become a fault.

Just as the laughter died down, Brenda's ear caught the sound of her cell phone ringing. She snatched the phone up from the coffee table and checked the caller ID.

Smiling, she answered, "Well, it's about time I heard from you."

"You know I was going to call eventually," Alexis said with a laugh.

"Yeah, but I was hoping it would be sooner rather than later. Y'all got in all right?" Brenda asked, leaving the living room so she could hear better.

"Tell her I said what's up," Darnell called after her.

Brenda nodded at him, then walked into the kitchen and leaned on the counter.

"Yeah, we got in around six. We're staying at a resort on the beach," Alexis said.

"That's Jamar's time-share?"

"His friend's time-share. It's pretty nice so far."

"Well, that's good. At least I know you guys are okay. Have you eaten yet?"

"Uh-uh. Jamar's in the bedroom, resting. We'll probably go to the boardwalk later."

"Well, that's good. We're over here at Dee and Chris's house. We just finished barbecuing."

"That's nice." A few seconds of uncomfortable silence went by before Alexis finally said, "I'll let you get back to your friends. I just wanted to let you know we were okay."

"Okay," Brenda replied, tapping the counter. She hated the awkwardness that passed over them every time she brought up Christopher's or Andrea's name. It was wearing her out. "What do y'all have planned for tomorrow?"

"Well, we were going to the beach tonight, but since it's getting late, we'll do it tomorrow. I also have to start looking for a wedding gown."

"Oh, wow! Can I help?"

"You better, since you're the maid of honor!"

They laughed, breaking some of the tension.

"Well, I'ma let you go spend some time with that fiancé of yours," Brenda said. "I'll call you tomorrow. Maybe Darnell and I will join you at the beach."

"That'll be good. I'll see you then."

Once the cousins hung up, Brenda joined the rest of the group in the living room.

"They doing all right?" Darnell asked.

"Yep," Brenda replied. "They checked into the time-share about an hour or so ago."

"That's good," Darnell said. He then chuckled a bit. "That girl doesn't do anything half-assed, does she?"

"What?" Brenda asked.

"Most people would just get whatever they can in this situation, but not Alexis."

"Who's Alexis?" Rayna asked.

"She's my cousin," Brenda replied. "She came up here, too, but she and her fiancé are making this little ordeal into a vacation."

"That's cool," Rayna remarked. "She's getting married, too? Maybe she can help me plan our wedding."

Byron shot her a funny look and squeezed her hand. "We'll have to see if she would be up to that."

"Why wouldn't she be?" Rayna asked.

Andrea sucked her teeth and began cleaning the glasses off the coffee table. "Anybody want more wine?"

"I'll take some," Christopher replied.

"Me too," Darnell added.

Christopher helped his wife carry the dirty dishes into the kitchen. Once they were safely out of earshot, he asked, "You all right?"

"I'm good," Andrea replied, placing the dishes into the dishwasher. She remained silent until the last glass was placed, and then suddenly she turned to her husband with venom in her eyes. "Chris, I'm trying. I really am. I told Brenda I would leave the situation alone, but it really bothers me how that bitch is always able to land on her feet. She nearly destroyed our marriage. Shouldn't that be bad karma?"

"I think she has had some bad karma," Christopher said. "She and Brenda almost stopped speaking over that. And that abortion—"

The look his wife gave him at the sound of that word made him stop short. Although she'd forgiven Christopher for his affair with Alexis, it was still hard for her to come to grips with the fact that he had gotten her pregnant and had paid for the abortion. Had that abortion never happened, she was sure she never would have found out about the affair.

"Yeah, she had an abortion. So what?" she snapped quietly, trying hard not to let her friend overhear their conversation. "In the meantime, she became a doctor, got engaged to a lawyer, and now, when she should be worrying about losing it all, she's living it up on the boardwalk. What kind of karma is that?"

Christopher grabbed his wife and hugged her tightly. "Baby, you're worried about the wrong thing. Do you believe I love you?"

She cut her eyes at him, ashamed of her spiteful feelings. "Yes."

"Do you believe I will ever risk our marriage again?" "No."

"Have you forgiven me?"

She met his gaze, trying hard to fight back her tears. "You know I have, but I can't forgive her."

"Nobody's forcing you to, but you've got to let that girl live her life. She can't keep paying for a mistake she made before she even turned twenty-one."

She nodded slowly. "I hear you." She turned away and grabbed another bottle of Riesling out of the refrigerator. Once she gathered more clean wineglasses, she forced a slight smile. "Let's go back and join our company before they think we've abandoned them."

"That's my girl," he said, picking up the glasses. He lightly tapped her butt as he followed her out of the kitchen.

***

"Jamar, why is the door locked?"

Her voice nearly made him jump out of his skin. He'd hoped to be off the phone by now, but when the automated voice told him that his credit card account was closed, he knew he would be in for a long day. He just knew it had to be a mistake. Maybe it was just a computer glitch caused by the confusion of Gustav. Maybe his name had been mixed up with some guy who didn't pay his bills. Whatever the case, he wouldn't stop trying until he got this situation resolved, no matter how long it took.

He stuffed his cell phone into his pocket and hopped up from the bed.

"Sorry, baby," he said once he let Alexis into the room. "Force of habit."

"What? You think I was gonna come in here and attack you or something?" she asked, walking past him. She opened the balcony door and stepped outside. The warm salt air caressed her espresso-colored skin. "My God, it's beautiful out here!"

Relieved that Alexis had changed the subject so quickly, Jamar smiled and joined her on the balcony. "It is nice, isn't it?"

"You think anyone can see us up here?" she asked, turning to him with a wicked smile.

"We're on the eighth floor, so probably not."

She smiled even wider and began unzipping his jeans, while Jamar looked at her in shock.

"Girl, what are you doing?"

"Whatcha think?"

"You better stop before you start something you can't finish," he said, making no attempt to stop her seduction. "I thought you wanted to go out to dinner?"

"Okay, I'll stop," she said, pulling her hand from his pants. "Let's go eat."

"Hold on. I didn't say you *had* to stop," Jamar pleaded, following her back into the room.

"No, you're right. We need to eat," she said while searching her suitcase for her toiletries.

"Oh, I'm hungry, but it's not for food right now," he remarked, walking right up behind her. He placed his arms around her waist and put his hands underneath her baby doll T-shirt.

"Well, you're gonna have to wait. The thrill is gone now."

"You're a cold woman," he said, shaking his head. He let her go and sat down on the bed. "You just remember we have some unfinished business when we get back."

Chapter 4

"What a beautiful day to be at the beach," Nikki said to herself as she stretched her long mahogany legs out in front of her and adjusted the scarf under her large straw hat.

The sun seemed to send its beams in all the right places. It was hot without being scorching, and the water looked fit to take its place in a "Wish You Were Here" Virginia Beach postcard.

In reality, though, Nikki longed for no one. Hurricane Gustav had given her the excuse she needed not to rush back to New Orleans. She could now recoup in style from the two-week, two-country modeling shoot she had endured. Make no mistake, the money was good, but she earned every dime of what the company spent on her. She was exhausted!

She was headed back home when she heard about the hurricane, and decided not to get caught up in the madness of trying to evacuate. Instead, she rerouted her trip to Virginia Beach to wait it out. The peace and quiet of being somewhere where she didn't know anyone would do her some good.

She hated to admit it, but these were the times when she was happy her ex-husband, Reggie Morgan, a former New Orleans Saints player, had gained custody of their son, DeShawn. Since he had him, she had been able to concentrate more on her modeling career. She no longer had to search for babysitters or schools; she needed to worry only about herself.

Yet as she watched a mother help her kids build a sand castle, she also had to admit that she missed her son. She was sure he would enjoy running around the beach with the other kids, and she would almost enjoy fussing at him for getting sand mixed into his little cornrows. A sad smile tugged at her lips and forced her to dig her cell phone out of her shoulder bag, which perfectly matched her multicolored bikini.

"What's up, Nikki?" asked a dry male voice.

"Hey, Reg," she replied, staring out at the water, pretending not to hear the sarcasm in her ex-husband's voice. "I just called to check on y'all and see how Shawn was doing."

"We're good. We got into Atlanta day before yesterday."

"That's good. I'm going to wait it out in Virginia Beach."

A few seconds of silence went by before Reggie responded. What followed was a bitterness that couldn't be hidden by the calmness his voice displayed.

"You don't think your son mighta wanted you to come be with him?"

Nikki rolled her eyes and pursed her lips. "Come on, Reggie. Don't do that. You know your family doesn't like me. I don't even think this storm is gonna be all that serious, so we'll see each other when it blows over. And even if it doesn't, I'll just fly in to see him for a couple days."

The bitterness still hung in the atmosphere. "You got it all figured out, don't you?"

"Fool, I care about my son, too," she snapped. "You don't hold the patent on how to love your son!"

"I know you do, Nikki," Reggie responded, some of the anger leaving his tone. "I'm not trying to argue with you today. Let me put DeShawn on the phone."

"Thanks, Reg," she said, pulling back some of her own attitude.

She knew she couldn't blame Reggie for his hatred. She had treated him terribly the last couple years of their marriage. She had cheated on him a lot, but who wasn't cheating? Everybody she knew had something on the side, and she had somehow convinced herself that Reggie was no different. Somewhere along the way, she'd forgotten that she'd actually married one of the good ones. By the time she'd remembered, it was too late.

"Hey, Mommy!" exclaimed a juvenile voice.

"Hey, Shawn," Nikki greeted with a smile, which she hoped her son could feel through the line. "How you makin' out?"

"Good. Daddy and I were playing on my Wii. I was beating him in football."

Nikki laughed at the thought of Reggie letting the boy win. There was no way in the world a professional football player could lose to a seven-year-old.

"How was your ride to Atlanta?"

"It was good. Miss Janet came with us, and we played this game where we had to count license plates, but most of them said Louisiana."

"Is that right?" Although Nikki had gotten over the breakup, it still slightly bothered her that Reggie was able to move on with his life so quickly. She'd seen this Janet character once, maybe twice. There was no way that chick could hold a candle to Nikki's beauty, but if that was what Reggie had settled for, more power to him.

"What are you doing?" DeShawn asked.

"Wishing you were here," she replied, thinking back to the postcard image she'd pictured earlier. She began watching the families and couples walk past her.

One particular couple caught her interest. As they drew closer, they seemed more and more familiar. She pulled her glasses down to get a better look.

"Are you havin' fun?" DeShawn asked, pressing.

"It's okay, but I'd rather be at home with you," she said absently, staring at the couple. The woman had espresso skin and long, wavy hair, while the man had more of a mocha complexion. They were walking with a couple she'd never seen before. The foursome was nearly right in front of her before it finally hit her. *I'll be damned,* she thought. "Sweetie, Mommy has to go, but I'll call you later this evening to tell you good night."

"Okay, Mommy," DeShawn said. "Love you!"

"I love you, too, baby," she replied. "Have fun with your daddy."

She hit the END button and threw the phone back in her bag, never taking her eyes off the couple. There was no mistake about it—it was Jamar and Alexis! *What the hell are they doing here?* She'd hoped her association with them had ended after her divorce proceedings.

It was all too much of an uncomfortable coincidence. Jamar was Reggie's lawyer, and Alexis was Reggie's ex-girlfriend from college. How the idiots didn't know this until Nikki brought it to light, she could never understand. Now they all hated her like she was the villain in this thing, when, in fact, she was the only person who had told the truth in the situation.

Now here they were in Virginia Beach, probably waiting out Gustav. Well, one thing was for sure: she would keep her presence unknown. She had enough drama in her life, and she would like to keep her mini-vacation as drama free as possible.

***

"Man," Darnell commented as they strolled down the beach, "seems like everybody and their momma is here today."

"I know," Alexis replied. "I've never seen so many bad-bodied people in one spot."

The group laughed.

"Well, everybody doesn't exercise," Brenda said. "Besides, being a doctor, you should be used to seeing that."

"Uh-uh," Alexis said. "I'm a pediatrician. I've seen nine-year-olds with more curves than some of these chicks."

"That's cold," Jamar said as the group laughed again.

"No, it's not," Alexis continued. "I can understand a person being big. Everybody doesn't have to be small. But some of these people—men and women—seem like they don't take the time to even walk."

"Keep talkin'," Brenda said. "You're not going to be perfect forever. You'll be knockin' on forty before you know it."

"But I'ma still look good," Alexis snapped, putting her hand on her hip and striking a pose.

"Aw, let me hurry up and marry this woman before her head gets too big to fit into her dress," Jamar joked, placing his arm across his fiancée's shoulders.

"Speaking of dresses," Brenda said, jumping back to let two little boys run past. "Have you found any shops yet?"

"I found a couple right around here," Alexis replied. "I was going to wake up early tomorrow and check them out."

"Okay," Brenda said. "A lady in church today told me about another shop in her neighborhood we could try, as well."

"Sounds good. Let's make a whole day of it."

"You hear that, Jamar?" Darnell asked with a smile. "The women are gonna be gone all day."

"I heard it, bruh," Jamar replied, rubbing his hands together. "Time for some *man* time!"

"Excuse me?" the ladies said together.

"Aw, relax," Jamar said, waving them off. "What kinda trouble you think we're gonna get into in the middle of the day?"

Brenda and Alexis looked at each other, then back at the men. "A lot," they chorused.

The group laughed and continued walking.

"Hey, cousin," Brenda said tentatively, glancing at her husband for support. She wasn't sure how this would go, but she had promised she would ask. Since they were all in a good mood, this seemed just as good a time as any.

"What's up?"

"Um, you remember Byron, don't you?"

"Yeah, your girl's brother-in-law, right?"

"Yeah. Well, he's getting married, too."

"That's cool," Alexis replied, shrugging her shoulders. They had never been the best of friends, so the announcement didn't mean much to her.

"Well, his fiancée wants to meet you and was hoping you two could go dress shopping together," Brenda said quickly before she could change her mind.

Alexis stopped walking and stared at her cousin. "Excuse me? Why would she want to do that?"

"She's excited about getting married," Brenda responded with a shrug.

"So what's that gotta do with me?"

Jamar jumped to his fiancée's defense. "Yeah, that does sound kinda funny. She ain't tryin'a start no mess, is she? I promised Alexis we wouldn't have any of that."

"I don't think it's like that," Darnell offered. "I talked to her last night, and she seems to really want to be friends."

"But why?" Alexis asked, still confused. She hadn't seen or talked to Byron since she left Virginia Beach fifteen years ago, and she hadn't left the best impression. Byron had originally had a crush on her, but she'd chosen to sleep with his very married brother. Not only that, but she'd left Byron to pick up the pieces when the truth came out. "I'm sure she hasn't heard anything good about me."

"You think I would let a room full of people bash you in front of me?" Brenda asked.

Alexis folded her arms in defiance. "No, but God knows what they had to say when you left the room."

"Like I said, I don't think you have to worry about that," Darnell said. "The only person who still seems to hold a grudge about that is Andrea, but Brenda told me she set her straight on that."

Alexis looked at her cousin appreciatively. "You did?"

Brenda smiled back. "I got your back. You know that."

Darnell continued. "I talked to Byron last night, and he said he's past all of that. Rayna, his fiancée, seems like a nice girl. She knows what happened back in the day, but she said if Byron is past it, then she's not going to keep the mess going."

Alexis nodded, taking it all in.

Jamar wrapped his arms around her in support and said, "Well, speaking as the only person who wasn't there when this thing happened, I can understand why Alexis would be hesitant, but I agree that we need to get past all of this. Too much time has passed."

Alexis nodded again. "It's fine. She can come. She's willing to go tomorrow? I'm sure all the shops are closed Sunday, and I'm hoping to be gone on Monday."

"She said she would if you wanted to go shopping," Brenda responded. "She's pregnant, so they had to move the wedding up before she got too big."

"Interesting," Alexis remarked. "So do I get to meet this Rayna person before tomorrow, since she's gonna be sharing my day?"

"Funny you should ask," Brenda replied with a smile. "We're going out tonight. You wanna come?"

Alexis looked at her and wrinkled her nose. "Who is 'we'?"

Brenda sighed. "Yes, Andrea's going, but you don't need to sit with her. And no, I'm not trying to fix things between you two. I just don't want you and Jamar cooped up in that hotel room all week."

"Have you *seen* my hotel?" Alexis asked. "It's the bomb. I will not be cooped up!"

The group laughed again.

"Come on, baby," Jamar said, kissing her neck. "Let's go out. I promise not to let you get into it with her tonight. We don't even need to be bothered with them."

Alexis cut her eyes at him and agreed to go under the condition that there would be no fake greetings or promises of friendship. Brenda gave Alexis her scout's honor that she would stay out of the situation.

Chapter 5

"Everything okay?" Janet asked, peeking into the bedroom where Reggie and DeShawn were going at it Madden style. The older Morgan and the younger Morgan both sat on the floor next to Reggie's full-sized bed with their legs crossed. Intent and determination were plastered on their faces as they stared at the thirty-two-inch flat screen sitting on top of the dresser.

"Couldn't be better," Reggie replied with his eyes still glued to the screen. He leaned in closer as he struggled to maneuver his player into a defensive move. The computerized man failed miserably, taking a nosedive into the Astroturf.

"Touchdown!" DeShawn exclaimed as his player easily trotted into the end zone. He threw his hands in the air, jumped up, and began an end zone dance that would put Deion Sanders to shame.

"How does a man spend eleven years in the NFL, earn a bachelor's *and* a master's degree, and lose to a seven-year-old boy in Madden twenty-oh-eight?" Reggie asked Janet, who stood by the door, laughing.

"Because you don't play this game twenty-four hours a day," she said. She walked over to the bed and lay behind Reggie's head.

"I don't think it's twenty-four hours," Reggie commented, playfully pushing the little boy's head. "The little con artist has to sleep sometime."

"Don't hate, Daddy. Appreciate," DeShawn replied with a triumphant smile.

Reggie and Janet hooted in laughter.

"He's too grown for me," she said, shaking her head.

"Shoot," Reggie said, careful not to use the word he really wanted to use, "too grown for me, too."

"Can I go get some milk?" DeShawn asked, placing his game controller next to Janet.

"Feel free, baby boy. While you're down there, ask your grandma what time dinner's gonna be ready."

"Okay, Daddy," the boy replied, running out of the room.

Reggie walked over to the door and made sure it was shut completely. He then turned to Janet and smiled flirtatiously.

"What are you smiling at?" she asked, although her face wore the same expression.

"I can't smile at my woman?"

"I didn't say that, but I know something is on your mind."

He lay back on the bed and pulled Janet on top of him. His hands began traveling down her back, resting at the curve between her lower back and her butt.

"The only thing on my mind is making love to the best thing that's happened to me in a very long time."

"Is that right?" she asked.

Janet smiled and ran the tip of her tongue across Reggie's thick lips. She still couldn't believe that a chance phone call requesting tickets would lead to her dating one of the most eligible bachelors in New Orleans. Not only was he handsome and educated, but he was generous with both his time and his money. He was great with his son and had a heart of gold with the ones he loved. Reggie was definitely one of the good ones. How his ex-wife, Nikki, couldn't see that, she would never know.

However, she did know that she planned on being with this man for years to come.

She pecked the tip of his nose, and Reggie reciprocated with a kiss. He ran his fingers through Janet's thick, chin-length hair. He loved the softness of her curly brown and black mane. It was always touchable, as if she worked extra hard to always look good for him. She wasn't high maintenance like Nikki, but he appreciated her beautiful girl-next-door looks.

"That's very right," he mumbled, giving her another kiss.

It was a good thing he hadn't let this woman get away. Janet was his former babysitter's sister, but she didn't live in New Orleans at the time she and Reggie met. She just happened to pop up while he was struggling with his divorce from Nikki and his rising feelings for his ex-girlfriend Alexis. Nothing had seemed to be going right in either situation. So when Janet called, looking for tickets to one of his games last year, he was ready to introduce her to Mr. Dial Tone, thinking she was just one more person who wanted something from him. He was actually about ready to call his babysitter and fire her on the spot for even giving out his number like that. Fortunately, he had had a change of heart and had given her the tickets, and when she called again to say thanks, he decided to get to know her. The rest, as they say, was history.

"You love me?" Janet asked, nuzzling her head between his head and shoulder.

"You already know the answer to that."

"I know, but a woman likes to hear the words every now and then."

Reggie sighed inwardly and stared at the ceiling. *Why do women always have to do this?*

They had a good thing going. They were an exclusive couple. They were happy. His son loved her. He'd even taken her to his family's house to wait out Gustav with him. Why did he need to say the words? He showed her every day.

"I can tell by your silence that you're still not ready to say the words," Janet said, sitting up.

Reggie looked at her without moving. She looked hurt, but there was nothing he could do about that right now. He'd told her that he loved her before, but he knew that continuing to say the words would quickly lead to questions of marriage, and he just wasn't ready to take that step. The last two years had taken him through an emotional wringer. Why couldn't she have sense enough to know he wasn't about to jump from one marriage to another? Not to say he would never get married again, but he needed to make sure that next time it would be under the right circumstances.

"Janet, you know I love you," he said quietly. "What more do you want me to say?"

A frantic knocking at the door stopped Janet from replying.

"Whatcha need, Shawn?" Reggie asked, holding his position on the bed.

"Grandma said she ain't no hired cook and you need to hurry yourself downstairs if you want something to eat!"

Reggie chuckled, knowing his son had quoted his mother perfectly. She probably had to edit herself to keep from cursing, but the words were definitely hers. "All right, baby boy, we'll be down in a minute."

"Okay!"

Once he was sure the boy had gone back downstairs, he turned back to Janet. "I guess you heard that. We'd better get on downstairs."

Janet sighed deeply and rolled her eyes. "Saved by the bell, huh?"

"What are you talking about?"

"Your momma called you. So, once again, you can avoid talking about our relationship."

"Damn, Janet. I told you I love you. You don't believe me?"

"Yeah, I believe you, but that doesn't mean I have to accept the crumbs you're dropping."

"What crumbs?" Reggie asked, rising onto his elbows. He glared into her eyes, already irritated with the conversation.

"You gave a woman like Nikki your all, but now that you have a real woman, you give me your crumbs," she snapped.

There, she'd said it. She'd been meaning to say it for months, and now, as she waited out a hurricane, the words blew out of her mouth like their own windstorm. And, like Gustav, her words were about to cause some damage.

"Janet, baby, you really don't know what you're talking about, so it's best you leave that alone," he said flatly.

"I think I *do* know what I'm talking about," she snapped. "I know you love me. I know you're committed to me. Yet when it comes down to discussing our relationship and where it's going, you freeze up. Are you holding out for someone better?"

"You know it's not like that," he said, rolling his eyes and rising from the bed. Without looking back at her, he asked, "Why can't you be happy with the way things are? I'm right where I wanna be."

"That's what you say, but you're letting memories of that bitch Nikki keep walls between us."

He leaned against the wall next to the door and folded his arms. He stared toward the window but couldn't focus on what was going on outside. The happenings inside the room consumed enough of his attention. The room seemed so much smaller than it had when he was growing up, like the walls were caving in. His eyes rested on the Deion Sanders poster hanging above his bed.

"So now you're a psychiatrist?" he asked finally, still not focusing on Janet. "You know all about the black man's mind and how it works? If you did, you would know you don't need to be calling Nikki out her name. I have my issues with her, but you don't know the mother of my child well enough to call her anything outside of Nikki."

Janet looked away, tears stinging the corners of her eyes. She knew she'd gone too far, but she had to speak her mind, and she couldn't apologize for that. Although she meant what she'd said about Nikki, she could almost halfway understand Reggie's point. How could he blame her for calling her a bitch, though? It was not like he spoke of her in glowing terms.

"You comin' downstairs to eat?" Reggie asked, breaking the silence.

She remained on the bed and stared out the window. It looked like a beautiful day. The setting sun cast beautiful golden sunbeams through the leaves in the trees. A few neighborhood kids ran up and down the sidewalk without a care in the world. She wished she could go back to those days. Being an adult was more stressful than it looked.

"You know we're not finished with this, right?"

"I know," he replied with a nod, "but we're not gonna finish it today. I just got off the phone with Nikki and her attitude, and I really don't feel like letting her poison what I have right here."

Janet turned away from the window and shot Reggie a quizzical look. Reggie understood.

"Yeah, she called and talked to Shawn right before you came up here."

"She okay?" she asked, not knowing what else to say.

"She's Nikki," he replied with a shrug. "I'll tell you about it later, but she's safe."

"That's good," Janet mumbled.

"You comin' to eat or what?" Reggie asked.

She sighed again and nodded. "Yeah, I'm coming."

She rose from the bed and approached the door. Before she could leave the room, Reggie pulled her into a tight hug.

"I love you, Janet, and I really meant it when I said you were the best thing that's happened to me. I'm not going anywhere."

"Okay," she said with a nod. "I'm holding you to that."

"I know you will," he replied, opening the door. He then ushered her out and down the steps, secretly thankful that he'd dodged a bullet.

Chapter 6

"This is what I needed!" Alexis exclaimed as she and Jamar walked into the club.

Her heart immediately began pulsating to the beat of Beyoncé's "Get Me Bodied." By the look of the crowded dance floor and the bobbing heads at the few tables in the place, it seemed like everyone else felt the rhythm, too.

Jamar wrapped his arm around her waist and pulled her closer. Smiling, he kissed her neck and whispered in her ear, "You glad you came out now?"

She looked up and returned his kiss.

"This place is pretty nice," she said, scanning the small club.

Its decor was simple, yet tasteful. Although it looked like nothing more than a strip-mall shop from the outside, the interior included plush sofas and an expansive bar. Since the club was located on the Virginia Beach oceanfront, Alexis expected the patrons to be dressed for the beach, but she was pleasantly surprised to see everyone in their after-five best. Of course, there were a few who looked like they were auditioning for a rap video, but many seemed to have taken their time putting their outfits together. Some ladies even rivaled Alexis, who wore a sleeveless denim jumpsuit that hugged her figure tightly. She had accented her outfit with a pair of gold stilettos that she'd purchased earlier that day.

"You ready to dance? You know Beyoncé is my girl."

"You don't wanna look for your cousin first?" Jamar asked, allowing his fiancée to lead him to the floor.

She shook her head no as she began gyrating to the beat. "They'll be all right," she said, turning her back to him and wrapping her arm around the back of his neck. Soon both their hips moved in perfect synchronization. Alexis got low, then popped up and faced Jamar seductively. He smiled back at her and danced closer.

It seemed as if "Get Me Bodied" would never end, but neither of them cared. This was their night to get their minds off the concerns they'd left back in New Orleans. Even if it was only for a couple of hours, they would forget that their livelihoods might not be there when they awoke the next morning. For a few fleeting moments, they would imagine all was well with their families and that everyone wasn't spread all over the South.

Meanwhile, Andrea and Christopher sat at a long table with Brenda, Darnell, Rayna, and Byron. The women flung their arms and chair danced, while their significant others tried their best to talk smack over the loud music.

Brenda continually watched the door, waiting for her cousin to come in, but Andrea relished the few moments of peace she had left. She had no idea why she was there. She didn't want to go to the club that night, and for the life of her, she wasn't sure how she'd let Christopher talk her into coming out. Although deep down she didn't want to be the odd man out when everyone spoke about going out, she knew she wasn't ready to face Alexis just yet.

Andrea looked around the club at all the people having a good time. Besides them, there were few couples in the place. It seemed that most of the patrons were in groups looking for other groups to hook up with. *I am so over this scene,* Andrea thought to herself.

"Looking at these folks," she told the other ladies, "I am so glad I'm married. You can see the lust in these kids' sex-depraved eyes."

Rayna squealed with laughter. "You ain't never lied, but the old heads aren't any better. Lookin' like they're searchin' for a young whippersnapper to take home."

The ladies' laughter sounded like cackles, but no one seemed to care. For Andrea, this was what felt right about the night. Hanging out with the girls. Chopping it up with their one and onlys. People watching. Dancing to music she had time to listen to only during the car ride to and from work. It couldn't get any better than this. Unfortunately for Andrea, it wouldn't.

Just as she threw her head back to recover from her laughter, she caught a glimpse of Alexis dancing with who she assumed to be her fiancé. The sight of the woman she'd hated for the last fifteen years made her stomach flip. Deep down, she would never admit that the years had been good to Alexis. All she could see was that tight outfit and those dance moves that would put a stripper out of business.

"She's still a slut," Andrea mumbled, her eyes transfixed on her archenemy. She instinctively moved closer to Christopher and placed her hand on the inside of his thigh.

"You all right, baby?" he whispered in her ear, while wrapping his arm around her shoulders.

She nodded silently, careful not to let Brenda see the look she was sure was painted across her face. She could feel her jaw lock. She loved her friend, but she could kill Brenda for putting her in this position. She really didn't feel like being fake, and she wasn't sure she had the capacity to do so.

Her efforts must have been in vain, however, because she could see from the corner of her eye Christopher following her gaze. Before she could turn away, he blurted, "Hey, Bren. Is that your cousin right there?"

Brenda looked over to where he pointed and replied, "Yeah, that's her! How long has she been here?"

"I don't know, but from the looks of that sweat rolling down her forehead, she's been here for a good minute," he replied.

When Andrea shot him a dirty look, he quickly looked to his brother for help. Byron silently lifted his eyebrows and sipped his drink, as if to say he couldn't help him.

"I actually forgot she could dance like that," Brenda commented as she stood up. "Y'all mind if I bring her over for a minute?"

"Please do," Rayna said quickly, noting and ignoring the silent plea on Andrea's face. "I wanna meet this famous chick if we're gonna be shopping together tomorrow."

Andrea sighed as she watched her best friend march to the dance floor to retrieve her cousin. The moment of truth had finally come.

"Dee, girl, stop trippin'," Rayna said once Brenda was out of earshot. "That mess happened two decades ago. You got your man."

"Mind your business, Rayna," Andrea snapped. "There are a lot of things you don't understand about this."

"I understand you're lettin' that shit eat you up, while Alexis seems to be livin' her life," Rayna replied. "You need to do the same."

Rayna glared at Andrea, disappointed in the way she had been acting. She felt like Andrea had taken on an entirely new persona ever since she found out Alexis was returning to Virginia Beach. She couldn't blame her for being upset, but she couldn't understand why anyone would hold a grudge for as long as she had. Alexis was practically a teenager when she did what she did. Couldn't Andrea give her the benefit of the doubt that she'd grown up?

To tell the truth, Rayna actually admired Alexis for all she'd accomplished over the years. She, like Byron and Andrea, wanted to hate Alexis for what she'd done, but when she heard that this so-called home wrecker, who'd gotten pregnant by a married man, had gone on to graduate from college with honors, complete medical school, become a doctor with a private practice, and survive a hurricane, she knew she had to meet this woman!

On top of all that, Alexis had found a professional man to share her life with. Although Rayna was happy with Byron, she secretly wished he would live up to his potential the way Alexis's boyfriend had. He didn't have to be a lawyer, but he had the potential to be so much more than a cook at a three-star restaurant. He could be a sous chef or even a head chef if he wanted to be! She hoped that if she could make friends with Alexis, maybe Byron and Jamar would get close. Maybe Jamar could even pass him a few contacts. She would move to New Orleans if they had to. At least she would if those damn hurricanes would stop.

"Hey, everybody," Brenda said, holding on to her cousin's hand with a near death grip. "Y'all remember Alexis? And this is her fiancé, Jamar."

The group murmured a hello as best they could over the music. Rayna snuck a quick look at Christopher and Andrea, who were trying their best to look nonchalant. It wasn't working. She could see their strained looks as clear as day.

"Alexis, this is Byron's fiancée, Rayna," Brenda said introducing them, seemingly oblivious to the tension.

"Hey, girl," Alexis said with a smile, also ignoring the tension. She reached out and lightly shook Rayna's hand. "I guess we're going shopping tomorrow?"

"Yep," Rayna replied, smiling back. "Just let me know when you're ready."

Alexis reached into her small purse and pulled out a business card.

"Call me in the morning, and we'll work it out," she said, handing Rayna the card. "Maybe we can make a day out of it."

"Sounds good," Rayna said, reading the print. *Impressive,* she thought as she read the letters *MD* beside Alexis's name.

"So why don't y'all sit down?" Christopher asked, standing suddenly.

"Is there room?" Jamar asked.

"We can try to find a couple of chairs," Christopher said. "You can have my seat, Alexis."

"Um, thanks," Alexis replied, noting how quickly Andrea snapped her neck to glare at her husband.

"Uh, yeah," Brenda interjected, taking her seat next to Darnell. "Y'all go on."

Byron and Christopher left the group in search of extra seating, giving them a chance to be alone.

"She looks good, huh?" Byron said once they were out of earshot.

Christopher shook his head. "Better than she did back in the day."

"You gonna be all right?"

"Hell, yeah. I'm not sweatin' that stuff. You think I'm willing to go through all that shit again?"

Byron chuckled a bit. "No, I'm not saying that. I'm just saying it's kinda awkward seeing her again after all this time."

"Yeah, but we've all grown up since then. Seems like she's doing pretty well for herself."

"Yeah, well, we'll see," Byron said, grabbing a chair from a table near the restroom. He spotted another empty chair at a table occupied by three women. "See if they're using that chair."

"You would send me to a table full of cacklers," Christopher grumbled, trudging toward the table. He looked helplessly at his brother, who had already headed back to their group. The women again laughed loudly just as he approached them. "Excuse me, ladies. Is this seat taken?"

"Not unless you're about to sit your fine tail in it," replied one of the ladies.

Christopher felt like he was being raped as he watched her eyes flirtatiously scan him up and down.

He smiled graciously. "Thanks, baby girl, but I'm a happily married man."

"Can't be too happy if you're in here," another woman chimed in.

"Girl, leave that man alone!" admonished the third woman at the table. She looked up at Christopher and smiled apologetically. "Excuse my friends. They have no home training."

"It's all good," Christopher said with a laugh. "But can I have the chair? My wife is waiting for me."

"Ummm, excuse me," the first woman said, waving her hand dismissively at him. "Go ahead."

"Have a nice night, ladies," he said, picking up the chair by its backrest.

He could feel the ladies' eyes on him as he walked back to his table. At one point in his life, he would have taken that woman and her friend home and turned them both out. Now he didn't think twice about them. It was times like these that he realized he'd truly grown up.

"Y'all good on drinks?" he asked once he reached the table. He placed the chair strategically between Alexis and Andrea.

"I'll take another Moscato," Andrea said, pushing away her empty wineglass.

"I like Moscato, too," Alexis said.

Andrea turned her head slowly to look at Alexis and replied, "Really?"

Jamar squeezed Alexis's thigh, signaling to her that he'd caught on to the icy comment.

"Girl, why did you let your great uncle come to the club looking like that?" Brenda asked, pointing to an older gentleman wearing a shiny, multicolored shirt with a red fedora. He commanded the dance floor as he gyrated slowly against a helpless woman who looked to be half his age.

The entire table hooted in laughter. Alexis was grateful for the temporary change in subject. She hadn't meant to trigger any animosity. She actually thought that with her comment, she would find common ground with Andrea. Instead, she guessed she succeeded only in bringing up bad memories. The way Andrea looked at her, she could swear she was thinking, *I guess you like everything I got.*

She looked up at Jamar, thankful that he would be by her side through this whole ordeal. If it weren't for him and Brenda, she would have left the entire situation an hour ago. However, she was determined to make the best of it for Darnell's and Brenda's sakes. This couldn't be easy for them, either.

"Yeah, I like Moscato, but I think I want a margarita if they have it," Alexis said.

"I got you, baby," Jamar said, rising from the table.

The other men took their women's drink orders and left the table, leaving the women to talk. Or at least try. Brenda did her best to keep the conversation flowing, while Rayna did what she could to chat with Alexis about their upcoming date to pick out wedding dresses.

Truthfully, Alexis preferred this rather than forcing a strained conversation with Andrea, but she was getting weary of hearing about wedding dresses. She understood why Rayna was so excited, because she was also excited about seeing herself in white. Well, ivory. Maybe gold. Still, it didn't mean she wanted to spend all night talking about it. She figured Rayna was just one of those girls who saw marriage as a happy ending rather than a stop on the path of life. She hoped the girl would put just as much energy into being a good wife as she was into being a beautiful bride. She looked toward the bar, wishing Jamar would hurry and return so he could rescue her from this nightmare.

Jamar, on the other hand, felt the heat of the spotlight that beamed on him as he stood in line at the bar with the Lee brothers. Darnell's easygoing presence made him feel a little more at ease, but he couldn't help thinking that Christopher and Byron were studying his every move.

He tried to study Christopher without the others noticing. He could see why Alexis had been attracted to him once upon a time. Christopher wasn't a bad-looking guy. He had the muscles that Alexis liked, and he was pretty clean-cut, with a neatly-trimmed mustache and goatee. Jamar would never go as far as to say

Christopher was better looking than he was, but he had to admit the guy was all right.

He smirked a bit at the way Christopher tried so hard to avoid eye contact with Alexis, while trying to play the attentive husband with Andrea. He wasn't sure if Christopher was trying to impress him, Andrea, Alexis, or even himself. Maybe it was a combination of all four of them, like a bad showing of "look how far I've come."

"So you from New Orleans, too?" Byron asked from behind.

"Yeah," Jamar replied. "Born and raised."

"You ever been to Vah Beach?" Christopher asked, pronouncing the abbreviation for Virginia "Vah." He continued to avoid eye contact for a moment, but finally locked eyes with Jamar.

"No, this is my first time here," Jamar answered. "It's cool so far. Y'all been here all your life?"

"Naw, we're from upstate New York," Byron responded.

"God's country," Christopher added with a smile.

Darnell and Jamar looked at each other and laughed.

"That's the first time I've heard that one," Darnell said.

"It's true," Christopher said. "People think of New York City when they hear New York, but Albany is where the ballers are."

The men began discussing the advantages of living in Albany versus the hustle and bustle of New York City. Once they reached the bar, they each ordered their drinks. Since they had reached a semblance of friendly ground, Jamar decided to bite the bullet once the bartender began preparing the drinks.

"You know it wasn't easy for Alexis to come back here," he said, leaning on the bar.

Christopher nodded silently, looking straight ahead at the mirror behind the bar.

"Yeah, Brenda had to practically beg her to come up," Darnell added.

"I don't blame her," Byron said, pushing his hands into his jeans pockets. "She caused a lot of shit here back in the day."

"Yeah, she told me about it," Jamar said. "Are y'all all right with her being here? I mean, I told her I wasn't going to let her get involved in any shit while she was here. We have enough drama going on with this hurricane."

"I'm cool," Christopher said. "Things are good with me and my wife again. I can't change what happened, but I can tell you it ain't gonna happen again. Besides, it was just as much my fault as it was hers. The question is, are *you* all right? It ain't every day that a brother comes face-to-face with his woman's past."

"And that's exactly what it is, bruh," Jamar said as the bartender placed the last drink on the bar. He pulled out his wallet and took out a credit card, being careful not to choose the one that gave him the problems when they checked into the hotel. "The past is the past. Alexis is past it, and we're dealing with everything just fine."

He was careful not to let on that Alexis was unable to have babies as a result of the affair. It really wasn't Christopher's and Byron's business, and he was sure she didn't want them to know. If she did, she would have told them long ago.

"That's gonna be sixty dollars," the bartender said.

"I got it," Jamar told them, handing her the card.

The bartender took the card and slid it through the scanner. Instead of hearing the printing noise Jamar was used to hearing when his credit card cleared, there was only silence.

"It was declined," the bartender said nonchalantly, looking him in the eyes.

Jamar took the card back, a wave of humiliation and confusion washing over him. "I don't know what the hell is going on."

"What's up, J?" Darnell asked.

"My card's not working. This is the second time since we got here."

Darnell pulled out his wallet and took care of the bill. "You better get that checked."

"You're damn right I will."

"You're not going to be able to check until Tuesday, at the earliest," Christopher said. "Monday is Labor Day, and even if you do call tomorrow, chances are they won't be able to do much until Tuesday."

"Shit!" Jamar exclaimed, placing his hands on his hips in frustration. "I forgot all about that."

"You think the storm has anything to do with it?" Byron asked. "I heard during Katrina people couldn't access their bank accounts or anything."

"I don't know, but I'll find out Tuesday," Jamar replied, picking up his and Alexis's drinks. "If I don't do anything else, I keep my finances straight. Thanks for covering for me, Darnell."

"No sweat," Darnell replied, picking up his own drinks. "You're practically family now."

"I feel for you, bruh," Christopher said. "First the storm, now your money?"

"That's what I'm saying," Jamar replied. "Just don't say anything about this around Alexis. She has enough on her mind, and I don't want her to know about this until I figure out what's going on."

"You ain't gotta worry about me saying anything," Christopher said. "My wife won't let me get close enough to her to so much as say hi."

They laughed as they reached their table. Once they passed out the drinks, they took their seats next to their significant others. The women were mostly quiet, except for Rayna and Brenda, who were still trying to get Alexis to begin wedding planning despite the loud music. Alexis held her head, looking weary of the entire situation.

"Damn, girl, give it a rest!" Byron told Rayna. "Y'all ain't gotta plan the whole wedding tonight."

"Who you talkin' to?" Rayna asked, whipping her head toward him.

"Girl, don't be tryin' to jump bad just because my people are around," Byron said with a smirk. He grabbed her hand and pulled her to the dance floor. "Let's dance."

The group laughed and then turned back to the table to finish their drinks.

Christopher leaned in and kissed Andrea behind her ear. "How you holding up?"

She shrugged and replied, "I'm good."

"You didn't try to jump across the table at Alexis, did you?"

She smiled slightly for the first time that night. "No. I told you I'm cool."

"Then you need to get that stank look off your face and enjoy yourself."

"Oh, so now I'm stank, huh?" Andrea asked, turning toward her husband.

"Yep," he replied, kissing her ear again. "About as stank as month-old collard greens."

Andrea contorted her face. "That's just nasty!"

"I'm just saying," he said, shrugging his shoulders in resignation. "Let's go dance."

Andrea smiled and accepted her husband's suggestion, leaving Darnell, Brenda, Alexis, and Jamar with the table to themselves.

"Are you enjoying yourself, Lex?" Brenda asked.

Alexis laughed and took a sip from her drink. "Actually, yes. This place is pretty nice."

"You didn't let Andrea get to you, did you?"

Alexis shook her head and took another sip. "I didn't expect anything else from her. I'm not worried."

"Wow, you *have* changed," Brenda said, staring at her cousin in disbelief. "There was a time when you woulda been ready to scrap if somebody gave you that much attitude."

Darnell and Jamar laughed.

"My girl finally has a good man," Jamar said as he placed his arms around Alexis. "That alone is reason for change."

Brenda smiled and leaned forward. "You saying she finally found her Boaz?"

Jamar smiled and contemplated Brenda's reference to the biblical story of Ruth. "Yeah, I guess she did."

"Who's Boaz?" Alexis asked.

The group let out a chorus of woos.

"Somebody hasn't been to church in a minute!" Darnell exclaimed, eliciting chuckles of agreement from the others.

"Laugh if y'all want, but who's Boaz?" Alexis persisted.

"I'll tell you later," Jamar said, patting her leg. "Tonight we concentrate on having a good time."

"Yeah, because Lord knows what we'll wake up to in the morning," Darnell commented.

"Well, I'm not thinking about that right now," Alexis said. When Soulja Boy's "Superman" began playing, she popped out of her seat. "I'm ready to get my dance on."

She trotted to the dance floor and fell in with everyone else doing the infamous dance. Jamar wasn't far behind her. Brenda and Darnell remained at the table and watched everyone's drinks.

"Sometimes I think that girl forgets she's in her thirties," Brenda said with a laugh.

"Ain't nothing wrong with that," Darnell replied. "That's what keeps them young."

Chapter 7

"Wake up, babe," Jamar commanded, shaking Alexis's shoulder. When she didn't move, he lightly slapped her espresso skin. "Lex, wake up."

"Uh-uh," she moaned, turning away from him. "We don't have anywhere to go."

"Girl, get up! They're talking about Gustav on TV."

Those words sent a jolt through her body that made her jump straight up. As she wiped the sleep from her eyes, she could just make out a journalist struggling against the fierce winds while giving his report. Jamar turned up the volume.

"Again, Hurricane Gustav has been downgraded to a Category Two, but it doesn't mean the Gulf Coast is out of the woods yet," the journalist shouted over the winds. "At any time, Gustav could gain momentum. That could mean disaster for New Orleans, which is still struggling to recover from Hurricane Katrina exactly three years ago."

Alexis shook her head slowly as she listened to the report. Behind the journalist, she could make out the statue of Andrew Jackson riding his horse in the center of Jackson Square in the French Quarter. It almost seemed stereotypical to be standing in the middle of the tourist district, but it made sense since the French Quarter was on some of the highest ground in New Orleans. It was probably one of the safest places to report from in terms of flooding.

"According to reports from FEMA, only about ten thousand residents remain in the city," the journalist continued. "About two hundred thousand residents evacuated from New Orleans this morning, after Mayor Ray Nagin, who shortened his appearance at the Democratic National Convention, issued a mandatory evacuation. It was obvious he benefited from a lot of lessons learned. In addition to the contraflow on all major highways, the city also contracted seven hundred buses to move evacuees to safety. Those who stayed in the city will not be going to the Louisiana Superdome or the Ernest Morial Convention Center for shelter."

"I guess that's a good thing," Jamar said. "Sounds like Governor Jindal and Mayor Nagin are working together this time."

"Yeah, it's not the madness we experienced with Katrina," Alexis replied.

Later, another reporter appeared on the screen. He stood next to the levee just under the Industrial Canal, which separated the Upper Ninth Ward from the Lower Ninth Ward. The Lower Nine, as many residents called it, made national news three years ago as the area hardest hit by Hurricane Katrina. Both Alexis and Jamar had family members who lost their homes in the Lower Nine. And now, just as the area was showing signs of revitalization, it seemed as if Gustav was coming to blow it all away again.

"One of the biggest concerns is if the levees are strong enough to withstand the winds, which are coming in at about one hundred and five miles per hour," the reporter explained. "Estimates say the levees can withstand up to a Category Three, and if Gustav doesn't get any stronger, that's good news. However, if the waters crest over the top, it could still mean flood damage for this troubled area of the city."

"That's right where my cousin Sheree used to live," Jamar pointed out.

"Yeah?" Alexis asked, turning toward him. "She moved back?"

"No. Some kinda way she wound up moving to Memphis. Some church group got her a house and she found a job, so she stayed there."

"That's good. Does she like it there?"

"That's what she told me, but she said it's nothing like home."

Alexis laughed. "I'll bet. There's no city like New Orleans."

Jamar smiled as memories began to wash over his melancholy mood. "You remember when Canal Street used to be the spot?"

"You know it!" Alexis exclaimed. "I used to go there every year, right before school started, so I could buy my Esprit schoolbag."

Jamar laughed. "All y'all girls used to sport those damn bags. We used to think the ones who didn't were outta style."

"Shoot, speaking of style, I used to go to Canal Street to buy my Christ-head rings and medallion earrings with my name across them. Now that was the style."

Jamar hooted in laughter. "I'll bet you used to wear stacks, too."

Alexis laughed so hard at the thought of the outlandish hairdo she and her friends wore in junior high that a tear formed in the corner of her eye. "How you know? My hair was so high, I looked like I had a spaceship on my head! But the real style came when I got to high school—the Get it, Girl!"

Jamar's laughter nearly made him run out of breath. He remembered very well the curly ponytail all the girls used to wear in school. Some had enough real hair to carry the look, but many resorted to weaves and told everyone it was real.

Alexis smiled and shook her head at the memories. "Yeah, I remember Canal Street. It seemed like it was only good for hanging out at night once the Plaza came on the scene."

"Oh, I used to love going to the Plaza," Jamar stated once he had caught his breath. "All the girls from Saint Mary used to hang out there after school. I used to get all kinds of phone numbers from those girls. They thought I didn't notice how they used to roll their uniform skirts up high."

"You know, my momma graduated from Saint Mary," Alexis pointed out. "She wouldn't let me go, because one, she couldn't afford it, being a single parent, and two, she said it just wasn't the same after the principal passed. She said she ruled that place with an iron fist."

"My momma went there, too, which is why I went to Saint Augustine," Jamar said. "That school still has it going on, but I think some of those boys only go there because of the band. Makes me wanna pop them upside their big heads."

"I hear you. I never thought I would say this, but these kids just don't understand. They come in and out of my office all the time, thinking they have it going on. Don't wanna listen to nobody."

"That's 'cause you're old, baby."

"Excuse me?" Alexis asked, cocking her head back in shock.

"Girl, calm down. I'm talking about you're old in *their* eyes. You can't tell them anything, no matter how many STDs they come in with. You just have to have faith that your words will eventually sink in when the time is right."

She nodded. "I guess you're right. I know I wasn't trying to listen to anybody when I was young."

"Yeah, that's how you got caught up with that clown down the street."

Alexis's mouth dropped in shock. "I know you didn't go there."

"No offense, baby, but Chris ain't all that. You couldn't have found a better man to give you all that drama?"

"You shoulda seen him back in the day. You're seeing the kinder, gentler Chris."

"If you say so, but from what I've seen of the men you've been with, I'm the best thing that's ever happened to your crazy ass. Hey!" he cried, his face feeling the effect of a pillow swat.

"I don't think it's possible for me to love you more than *you* do," Alexis remarked with a smirk.

They laughed together as Alexis's cell phone rang. She snatched it from the nightstand and checked the caller ID. Seeing the 281 area code, she figured it was her mother or Roman calling to check on them.

"Hey, we're safe and sound," she announced once she hit TALK.

"I'm glad to hear that."

Eyebrows scrunched in confusion, she pulled the phone away from her ear and studied it, as if the origin of the strange male voice would somehow be revealed.

"Who is this?"

"I know it hasn't been that long, Alexis," the man said.

A pit formed in her stomach and her heart nearly skipped a beat once she realized to whom she was speaking. *I'll be damned,* she thought. "Tony?"

She stole a quick glance at Jamar, who watched her with concern. He turned away, as if trying not to look jealous or nosy. Too late for that, but she understood. She'd be looking at him the same way if his ex-fiancée had called.

"So you haven't forgotten me," he said, his voice dripping in condescending honey.

"Uh, yeah. What brought on this unexpected surprise?"

Tony chuckled. "I just wanted to see if you were okay. I saw the news this morning."

"We're fine. Thank you. You didn't have to call."

"Yes, I did. Believe it or not, I do still care what happens to you."

"Is that right?" Alexis challenged, momentarily forgetting that Jamar was still in the room. "Where in the hell was all that care three years ago, when you made me drive back to New Orleans by myself?"

"Come on, Alexis," Tony said with a hint of laughter in his voice. "You're not still mad about that, are you? We both said and did some things we shouldn't have."

"Bullshit!" she shot back. She was just about to light into him but caught a glimpse of the concern written across Jamar's face. He must have turned back over once he heard the commotion. She rolled her eyes and shook her head. "You know what? I'm not tryin'a argue about that."

"That's good, because I don't wanna argue about it, either," Tony replied, taking a sigh of relief. "That was a long time ago. I'm not proud of how I treated you, but I'm not going to sit here and let you keep punishing me for it."

"Tony, ain't nobody tryin'a punish you, but it's not like you ever called to apologize about it. You never even called to see if I made it back safely. I coulda had my head bashed in, been bleeding and dying on the side of the road, for all you cared."

"Just because I didn't call doesn't mean I didn't care. I knew you made it back safely. I hear you even have your own practice now. I'm proud of you."

"How—" she began but stopped herself. She knew Tony still had friends at Touro Infirmary, the hospital where she worked when they met. He could have easily been informed by one of them as to her status. If that was the case, he probably knew about her engagement, as well. Come to think of it, that could be the real reason he called.

Tony sighed, seeming to read her thoughts. "Like I said, I'm sorry about how we ended, but I'm glad things have worked out well for you."

She laid her head on Jamar's chest and scooted closer to him. "Yeah, thanks. So you married yet?"

She quickly cut her eyes at Jamar, who impatiently stared straight ahead at the television. She knew she was wrong for asking the question. Outside of curiosity, she really didn't care, but she could think of no other way to fish for whatever information he had on her. She would just have to deal with the attitude she was sure she'd receive when she hit END on her cell.

Tony laughed nervously. "Actually, yes. I got married about a year ago. We're expecting our first child in March."

The word *child* hit Alexis with the force of a Mike Tyson right hook. Immediately, the last words she remembered Tony saying to her flooded her memory. She bit her lip to mask the pain. "It wasn't like you were gonna give me any kids, anyway," he had told her when she announced she would return to New Orleans with or without him.

"Looks like things worked out for you."

He cleared his throat, as if realizing the pain he'd caused her. "Um, yeah. I, uh, heard *you're* getting married soon."

"You just have all the four-one-one, don't you?" she mumbled. "Yeah, we're getting married about the same time you have your baby."

Jamar lifted his eyebrows and instinctively stroked her hair. She smiled in gratitude and decided to end the call.

"Look, Tony, it was good talking with you," she said, sitting up, "but my fiancé is waiting for me. We're actually in Virginia Beach, waiting out the storm."

"Oh, that's nice," he said quickly. "Well, like I said, I was just calling to check on you. I'm glad you guys are safe."

"We are. Thanks. By the way, my mother and her husband are out there in Houston."

"Oh, okay. Well, tell them to call me if they need anything."

Alexis held back a laugh. He knew as well as she did that neither Mary nor Frank could stand him. And if her stepbrother, Roman, ever saw him again, he swore he'd kick his ass for how he treated Alexis.

"I doubt they'll call, but I'll let them know."

Tony chuckled and bade his good-bye.

"You all right?" Jamar asked once Alexis placed the phone back on the nightstand.

"Most definitely," she replied scooting closer to him. "Can you believe he had the nerve to claim he cares about me?"

Jamar shrugged. "Seems like all your exes can't forget you."

Alexis laughed and sat up. "What's that supposed to mean?"

"Girl, this trip ain't even three days old yet, and I've already experienced two more of your ex men. Not to mention that clown Reggie back in New Orleans. I'm sure he's bound to call sooner or later."

"So now he's a clown, huh? Just last year you were calling him champ."

"That's until that motherfucker tried to take my woman right from under me."

"Well, it didn't happen. You should be over that."

"Ain't like he said he was sorry," Jamar said, throwing Alexis's words to Tony right back at her. Before she could reply, he grabbed her and kissed her deeply. He then drew his head back and smiled. "Looking at that lineup, I'm sure I'm the best thing that's ever happened to you."

He was, but she would never inflate his ego by telling him so.

Andrea sat on a nearby bench, watching Elizabeth and Latrise study the tiger shark exhibit at the Virginia Aquarium and Marine Science Center. She smiled as the girls marveled over the predators' large size and curious stripes.

"It kinda does look like a tiger," Elizabeth said as a shark swam past her.

"Yeah," Latrise agreed. "We came here for a field trip last year, and my teacher said they can weigh up to two thousand pounds."

"Wow! I wouldn't want that thing on me."

"Yeah, it could eat you whole."

The girls giggled, and Andrea smiled right along with them. Their innocence made her long for the good old days, when life was easier. It was certainly true that youth was wasted on the young. So many kids rushed to get older, thinking life would be easier and carefree, yet once they reached adulthood, all they found were bills, jobs, and problems. They just didn't know how good they had it.

Andrea was thankful she could spend her Saturday kicked back at the aquarium, but the reality was that the first day of school was quickly approaching. The solace of her pristine hallways would soon be replaced by fast girls, thuggish boys, and a plethora of personalities. Back to reality. She really loved being a principal, but she had to admit that it was not a job for the weak at heart. It took lots of mental preparation to deal with such budding minds. It was the type of preparation she should have used to get ready for the reality she faced this weekend.

She wished she could play it cool when it came to Alexis. She didn't understand why that woman got to her the way she did. Nor did she want to get over it, like Brenda and Christopher seemed to want her to. Weren't they there when Alexis tore her life apart more than a decade ago? Didn't Christopher hate Alexis as much as she did? If not, why the hell not?

Of course he didn't. She'd seen the lust in her husband's eyes when Alexis and her new man showed up at the club last night. She wondered how long it would be before his mind would go back to the illicit rendezvous they'd had. The ones they'd had right under her nose. In her house. In the room that was now Latrise's domain. Each time Andrea thought of the time it took to strip those terrible memories from her home and replace them with juvenile innocence, she wanted to scream.

She loved her husband. With time, she had even learned to forgive him for what he'd done. He'd worked hard to reenter her good graces. Yet she couldn't help but wonder if he would relapse now that the bitch was back in their lives.

She hoped last night would work in ensuring those fears never became reality. The way she'd worked it when they returned home from the club was a thing of beauty. Even when she grew exhausted, she was relentless in her pursuit of Christopher's satisfaction. Although he'd vowed never to repeat his indiscretion, she needed to be sure he wouldn't even consider it.

Andrea couldn't help but hate Alexis. Why couldn't karma bite her in the ass? Here she was, a woman who had torn a family apart by getting pregnant by a married man. She'd even treated her supposed boyfriend at the time like crap. So much so that he broke up with her just to save face. Yet she still finished college, became a doctor, and was now marrying a successful lawyer. Where was the justice in that?

Okay, she was a little jealous, although she would never admit that to anyone but herself. Although she had no desire to be a doctor, and would never trade her husband for anyone, she just wished she had even a piece of the self-confidence and drive that Alexis had. While Andrea writhed in the pain that Alexis and Christopher had caused her, Alexis seemed to use it as fuel to do better. Have an abortion? Become a doctor. Lose a good boyfriend? Marry a lawyer. Get your feelings hurt? Pretend it never happened. Hurt someone else? Never apologize! Why couldn't Andrea have that type of attitude, instead of letting anger eat her from the inside?

"Mommy, can we get a soda or something? We're thirsty."

"What? Oh, yeah," Andrea said dryly, wakening from her thoughts. She took each girl's hand and walked them over to the concession stand, a pretty decent walk considering the concession stand and the shark exhibit were on opposite sides of the building.

"Maybe when we finish, we can go play with the stingrays," Elizabeth suggested.

Andrea enjoyed that part of the aquarium most. The Virginia Aquarium boasted touch pools, in which patrons could actually touch some of the marine life. The stingray pool was the magnet that kept Andrea coming back. She loved the way they flapped when they came close to the edge of the pool. And their wet skin felt eerily smooth.

However, the thought of touching potentially dangerous sea life couldn't keep her mind off of her nemesis. Alexis. Even her name sounded slutty.

She wondered what that Jamar guy even saw in her. From what she'd gleaned from Brenda, Alexis had tried to play him with her ex-boyfriend Reggie, who, believe it or not, was the man she'd cheated on when she bedded Christopher.

Who was Jamar, anyway? He looked okay, but what man would put up with the stuff Alexis had put him through and still propose? Was he up to something? Was Alexis up to something? Even if she wasn't, Andrea doubted the marriage would last very long. Who could live with a woman like her? She was sure Alexis would step out on him as soon as she found a better deal. Her track record was already proven. The thought of the divorce that would soon follow nearly made her chuckle. She nearly laughed aloud when she thought of the possibility of Alexis screwing up the relationship before she even had time to look at the aisle, let alone walk down it!

Andrea glanced at her watch. It was nearly eleven. She was sure Brenda and Rayna were already shopping for wedding gowns with Little Miss Alexis. She had nearly choked on her coffee when Brenda asked her over breakfast if she'd like to go.

"You can't be serious," Andrea had told her.

Brenda had smiled at her. "I'm not, but I was hoping you had warmed up to her a little after we hung out last night."

"Nope. She's just as much my enemy now as she was before," Andrea told her, shrugging her shoulders.

"*Enemy*'s a pretty strong word."

"Yes, but it's also a truthful one right now."

Brenda put down her coffee cup and looked her friend in the eyes. "Tell me this. You told me when I first got here that the reason you hate her is that she never apologized for what she did. If she did, knowing the way you feel about her, could you forgive her and get past it?"

Andrea still didn't know the answer to that question. She knew as a Christian, she should forgive Alexis, but as a human, she also knew it wasn't that easy. As she pulled out twenty dollars to pay for three sodas and a large order of french fries, she knew she wouldn't find the answer right now. Time to get back to reality.

"That's the one," Brenda said as Alexis emerged from the dressing room.

"You think so?" she asked, stepping onto the small platform in front of the three-way mirror.

The satin, A-line Vera Wang design fit her like it had been stitched with only her in mind. Alexis twirled back and forth, trying to see it from every angle. After kissing seven different frog dresses, she'd finally found the one.

"I agree, Alexis. It's beautiful," Rayna chimed in.

"I do like it," Alexis replied, her eyes still glued to the mirror, "but you don't think I should try on a few more styles just in case?"

"Girl, just in case what?" Brenda asked, laughing. She took a sip from the champagne the store manager had given them. "Just in case you find something more expensive? You're gonna spend all that money for a dress you're going to wear only once? I say go for the one that looks good on you—that one right there—and spend the rest of your funds on your honeymoon."

"I know what you're saying, but I'm only planning on doing this once," Alexis said, turning to face her cousin. "It might just be one day, but it's the only day I'll have. Why not look like a million bucks?"

"Why not look like a million and have spent only one thousand?" Brenda replied with a shrug. "You know what Grandma used to say. 'Get a Cadillac on a Ford budget.'"

The ladies laughed at the century-old saying. Even the store manager had to smile.

"Dr. White, the dress is lovely," the manager said. "I do have a few more in the same price range if you want to try on a couple more."

"See?" Alexis said, pointing at the manager. "She knows how to sell dresses. Now, let me do me, please."

Brenda smiled and held up her champagne glass at her cousin. "It's all you, girl."

Rayna took a seat next to Brenda as Alexis disappeared into the dressing room. "She's making me feel like I chose my dress too quickly."

"You did the right thing," Brenda assured her. "This store is full of beautiful dresses. You could spend all day second-guessing yourself. Take it from a married woman. You still have to live once the wedding is over."

Rayna nodded. "I hear you."

Alexis paraded in and out of the dressing room, modeling different styles from different designers. An hour later, she finally decided on the Vera Wang she'd worn earlier.

"Not a word," Alexis told her smiling cousin.

"I didn't say anything," Brenda said.

"I know, and you can stop thinking it, too."

She and Rayna carried their dresses to the register. Since the store was a small local business, they didn't have a seamstress on site, so Rayna decided to take her dress to her aunt for alterations. She was careful to buy the dress two sizes bigger, knowing her rising belly would soon make her correct size a thing of the past. At least if she got it too big, her aunt would have an easier time taking it in than letting it out.

Alexis, on the other hand, decided to take hers back to New Orleans. She would get her favorite tailor to alter the dress there. Now all she had to do was buy shoes and choose a hairstyle, and that could be handled in New Orleans, as well.

A part of her wondered if she should be spending this much money while she and Jamar were technically in the middle of a crisis. After all, they had taken an unplanned trip to Virginia Beach, were living in a hotel, and were eating out every day. Should she really be planning a wedding right now? Especially since Gustav would probably affect her patients' ability to play, just as Katrina had done. She quickly shrugged off the thought. Jamar wouldn't have encouraged her to go dress shopping if he didn't have a plan, would he? Besides, those couple of years of living with her parents had allowed her to build a decent nest egg. On top of that, Jamar was doing well with his law practice. They would be able to get by, wouldn't they?

"So what do we do now?" Rayna asked once they left the shop.

"How about some ice cream?" Brenda suggested.

Alexis made a face at her. "Brenda, you are so wholesome. Live a little. Let's go get a drink."

Rayna laughed. "That's what I'm talking about."

Brenda rolled her eyes at them. "I'm not as wholesome as you think. I'll go get a drink."

"And I'm not talking about the white wine mess you had at the club last night," Alexis snapped. "Iced tea for all. From Long Island, that is. Well, except for Rayna. She gets real iced tea."

Rayna laughed again. "Alexis, I'm starting to like you more and more."

"You better ask somebody," Alexis shot back, posing with her hand on her hip.

"Oh, goodness," Brenda said, rolling her eyes. "The true, blue Alexis is back."

"I never left. Now come on."

Chapter 8

The day was gorgeous. A slight breeze blew gently through the sun's blazing rays. The beach seemed unusually crowded for a Monday. Nikki would have thought more people would be in school or at work.

She scanned the beach, searching for a place to set up her little perch. People watching in the sand had become her favorite pastime. Unfortunately, the number of people strolling the beach and running in and out of the water would make finding a spot a challenge. She gave up and decided to shop for mementos, which she knew she'd never have any use for once she returned to New Orleans. Seashell necklaces and Virginia Beach coasters only seemed like a good idea on vacation, and she knew deep down that crap would get tossed to the back of her closet once she returned home. *Home.* What a beautiful word. As much as she was enjoying her mini-vacation, she really couldn't wait to get back to the familiarity of home.

This wasn't the same as the time she'd evacuated with Reggie and DeShawn. That time, she'd been in the comfort of her second home in Atlanta, while Reggie traveled with the Saints. Her in-laws were just a phone call away, and her own parents stayed in the house with her. Now she was alone. Her parents had chosen to evacuate to Baton Rouge this time, believing that nothing could be as bad as Katrina. On top of that,

Reggie was living it up in Atlanta with their son and his new woman.

Nikki rolled her eyes at the thought of Reggie and then shook off the thought as she tried on a sarong in a surf shop. She modeled in front of the mirror, inspecting the way the colors contrasted with her caramel-colored skin. She smiled and took the sarong to the register.

"That'll be all for ya?" asked the young cashier. He was a blond-haired, blue-eyed cutie who sounded like a stereotypical Valley boy, which made Nikki smile even wider.

"Yeah, that's it," she replied as she tied her old pink sarong around her waist, concealing the bottom of her floral bikini.

The Valley boy's eyes rested on her cleavage before he rang up the price on the register. "You enjoying your time here?"

"How you know I'm a visitor?"

The Valley boy laughed. "The locals don't shop here."

"I guess that's true," Nikki remarked with a smile. She waved the boy off as she grabbed her bag off the counter. Her eyes then landed on a display filled with saltwater taffy. She pointed at it with her French-tipped index finger. "Is that stuff any good?"

"I like it."

She smiled at him flirtatiously. "Then it must be good."

The Valley boy laughed as she grabbed two boxes and placed them on the counter. He silently rang up the price and then placed them in the bag with her sarong.

"This is the good stuff," he told her. "This was made by Forbes, and it's made right here in Vah Beach."

"Vah Beach?"

"Yep, that's what we call Virginia Beach for short."

"I see," Nikki replied, moving toward the door. "I feel more like a local already."

"You wanna feel more like a local, you need to get off the oceanfront and check out the rest of the city. Maybe even go to Norfolk or Portsmouth."

"I'll remember that," she replied before leaving the store.

She thought back to how the cashier had stared at her breasts. Lustful looks like that were a constant in Nikki's life. So much so that she rarely told anyone her real age. Most modeling agents still sought the nine-teen-and twenty-year-olds, so she had to make sure she could still compete. Although she was thirty-five, her slim, but muscular legs could put many younger women to shame. She always made sure her shoulder-length, bone-straight hair and her natural, half-inch-long nails were styled to perfection. Even without makeup, she looked as young as twenty-three. Heck, the few twenty-year-olds who knew her real age always told her that they hoped to look half as good as she did when they were older.

Nikki pulled her shades from her purse and placed them over her squinted eyes. The sun was relentless. She looked around for a respite from the heat and found it in the form of a lounge facing the beach. The walk signal appeared just under the stoplight, so she scampered across the street and walked into the bar. She found a table and took a seat.

"What can I get you?" asked a waitress, who seemed to appear from nowhere.

Nikki looked up and found an attractive brunette wearing a pair of jeans and a tank top. She guessed the lounge didn't have a strict dress code for its employees since it was located on the beach. "Uh, yeah, can I get a margarita?"

"Original or strawberry?"

"Original, of course."

"Anything else for ya?"

"No, I'm good," Nikki replied while stretching her legs out in front of her.

"Got it," the waitress said, scribbling on her notepad. "You enjoying your holiday?"

"Holiday?"

"Hello?" the waitress sang sarcastically. "Labor Day?"

Nikki drew back her head as the realization of time sank in. "Oh, yeah. Is that why it's so crowded out here? I forgot all about that."

The waitress chuckled. "Be right back with your drink."

Nikki stared out the window at the pretty beach. The light brown sand and the sapphire-colored water were a stark contrast to the dank waters that threatened to flood her city once again. She had seen the reports this morning and knew well the danger that could befall the city. She wasn't so sure the levees would hold, but she had to have faith. As much as Nikki loved traveling, there was definitely no place like home.

A couple of boys playing with a soccer ball on the beach caught her attention. If DeShawn were there, he would be begging to join them, knowing he hadn't played soccer a day in his life. He was strictly his daddy's boy, a football player in the making. Although soccer was known as football in other countries, it was a completely different game as far as Nikki was concerned.

Yet DeShawn wouldn't have cared. He would have just been happy to play. He was one of the friendliest kids in his school, partly because his daddy's celebrity status made him one of the most popular. At seven years old, DeShawn hadn't gotten to the age that made him wonder if people liked him because of his daddy. She only hoped that having an ex-football player as a daddy and a model as a mommy wouldn't have an adverse effect on how he saw himself. Maybe if he continued being the social butterfly that he was, she would never see a plunge in his self-esteem.

By the time her drink arrived, Nikki had nearly drowned in her thoughts of her son. She could kick herself for letting her selfishness cause her to lose him, but as long as he was happy and being taken care of, there wasn't much she could do about the situation.

She pulled out her cell phone and dialed Reggie's number. As she waited for an answer, she wondered why he hadn't called her to check on her, but then dismissed the thought. *Ain't nothing worse than a petty man,* she thought.

"Hello?" answered a woman's voice.

Nikki drew her head back in surprise. "Who's this?"

"This is Janet. May I help you?"

"Janet?" Nikki repeated, tapping her fingers on the table. She took a sip from her drink and tried her best to keep the attitude from invading her tone. "Well, um, this is Nikki, DeShawn's mother?"

A second of silence went by. "Nikki? Hi. I'm Reggie's girlfriend. It's really nice to meet you."

"It is, huh? You two must have gotten pretty close if you're already answering his phone."

"Well, we've been together for a while now, so I guess so."

Nikki wanted to curse the woman out for her non-chalance but decided against it. *I didn't call to speak to this bitch*, she thought. *She's inconsequential, anyway.* "Is DeShawn there?"

"Oh, yes," she replied, in a tone that was a little *too* friendly for Nikki's taste. "I'll get him for you."

Nikki listened as Janet called her son, having the nerve to call him "sweetie." Who was this woman who was trying to be Mommy in DeShawn's life? *I'll be damned if she comes in tryin'a play that role.*

"Hey, Mommy!" DeShawn greeted excitedly.

"Hey, baby," she said with a smile, momentarily forgetting her irritation. "Whatcha up to?"

"I'm about to help Daddy wash the car. Then he's gonna take me to see a movie."

"That's good. Where's your daddy now?"

"He's downstairs talking to Grandma."

"Oh, okay." She took another sip from her drink. "Are you scared about the hurricane?"

"No. Daddy said there's nothing to worry about."

"Well, he's right," Nikki agreed, wishing she had as much optimism as her son. She glanced at the television, but only news from the Republican National Convention was being broadcast. "We'll be back home soon, and when we get back, we'll have to do something special."

"Like what?"

"I'll tell you what. Make a list of some things you want us to do together, and when we get back, we'll pick something."

"I can do that."

Nikki and DeShawn spoke for a while longer, laughing and chatting in ways only a mother and son could understand.

"Well, baby, I'm going to get off now," Nikki said. "I was just checkin' on you."

"Okay, Mommy. You want me to tell Daddy you called?"

"No, you don't have to. I was just calling for you."

"Okay, Mommy. Have fun in Virginia," DeShawn said. "I love you."

"Love you too, baby," Nikki replied.

She smiled as she pressed END, and then dropped the phone in her purse. A wave of pride washed over her as she thought of how she had handled herself with Janet. She could have cursed her out and demanded that she speak to Reggie, then cursed him out for letting that woman spend so much time with their son. Yet none of that had happened. Not that it would have solved anything, anyway.

She wished she and Reggie could get along. She no longer entertained thoughts of them getting back together. That was just wasted energy. All she wanted was a relationship with her son. Although she and De-Shawn got along famously, she feared that the tension between her and Reggie would eventually spill over into the harmony between her and DeShawn.

He really needed to get over what had happened in their marriage. So, what? She'd cheated on him one, two, twenty, or thirty times? At least she was woman enough to admit it. At least she could come to terms with the fact that she just wasn't the marrying type. Reggie was a good guy, a great husband, and an even better father, but he didn't need to be with a woman like her.

Nikki was like an eagle. She needed to fly free. Land where she needed to until the time came for her to move on. She owed Reggie a lot for helping her to get the lifestyle she desired, but there was no way in hell she could stay married to his softhearted ass. Now, maybe if he had agreed to the open marriage idea, things would be different, but that would never come into fruition.

An attractive man wearing white cotton slacks and a Hawaiian button-down shirt walked into the lounge, catching Nikki's attention. His dark hair and olive skin suggested he might be of European descent. He caught Nikki's gaze and smiled as he sat at the bar.

Nikki lifted her eyebrows in response. This was why she needed to be single. Had she been married, her flirtation would have been disgraceful, as her grand-mother would say. However, as a single woman, she answered to no one. She was flying free!

She smiled and licked her lips while swirling the straw in her melting margarita. *I'm a bad girl,* she thought as she crossed her legs.

"Can I get you anything else?" the casually dressed waitress asked, again appearing from nowhere.

"Girl, if you don't stop sneaking up on me," Nikki said, laughing.

The waitress laughed, too. "I'm sorry, but you looked like you were in outer space for a minute."

Nikki smiled. "I was, but I'm back. Can I get another margarita?"

"No problem."

Once the waitress walked away, Nikki again glanced at the television, deciding not to give the European man more energy than he deserved. If he wanted to talk to her, he would get his hot tail up and join her at her table. She studied the images moving around on the TV. The sound was turned down, so she had to depend on the headlines scrolling at the bottom of the screen.

The image now showing on TV looked very familiar. A reporter stood in front of the levee near the Florida Avenue Bridge in the Lower Ninth Ward. The bridge was only about a five-minute drive from her parents' home. Their first house in the Lower Nine had been destroyed by Hurricane Katrina, but they had refused to rebuild anywhere else. The Lower Ninth Ward, the area stretching from the Industrial Canal to St. Bernard Parish, nearly 100 percent black, was the neighborhood they would always call home.

They had rebuilt their home a few blocks from Fats Domino's home near St. Claude Avenue. The Lower Nine still had a long way to go, but the residents who had returned to the area were working hard to bring the area back. Brad Pitt had even begun a project to build 150 homes in the area. Other volunteers had also thrown their hats into revitalizing the Lower Nine. People were returning every day. It had never been a prosperous neighborhood, but it was one filled with pride. This was why people like Fats and Nikki's parents longed to remain there.

Yet the neighborhood still had a long way to go. Many of its schools still had not reopened. A number of businesses hadn't returned. Many residents who owned property there still had not returned to demolish their blighted homes, which gave the area a constant look of devastation. Mayor Ray Nagin had threatened to use imminent domain to seize the blighted properties, but only time would tell if revitalization efforts would win over.

However, it seemed as if Gustav threatened to take away what little progress they'd made. That didn't seem to be the case, though, according to the images Nikki saw on television. Instead of flooded desolation, she saw waves from the mighty Mississippi lapping over the steel walls of the levee. The waves seemed mean, but the walls held firm. The levees were holding!

She strained her eyes to read the words at the bottom of the screen. Once the reality hit her, she covered her mouth with both hands. A tear of joy slid slowly down the crease of her nose. Water spurted through a few cracks, and there was minimal flooding in the Upper Ninth Ward, but her city was safe. Gustav had not been strong enough to breach the levees.

The waitress set her margarita in front of her and took away the empty glass. Nikki barely noticed her. All she cared about was getting back home to her son and helping her parents get back into their home. She smiled under her hands and tried to fight back the tears.

Once she noticed the full margarita in front of her, she held it up as if to say, "Cheers." This was truly a celebration. She was going home! She was so busy celebrating that she didn't notice the company she had standing over her.

"May I join you?" asked a male voice, drawing her face upward.

It was the European man who'd walked into the lounge earlier. She welcomed him to her table by nodding and indicating the chair across from her. He smiled and took a seat.

"You are one beautiful woman."

"Thank you," she said, a flirtatious smile covering her face.

The compliment became the precursor to a conversation that lasted into the late afternoon. They sat so long that they ordered dinner. Turned out the man's name was Clarke, and he was an Italian businessman who owned a gourmet restaurant on the strip. The restaurant, according to him, was doing quite well. He'd come into the lounge only for a change of scenery, but meeting Nikki made him want to stay longer.

"How much longer will you be visiting the Beach?" he asked.

"Just a few more days," she replied. She didn't want to tell him that she was from New Orleans, because she was tired of questions like "How's your family?" or "Did you lose your home?" She'd been having those conversations for the last three years, and she hoped to take a brief respite just this once. "Just taking a quick vacation before going back to reality."

Clarke laughed lightly. "I understand. Tell me, Nikki, is this your first time to Virginia Beach?"

"Oh, no, I've been here lots of times," she lied. She had enough street smarts not to let some stranger know she was a rookie at this game. In truth, she couldn't find her way to the nearest mall, but she'd never let anyone around here know that. "I love this area."

"I wish you had eaten at my restaurant during one of your visits," Clarke said with a smile.

"How do you know I haven't?"

"Oh, I'm sure I would remember seeing your beautiful face in my restaurant."

Nikki smiled, drinking in all of Clarke's compliments. His intentions of getting her into bed were embedded in his every movement. His gestures were slow and deliberate; his eyes never left hers. She knew what he wanted, but she also knew he wouldn't succeed. As much as she enjoyed a good one-night stand, there was no way in hell she would give it up to someone being this obvious.

Her mind began to wander as Clarke continued showering her with compliments. She wondered how much a ticket flying her back to New Orleans tomorrow would cost. She tried deciding between taking DeShawn to the Audubon Aquarium of the Americas in New Orleans or driving him to Biloxi, to the beach. Well, maybe not the beach.

"You are too funny," she sang, trying to fake enjoyment with the conversation. As beautiful as she felt she was, she actually got tired of hearing it all the time. These men really needed to learn to change the subject every once in a while.

Her eyes scanned the lounge, more out of boredom than curiosity. She turned back to Clarke, who was rattling off the benefits of owning a business in Virginia Beach. He didn't even seem to notice she'd drifted into outer space. *This clown is more interested in himself than he is me,* she thought. *I'm not having that. He must not know who the hell I am!*

She wanted to just disregard him altogether and get out of there. However, she didn't want to be rude. She never knew when she might need him later. Money and good sex could sometimes be hard to come by. It wasn't like she'd seen any other prospects in the last couple of days. On the other hand, it was sleeping with an Italian that had gotten her in trouble once before. She still hadn't figured out how Reggie had found out about her one-night stand while they were separated, but she would never forget how he used it as a surprise move in court to win custody of their son.

"Clarke, honey," she said with the most Southern-belle charm her Lower Nine edge would allow, "it's gettin' a little late, and I want to get a little more shopping in before I go home in a few days."

He smiled, picked up her hand, and gently kissed it. "I understand, lovely lady. You know, you never did tell me where home is for you."

She smiled back and winked. "Why do you wanna know? You plan on visiting one day?"

"Possibly, if the opportunity arises."

"I'll tell you what," Nikki said, rubbing her finger across his cheek. "You keep charming me like that and I might let you do a lot of things."

Clarke shot her a sexy, toothy smile, seeming to totally forget that she hadn't answered his question. "If you're available tomorrow, I'd like to get you away from the beach."

"To where?"

"You said you wanted to go shopping. I thought I might take you to the mall and let you get a few things that don't have Virginia Beach written all over them."

She smiled and nodded. Maybe old Clarke would have some use, after all. "I'm with that."

They exchanged phone numbers, then bade each other farewell. After going their separate ways, Nikki decided to stroll the beach for a while longer before heading back to her hotel room. These were the days when she was thankful that she didn't have a nine-to-five. Between the money she'd secretly saved during her marriage to Reggie and the dollars she earned from her modeling career, she was free to chill out for as long as she wanted. If it weren't for DeShawn, she could have stayed in Virginia Beach for at least another week.

"What you smiling about?" Reggie asked, eyeing Janet as she descended the steps.

"Nothing," she replied, taking a seat next to him on the couch. Her eyes rested on the back of DeShawn, who lay on the floor, watching *SpongeBob*. The fact that the child had maintained his childlike innocence through three major hurricanes and a divorce was surprisingly comforting, but it wasn't enough to take her mind off of what was really on the forefront.

She could have told him about Nikki's call, but why? He'd hear about it soon enough from DeShawn, and even if he didn't, he didn't need to know about the jealousy she was sure she'd heard in his ex-wife's voice. Really, he didn't need to know about the sense of triumph Janet had felt as a result of that jealousy.

All this time Janet had felt like she was competing against a memory. A memory she felt she'd never live up to. She'd seen Nikki on TV and in a couple of magazines. The bitch was gorgeous, with a body to kill for. Janet was no slouch herself, but next to Nikki, she felt plain and secretly wondered how Reggie really saw her. Was she merely the woman he'd settled for when things didn't work out with either Nikki or his college sweetheart, Alexis? Was he really serious about her, or was he passing time until the next glamour girl came along?

She could only hope he appreciated the fact that she treated his ornery ass better than any woman he'd been with in recent years. And his son, with his cute self, loved her like a second mother. At least *she* thought so. Unfortunately, it was well known that love didn't always win the man's heart. A woman could cook well, sex well, and connect on nearly every level, but if a man had it in his mind that he didn't want to commit, there was nothing she could do to convince him otherwise. She could only pray that he would receive a mental kick in the ass to make him see the treasure he had before him.

Janet hoped it wouldn't come down to that with her and Reggie. She was crazy about him, issues and all. Reggie had been through hell and back with respect to relationships, so she tried being patient with him.

Maybe it wouldn't take him a year or three or four to realize he'd finally found the right thing.

"You're not watching the hurricane coverage?" Janet asked, laying her head on Reggie's shoulder.

He shook his head no. "Can't watch that shit right now. It's too depressing."

Janet nodded in agreement. She still hadn't finished rebuilding her house after Katrina. Would the little progress she'd made with the little insurance money she had withstand another hurricane? It was a question she didn't even want to think about answering, so *SpongeBob* seemed just as good a choice as any to get her mind off of home.

DeShawn laughed out loud.

Janet smiled. Even at thirty-three years old, she thought *SpongeBob* was one of the funniest cartoons out there. "I can see why you chose to watch this."

Reggie stifled a chuckle. "I don't even know why I let Shawn watch this anymore."

"Why do you say that?"

He glanced at his son and then faced Janet with a smile. "Remind me one of these days to let you know why it's too much of a coincidence that a sponge runs around with a starfish and a squirrel in Bikini Bottom."

"Huh?"

He smiled again and patted her on the thigh. "I'll tell you later."

Before Janet could put much more thought into the strange riddle, Reggie's mother, Shirley, rushed through the front door.

"Did you see the news?" she asked, excitedly shifting from one foot to the other.

"What, Momma?" Reggie asked, jumping from the couch. DeShawn and Janet followed suit, each wearing fearful looks on their faces. "You all right? What happened?"

"Gustav!" she exclaimed. "It's . . ."

"It's what?" Reggie pushed.

"Just turn the damn news on!" Shirley shouted.

Reggie did as he was told, expecting the worst. Had his worst nightmare come true? Would he have to start all over again? He'd lost nearly everything once. He couldn't bear to think about going through that again so soon.

"The worst has passed," the reporter said, as if on cue.

"Shit! The levees held?" Reggie asked happily. He folded his arms and watched the television with a content smile on his face.

DeShawn screamed in jubilation, jumping up and down while pumping both arms in the air.

"Thank you, Jesus," Shirley declared, but Reggie barely heard her.

All he could hear was the reporters telling him that his home was safe. He would return to New Orleans and take his new job as a New Orleans Saints commentator. DeShawn wouldn't have to switch schools. He could go back to life as he knew it. They would finally get to live as father and son—two bachelors living it up.

He stared at the TV so hard that he hadn't noticed Janet's arms snaking around his waist from the back. He nearly jumped once he realized she was holding him. That made him feel bad. Not once in his private celebration had he thought about Janet. Did she actually have a place in his future? She was a good girl, but was he ready for her yet?

"Looks like we can go home," Janet said softly.

"Y'all ain't gonna rush off tomorrow, are you?" asked Shirley, who had taken a seat in the same spot Reggie had vacated after her abrupt entrance. DeShawn walked over and snuggled next to her.

"Of course not, Momma," Reggie replied, turning and placing his arm around Janet. "You think I would cut short my visit with my favorite mother?"

Shirley sucked her teeth and cut her eyes at her son. "I'm your *only* mother, boy, and don't you forget it."

Chapter 9

News about Gustav didn't get past Darnell and Jamar, either. The ladies had gone out again, so Darnell hung out with Jamar at the hotel.

"Looks like we can head home soon," Darnell said before taking a bite of his burger.

"I hope so," Jamar said. "I don't know what's going on with my credit cards, but I do know I could take care of the situation a lot better if I was at home."

"You ain't called the bank yet?"

"No. I was trying to wait for Alexis to leave."

"You haven't told her yet? Whatcha waitin' on? For all your money to be gone?"

"No, man," Jamar replied in exasperation. He looked down and rubbed the back of his head with both hands. "I just don't want to say anything until I figure out what's going on. If I can handle this without her knowing, that's less stress for the both of us."

"I hear you, bruh, but you know as well as I do that Alexis doesn't like being in the dark about anything," Darnell said. "Besides, if we're heading home soon, you're gonna need those cards on the road."

"I know, baby boy, I know. That ain't even the bad part. I gotta call downstairs and try to talk these people into lettin' us stay a couple more nights. I'm praying they don't make me pay for the extra nights in advance."

Darnell thought for a minute. "Maybe they'll give you a break if you let them know you're a Gustav evacuee."

Jamar cursed and shook his head. "I feel like a fuckin' bum! I ain't never had to make no excuses for money!"

"Bruh, sometimes you've gotta put your pride in your pocket and do what you gotta do."

The men sat in silence, watching the news reports on Hurricane Gustav. The winds had knocked out much of the power in the city. Cleanup efforts would begin soon. The Republican National Convention had been truncated due to the troubles on the Gulf Coast.

"When do you think you're gonna head back home?" Jamar asked, swirling a couple of fries in a splotch of ketchup.

"Soon as my job gives me the thumbs-up."

Jamar looked up at his friend. A friend he probably never would have met had it not been for Brenda and Alexis. "How did the navy let you leave, anyway? You didn't have to stay back for rescue efforts or anything like that?"

"Man, I'm on my way out," Darnell replied, stretching his legs out in front of him. "Everybody knows I'm dropping my retirement papers soon. Besides, I don't have that type of job. Right now I'm considered nonessential personnel, which means I'm free to go to make sure my family is okay."

"That's all right," Jamar said, nodding his head. "Must be nice."

"Hey, being a navy chief has its privileges."

They laughed and shook hands. Jamar and Darnell had been friends for only a few months. They'd met once Alexis had finally gotten over her shell shock from relationships and had accepted his proposal of marriage. Only then had he been free to get to know anyone in her family. Until then, Darnell and Brenda were only names in fleeting conversation.

The two men had immediately hit it off. Both had been through obstacles trying to win their women over. Both were serious about their careers. Both enjoyed a good, stiff drink after a hard day at work. Over the months, they'd learned to become great friends.

"I just don't understand it," Jamar said, bringing the conversation back to his problems. "I pay my bills religiously every month. I keep my checkbook balanced to the penny. A brother got stock, mutual funds. How in the hell do I have two credit cards closed and an empty bank account right out of the damn blue? Come to think of it, I ain't even checked on my stocks. That shit's probably fucked up, too!"

Darnell shrugged. "Maybe it's like we said. It could have something to do with Gustav. The same thing happened to a lot of people during Katrina."

Jamar shook his head. "Ain't the same, bruh. A lot of that didn't happen until after Katrina hit. My shit was fucked up before Gustav even hit New Orleans. This is some other shit."

"Anybody else have access to your accounts?"

"Not even Alexis."

"You piss anybody off lately?"

"Nobody smart enough to know how to get into my accounts," Jamar replied with a chuckle.

Darnell's face remained serious. "You sure about that?"

Jamar thought back. He was sure it wasn't a woman. He hadn't been involved with anyone since his early days of dating Alexis. Even then, he had been straight up with everyone he dated. That it was just that—dating. His focus was his career and nothing else. The love he sought was the love of money. Sex was good, and many times it was off the chain, but he really didn't want or need it every day. He enjoyed the days when he could come home alone, work on a case, have a Jack and Coke, then hit the sheets without the nagging of a woman.

Believe it or not, that was what made him fall in love with Alexis. She was just as serious about her career as he was about his. Popping up in the middle of the night? She didn't think so. Nagging him about spending more time together? Not Dr. Alexis White. She had her own thing going on, and he loved it! Her independence turned him on, made *him* nag *her* about spending time together. It wasn't easy. Still, he got her and intended to keep her.

"This ain't got nothin' to do with no woman," Jamar said confidently, leaning back on the couch. He crossed his feet on top of the coffee table, careful not to kick over his leftover fries.

"Maybe it's not a woman," Darnell said, leaning forward. "You're a lawyer, and you're damn good at what you do. Maybe somebody's trying to get some payback."

"Boy, don't even play like that," Jamar responded, glaring in anger. "I wish somebody would try to mess with my finances over some bullshit. I ain't the one who made them break the law or cheat on their wives or embezzle funds, or whatever else they did. All I can do is my job."

"I feel you, but some might think you do your job well while standing on the necks of those who can't afford you."

"That ain't my problem," Jamar replied, stretching his arms out in resignation. "Besides, most of the people who can afford me are going against people who can afford just as good or even better. And even if they couldn't afford me, what am I supposed to do? Hold back? Take my clients' money without doing everything I can to win? I don't think so, bruh."

"I know what you're saying, and I agree with you, but that doesn't stop somebody from trying to get revenge."

Jamar sucked his teeth. "That shit only happens in the movies. In this case, somebody at the bank done messed up."

"At three different banks?" Darnell pointed out, raising his eyebrows.

"Coincidence."

"If you say so," Darnell replied, sitting back in his chair. He began pulling at his white polo shirt in an effort to fan himself. "It's getting hot as hell in here."

"It is, huh?" Jamar agreed, rising from the couch. He walked over to the thermostat and turned it down to sixty-five degrees. "You want some water or something?"

"Yeah, that's cool."

Jamar walked to the kitchen and grabbed two bottled waters from the refrigerator. After tossing one to Darnell, he took his seat back on the couch and thought about everything his friend had told him. Could someone really be trying to get him? If so, who? Whoever it was, he damn sure had better put an end to this game quick. The rest of his life depended on it.

Depression had destroyed Jamar's entire swagger. He was no longer the streetwise, happy-go-lucky lawyer who sat on top of the world. That persona had blown away with Gustav and had been replaced by a defeated brother with no credit. He wasn't even sure how he would pay for the time-share unit. When he called to extend the room for a couple of days, the card he'd used for approval had been canceled. He felt like a squatter waiting to be caught. It pained him to do it, but he decided to take Darnell's advice and play the Gustav card. It worked, but it didn't make him feel much better. It only put a Band-Aid on the already hemorrhaging situation.

He'd called all three of his banks, but just as Christopher had predicted, he couldn't reach a human being to save his life. All he could do was press the buttons that would report his cards stolen. He still had the cards in his possession, but he figured his numbers must have been stolen. What explanation would befit the cancellation of all his cards at the same time?

It was amazing how life worked sometimes. He had moved heaven and hell to get the woman of his dreams, and now it seemed like they would be stuck in the time warp of her past because he couldn't keep his finances straight. It just wasn't right.

He'd always prided himself on keeping his business straight. That was why he graduated magna cum laude from Xavier University and coasted through Howard University Law School with a constant 4.0 average. It was what made him the owner of not one, but three properties by the time he was thirty-five. It was what made the hardest-hearted woman—next to her mean-ass mother—in New Orleans finally fall in love with him. This shit that seemed to come out of nowhere was not going to make all that crumble to the ground. Whatever was going on, he'd damn sure get to the bottom of it . . . or die trying.

Darnell did his best to get Jamar's mind off his problems.

"Once upon a time, I knew a brother who had let all his problems consume him," he told Jamar. "From what I heard, a night out with the fellas did him hella good."

"Come on, D," Jamar replied, his lips pursed in frustration. "What little bit of money I do have needs to be saved until my firm can come through with some emergency funds to get us back home. Thank God I have some damn pull at that place."

"Now, what type of brother do you think I am?"

Jamar looked at his friend in confusion.

"How you think I'ma invite you out and make you pay for it, knowing what you're going through?"

Jamar shook his head and stared at the television, refusing to face his friend for fear of tears invading his tough exterior. He wiped his face with both hands and took a deep breath. "I can't let you do that, man. You're an evacuee just like I am."

"You don't need to be worried about that," Darnell said. "My wife would never let her cousin suffer, so I can't let her cousin's fiancé suffer. Besides, a few drinks and a ride around the city aren't going to break us."

"I appreciate that, baby boy, but I think I need to stay here and figure this shit out."

"J, you're not going to solve this in one night," Darnell replied, rising from his chair. He walked over to the phone and began dialing. "You need to get your mind off of this for a couple hours. This shit's been eatin' you up since you got here."

Jamar nodded, knowing his friend was right. But what else could he think about? How the hell could a man be the provider and protector for his woman like this?

"Who you callin'?"

"Byron. If anybody knows his way around this city, it's him."

Jamar's eyebrows rose, but he remained silent. He appreciated what his friend was trying to do. Still, he wasn't sure he wanted to hang out with Byron. He didn't feel right hanging out with a piece of Alexis's past.

"All right, he'll be over in an hour to scoop us up," Darnell announced a few minutes later. He returned to his seat and crossed his feet on the coffee table. "Said he's bringing Chris, too."

"I don't know about hanging out with those two," Jamar admitted.

Darnell sighed and took his feet off the table. He then leaned forward and looked his friend in the eye. "I understand why you're feeling that way, but I can assure you that they're not keeping that bull going."

"D, I know you try to see the best in people, but I'm a lawyer. I can look in a brother's eyes and see when he's not saying what he's thinking." Jamar matched Darnell's gaze before continuing. "Your boy, Byron, he's cool and all, but it's deeper than he's letting on."

"Whatcha sayin'?"

"I can't put my finger on it, but he's definitely not happy to see Alexis back in town."

Darnell shrugged. "Can't see why not. I know he used to have a crush on Andrea back in the day, and that made him a little protective of her, but I thought he'd gotten over that."

"You serious?" Jamar asked, scooting forward on the couch. His eyes bugged in shock. "Your boy used to crush on his brother's wife?"

Darnell held up his hands in defense. "Hold up now, bruh. That's not what I said. Byron liked Andrea way before she married Christopher. I just said he's protective of her. He's probably waiting to see if something's gonna pop off between Andrea and Lex."

"Well, *I* can assure *you* I'm not lettin' that happen. If Alexis doesn't listen to anything else I tell her, she's gonna heed this—she *will not* start shit with Andrea."

Darnell laughed. "All right, then. You're the man."

"And she better know that."

"You sure can talk a lot of shit when your woman ain't around," Darnell noted with another laugh.

"Shit, let you tell it. I'm the man in this household."

"A'ight, I'ma see if you repeat that when Lex gets back."

"You ain't gonna be able to do that."

"Why not?" Darnell asked, looking confused.

"'Cause we're gonna be out with the boys, remember?"

The men laughed together and slapped hands.

"On the serious tip," Jamar said once they recovered from their laughter, "you've been in this family a lot longer than I have. Got any tips for me?"

"I don't know," Darnell replied, scratching the back of his ear. "You gotta remember that as much as Brenda and Alexis try to act like sisters, they're really cousins. I only get a glimpse of Alexis's family life every once in a while."

"Yeah, but you've seen more than I have. My woman wouldn't let me anywhere near her family till Christmas."

"Yeah, I remember that. You missed a helluva Thanksgiving."

"Man, fuck you!" Jamar exclaimed, throwing a pillow at his friend. They laughed again.

"Seriously, though," Darnell continued, "you pretty much saw the real thing. Aunt Mary ain't nobody to play with. She's cool when you're on her good side, but that woman can be mean as hell when she wants to."

"Man, don't I know it!" Jamar agreed. "That woman will curse you out up one side and down the other. I've seen her do it. Hell, she cursed Lex out before we left because she forgot to pay the electric bill. Told her she needed to get her priorities straight and stop worrying about that ole nappy-headed-ass boy."

Darnell howled in laughter as Jamar asked, "Can you believe that? How she gonna call a brotha nappy-headed? Shit, I look good." He rubbed his goatee with his thumb and forefinger.

"I'm glad to see you're feeling better."

"Yeah, well, the shit's still on my mind, but like you said, I can't solve it in a day," Jamar remarked, rising from the couch. He walked to the bathroom and called out, "Might as well have a night of fun. I'ma be just as broke tomorrow."

"You're gonna be even broker if you keep thinking that way," Darnell yelled back.

Chapter 10

By the time they reached the oceanfront, Alexis realized she had warmed up to Rayna much more than she thought she would. The young woman was pretty cool once she got to know her. Alexis guessed the initial nerves just needed to wear off so both their true selves could show.

Alexis really hadn't wanted anything to do with Rayna at first. Truthfully, she didn't expect much out of any woman willing to marry a player like Byron. She didn't know him well, but she did know what she remembered. He had his way with the women, but he was a hard-core hater with a serious chip on his shoulder.

She figured a woman willing to put up with someone like that was either weak-minded or strong-willed. Alexis had guessed the former when she first met Rayna. She just seemed way too happy-go-lucky, and her mouth seemed to move at the pace of the Road Runner. There were some moments when she just wanted to snatch the girl by her long blond locks and tell her to shut the fuck up!

However, after spending more time with her, she realized Rayna was a bright young woman who happened to meet a man who was bringing his player days to an end. She wanted more out of life than to just say she had a husband. She wanted a career and a partner in life and love. From what Alexis could tell, Rayna saw her as the example of what she wanted out of life.

"This place serves pretty good drinks," Rayna said, pointing to a bar facing the beach. "Let's stop here."

"Lead the way," Alexis replied, shrugging and throwing up her hand to let Brenda and Rayna walk in ahead of her.

They were seated at a table near the middle of the restaurant. After ordering dinner and a round of drinks, the ladies chatted about all they had done over the past couple of days. Alexis had almost felt badly about not spending the holiday with Jamar, but when he called to say he would hang out with the guys, she felt better. Truthfully, it felt kind of good to be a part of a mini sister circle. She had only one close friend back home, so this was a different experience for her.

Brenda's cell phone rang, interrupting the flow of conversation. She reached for her purse and began a frantic search when she didn't find the phone in its usual spot, attached to the top of the opening. She mumbled, "Coming, coming," as the digital rings became more relentless.

Rayna giggled and Alexis snorted while watching Brenda's frantic search.

"That's what you get for carrying around those big-ass purses," Alexis commented.

"Shut up," Brenda snapped just as she found the phone under her wallet and a folded stack of papers. She pressed TALK as she raised the phone to her ear. She knew who it was. "Hey, baby. . . . Yeah, we're having a good time, except your cousin-in-law is being mean to me," she replied, cutting her eyes at Alexis. Her cousin responded by smiling and waving.

Rayna giggled again. "You two always go back and forth like that?"

"Girl, yes," Alexis replied. "Brenda and I are more like sisters than cousins. We pretty much grew up together."

"That's cool," Rayna said, nodding in approval. "I can tell you two are close. Y'all grow up in the same house?"

Alexis shook her head no and then explained that because the two of them were only children and their mothers were so close, they naturally drifted together. In fact, Alexis pointed out, Brenda was her inspiration for going to medical school.

"Aw, sister-cuz," Brenda said, clipping her phone in its rightful position, "you never told me that."

"It's true," Alexis said as the waitress set their drinks in front of them. She thanked the waitress before continuing. "As I used to listen to your nursing stories about how you helped all these kids, I knew then that I wanted to work in the medical field. Then, when I came here to see you and saw how you were living and got to see you work, I said to myself, 'I really want to be a doctor.'"

She left out the fact that the complications from her abortion had cemented her decision to go into the medical field. She knew before that she wanted to be a doctor, but what she went through made her heart go out to other young women her age who had no one and treated abortions like a form of birth control.

"You know, I've never regretted my decision to become a pediatrician," Alexis said, nearly in a whisper, as she swirled her straw around in her drink. She took a long sip, smiling at the lemony tartness as it warmed her throat. "I don't have my own kids, but the kids I treat in my office are like my own."

"Listen to my little cousin growing up right in front of me. Never thought I'd see the day."

"Aw, shut up, Brenda," Alexis snapped playfully. "Why you gotta ruin the moment?"

The ladies laughed again, before Rayna brought their attention back to the subject at hand. "You ever plan on having any kids of your own?"

Alexis shrugged absently. No matter how resigned she'd grown to the fact that she'd never have children, that question never failed to sting. An abortion resulting in a barren womb was another aftereffect of her ill-advised decision to sleep with Christopher. She was surprised this was the first time she'd thought of it since her return to Virginia Beach. She'd been so worried about how Andrea would treat her, she'd nearly forgotten all about it.

Thank goodness for Jamar. He loved her so much that he wanted her despite her inability to bear children. They even planned to begin the adoption process once they returned from their honeymoon in Bermuda. *How did my mean tail get so lucky?* she wondered. True, Jamar had his faults. For instance, he could be bullheaded as hell, and she constantly had to pick up his dirty clothes from behind the bathroom door. However, he really was perfect for her. Not everyone could handle a woman like Alexis. Although she had calmed down since her college days, she hadn't completely lost her attitude. When called for, she could call on the spirit of Mary from deep within and go clean off!

Maybe she had found her . . . What was that name they used yesterday? *Bo something? Boaz! That's it.* She made a mental note to search the Bible later for his story.

"So what do you want?" Brenda asked Rayna, probably noticing the stress lines appearing in her cousin's otherwise smooth forehead. "A boy or a girl?"

Alexis shot her cousin a look of gratitude as Rayna placed the spotlight on herself. The young woman rattled off the virtues of having either a boy or a girl. A boy, she said, would be great because she wouldn't have to worry about combing hair every morning or stress about teen pregnancy in a few years. On the other hand, she felt if she had a girl, she could establish the mother/daughter bond she never had the opportunity to forge with her own mother.

"That's deep," Alexis said. "I can't imagine not being close to my mother. Even on the days when I thought she was overbearing and cruel, I would never have wanted to trade her for anyone else."

"I feel you there," Brenda said. "You never knew what you'd get with my mother. Sometimes she was sweeter than pecan candy, but other times, like when she got really pissed, you could tell why she and Aunt Mary were sisters."

Brenda and Alexis laughed at unspoken memories they knew Rayna would never understand.

"Well, don't get me wrong," Rayna interjected. "My momma and I are cool, but she was the kinda momma that didn't believe in being touchy-feely. She hardly ever hugged us. She didn't even hug Daddy. At least not in front of us, she didn't. That's kinda why I'm under Byron so much. That man loves to hug and kiss."

Brenda's phone rang again. She promptly snatched it from its rightful position on her purse and checked the caller ID.

"Dee," Brenda announced before pressing TALK. After a few seconds of silence, she said, "Hey, girl, whatcha up to?"

Alexis took a large sip from her drink and was about to chat with Rayna when she heard something horrifying. Brenda was actually inviting Andrea to join them!

What could she be thinking? This woman must really be trying to ignite some drama this week.

"Your cousin is really trying hard to fix things between you and Andrea," Rayna pointed out before sipping on her own drink.

"You see it, too, huh?"

"I am not trying to fix anything," Brenda protested. No one had noticed she had finished her call and had clipped her phone back on her purse.

"Then why did you invite her here?" Alexis asked. "You know that woman doesn't like me. We've had a nice day, and now she's gonna come here and dampen it for everyone."

"I don't think it's going to be like that," Brenda said. "Besides, I came here to spend time with my oldest and dearest friend. I also wanted to spend time with my favorite cousin, whom, before a few months ago, I hadn't spent any time with in about two years. I am too old and too weary to split my time all week, so can you two please put your attitudes in your pocket for a while?"

Alexis and Rayna looked at each other. The waitress set their meals in front of them and hurried away, probably sensing the growing tension between the ladies.

"Guess she told you," Rayna said before quickly taking another swallow of her iced tea. She picked up her fork and stabbed at a french fry.

"Shut up," Alexis snapped. She turned back to her cousin. "So is your girl coming or what?"

"She'll be here in a few," Brenda replied.

Alexis looked toward the window. The sun was setting. Its rays looked like golden butter had spilled down the ocean's smooth surface. A few die-hard beachcombers still strolled the shore. However, the crowd that had converged on the beach earlier had largely dispersed. She summoned the nice girl she had hidden deep inside of her to come on out. She'd need her to get through the rest of the night.

Nikki returned to her hotel room loaded down with more packages. She set the bags on her bed and looked around. The room was a mess! It would take all night for her to pack. Maybe if she stayed one more day, she could take her time and pack without running the risk of rushing and forgetting something.

That thought made her smile. The mess in her room was not calling her name, so she felt no need to invite herself to its party. Instead, she kicked the bags to the side and flopped on the part of the bed she'd just cleared for herself. Maybe a little TV would calm her nerves.

When she reached for the remote control, she realized housekeeping had moved it to the entertainment stand. Rolling her eyes, she begrudgingly got up and walked over to the television. After grabbing the remote, she still turned on the TV by hand. The screen sprang to life, showing advertisements of the amenities the hotel offered.

"Definitely not trying to watch that," she mumbled as she walked back to the bed. She lay down and flipped through the channels in pursuit of something that would hold her interest. It was between the news and a rerun of *Clean House*. She loved her some Niecy Nash; however, she felt it was her civic duty to first get an update on what was going on in her city.

It was nothing she wanted to hear.

Instead of the mass reentry back into the city that she thought she'd see, all she saw were reports stating it still wasn't safe to come back home. Electrical, water, and sewer systems still weren't running on full power. A dusk-to-dawn curfew was in effect for the ten thousand or so people who had remained in the city. It seemed that the mother of all storms had been downgraded, but it wasn't going out without wreaking at least a little havoc.

Nikki stared at the television in disbelief. The high she'd experienced earlier, when she thought she would be leaving, came crashing down. She almost knew what a crackhead felt like once the drugs had worn off. Empty. Let down. Nauseated. Disappointed. Down-right pissed. What would she do now?

She wanted to cry, but the tears refused to form. Only a burning sensation visited her eyes as the thinning air in the room hit them. She couldn't blink the burn away. In fact, she refused to blink. Blinking would mean that she'd have to admit this wasn't a dream turned night-mare.

"So when can I go home?" she pleaded with the televi-sion. Her cell phone rang. She quickly fished her purse from under the bags that remained on the other side of the bed. A check of the caller ID revealed her father's cell phone number.

"Hey, Daddy," she greeted dryly.

"Whatcha say, baby girl," greeted Earl Howard. "How you makin' out?"

"Not too good, Daddy. I just found out we're not go-ing to be able to go back home yet."

"You just finding that out? That's been on the news all day."

"I been out all day, Daddy," Nikki whined. She couldn't help but go into child mode whenever she spoke to Earl. She was the youngest child of four, which would always make her his baby girl.

"Spendin' money you shouldn't be, huh?" Earl stated.

"Not really," she protested.

Her father always could see right through her. She didn't even know why she tried to bend the truth. He was the only one in the family who knew her marriage to Reggie would never work. "I love you to death, baby girl," he'd told her, "but that boy is too softhearted for you. I don't think he has a hard bone in his body. I know you don't like to listen to me, but mark my words."

Of course, she didn't listen, and when she and Reggie divorced, Earl made his point by raising his eyebrows and winking at her. *Maybe he should choose my next man,* she thought.

"Well, kind of," Nikki continued after reflecting on her father. "I bought y'all some presents on the beach today. I thought I was goin' home tomorrow, so I figured I'd get all my souvenirs today."

"Well, you better hold tight for a couple more days," Earl warned. "Ain't no power in the city yet."

"I heard. You hear of anybody getting killed this time?"

"No, thank God. I think most everybody got out the city, and since the levees wasn't blew up this time, I think we'll be all right."

Nikki laughed. "Daddy, you need to stop with that. Those levees weren't blown up."

"Maybe not all of 'em, but I bet you a dime to a doughnut that the ones around the Lower Nine was."

"Y'all need to stop saying that. Those levees were just as old as the rest of the levees in the city. Ain't nobody blow them up."

"Now, baby girl, I been living a long time," Earl said. "I lived through Betsy, Camille, Katrina, Rita, and now Gustav. I also lived through segregation and hate that you can't imagine, right there in New Orleans. I know what people's capable of. If they blew the levees in the forties, what makes you think they wouldn'ta did it again?"

Nikki meditated on her father's words. She knew there was no use in arguing. Earl Howard would believe what he wanted to believe. He, like many other Lower Ninth Ward residents, as well as other blacks in the city, would always believe that blacks were intentionally held down in New Orleans. To them, having an African American mayor for the last ten years—and the fact that the city was more than 80 percent black before Hurricane Katrina hit—didn't make a bit of difference. The conspiracy against blacks in New Orleans would always stand.

Even after Katrina, the distrust only grew. Many believed it was no accident that most of the people stuck in the Louisiana Superdome and the Ernest Morial Convention Center were poor and black. It was by design that the urban neighborhoods were populated with wooden homes that could barely withstand a hard wind, let alone a hurricane. And the fact that much of the reconstruction work was awarded to Mexican immigrants only sealed the belief that blacks were being pushed out of New Orleans in the name of urban renewal.

Nikki didn't have a stand on the issue one way or the other. As long as it didn't stop her from booking modeling jobs and getting a slice of the finer life, she really didn't care who ran New Orleans. She knew she *should* care, but she never wanted to take the time to get educated so she *could* care. Maybe once she returned home, she'd do some research.

"Whatcha got goin' for the rest of the night?" Earl asked, changing the subject.

"Nothing," Nikki replied, leaning back on her pillows. "I been out all day, and now this news about New

Orleans got me all depressed. I don't feel like doing anything now."

"Look, baby girl, don't let this stuff get you down. We were blessed to have our city spared. If that means we can't go home for a day or two, I think that's a small price to pay. At least we got a home to go back to this time."

Nikki smiled. Her daddy always knew the right words to say. And he was right. She *did* have a home to go back to. Three years ago, she and Reggie had to collect what they could from their destroyed home in Eastover and search for a new place to build memories. This time, she didn't have to worry about that.

This time when she went home, she could pick up right where she'd left off. That mail she'd left on the coffee table would still be there, waiting for her to carry it to the mailbox. She'd still be able to keep her massage appointment, which she'd been waiting for the past two weeks. DeShawn, if his daddy didn't decide to keep him in Georgia, would be coming to visit this weekend.

The thought brought a slight smile to Nikki's face. She was still disappointed, but Earl made a lot of sense. Maybe she would go back out. It would be better than sitting in her hotel room, thinking about her problems.

"Thanks, Daddy," she said with a smile.

"I love you, baby girl."

"Love you, too."

They stayed on the phone for a while longer, catching up on the rest of the family and their plans for moving back to New Orleans. As they spoke, Nikki looked in the mirror and touched up her hair and makeup. She was sure there wasn't a club open, but maybe she could find another lounge to hang out in. Either that or she'd call the Italian she'd met earlier. He might be up for a good time.

Once she hung up with Earl, she slipped on a pair of jeans over her bikini bottom, slid her pedicured toes into her stilettos, grabbed her purse, and strolled back out of the hotel room. Once she reached the lobby, she peered around for anyone who even looked like they were searching for a party, but found no one. *This is definitely not New Orleans,* she thought.

She walked outside, the familiar salt air washing over her face. The boardwalk was empty compared to earlier, which allowed her to fully appreciate its beauty. The sun setting in the background gave it an almost romantic feel. The thought was nice, although a bit disconcerting. She had no one to share the romance with.

She strolled slowly down the boardwalk. There weren't many shops on this side of the street. Mostly restaurants and hotels. She looked into the windows as she passed, hoping to see what looked to be a jovial atmosphere. There was none.

"These people are dead," she grumbled.

Finally, she came upon a restaurant that had a few black people sitting toward the center of the dining area. Upon closer examination, she saw all four were women, and they seemed to be having a great time. She didn't usually hang with women, but maybe their good time would rub off on her.

She walked into the restaurant but stopped dead in her tracks. One of the women was that bitch Alexis. *Not again,* she thought.

Chapter 11

Nikki started to turn and leave, but something made her stop and slip into a nearby booth. Her curiosity piqued, she wanted to find out just what this woman had been up to. She hoped Alexis hadn't noticed her, but soon dismissed the thought. If she had seen her, Nikki was sure she would have said something or at least stared in her direction. Alexis did neither, so she must have been too caught up in her conversation to notice Nikki's entrance.

"What can I get you tonight, ma'am?" a waiter asked, approaching Nikki's table.

Nikki looked up at her server. *Nice.* His blond hair had been slicked back with mousse, and his brown eyes shined. She smiled and crossed her legs. "Lemme get a Sex on the Beach."

The waiter smiled back. "Popular drink."

"That's because it's damn good," she replied, winking. She licked her lips to add an exclamation point to her innuendo.

"Whoo," he said as he exhaled, shaking his head. He lowered his notepad, probably trying to cover his erection. Nikki was sure other women had flirted with him, but she doubted any of them looked as good as she did. "I'll be right back with that drink."

"You do that," she whispered once he turned away. She wished she could have kept the game going longer, but she didn't want to attract any more attention. She especially didn't want Alexis to know she was there. And she damn sure didn't want the waiter thinking she was taking him home!

She listened carefully to see if she could hear any of the conversation coming from Alexis's table. Unfortunately, only rumblings could be heard. How could she switch tables without being noticed? *Shit, shit, shit.*

As she sat thinking, she noticed Alexis walk past her. Now was her chance, but where could she go? If she sat too close, she was sure to be noticed. If she sat too far away, she wouldn't be able to hear anything. Not to mention, she might get caught.

The cute blond waiter walked past, no drink in hand. She signaled for him to come over.

"I'll have your drink in a minute," he told her. "The bartender's a little backed up."

"That's okay. It's no rush," she said. "I was just wondering if I could move to a different table."

"Something wrong?"

"No, I just wanted to get a different table," she replied, unable to think of a lie. She shouldn't have to, anyway. She was the customer, and the customer was always right, right?

He shrugged. "There's a couple of tables open. Take your pick."

"You still gonna be my waiter?" she asked while rising from the booth and looking toward the ladies' room. No sign of Alexis.

"If you want me to be," he replied, smiling.

She quickly dipped into the booth just behind Alexis's table. She could definitely hear from there. Now, to keep the waiter standing there so he could block Alexis's view should she pass by . . .

"What's your name, sweetie?"

"Tim," he replied, leaning on the top of her booth. He smiled, flashing his pearly whites. "And yours?"

"Lakisha," she lied. She couldn't risk Tim saying her name.

"Nice to meet you, Lakisha." He looked back toward the bar and then looked toward the door. "I'd better get back to work. You seem like the type of woman who would get me into trouble."

"Yeah, but you would enjoy every minute of that trouble."

Tim raised his eyebrows and scratched his head as he turned away from the table. It didn't matter. He'd served his purpose. Alexis had already walked past and was now with her friends.

"Took you long enough," Nikki heard one of the women remark.

"Why you timing me, Brenda?" Alexis snapped.

"I'm just saying."

Nikki had positioned herself so she couldn't be seen, but that position precluded her from seeing the women. She'd have to depend on her powers of active listening to keep up with what was going on. She'd keep her ears perked to find out.

"Here's your drink, Lakisha," Tim announced, setting her glass in front of her.

"Thanks, sweetie," she replied, glad she hadn't given Tim her real name. He would have blown her cover before she could get started.

"You need anything else?" he asked, hovering over her table.

"No, I'm good," she answered quickly.

He felt the sudden frost from her shoulder and walked away without another word.

"So I bought it two sizes too big so I'll have enough room to alter it," one of the ladies said. "I don't know how big I'll be before the wedding, but I don't want to take any chances."

So, one of them, probably the one with those ugly-ass blond dreadlocks, is pregnant and getting married, Nikki thought. It couldn't be the other woman with them, because Nikki had just seen her with a man, and she looked nowhere near being pregnant. Now, if only someone would mention names. She couldn't tell which woman was Brenda, although she was sure it wasn't the loc lady, because her voice didn't sound like that of the one who had made the bathroom comment to Alexis earlier.

"Sounds like you have it all planned out. That's good."

"So, anyway, I guess the next step is finding a church."

"You haven't done that yet, Rayna?"

"No."

"Backward bitch," Nikki mumbled, taking a sip from her drink. "How the hell do you buy the dress before you find a place to wear the thing?"

The other lady echoed her sentiment.

"Well, when we found out I was pregnant, we were thinking of just going to the justice of the peace, so I didn't worry about looking for a church," Rayna explained.

"What changed your mind about having a wedding?" Alexis asked.

"Believe it or not, I saw a pregnant chick on that show *Whose Wedding is it Anyway,* and I figured if she could pull it off, I could, too."

"This simple bitch," Nikki mumbled again. "Livin' her life based on a damn TV show."

"I like that show, too," Alexis said.

"You would," Nikki whispered with a sneer.

This conversation seemed to be going nowhere fast. There was obviously no juice for Nikki to sample, so she decided to leave. She prayed she would never become that boring. She signaled for Tim just as he walked by.

"Can I get the check, sweetie?" she asked, bringing the charm back to her voice.

"You done for the night?" he asked.

"Yeah, I think I'm going to head to bed."

"Really? It's still early."

"Yeah, but it's been a long day."

Tim smiled. "Okay, I'll be right back."

Nikki yawned and tapped her nails against her empty glass. That check couldn't come quickly enough. She would rather spend the evening watching TV than listen any longer to the black Stepford wives.

"Andrea, I'm gettin' real fuckin' tired of you cuttin' your eyes at me every five minutes," Nikki heard Alexis say all of a sudden. "Didn't nobody make your little up-tight ass come here tonight!"

Nikki sat up in her seat and cocked her head slightly to the left so she could hear better. Maybe things were looking up, after all.

"Excuse me?" Andrea asked.

"You heard," Alexis snapped. "You think you have command over being honest and wholesome? So I guess Chris took it real well when you told him you tongued down his brother, huh?"

"Whoa," sang the ladies at the table. They just didn't know that Nikki sang right along with them.

Tim placed the check on the table and turned away when Nikki didn't even give him so much as a head nod. The drama at the next table had suddenly taken precedence over the cute white guy she had never planned on sleeping with, anyway.

"You need to mind your business, Alexis, because you don't know what the hell you're talking about," Andrea told her.

"Oh, I don't, huh? Tell me why you tried to pretend all these years that you never kissed Byron after you found out Chris and I slept together?"

"Alexis!" Brenda snapped. At least Nikki thought the woman sounded like Brenda. "What's wrong with you?"

"When did you kiss Byron?" Rayna asked.

"Brenda, you're always trying to protect Andrea's feelings," Alexis said before anyone could answer Rayna. "This bitch is not made of porcelain."

"You've got one more time to call me a bitch, Alexis," Andrea said, "and I'ma show you how fuckin' fragile I am."

Nikki wished like hell she could turn around in her booth and watch the action. It seemed like everyone else in the restaurant was. Every table in her line of vision seemed to hold patrons who were transfixed by the four black women in the center of the dining area. She pictured them standing around the table, holding their silverware like they were about to go to battle at any moment. She wasn't exactly sure what was going on, but it sounded like Alexis had opened a serious can of worms.

"Andrea, cool out," Brenda said, trying to keep the peace. "Alexis was wrong for bringing this out, but fighting in the middle of a restaurant is not the answer."

"No, Brenda, let her come across this table," Alexis said. "I'll bet her ass will limp back. I guess you forgot where I'm from."

"And you forgot I'm from New Orleans, too!" Andrea retorted. "You think I'm supposed to just let you talk to me any kinda way? I didn't take that shit before, and I'm damn sure not taking it now. I will wipe the floor with your trashy ass!"

"Hold on," Rayna said. "Neither one of you is going to do a damn thing except tell me what the hell y'all are talking about."

"All right, Rayna," Alexis replied. "You wanna know so bad?"

"Shut up, Alexis!" Brenda pleaded.

Alexis ignored her. "Your future sister-in-law was so distraught over my so-called affair with her husband that she figured she'd get him back by kissing his brother."

"Dee?" Rayna asked. To Nikki, the woman sounded like she was about to burst into tears.

"That is not how it happened, Rayna," Andrea said, embarrassment dripping from her voice.

"Then tell her how it happened," Alexis taunted.

"Shut the fuck up, you stupid whore!" Andrea snapped.

"You know what?" Alexis asked. "I will. Brenda, I'm sorry it had to come out this way, and I know you meant well, but Andrea and I will never be friends. So, if she can hold on to the past, then she needs to get a tight hold on everything in the past. She's got to remember that she's just as flawed as the rest of us."

Well, all right, Nikki thought. *Ms. Alexis has some fire in her, after all.* She watched as Alexis stormed out of the restaurant, leaving the other three women to pick up the pieces.

"I'm sorry, Rayna," Andrea said. "She didn't even have to go there tonight. That kiss was a long time ago."

"Then when were you going to tell me about it?"

"I wasn't, because that was all it was. Nothing happened between us."

"She's telling the truth," Brenda said. "Byron and Dee are like brother and sister."

"That's funny, because I don't remember *ever* kissing my brother."

An uncomfortable silence followed, which made Nikki giggle. She peeked around her booth to find Rayna standing over the table with her arms folded, while the other two women sat and looked pitiful. At least she figured they looked pitiful, since their backs faced her. She smiled as she watched the women stew in the aftermath of another woman's wrath.

Alexis is one bad girl.

Chapter 12

Jamar wasn't sure how he'd let the fellas talk him into going to a strip club, but he was damn glad he did. None of the women he watched could even come close to Alexis, but they did a hell of a job getting his mind off his problems.

The club wasn't the dark, seedy spot that he'd expected. In fact, he was rather impressed with his surroundings. Plush sofas lined the walls, while a few wooden tables and chairs sat sparsely around the rest of the club. The light-adorned dance floor sat in the center of the room, surrounded by a rail that kept the patrons from swarming the dancers. This was probably a good thing, because the women performed moves that would put a pretzel to shame!

The bar sat toward the back of the club, but waitresses clad in tiny satin shorts and low-cut tops strolled the area, catering to the men's whims.

"This is a pretty nice place," Jamar said, leaning toward Byron. "Not really what I expected."

Not allowing his eyes to leave the six-foot-two-inch, hazel-eyed beauty gyrating in front of him, Byron replied, "This is how we roll, baby boy."

Jamar laughed and sat back in his seat. The hazel-eyed amazon twirled her hips nearly in slow motion to Lil Wayne's "Lollipop." Her hips continued twirling as her right leg slid closer to the edge of the stage. All of a sudden, she dropped into a perfect split, sending the men into a wild frenzy.

"That girl's got some skills!" Byron shouted, jumping from his seat and applauding. "I'm definitely buyin' this one some books tonight!"

He dropped a few dollar bills at the woman's feet to show his appreciation.

"I ain't mad at her at all," Christopher agreed. He held his seat, but shook his head in approval.

The dancer recovered from her split and gave an innocent-looking curtsy before collecting her tips and leaving the dance floor. Before anyone could recover, Flo Rida's "Low" blasted from the speakers and a five-foot ebony-colored woman ran onto the floor, placed her hands on her knees, and made her behind pop in ways Jamar had never seen before.

"I need to get out more," he said to himself, shaking his head.

It wasn't like Jamar didn't go out in New Orleans, but he'd made it a rule for himself not to frequent strip clubs. He just didn't get anything out of watching a woman take off her clothes unless she'd be crawling into bed with him. Besides, most of the regular strip clubs were on Bourbon Street, and he had made it a rule not to go there, either.

He looked over at Darnell, who didn't seem to be paying anyone any mind. He sipped from his drink and studied the dancer's movements, as if memorizing them to take back to Brenda. Jamar chuckled at the thought of his friend telling his wife, "Do your butt like this."

He looked back at the Lee brothers, silently thanking them for going through with this. The evening had started out a bit awkward, no one knowing what the other would say. He also wasn't sure if they would hold his financial problems against him. Fortunately, they'd seemed cordial when they picked Darnell and him up from the resort.

"Hey, man," Christopher had told him as they rode to the club, "I know you sweatin' a lot of shit right now, but tonight, do you."

Jamar had nodded in appreciation. This Christopher guy didn't seem to be so bad, after all. However, he noticed Byron remained silent during much of the ride. He contributed to the conversation at times yet became mute whenever the subject of their women came up. Or maybe it was just when they were on the subject of Alexis.

Just before they'd pulled up to the club, Darnell had joked, "Byron, your woman lets you come here? I thought for sure she had cracked the whip on you."

"Man, whatcha talkin' about?" Byron had replied with a smile. "I thought you knew I wear the pants in this household. You must have me mixed up with Chris."

"Believe that if you want," Christopher commented. "My woman ain't got no whip on me. She can be mean sometimes, but she knows who's the man."

The men laughed, and then Darnell added, "Just make sure Rayna and Andrea don't try to team up on you, like Brenda and Alexis do."

Christopher laughed again. "I can imagine them trying to be the dynamic duo or some shit."

Everyone laughed, but Byron grew silent. "We better get inside. The show's about to start."

No one else took notice of Byron's sudden attitude change, but Jamar certainly did. He knew right then that he'd have to keep an eye on Byron for the rest of the visit.

However, since they'd been in the club, Byron had seemed a lot more relaxed. It was amazing the power a shaking booty could have over a man's spirit. Yet when that booty was attached to a brown-haired, brown-eyed cutie like the one currently on the dance floor, the power was understandable.

No lap dances were given at this club, because it was against the law to touch the dancers. Instead, the men threw the money on the floor or made it rain, which meant they quickly shuffled dollars bills around the dance floor. Those who wanted a closer look had to hold the dollar bill in front of them and wait for the dancer to approach them. She would then perform a trick and take the dollar from his horny fingers.

This would be a turnoff to most men, but Jamar actually appreciated the rules. At least he wouldn't go home smelling like cigarettes and cheap perfume. Cigarette smoke could be explained away, but he really didn't want to address perfume and makeup stains with Alexis later.

"Looks like I'ma have to buy this one some books, too!" Byron exclaimed as the dancer shook her behind in his direction while holding her ankles. She demonstrated her flexibility by keeping her legs as straight as a soldier's.

"Boy, what are you talking about?" Darnell asked, laughing.

"You don't know?" Byron asked. "Chris, you better school 'em."

Christopher laughed and then explained, "You know how they say a lot of these girls are stripping to get through college? Well, we're just doing our civic duty when we come here. The way they dance determines whether they get new books or used books."

Everyone howled in laughter, including a couple of men who sat nearby.

"I like that, man," said a younger man who looked just old enough to meet the club's age restriction and large enough to block the sun from shining. He shook hands with Christopher. "I'ma use that shit."

"Just tell 'em where ya got it," Christopher told him and then turned back to his brother and friends. "I need to patent that shit."

The group chuckled in agreement. Byron pulled his phone from his pocket and looked at the screen.

"Aw, shit," Byron said aloud.

"What's wrong, baby bruh?" Christopher asked, taking his seat.

"Rayna just texted me, talkin' about we need to talk."

"That ain't never good," Darnell commented. "You never want to hear those four words coming from your woman."

"You ain't never lied," Byron agreed.

"You gonna call her back?" Christopher asked.

"Hell, naw," Byron replied, shoving the phone back in his pocket. "If I call her now, the night is over. I'll deal with it when I get home."

"You sure it's not an emergency?" Jamar asked.

Byron shook his head. "If it was, she woulda said it. It can't be too bad. She's been hanging with y'all girls all day."

"In that case, you better call her now," Christopher said. "You never know what will happen when all of them get together."

Just then, Christopher reached for his own phone. He pulled it from his pocket and checked the caller ID. "Damn. Now Dee is calling."

Jamar and Darnell quickly reached for their own phones to see if they had any missed calls. Brenda had called Darnell, but Jamar's screen displayed only the time.

"Guess it's time to go," Darnell said with a shrug.

Byron rolled his eyes and stood up begrudgingly. "I got a feeling this is gonna be a long night."

"You ain't bullshittin'," Christopher said, rising from his own chair.

The ride from the club took nearly twice as long as it should have. No man was eager to find out the drama that had caused all the women to call. That is, all the women except Alexis. The fact that she was the only woman who hadn't called or sent a text weighed heavily on Jamar's mind. *Isn't she with the rest of the women? Or did she go off by herself? Maybe she's trying to play the hard role and pretending she doesn't need to confide in her man, like everyone else seems to be doing.* He let out a quiet half laugh at that thought. *Leave it to Alexis to revert to her tough exterior just to try to prove a point.*

Although he tried to comfort himself with that reasoning, he couldn't help but wonder if something else might be wrong. Maybe tensions had finally escalated to the point where they boiled over. This was the last thing he wanted or needed. If Alexis had blown her top, it was more than likely that she would be ready to leave. And with his financial situation in shambles, he would not be able to accommodate that wish. He wouldn't even be able to buy her a Happy Meal if things didn't change soon.

Leaving Virginia Beach was exactly what stood in the forefront of Alexis's mind. She sat on a bench on the boardwalk, contemplating her next move.

She felt bad for Rayna. She was beginning to warm up to the younger woman and had even entertained the thought of them becoming close friends. She also felt bad for Brenda, who had become a helpless casualty in the verbal attack. All Brenda wanted was to make the best of a bad situation, but she had failed to overcome the hatred her best friend felt for her favorite cousin. Unfortunately, Andrea's hatred and Alexis's short temper might have created an irreparable rift between childhood friends. A wave of guilt chilled her spine, but her regrets weighed nothing compared to the contempt she felt for Andrea.

She knew she was wrong for putting out Andrea's business, especially in front of Rayna, but she couldn't take another minute of her self-righteous attitude. She was tired of tiptoeing around Andrea's feelings and trying to pay restitution for something she did when she was young and irresponsible.

Granted, sleeping with a woman's husband was definitely grounds for hatred, especially when the sleeping was done on sheets that the wife had paid for. Granted, Alexis did initiate the affair. Granted, Alexis accidentally succeeded at something in two weeks that Andrea hadn't been able to do in three years—she got pregnant. All of that put together was like swallowing a horse pill with no water.

Why couldn't Andrea accept the fact that Alexis had grown up? Couldn't she see that she wasn't the same person who had waltzed into their lives all those years ago? Better yet, couldn't she see that Alexis and Christopher had both gotten past the affair and had moved on? He'd finally given Andrea the baby she'd always wanted, and Alexis was marrying the man of her dreams. They really weren't checking for each other.

Alexis stared out at the ocean. It wasn't exactly Lake Pontchartrain, her favorite thinking spot in New Orleans, but it would have to do. The dark sky over the dark water looked like a black satin sheet. The water looked peaceful. Smooth. Quiet. A complete contrast to the turmoil boiling inside of her.

This was exactly what she didn't want. Who needed this type of drama? She had enough going on in her life. Which reminded her—she needed to call her nurse, Ms. Kay, in the morning and check on her. Ms. Kay and her cousin Latanya were the driving force behind Alexis's private practice. Had it not been for them, she was sure she would have closed her office and resorted to working crazy hours in the main hospital long ago.

She hoped to God that wouldn't be her fate once she returned home. Her all-day adventure with Brenda and Rayna hadn't allowed her to keep up with the news, so she had no idea where her city or her business stood. She needed to get home so she could find out.

Her earlier fears of her clients not being able to pay returned. Things had just started to improve only a year before Hurricane Gustav threatened the city. She was sure many of her patients' families had used whatever little money they had left to evacuate. If any of them bothered to keep their appointments after returning to the city, she would be surprised. And of those who did, she wondered how many would come up with a sob story about why they wouldn't be able to pay her until next week. Every bit of her being wanted to shout, "Then why didn't you reschedule for next week?" but she always lost the heart. No child should have to suffer because their parents couldn't pay.

She stood quickly and took two steps toward her resort but stopped. How could she face Jamar right now? She was sure he'd heard about the drama by now.

If Brenda hadn't said anything to him, Darnell surely had. He would probably yell at her for sinking to such a low. "Why would you let her get to you?" he would ask. "I told your ass no drama this week."

"Ugh!" she groaned loudly as she sank back on the bench. An older white couple walking past looked at her curiously, but she didn't care. "This is some bullshit."

"You know, all that language ain't called for."

Alexis looked around for the owner of the female voice, the person who had admonished her. The way she felt right now, she welcomed the opportunity to curse someone else out. Yet once she found the owner of the voice standing over her, her mouth just hung open in shock. Standing over her, wearing a floral bikini top and tight jeans, was what had to be an anger-induced hallucination. What else could explain this woman appearing from nowhere?

"You've gotta be fuckin' kidding me," Alexis mumbled, shaking her head. "Nikki?"

Chapter 13

"So you do remember me," Nikki replied, smiling like she knew she had the upper hand. She ran her fingers through her flowing straight hair, letting it fall neatly over her left shoulder.

Alexis sucked her teeth at the sight, convinced it was a weave. She then ran her fingers through her own naturally curly, shoulder-length hair and scratched her scalp. Was she dreaming?

"What are you doing here?"

"Probably the same thing you're doing here," Nikki replied, taking an uninvited seat next to Alexis. She set her bag near her feet and crossed her legs.

Alexis rolled her eyes and shook her head. "What are the fuckin' odds?"

"You're full of that language, aren't you?"

"I don't think you need to be worried about what's coming out of my mouth."

Nikki seemed not to be fazed by Alexis's attitude. Instead of getting insulted and leaving, like Alexis hoped, she only smiled and lifted her eyebrows, like she knew some burning secret. The look made Alexis uncomfortable, and her discomfort pissed her off even more.

"Nikki, I don't know what made you think I wanted you sitting next to me, but I can assure you that I'm not the one to be played with right now," she said, glaring at the woman. Nikki only matched her gaze with that same shit-eating grin. "Damn, bitch! Did you hear me? Walk the fuck on!"

Nikki chuckled and folded her arms. "I'm well aware that you just finished cursing some ladies out, so I'm going to excuse that little attitude of yours. But you might want to calm down, because I may be the only friend you have here right now."

"What?" Alexis asked, her eyebrows scrunched in anger. She was sure Nikki couldn't have been privy to the argument she'd had with Andrea in the restaurant, but even if she was, that wasn't the point. "Skip that. I don't know what the hell you're talking about. You just need to leave me alone right now. This really ain't the fuckin' time."

"You know, for an educated woman, you sure have a commanding grip on the English language."

Alexis was about ready to get a commanding grip on that weave and snatch it out of that woman's hair.

"What's up with you!" she exclaimed, jumping up from her seat. "Why are you so worried about what I'm saying? What you need to be worried about is leaving me alone before I throw your ass in that fuckin' ocean! I really don't need one more bitch blaming me for the problems in her marriage."

Nikki stood up and fearlessly looked Alexis in the eyes. She stood about half a foot taller than Alexis's five-foot-four frame, so she had to look down on her. Her smile had dropped slightly, but it hadn't disappeared. Alexis noticed a glimmer in the taller woman's eyes that nearly unnerved her, although she refused to show it.

"Alexis, I haven't blamed you for anything," Nikki said calmly. "Still, let's get something straight. You probably don't know it, but I'm from the Lower Nine. So, if you think I'm going to take much more of you cursing at me, you're out your damn mind. And you're even crazier if you think I'm just going to stand here and *let* you beat my ass. I thought you were more of a lady than that. Now, as I said before, I can understand you being pissed, which is why I was willing to put up with your attitude. If that Dee bitch or Andrea bitch, or whatever the hell her name is, was cuttin' her eyes at me all night, I probably woulda snapped, too. But you really need to calm down. I don't see not a damn one of those chicks out here, consoling your ass. So, like I said, I might be your only friend tonight."

Alexis cut her eyes into slits, wanting to curse Nikki like a voodoo queen, but the words refused to come. How did she know about her argument?

Seeming to read her mind, Nikki said, "Yes, I was in the restaurant. I heard the whole thing."

Alexis closed her eyes and swallowed a gulp of salt air. This could not be happening. Could this night get any worse? The day had started off so nice. She'd made love to her fiancé, gone shopping for a wedding dress, eaten lunch, and laughed it up with her cousin and her new friend. Then she'd ended it all by cursing out her cousin's best friend and alienating a future friend. Now, to top it all off, her ex-boyfriend Reggie's former wife had popped up from out of nowhere and had positioned herself to be Alexis's only ally. How did it go to hell so quickly?

She really had no reason to hate Nikki the way she did. The woman had never done anything to her personally, except marry the man Alexis had cheated on back in college. Although she had tried to go on with her life, Alexis had spent years being jealous of Nikki, wishing it had been her—or, better yet, knowing it should have been her. When Reggie waltzed back into her life and announced that he was divorcing Nikki because of her infidelity, the hate took on a whole new intensity. How could Nikki hurt a man like Reggie that way? At least Alexis could blame youth and immaturity as her reasons for hurting him. But Nikki was a grown-ass woman!

The hate intensified once Nikki found out about Alexis and Reggie's friendship. Convinced that they were sleeping together, Nikki began using their son as a bargaining chip to keep them apart. How stupid! They were only friends. Had she dug a little deeper, she'd have known that Alexis wasn't leaving Jamar, nor would she cheat on him. She'd learned from her past mistakes. Why couldn't Nikki?

When she really looked at it, life had come full circle. Virginia Beach was the city where Alexis had unknowingly come to change her life. Before coming here, she felt she had the world in the crook of her pinkie. She didn't care who she hurt, so long as her needs were met. She liked Reggie, but back then, she saw him as nothing more than a good-looking conquest.

Christopher had taught her a lesson she would never forget. She'd thought he would be something to do until she returned to New Orleans and stepped into Reggie's waiting arms—because he would definitely be waiting. However, she had never considered the fact that she'd get pregnant. She'd never entertained the thought that Christopher cared nothing about her. He'd thought of her as just as much a throwaway as she'd thought he would be, only worse. It never even occurred to her that she nearly broke up a marriage.

Now here she was, fifteen years later, back where it had all started, and the wounds still hadn't closed. In fact, she thought her return might have just added salt to the still fresh lesions. Andrea hated her, and after tonight, she probably always would. Christopher and Byron tiptoed around her, careful not to say two words to her. Who could blame them after she'd just brought up a nearly two-decade-old secret that could possibly break up another marriage, one that hadn't even happened yet? Poor Brenda, trying to be the peacemaker, was once again caught in the middle with nowhere to go.

Then there was Jamar. He'd promised that there would be no drama. Yet, the shit hit the fan as soon as he wasn't around. Even if he wouldn't be pissed when he found out, she'd still be too embarrassed to tell him what had happened.

Nikki was right. She was the only friend Alexis had right now. Yet she wasn't totally sure she could trust her. Could she just be fishing for something to hold over her head? Maybe she was just trying to make her life miserable as payback for the way things went down with the divorce. Tit for tat.

Then again, what could Nikki possibly do to Alexis? Absolutely nothing but dislike her. Jamar disliked Nikki as much as Alexis did, so there was no way Nikki could come between them. She darn sure couldn't mess with her job, although she wasn't so sure Nikki was smart enough to try something like that, anyway.

She wanted to push the woman to the side and go back to the resort, but she still wasn't sure she was ready to face Jamar. Her phone had buzzed twice since she'd been sitting outside, but she couldn't bring herself to answer it. Anyone who was calling was probably calling about the scene she'd caused, and she really didn't want to hear any lectures. She looked toward the resort, then back at Nikki. What could she lose?

"What's up, Nikki?" she sighed, dropping helplessly back onto the bench.

The friendly smile returned to Nikki's face as she took a seat next to Alexis. At least Alexis thought it looked friendly. She wasn't so sure, but it would be a relief to talk to a disinterested party. Maybe Nikki, since she didn't know anyone involved in this whole mess, would see things differently and give her some perspective. Help her to find that speck she continually cleaned around.

"Nice night, huh?" Nikki asked, looking out at the same horizon Alexis had just been staring at. She tugged up on her bikini, ensuring that the dark skin of her areolae didn't show.

Alexis shot Nikki a perplexed look. *Didn't this woman just say she was trying to be a friend? Why the hell is she trying to talk about the weather? If you're going to try to be a friend, be a damn friend!*

"I guess," Alexis muttered.

"You guess? Look around. It felt like the devil was leaning on our shoulders earlier today, and now it's actually bearable outside. The water, even at night, is beautiful. And look at that ship sailing in the distance."

Alexis looked out across the water and immediately spotted a cruise ship passing by. It sailed right into the moon's golden beam, looking like a scene from a postcard. It was too far off for her to see into the windows. Still, she was sure there were people dancing and having the time of their lives. She wished she could be one of them. She would dance her cares away in a city where she knew no one and no one knew her.

"You've gotta start appreciating the little things," Nikki continued, interrupting Alexis's thoughts.

"Since when did you get so wise?"

"Since today, really. I thought I would be leaving tomorrow, since the hurricane wasn't too bad."

"Why won't you?"

Nikki stared at Alexis in shock. "Ain't you been watching the news?"

"Not since this morning."

"Girl, your house and business coulda been in jeopardy," Nikki admonished. "I know you were out doing your thing and all, but you still need to keep up with what's going on in the world."

"What happened?" Alexis asked, more annoyed than curious. Who was this woman to tell her about keeping up with the world? What did she know? Wasn't this the same woman who made a fortune sleeping with half the NFL while posing for a few raunchy magazines?

The look on Nikki's face told Alexis that she recognized the attitude in her voice. A single raised eyebrow, coupled with skintight lips, told Alexis that Nikki would not put up with much more of her shit. Alexis decided to try to keep some of the contempt out of the conversation.

"Well, if you'd seen the news, you'd know that the city didn't flood, but Mayor Nagin isn't letting anyone come back into the city until the electricity is restored and they're sure the city is safe," Nikki reported. "So you might be stuck here for a couple more days."

Alexis rolled her eyes, laid her head back, and blew out frustrated air. "This is fucked up."

"Tell me about it. I was ready to go home, too."

"Yeah, but at least you don't have to put up with half the stuff I'm going through."

Nikki looked at Alexis intently; her interest was once again piqued. "What happened in that restaurant, anyway? Obviously, you've been here before."

Alexis rolled her eyes and unloaded the burden she'd been carrying for nearly two decades. At first, she thought it would be awkward telling this woman she barely knew and hardly liked such personal information, but the more she spoke, the lighter she felt. She slowly realized that Nikki had no room to judge anything she'd done in the past. Instead of the smirks and laughs she thought she'd get, Nikki instead offered understanding nods and friendly agreements. As the conversation went on, Alexis no longer saw an enemy. She saw an unlikely friend.

"That Andrea chick ain't nothin' nice," Nikki said.

"I know, huh?" Alexis agreed.

"So she actually lip-locked her brother-in-law, tried to hide the shit, and her husband still doesn't know about it?"

"Nope, but I'll bet you he knows by now."

"No shit."

"My thing is, how is she gonna get all pissy with me for what I did when she did dirt, herself?" Alexis asked, turning her body toward Nikki.

"Well, granted, she never slept with her brother-in-law," Nikki replied.

"Yeah, well, in my book, kissing your husband's brother is just as bad," Alexis pointed out. "Especially when you know your brother-in-law is feeling you like that. Who's to say she hadn't wanted to kiss him for years and just used what Chris did as an excuse?"

Nikki lifted her eyebrows, as if to tell Alexis that she had a point. "I feel what you're saying, but that was bad business to bring that out in front of the boy's fiancée."

"I know, and I feel bad about it. Poor girl will probably never speak to me again."

"Why not?" Nikki asked, surprised. "Hell, you didn't push Andrea's and Byron's heads together and make them kiss. She might have her feelings hurt for a minute, but that child will live to see another day. Once she gets over it, she'll realize it wasn't your fault. Andrea shouldn't have been acting stank like that. But if your girl doesn't get over it, fuck her. It's not like you knew her all that well, anyway. Were you planning on coming back here for the wedding or something?"

Alexis shrugged. She really hadn't even considered whether she'd come back to Virginia Beach to attend the wedding. She wasn't even sure Byron would allow her to come. Her phone buzzed before she could verbalize an answer. It was Jamar again. She knew she needed to answer the call. If she ignored him one more time, she was sure he would send a search party out after her. She pulled her phone from her purse and pressed TALK.

"Hey, baby."

"Girl, where the hell are you?" Jamar shouted. "I called your ass four times, and your cousin has called here twice."

"I'm okay," Alexis answered quietly.

"That was obvious when you answered the phone," he snapped. "What's going on?"

"I just needed to clear my head for a minute. Did Brenda tell you what happened?"

"Yeah, she told me, but we can discuss that later. When are you coming back home?"

Alexis's shoulders jumped from stifled laughter at the way her fiancé referred to the resort as home. Home looked nothing like that two-room, "barely an apartment" spot they were staying in. The time-share unit was great as a vacation spot, but it was nothing like home. For her, home was, and would always be, in New Orleans. Home had family, not a few people she barely knew. Home had a river walk, not a boardwalk. Home had a river and a lake, not an ocean. Home was the place they wouldn't be able to return to for at least two or three more days. Home was the place she wanted to be.

"I'll be there in a few. I'm just sitting on the boardwalk."

She wanted to tell him that she was talking with a friend, but she really didn't feel like explaining how Nikki had materialized from nowhere. It would be hard enough trying to explain how they'd so suddenly become friends when they'd hated each other just hours ago. The mess with Andrea and Brenda would weigh down the conversation enough.

"You're sitting on the boardwalk?" Jamar asked in disbelief. "Alexis, it's almost midnight."

"I know what time it is, Jamar," she snapped. She shot a look of embarrassment at Nikki, who had gone back to studying the moonbeams gleaming over the ocean. She looked like she was trying hard not to pay attention to the conversation. "Last I checked, I was a grown-ass woman who knew how to tell time. I said I'll be back in a few. You can understand that, right?"

He sucked his teeth loudly and sighed. "You got twenty minutes, or I'm comin' to look for your ass."

"Jamar, go take a shower or lie down or something. I'll be back before you know it."

"You heard me, Alexis. You've got twenty minutes."

She pursed her lips and reluctantly agreed to Jamar's time limit. She rolled her eyes as she dropped the phone into her purse.

"I don't know how I hooked up with such an overprotective man," she told Nikki, shaking her head.

"If you didn't like it, you wouldn't be with him," Nikki commented, keeping her eyes on the ocean.

Alexis cocked her head to the right, agreeing with Nikki's assessment. She fell in love with Jamar because of his take-charge attitude. She couldn't change her mind because it happened to be working against her at the moment.

"You better get back to your man," Nikki said after a moment of silence. "I ain't gonna be the cause of you two breaking up."

"That's not gonna happen," Alexis said, rising from the bench. She looked pensively toward the resort, wishing for peace once she walked through the door. She knew that was the last thing she'd be getting tonight.

"What?" Nikki asked, rising and grabbing her purse. She adjusted her bikini top again and then oriented herself toward her own hotel. "You two breaking up, or me being the cause of it?"

"Neither, boo," Alexis replied, smiling for the first time in hours. "We're tight."

"If you say so," Nikki responded with a shrug and then started walking slowly toward her hotel. "I'll see you later."

"Hey!" Alexis called after her. Once Nikki turned back toward her, she said, "Thanks."

"It's all good."

"You wanna talk tomorrow?"

"You're willing to talk to me again?" Nikki asked, staring at Alexis through scrunched eyebrows.

Alexis smiled nervously. "Well, I figured since I told you all my business tonight, you could return the favor by telling me all yours tomorrow."

The two women stared at each other silently for a few uncomfortable moments. Alexis wondered if the friendship had passed and Nikki had returned to her hateful ways. She had just decided to turn and leave when she noticed a slight smile tugging at the corners of Nikki's lips. She scratched behind her ear and ran her fingers through her hair.

"I might take you up on that," Nikki said before turning and walking away.

Alexis smiled back, glad that something had turned out halfway good that night.

Chapter 14

Andrea sat at her desk, staring at the empty wall in front of her. She'd been meaning to decorate her sparse office for months, but life just kept interrupting her plans. If she had had the time, her walls would be adorned with portraits, her shelves with leafy green foliage, and her floor would be covered with Asian splendor. Instead, her calendar was filled with appointments she didn't want to keep, her couch with parents pleading to keep their bad-ass kids in school, and her voice mail with requests she wouldn't dare fulfill. Cox High School was nowhere near Joe Clark's Eastside High, but every day was still an adventure.

None of that had yet come to fruition, since it was the first day of school, but she knew it was only a matter of time before the beatings would begin. Being the principal of a high school, she never went to school wondering *what* would happen, but *when* it would happen.

A knock at the door signified that the drama would soon begin.

"Yes?" Andrea called out, her eyes remaining on the empty wall in front of her. Maybe a coat of paint would lift her mood. *Sunshine yellow?*

The door opened, and Marguerite Foster, one of the secretaries, poked her head in. Mrs. Foster, as everyone called her, because no one dared call the thirty-year veteran by her first name, was the employee everyone hated. Still, they couldn't help but respect her. She never seemed happy, and her eyes, which looked like they could strip paint, made even the toughest students cringe in fear. Yet she remained at the school, because despite her tough exterior, she loved the students and knew the institution both inside and out. Andrea might have been the principal, but she had the good sense to understand that it was really Mrs. Foster who ran things.

She approached Andrea's desk with the urgency of a woman on a mission and dropped three sheets of paper on it. "That's your absentees for the day."

Andrea's eyes dropped to the pages, but she barely glanced at the names listed on them. She'd been a principal for two years, but she still could never understand how kids could ditch the first day of school. If anything, they should be at least curious as to who would be teaching them for the next year. Yet, as much as the absentee list irritated her, she couldn't wait to see the excuse slips that would fill her in-box the next day. Some might even be signed by real parents.

"You call their houses yet?"

"I didn't, but the computer did."

Andrea glanced at the woman, whose expression remained cold. "You know what I mean, Mrs. Foster."

She let out a sound that seemed to be a cross between a laugh and a cough. "Say what you mean, mean what you say, Mrs. Lee."

"I'll keep that in mind, Mrs. Foster," Andrea replied with a half smile.

She really wasn't sure she liked Mrs. Foster. Nor was she sure Mrs. Foster even respected her as the principal. Whenever the older woman was around, she felt like a little girl playing the boss. She was sure Mrs. Foster could smell her insecurity.

"Anything else?" Andrea added.

"Not right now," the older woman replied, backing toward the door.

"Okay," Andrea said, looking back down at the list. "Can you remind all the teachers about the meeting this afternoon?"

"Already did, Mrs. Lee," Mrs. Foster replied, walking out and closing the door behind her.

"*Already did, Mrs. Lee,*" Andrea mocked, contorting her face in irritation. God, how she hated that woman. Today was just not the day for the old lady's attitude. The way she was feeling, the secretary might get cursed out up one side and down the other.

Andrea tried to put up with her, because she remembered dealing with secretaries just like her during her high school days at John F. Kennedy. She remembered one Evileen who would look at students with a menacing stare and mumble, "I don't do double work." If the poor kid, who many times was Andrea, had misplaced paperwork or needed a late pass, he or she would have to choke on swallowed pride while trying to beg the woman for help.

Mrs. Foster didn't have quite the attitude that the sista back at Kennedy did, but she knew how to strike fear in students' hearts in her own way. She didn't need to make cutting remarks; those paint-stripping eyes were known to make many a freshman suffer from a case of the shakes. Sophomores had less fear because they'd grown used to those eyes. Yet they trod lightly on their occasional visits to the office. Juniors still trod lightly, but by then, they had worked up the courage to mutter a hello when she passed. And seniors? They paid her little or no mind, because the only cares they had were prom and graduation.

Andrea pushed the list to the side and checked her e-mail. She sometimes wished she could evoke the same fear in the students that Mrs. Foster did. Yet her looks seemed too young and her eyes too friendly for her to reach that level. Her only saving grace was her tough, but fair demeanor. Students knew and understood the consequences of their actions when she had to deal with them. She took a stern, but caring approach, and it had served her well for the past two years as a principal, and even through her time as a teacher.

Unfortunately, that approach hadn't kept her from arguing with Alexis. Nor had it kept the proverbial shit from hitting the fan once she got home. She'd tried to get Christopher home before the news hit his ears the wrong way. But, apparently, Christopher was the one driving last night. He'd dropped off Jamar and Darnell at Jamar's resort and then driven to Byron's apartment. Rayna was already there, waiting for him, and as soon as she saw the car pull up in the driveway, she went off!

Andrea had called Christopher when he hadn't made it back to the town house. Someone had pressed TALK on his cell phone, but no one had answered. Instead, she'd heard shouting and shuffling. Once she clearly heard Rayna yelling, "You wanna fuck her?" she knew it was time to get over there. The secret had come out. Andrea fought back fresh tears as she replayed the scene in her mind.

The argument had moved inside of Byron's apartment by the time Andrea arrived. Byron let her in, but his eyes were fixed on the floor. She walked into the living room, to find Rayna sitting on the couch, her makeup streaked from dried tears, her face still contorted in anger. Christopher stood leaning against the wall with his arms folded. The look on his smooth ebony face told his wife that he definitely wasn't happy.

The living room was dark except for streaks of light coming from the kitchen. The coffee table was over-turned, and a couple books and a few pieces of mail were scattered across the floor, but aside from that, everything else seemed to be in order. Andrea wondered if Rayna had tried to take a swing at Byron and had knocked over the table instead.

Byron took a seat next to Rayna, but she shot him a look so lethal, he immediately scooted as far as he could to the other end of the couch.

"Baby, you got this shit—"

Rayna closed her swollen eyes and immediately held the palm of her right hand toward him, shutting him up mid-sentence. She looked up at Andrea, scorn seeping from her pores. "Tell me this shit."

Andrea stared back quietly, afraid of the pending question. She glanced at Christopher, but he took a breath and looked away.

"Do you or did you have anything going with Byron?" Rayna asked, her voice shaky as she tried with what seemed to be all her strength to keep calm.

The question sounded more like an accusation, but attitudinal defensiveness was not the best course of action at this point. She measured how many steps it would take for Rayna to get to the kitchen to grab a knife and get to slicing if she heard the wrong thing. All of a sudden, she felt alone. No one in that room was her ally.

"I'm listening!" Rayna demanded.

Andrea had never seen this side of her future sister-in-law. At least she hoped she was still her future sister-in-law. This wasn't the Rayna she knew. This new woman sitting before her with the wild golden locs looked a lot like Rayna, but she couldn't be the talkative and friendly buddy she was used to.

"Rayna, Byron and I have always been just friends," Andrea said slowly and quietly. "We're brother and sister. You know that."

Rayna's shoulders jumped in a stifled chuckle. "That's funny. I have a lot of fuckin' friends. You used to be one of them. I ain't never lip-locked one of them unless I knew it was going further. By then, the man wasn't much of a friend anymore. He was a fuck buddy."

"Baby, it's not like that," Byron pleaded. "Listen to me. Don't let Alexis come between us over some bullshit that doesn't even matter anymore."

"What's bullshit is the two of you keeping this from me all these years," Christopher added finally. "You know I couldn't trust you around Dee for a long time after we got married. I knew your ass liked her, but you convinced me it was in my head and you would never go there with her. Now this shit comes up."

"Chris, man, I didn't go there with her," Byron said, jumping from the couch and facing his brother.

"Listen to him, baby," Andrea pleaded, looking back and forth at the only people in the city she could call family.

"And you might not wanna say anything right now," Christopher said to Andrea. "You punished me for years for what I did with Alexis. I knew I was wrong, so I accepted it. But while I was kissing your ass, trying to get you to trust me again, did you ever bother letting me know you kissed my brother?"

"That's some fucked-up shit," Rayna mumbled.

"We coulda told you, Chris, but what would that have solved?" Byron asked, holding his hands out in resignation. "You and Dee were workin' on hookin' back up. You and I were cool again. There was nothing gonna happen with me and Dee. It didn't make sense to say anything."

"Well, your ass could have told me so I didn't have to find out in the street," Rayna snapped.

Byron turned back to his fiancée. "Rayna, the shit happened almost fifteen years ago. Why would I bring that shit up now?"

"If he had, would it have changed how you felt about Byron?" Andrea asked.

Rayna rolled her eyes and looked away. "I guess I'll never know. Y'all lying asses took away my freedom of choice."

Everyone fell silent as the weight of Rayna's words fell upon them. Andrea looked helplessly at her husband, but he refused to match her gaze. Truthfully, she was surprised at how calm he was through this whole ordeal. She'd always thought his wrath would show no mercy should he ever find out about that kiss. It was true that he had never trusted his brother around her. Byron's attraction to her was too obvious for comfort. He had never tried to act on his feelings, but Andrea guessed that Christopher knew something she didn't.

"Look, Rayna," Byron said, his voice stern. He sat next to her and gently turned her face toward his, forcing her to look into his eyes. She concurred, but her expression remained hard. "This goes for you, too, Chris. I can't change the past. There was a lot of shit going on back then. Chris and Dee were separated behind that Alexis shit. All I was trying to do was look out for the both of them. I went over there to check on her, she was crying, and we got caught up. All I can do is tell you that I regret it and the shit ain't gonna happen again."

He looked even harder into Rayna's eyes. "That was then. We put the shit behind us. You gonna leave me over something that happened fifteen years ago?"

Rayna rolled her eyes and looked away. Before she could reply, however, a slam shook the windows, making them nearly jump from their seats. Christopher was gone. Andrea stood near the door, crying.

"I have to go," she said through her sniffles, wiping her eyes. She couldn't even look at them. "I'm sorry."

She scooted out of the door before either of them could say a word. She was embarrassed. Frustrated. Scared. And there was nothing she could do to fix it.

Christopher's truck was gone by the time she reached the parking lot. She could just see his brake lights flash before he turned the corner. Was this symbolic of what was to come? Would Christopher really leave her?

Fortunately, the truck was parked in their driveway, right next to Brenda and Darnell's, once Andrea returned home. She pulled her little Celica behind Christopher's truck, half hoping that if she blocked him in, he wouldn't be able to leave later. What could she expect once she walked in? Disdain from her husband? Sappy apologies from her so-called best friend? Why couldn't Brenda keep her big mouth closed, anyway? She understood that Brenda and Alexis were close, but did she have to tell her all her business?

"I really don't want to go in there," Andrea mumbled, spotting the light coming from her bedroom. The rest of the house was dark, which told Andrea that no one was waiting up for her. That was a relief. Maybe she could get a couple of hours in before starting her first day of school. But then, how could she sleep when her entire life had gone from sugar to shit in a matter of hours?

Finally, she willed herself to go inside. Just as she thought, no one waited with axes, torches, and hatchets in the living room. The house was completely quiet, so she crept upstairs to her bedroom. Christopher lay facedown on their bed, still wearing his street clothes. He didn't even flinch when she walked in. She quietly changed into her nightgown and lay next him, afraid to touch him.

Back in the moment. Andrea opened her mouth as wide as she could and yawned, still reeling from last night's events. That couple of awkward hours of sleep did nothing for her. Especially since she woke up at the crack of dawn and shuffled out before anyone woke up. She just wasn't ready to face anyone.

Now here she was, struggling to make it through the day so she could go home and try again. She'd nearly yawned during the welcome address to the students that morning. Between that, the circus going on in her head, and Mrs. Foster's attitude, she wasn't sure how much she could take. She really hoped no one would be in her house when she got home so she could just go straight to bed and pull the covers over her head.

"You tellin' me that's the best you can do?" Jamar asked, bumping the tabletop nervously with his fist.

The sun shone brightly over the ocean, making the tops of the waves sparkle like diamonds. A slight morning breeze cooled the steam swirling from Jamar's coffee, but it could do nothing about the steam blowing from his ears.

He'd called all three of the banks holding his accounts, and all three had the same story. Each showed his accounts as closed, but no one could explain why. No one had any record of him or anyone else calling to close the accounts. His mailing address was the same. All had received his last payment. Yet the computers all showed his accounts as being canceled.

"I'm sorry, Mr. Duplessis," said the customer service rep, who sounded like the sweetest version of gay that Jamar had ever heard. "I wish I could help you more. I've arranged to have a packet sent out to you so you can make a fraud claim, but until we get the packet back, there's not much more we can do."

"This is some bullshit," Jamar mumbled. "I'm not happy."

"I'm sorry, sir."

"Ain't no fuckin' need to apologize," he snapped. "Ain't like you closed the damn account."

"Sir, I'm just trying to help," the man said, the strain to stay professional evident in his voice. "There's no need for that type of language."

"Try livin' what I'm going through and then say that!" Jamar yelled. He glanced back, hoping he hadn't awakened Alexis with his outburst. He then shook his head, a tinge of guilt nagging at him for how he was treating the poor rep. It really wasn't the rep's fault that someone in his organization had messed up. "Look, I'm sorry. I'm just stressed right now. Between this damn hurricane and my financial situation, I just got some shit about me right now."

"I understand, sir. I'll get those papers out to you as soon as possible. Do you want them sent to your hotel in Virginia?"

"Yes. Can you overnight them?"

"I've placed a note on your account. You'll have them by noon tomorrow."

Jamar sucked his teeth. "All right."

It was the same story with all three accounts. Maybe he would have felt better if at least one bank had told him something different. He thanked God that he had pulled out enough cash to get by for the next couple of days, but what would he do when it was time to return home? And worse, what would happen once the charges for the room came in? The evacuee excuse wouldn't hold up forever.

How was he going to talk Alexis into staying for another two or three days? After her drama last night, she was ready to get out of the city as soon as she possibly could. Soon meaning today.

Mayor Nagin had announced that people could return to New Orleans temporarily on Thursday to inspect their damage, but no one could stay permanently until the power was restored. Jamar knew it was important for them both to get back so they could inspect their businesses and home, but with his credit shot, he couldn't even afford to get them to North Carolina. And knowing Alexis, she would want to stay in Louisiana, even if it meant getting a hotel in Gonzales just so she could be close to home. That would be even more money. He was definitely wedged between a rock and a hard place.

Fortunately, he had been able to get in touch with one of the partners in his firm and had talked him into sending him five hundred dollars. He explained that his wallet had been stolen while he and Alexis were on the beach. It was a bad lie, but it was better than the alternative of admitting that his credit accounts had been closed. He had no idea how to explain that without looking and sounding like a deadbeat. It was bad enough that Christopher and Byron knew, but what could he do when they were right there when his card was denied at the club? He probably didn't have to explain anything to them, but he'd been so consumed with embarrassment that the truth seemed to be the only option. The partners at the firm, on the other hand, knew him as a responsible, cutthroat attorney who always had his act together. A credit situation was sure to change their view of him, and he wasn't willing to risk that.

The partner had agreed to send him the money by Western Union, and he would receive it later that day. That was a relief, but it wouldn't cover all their expenses. He still had to settle the bill on the resort. They still had to eat. They still had to put gas in the car. Not to mention that wedding dress Alexis bought yesterday. The money would help, but it certainly wasn't the answer to his prayers.

"J?" Alexis called from the bedroom.

"Out here," Jamar called back, not taking his eyes from the ocean. He noticed the beauty of the coast for the first time. It was a shame that problem after problem had kept him from enjoying such splendor. The hotel had fast become his private sanctuary.

A slender arm snaked around his shoulders, followed by his fiancée's familiar kiss behind his ear. She took a seat on his lap and laid her head on his shoulder. "Good morning."

Jamar kissed her on the lips and laid her head back on his shoulder. He smiled at the sight of her still dressed in her blue teddy. "Morning, baby. You sleep okay?"

"No. You still mad at me?"

"To tell the truth, I don't know what to be mad at. You started some shit we agreed we would leave alone, you ignored my calls, and you stayed out for hours without as much as a phone call."

"I said I was sorry."

"Sorry don't always cut it, Alexis. We don't know anybody around here, and you pissed off the few people we do know."

"You act like you don't know by now that I can think for myself," Alexis snapped, lifting her head and facing her fiancé. "I can also take care of myself."

"I didn't say you can't, but it's not just you anymore," Jamar told her. "If not for accountability, it's about courtesy. You knew I had been calling you all night. Last night all those guys got a call but me. How was I to know your ass wasn't lying in a ditch somewhere?"

"Because my name is Alexis, that's why!"

"Okay, *Alexis,* but the Alexis I know wouldn't have let herself get caught up in some shit that wasn't worth the energy," Jamar challenged. "Who the hell cares if she was rolling her eyes at you? That just goes to show who the bigger person was."

A wave of hypocrisy rippled through Jamar's stomach as he continued lecturing his fiancée. *It's not just you anymore?* He should have been telling himself that! He wanted Alexis to see him as a full partner in this relationship, yet he couldn't confide in her when he, himself, had a personal crisis. He had convinced himself that it was because he was the man in the relationship, and although he was engaged to a professional, it wasn't her responsibility to be the caretaker. That was his job. It was what he was taught as a child, and it wouldn't be easily changed now. Yet, he tried to tell himself, if she were a good woman, a real woman, she would support him in his crisis. She would understand and would step up to hold them up until he could get on his feet. Maybe once they got through this mess with Andrea, he would test that theory.

"Why do I have to always be the bigger person?" Alexis demanded, standing up. She leaned on the railing of the balcony. "You weren't there watching her cut her eyes and make her little dry-ass comments every time I opened my mouth. You don't know what it's like to have somebody think you can do no right."

"On the contrary, you ever think she might be a little jealous of you?"

"Jealous of what? Chris isn't checkin' for me, and I'm damn sure not thinking about him."

"Maybe it's not just about that."

"Then what? She's the one with her nice little job, her comfy little house, and her cute little daughter. I don't have any of that yet."

"Maybe she's not looking at that."

"Then what else is there?" Alexis asked, holding out her hands. "Because I damn sure don't see it. If anything, I was the biggest loser in that whole situation. I'll never be able to have kids because of the shit I did."

She turned away from him. The crack in her voice told him that she was fighting back tears. He walked over and wrapped his arms around her, knowing how she hated showing such vulnerability.

Alexis was tough. As far as he knew, she'd always been a fighter. She had never been one to settle for the easy no and would combat the devil for the hard yes. Very few times did she show the type of emotion she displayed now. Most times, her feelings came out in the form of venomous fury, but her inability to have children was her Achilles' heel. It was the only elixir for the venom.

"Shhh," he whispered in her ear, spreading kisses over her neck. It was times like these that made him fall in love with Alexis. Very few people had ever witnessed this side of her. He felt honored that she trusted him enough to strip down to her true feelings in front of him. Maybe now wasn't the time to test his theory. "Calm down."

He turned her around so she faced him. He held her face in his hands and kissed her on the lips. "I know it's hard thinking about that, but I've already told you I'm here for you. I'm not marrying you to have kids."

"I know that," she replied, a tear rolling down her left cheek. "But this isn't just about you. Only a woman can reproduce. You might fertilize the egg, but it's the woman's job to carry the fetus and nurture it until she delivers the baby. I'll never be able to do that. I had one chance in this lifetime to do that, and I threw it away. Now I'll never be able to make it right."

"It's not just a woman's job to have a baby," Jamar said. "A woman is the person who raises a child to be a man. She inspires a little girl to be a strong black woman. You can still do that. You do it every day. I've seen how much your patients look up to you. They love and respect you. There are women who can have babies who can never hold the badges you wear."

"That's the bad part," she sobbed. "There are women out there who don't give a shit 'bout their kids. Some of them just have babies so they can keep getting paid by the government. Then you have someone like me who would love to be a mother, and I can't!"

"Yes, you can!" Jamar pleaded. "You may not be able to carry a baby or deliver a baby, but you can damn sure raise one. Hell, we'll adopt five if you want to. I told you a long time ago we could be the reverse Huxtables."

Only if I can get this money situation worked out.

Alexis smiled sadly and slapped him lightly on the chest. "You're so crazy."

"Crazy for you," he replied, kissing her on her hand. "Now, come sit down." He led her back to the table and sat her down. "You want some coffee?"

She shook her head and rested her foot on his empty chair. "I'd rather have juice."

He disappeared into the kitchen and came back a few minutes later with a large glass of orange juice. After setting the glass in front of her, he took her foot into his hand and sat down.

"So you never told me what you were doing all night on the beach," he said, digging his thumb knuckles into the ball of her foot.

"It wasn't all night," Alexis replied, laughing slightly. "I got home around one."

"That's late enough."

"How do you figure? All night is coming home at five or six in the morning."

"Actually, when you've been gone since morning and you don't come home until fourteen hours later, that constitutes all night," Jamar corrected, digging deeper into her foot.

"Damn, that feels good," Alexis said, her foot twitching.

"Give me your other one," he commanded, placing her foot on the floor. Once Alexis obliged, he grabbed it and immediately went to work. He watched her roll her eyes into the back of her head, but he hadn't forgotten the point. "You never answered my question."

"What question?" she asked, her head resting against the backrest of the chair.

"You know what question. What were you doing all night?"

She lifted her head and smiled hesitantly. "Believe it or not, I was talking with Nikki."

Jamar scrunched his eyebrows. "Nikki who?"

"Nikki Morgan, Reggie's ex-wife."

"Reggie? Your ex-boyfriend Reggie?" Jamar asked, letting go of her foot.

"What other Reggie do I know?"

"Hell, I don't know, but I didn't think you and Nikki had become friends. What's she even doing here?"

"Apparently, she's here waiting out Gustav just like we are," Alexis replied, crossing her legs and taking a sip from her juice. "I didn't even know she was here. She kinda just walked up on me last night."

"Walked up on you?"

"Yeah. Apparently, she was in the restaurant when I went off on Andrea last night."

"Is that right? That's a lot of *apparent* shit."

Alexis chuckled. "I guess it is."

"I don't know if you can trust her. You saw how scandalous she was during the divorce. She tried to take Reggie to the poorhouse because of you."

"Yeah, I seem to have that effect on women, especially when it comes to their men."

"Just be careful," Jamar warned, sitting back in his chair. He took a sip from his coffee and frowned when he realized it had gotten cold. He immediately rose and took the cup to the kitchen.

"So who were you on the phone with earlier?" Alexis asked, following him.

"Huh?" Jamar responded, his eyes fixed on the coffeemaker. He avoided eye contact as he poured the steaming hot liquid into the cold contents of his coffee cup, hoping the mixture would turn out to be just the right temperature. Suddenly, he looked up, as if noticing her for the first time. "You said something?"

"I heard you on the phone earlier," she said, leaning on the counter.

He shrugged, watching intently as he added a teaspoon of sugar to the cup. He racked his mind for the right words as he studied the granules descending slowly into the coffee. Nothing came except more stall techniques. "Nobody special."

"You sounded like you were shouting for a minute."

"Shouting?" he repeated, grabbing a packet of creamer from the courtesy basket. "No, I ain't got nothin' to shout about."

Andrea squinted at him through confused eyes. Her gaze made Jamar nervous.

"You all right?" she asked. "Why are you acting all guilty?"

"Whatcha talkin' about, girl?" he asked, trying to laugh it off. He took a sip from his coffee. Although it was indeed the right temperature, he could barely taste it over the tension he felt in the back of his head.

"You know what I'm talking about," Andrea said, folding her arms. She stared harder at him. "Were you on the phone with some chickenhead or something?"

Jamar sucked his teeth and set down his coffee cup. "Girl, no. How you gonna ask me something like that?"

"You're the one acting all funny. What am I supposed to think?"

He wanted to say something flippant and flip the script on her, but he knew Alexis was too smart for that. She would flip that script back so quickly, he wouldn't have a chance to respond. Besides, getting smart would only make things worse. Fortunately for him, she wasn't in the mood for debate.

"I'm gonna leave it alone for right now," Alexis said, rolling her eyes. She turned and walked back out on the balcony. "But just know this ain't over, and that better not have been no woman on the phone."

"That is one mean woman," Jamar mumbled before taking another sip from his coffee.

And he knew she would just get meaner if he didn't level with her soon.

***

Jamar and Alexis decided to have a lazy day in which they would stay in the hotel all day, eating, sleeping, and making love. They had just finished the making love part and had fallen into a satisfied stupor. Jamar awoke first, but instead of waking up his fiancée, he propped his head on his fist and watched her sleep. He loved how peaceful she looked. Even though they'd fought earlier, they both knew they had a deep love that wouldn't change.

This was really what confused Jamar. He knew they had something solid, but something wouldn't let him level with his future wife about his situation. He was sure she wouldn't leave him, and she had too much class to hold it over his head. It was really a problem that lay with him.

All his life, he had been the man. He knew the right words to say, the right actions to take. When he saw what he wanted, he went after it. He'd worked hard to get Alexis, independent in her own right, to trust him enough to depend on him. He always wanted to be the man in her eyes. This crazy situation with his credit threatened to ruin all of that. How could he have spent so much time getting her to lean on him, only for him to back away and ask her to let him do the leaning? Sure, she loved him. Sure, she was financially able. But he was the caretaker. He was the man. He'd also promised not to let his woman go through any more stress than she had to during this time revisiting her past. He would have to handle this situation by himself.

Alexis stirred and slowly opened her small brown eyes. She smiled when she looked up and saw her fiancé watching her. "Hey, how long you been awake?"

"Not long."

"Why you staring at me like that?"

"Because I love your mean ass," he said with a chuckle. "You feeling better?"

Alexis nodded. "You know it takes more than your attitude to get under my skin!"

"And puttin' on you like a champ doesn't hurt much, either!"

They laughed, and Alexis shook her head in spite of herself.

"Actually, fussing with you keeps my mind off of other things," Alexis admitted.

"Like what?"

She sighed. "With all the mess going on here, I still can't keep my mind off the state of my practice. I'm not sure what I'm going to find when I get back. You remember how it was when I had all those patients who couldn't afford to pay? What if I go back to that?"

This time, Jamar did the sighing. Not once had he considered that Alexis had her own concerns about the future. Before, her only show of concern was about her city and how Andrea would handle seeing her again. She had never talked about work. He was almost glad to see that she had financial concerns, as well.

She continued. "You know, I actually considered not buying that dress. I figured I would need the money to keep my practice going when we get back."

Immediately, the caretaker took over. "Baby, you keep that dress, and you better wear the shit out of it at our wedding. We will be all right."

He wasn't sure if that was totally true, but he knew he would do everything in his power to make it so. Alexis had shown him that they were a team. Maybe it was time he swallowed his pride and leveled with her about his problem. The timing wasn't right, but since they were talking about finances, she was in the right mind-set to help him come up with a solution.

"Baby, I know things are kind of rough right now, but you have to have faith that things are going to work out," he said. "It hasn't been easy for me, either."

She gave him a curious look. "What do you mean?"

Knock, knock, knock.

"Shit!" Jamar exclaimed. "You expecting anybody?"

Alexis shook her head no, remaining under the covers since she was still naked.

Knock, knock, knock.

"All right, all right," Jamar mumbled, wiping the leftover sleep from his eyes. He trudged to the door, wearing nothing but a pair of boxer briefs. "Who is it?"

Whoever it was, he would get rid of them before they could even *think* about staying too long.

"It's Brenda!" came a voice from the other side of the door.

"Ahh, shit!" Jamar grunted in a loud whisper. There went that idea.

"I heard that, Jamar. Now, let me in!"

He looked back at the door in shock. That woman had ears like a Southern grandma.

"Don't worry, J," Darnell called through the door. "I'm here, too."

"Hold on," Jamar yelled back, shaking his head and moping back to the bedroom.

Alexis had just gotten up and was walking into the bathroom, still dressed in her teddy.

"Who's at the door?" she asked, leaning over the sink to check her hair.

"Who the hell you think?" he grumbled. "Get dressed."

"Damn," she said. "You ready for some drama?"

"Whatever, man."

He pulled on a pair of jeans and rifled through the drawer. After pulling out a black T-shirt, he slipped it on and walked back to the front door. He opened it and immediately walked to the love seat and propped his foot on the coffee table.

"Hello to you, too, Jamar," Brenda remarked, walking into the room, Darnell following close behind. "Thought you were never going to open the door."

"That's what happens when you show up at a person's spot without calling first," Jamar mumbled. "You catch folks when they're not ready for company. When they might be busy."

"Sorry about that, J, but these two need to talk," Darnell said, taking a seat on the couch. He patted the spot next to him, inviting his wife to sit, but she remained standing, with her arms folded.

"This about that shit last night?" Jamar asked.

"What else?" Darnell replied.

"Don't minimize this," Brenda snapped, pacing back and forth. "This goes way deeper than Andrea's feelings being hurt. This is about trust."

Jamar and Darnell looked at each other and sighed. It seemed like both of them knew there would be no peace for the rest of the morning. Brenda caught the gesture and rolled her eyes.

"Y'all can think I'm crazy all you want, but I trusted my cousin to keep this to herself." She started pacing more rapidly. Jamar wondered if she would get dizzy from all the back-and-forth action.

"You mean the same way I trusted you to keep it to yourself when I told you?" Darnell challenged, prompting Jamar to snort a suppressed chuckle.

"Shut up, Darnell," Brenda snapped. "Don't act like you're the victim in this. Andrea and I have been friends since we were sixteen. You don't think she told me about that kiss way before you did?"

Her husband looked away in defeat but then looked back with new vigor. "That's bull and you know it. You and Andrea weren't even speaking when that happened. The day it happened, Byron came straight to my place and told me about it. I told you about it a couple days later, and the first thing you did when you and Andrea started speaking again was open your mouth."

Brenda stopped pacing and faced Darnell, her mouth agape.

"That's right. I know," he said, nodding his head with confidence. "So your cousin isn't the only one spilling secrets. How you know Byron even wanted his business put out like that?"

"If that's the case, you shouldn't have told me," she replied, rolling her neck with each word.

"And you shouldn't have told *me*," Alexis added, walking into the room. "I don't even understand why you felt the need to let me know about that, anyway. It's not like I care what Andrea does with her life."

"I told you because I didn't want you punishing yourself anymore over what happened between you and Chris," Brenda explained, her hands firmly on her hips. "But if I had known you were going to use the information against her, I wouldn't have said anything."

"Yeah, because Andrea's so innocent and she never holds anything against anyone," Alexis commented with one hand in the air and the other lightly over her heart, as if performing Shakespeare. She then leaned against the wall with her arms folded, her lips pursed so high they nearly touched her nose.

"She's got a point there," Jamar said. "Andrea's been acting stank with her since we got to town."

Brenda sighed, frustration written all over her face. "I'm not saying Dee is innocent. I'm not even saying she didn't deserve you yelling at her last night. What I am saying is what you said wasn't your business. It had nothing to do with you, and it wasn't your place to put that out there like that."

"I'll give you that," Alexis agreed, nodding her head. "Still, as long as she's been holding that shit against me while she's been hiding her own dirt, she deserved to see how it feels to have your past thrown in your face."

"And it didn't matter that in the process you destroyed the trust you had with me?"

Alexis waved her hand at her cousin. "Don't be so melodramatic, Brenda. You know we'll be confiding in each other again as soon as we get back to New Orleans."

"Maybe so, but you have me thinking hard about trusting you again. How do I know you won't throw some of my dirt in my face—"

"What dirt do you have?" Darnell interrupted.

"Darnell, please!" Brenda exclaimed. "I'm just making a point."

"Yeah, Darnell," Alexis added, "Brenda's almost as perfect as Saint Andrea herself. She couldn't have dirt if she tried. She would vacuum it up before it could even have the chance to turn brown."

Jamar burst into laughter but quieted once he realized he was the only one laughing. "My bad."

"I'm not perfect," Brenda continued. "I've made mistakes in the past, too. You know that, and Darnell knows that. But that's exactly what they are—mistakes. We can't keep reliving them."

"Tell that to your girl. Tell that to Byron's bitch ass. He hasn't spoken to me at all since I've been back," Alexis said, walking closer to her cousin. "It's like he's taking this stuff more personally than anyone else. He's the one who really had nothing to do with it."

"Well, actually," Darnell interjected, "Byron and Chris stopped speaking for a long time after the affair came out. Chris accused Byron of plotting to tell Andrea so he could get with her later."

"Excuse me?" Alexis sneered. "Are we living in a soap opera or what?"

"He can't still be holding on to that," Jamar added.

Darnell shrugged. "A bond between brothers can be strong, especially when they think just alike. Maybe Chris knew he would do the same or worse to Byron if the situation was reversed."

"That's silly," Alexis remarked, flicking her wrist at them. "Let me know when they grow the hell up."

"Well, anyway, that's their issue," Jamar announced, rising from the love seat. He walked until he was in the middle of the group. "We need to deal with our issue right now. Are y'all cool?"

Brenda and Alexis folded their arms at the same time and looked away. Darnell rolled his eyes and glared at the two women.

"I know you two aren't gonna stop speaking over some old shit," Jamar said, looking back and forth between his fiancée and his future cousin. "I'm sure you two are gonna disappoint each other a lot more than this as the years go on."

"It's not just that," Alexis pleaded. "It's also Brenda's incessant need to feel like she has to fix everything. I don't know why she had to invite Andrea to the restaurant, anyway."

"I told you why," Brenda replied in exasperation. "I can't keep splitting my time between you two. I love both of y'all, but I'm only one person."

"I understand that, but you're staying with Andrea. You see her every night, so stop trying to throw us together. It didn't work in the club, and it damn sure didn't work last night."

Brenda hugged herself and contorted her face, showing that she was deep in thought. Finally, she nodded. "I hear you. I guess it will get easier, anyway. Andrea went to work today, so we can hang during the day, and I'll hang with Dee at night."

"Sounds good to me," Alexis told her.

"So y'all cool?" Jamar asked again.

"I guess," Alexis said with her arms still folded tightly.

"You guess?" Darnell asked. "Ain't this your so-called sister-cuz?"

"Look, I'm bending for you, so you damn sure need to bend for me," Brenda told Alexis.

It took a few minutes of pouting and threats, but finally, Alexis bent to better judgment and hugged her cousin. They couldn't stay mad at each other even if they tried.

"We're cool, but you really need to learn when to keep your mouth shut, though," Brenda snapped once they broke their embrace.

Chapter 15

Forgiveness wasn't such an easy sell in the Lee household. Andrea came home from work to find an empty driveway. She walked inside and found no signs that her husband had even been home in recent hours.

She glanced at the clock. It was nearing five. She had hoped by staying out for an extra hour or two, her husband and best friend would wonder where she was and maybe look for her. It seemed the joke was on her. No one had called. No one was waiting for her. No one seemed to care.

Oh well, she thought, tossing her mail on the kitchen counter. She still had an hour before she would have to pick up the girls from Latrise's after-school program, so she might as well try to enjoy the peace while she could.

Who could blame Christopher for being upset? To him, she and Byron had gone for years hiding an affair. Nothing had ever happened beyond that kiss, but how was he to know that? He had always believed Byron wanted more than a friendship, anyway.

Even if he still believed that, why couldn't he trust his wife enough to know that she would never let anything like that happen? Yes, she had slipped once and kissed his brother, but that was right after she'd found out about his affair with Alexis. What did he expect? For her to throw a party? He'd cheated on her. With her best friend's cousin! He might be the model husband these days, but with all the mess he'd put her through back in those days, he should be thankful she hadn't done more than just kiss Byron!

"It's not like I did the shit on purpose," she mumbled to herself as she trudged upstairs. "It's one of those things that just happened."

It should have gone to the grave with her. Christopher never should have known about this. It really wasn't worth mentioning, but that bitch Alexis just had to open her mouth, she thought. The more she thought about last night, the angrier she grew. How could Alexis do that? Her little outburst just proved she still hadn't grown up. She was still the same immature little girl who thought the entire world revolved around her. If things didn't go her way, no one deserved to be happy.

As she thought about it, she realized Alexis was the same way when she was a kid. There was one time when Alexis wanted to tag along with her and Brenda to Canal Street to go shopping. Brenda wouldn't let her go, because she didn't want to have to keep up with her while still trying to have fun. Besides, what if they met a couple of boys? That "what-if" would never come to fruition, though, because Alexis threw such a tantrum that Brenda's mother, Ms. Ernestine, told them both to stay home.

Alexis always has been a big baby, Andrea thought as she lay faceup on her bed.

For the life of her, she couldn't figure out why Brenda had felt the need to tell Alexis anything. Nothing in that situation was any of her business. Didn't Brenda realize that telling her something like that would only justify in her mind the wrongs she'd created? By hearing that Andrea wasn't perfect, she could somehow feel better about her own sins.

Yet Alexis took it a step further. Not only did she feel better about what she did, but she filed the information away so she could use it against her later. And with one fell swoop, she ruined three relationships at once. How evil could she be? She had everything she wanted in life. What was wrong with other people being just as happy?

She stared at the phone, wondering if anyone would call. Yet, as much as she wished it would ring, she wasn't sure if she was ready to talk to anyone. Talking to her husband would bring a hodgepodge of embarrassment, anger, and frustration. If Brenda called, her inability to confide in her best friend would make her angry and defensive. She didn't want to go there with either of them.

These were the days when she wished she and Sheila were still speaking. Aside from Brenda, Sheila and Andrea had been best friends and could count on each other for anything. She could always trust Sheila to tell her the straight-up truth. Unfortunately, her truthfulness was what tore them apart. Sheila had a front row seat to the emotional roller coaster that Andrea rode on during the Christopher/Alexis ordeal, and she couldn't accept it when Andrea and Christopher tried to reconcile. She tried being civil, but she eventually couldn't look at Christopher without seeing the pain he'd caused Andrea. Over time they drifted apart. They hadn't spoken to or seen each other in eleven years, which was unfortunate, because Christopher and Sheila's husband, Lewis, used to be best friends.

The sound of the seal breaking on the front door woke Andrea from her brooding session. She popped up but refused to move from the bed, still not ready to face anyone. Only one set of footsteps sounded from the stairs. It had to be Christopher.

"Hey," Christopher said, entering the room. He tossed his keys on the chest of drawers and walked into the bathroom without looking at her.

Andrea looked down at the bedspread, contemplating her next move. She wanted to ask him how he felt, but feared getting into an argument. Last night's ordeal was sure to still be fresh on his mind, as it was on hers. Forcing reconciliation would only drive them further apart.

Christopher left the bathroom and walked into their closet, still refusing to utter a word. He came out a few minutes later with his gym bag and headed for the door.

"Going to the gym," he mumbled over his shoulder.

She stared at his back as he shuffled down the steps. The cold stranger who had entered and left her bedroom looked a lot like her husband, but she hadn't seen this side of him in years. This wasn't a husband who had drifted in and out. It was a roommate. A boarder. A guest. Someone who owed her nothing. There was no need to report his whereabouts to her.

In that brief exchange, Andrea thought she saw the beginning of the end. She had experienced life without her husband once before and wasn't willing to go through that again. In a panic, she rushed out of the room and scampered down the steps. She could just make out her husband standing near the door as she reached the bottom step. She ran her fingers through her short hair and sighed in an effort to regain her composure.

Christopher turned his head to look at her, his face rigid. To Andrea, he looked like the marine from the Toys for Tots commercial. She swallowed and walked toward him, praying her desperation didn't show in her eyes.

"What's up?" he asked. His hand remained on the doorknob, signaling to his wife that he was leaving no matter what she had to say.

"You, uh, gonna be back in time for, um, dinner?" Andrea stammered. She placed her hands in her back pockets and shifted her weight back and forth, fully aware that she looked like one of the girls who had been sent to the vice principal's office for punishment.

Christopher rolled his eyes and looked away. "I don't know. You don't need to cook."

"You still mad at me?"

He sucked his teeth and cut his eyes at her. "What do *you* think?"

Andrea drew in a breath. She rubbed her neck, wondering what to say next. "Who are you going to the gym with?"

"Nobody. I just need some air. Had a long day at work, and truthfully, I'm not ready to come home yet."

"What do you mean, you're not ready to come home yet?" Andrea snapped. "You're moving out?"

Finally, Christopher turned around and faced her, but instead of moving closer to his wife, he leaned against the door and folded his arms, his gym bag hanging over his shoulder.

"Don't be so melodramatic, Dee. I'm not going anywhere but the gym."

She let out a slight sigh of relief and rubbed her hands together. "Look, I'm sorry you had to find out about things the way you did, but do you believe me when I say that nothing happened?"

He shrugged. "I don't know what to believe anymore. That's part of the reason I need to get out of this house."

"I kinda think we should talk."

"We will, but just not right now."

"Why not?"

The glare he responded with nearly made her tremble. She'd never seen such a look from her husband. It was almost as if he hated her, and the words that followed seemed to confirm her thoughts.

"Because if I even think about talking to you right now, I might say something both of us will regret."

The words sent a chill up her spine that she couldn't shake off. Wasn't this the same man who had begged to come back home years ago, when she put him out after his affair? Wasn't this the man who claimed to love her forever through thick and thin? Wasn't this the man who, since he'd moved back into the house, had worshipped the very ground she walked on? Her eyes widened as she beheld the stranger who now stood before her.

The same panic that had visited her earlier overtook her. She'd be damned if she would let it go down this way. She threw her arms around his neck and kissed him as hard as her trembling lips would allow. The move shocked Christopher, who quickly stepped back, dropped his bag, and tried to pull her arms away from him.

"What's up with you, Andrea?" he demanded, holding her back at arm's length.

"Chris, I'm not gonna let you walk out on us over something that happened fifteen years ago," she cried, struggling to get out of his grasp. "And I refuse to let that bitch Alexis ruin our marriage yet again!"

"You don't get it, do you?" he said, his voice shaking, as if he was trying with all his might to stay calm. He let her go and walked into the living room. Instead of sitting down, he stood near the coffee table with his arms folded. "This doesn't have a damn thing to do with Alexis, and it's not about that fuckin' kiss."

"What is it, then?" Andrea asked, clinging to her spot in front of the door. She was afraid if she moved, she would give him the green light to leave. If he did manage to walk out that door, she was afraid his retreating back would be the last view she would ever have of him.

"You really don't know? You don't understand?"

"Enlighten me, Chris!"

He sighed while looking around at the furniture, as if it could give him support. "Look, let's not do this right now."

"Talk to me, Chris!" Andrea pleaded, tears streaming down her cheeks.

"I can't," he said quietly, walking back toward her. His bag remained in the same spot where he'd dropped it. He silently picked it up and walked toward the door, but he stopped short when he realized his wife had never moved. "Let me go, Andrea."

She shook her head no and leaned against the door.

He rolled his eyes and shook his head. "Dee, please don't make this difficult. I'm not leaving you. I love you just as much now as I did yesterday, but I need some time by myself. Can you give me that, please?"

Was he just saying what she wanted to hear? How could she be sure he wasn't saying what he needed to just to get her out of the way? The fact that he held a bag that contained only a few sweaty gym clothes should have been indication enough, but she didn't have the time to think rationally.

"Are you sure you're coming back?" she asked, feeling like a little girl trying to get her daddy to keep a bogus promise. She felt stupid, but she was in too deep to back off.

Her feelings seemed to be lost on her husband. And, instead of softening his stance, anger took over. Cursing, he threw his bag to the side and punched at the air.

"Dammit, Dee, this isn't a fuckin' game! I told you I was coming back, and that's just what the fuck I meant! Now, let me get some fuckin' air!"

Andrea recoiled at the rage but couldn't help but strike back. "Who are you cursing at? I know you're mad, but I will not have you talking to me like some bitch off the street!"

"This is precisely why I didn't want to get into this with you right now!" he shouted back, pointing his finger at her. "You just had to push the damn issue! Why is it okay for you to go running off to your girls or to pout in our room when you need time to think, but when I want time to think, it has to be a goddamn issue?"

The two went back and forth, each trying to pin the biggest wrong on the other. Neither of them heard the lock turn on the front door. It wasn't until the doorknob poked Andrea in the back that either of them stopped shouting long enough to see what was happening.

"Okay, you two need to calm down before I bring these two girls in the house," Brenda said, closing the door behind her.

"Where are they?" Andrea asked.

"Out in the driveway with Darnell," she replied. "There was no way in the world I was going to bring them into this battle zone."

"You need to talk to your girl," Christopher snapped, pointing at Andrea. He then picked up his bag and shuffled out of the house before either woman could reply.

"Hi, Daddy," Latrise greeted with a wave once he was safely outside. She ran up to him and gave him a hug.

"Hey, sweetheart," he replied, hugging her back. "How was your first day of school?"

"It was good!" she exclaimed. "Two of my BFFs are in my class."

"What in the world is a BFF?"

"Come on, Daddy, you've got to get with it."

"Yeah, Chris." Darnell laughed. "Even I know what a BFF is."

"Well, do you mind letting me in on the big mystery?" Christopher asked, looking up at his friend.

"It's a best friend forever!" Elizabeth broke in, giggling. "I can't believe you didn't know that."

"Don't get smart, peanut head," Darnell admonished his daughter, lightly plucking the top of her head.

"Daddy!" she shrieked, rubbing her head. "I told you not to call me that."

"Oops, my bad," he replied, shrugging his shoulders. He looked back at Christopher, who had stood upright and was holding hands with his own daughter. "You all right, man?"

"Not really, but I'm sure they'll fill you in when you go inside."

"You leaving?"

"Hell, yeah," Christopher replied, nearly forgetting about the kids in the vicinity. "Lizzy, why don't you and Latrise go ahead and go inside?"

"Okay, Mr. Lee," Elizabeth replied obediently. She then turned to her friend. "Let's go play *Cooking Mama*."

"Okay," Latrise agreed.

Christopher watched the two girls scamper inside, then turned back to Darnell. "She's gonna make me say something I don't need to."

Darnell nodded in understanding. "Where you going?"

Christopher shrugged. "Just to get some air. I was gonna go play basketball, but I'm not in the mood anymore."

"I hear ya. Just be careful out there."

"I ain't goin' far. I'll be back in a couple of hours."

"Can you be back about seven thirty? I'm taking my wife and her cousin and Jamar out to dinner."

"You trying to leave Elizabeth here?"

"You don't mind, do you?"

Christopher looked back at the house and lifted his eyebrows. "You sure you wanna leave her in all this drama?"

Darnell chuckled. "Y'all gonna be all right. You're not really that pissed over something that happened ages ago, are you?"

"You damn right I am. She put me through hell when she found out about Alexis. I can even understand her trying to get some payback, but with my brother?"

"I don't think it was like that, Chris."

"Then how was it?" he asked, folding his arms and leaning against Darnell's truck.

"Now, you know Byron is my boy and we were pretty tight back then," Darnell said, leaning next to Christopher, ensuring that there was a respectable amount of space between them. "I think it was just a matter of emotions getting the better of both of them."

"Come on, Darnell!" Christopher exclaimed, throwing his hands in the air. "Is that shit supposed to make me feel better—"

"Hold on. Hear me out," Darnell cut in, holding his hands out in retreat. "You know as well as I do that Byron had always had a crush on Andrea. He never did anything about it, but it didn't stop him from looking out for her. Then, when that stuff with Alexis came up, he kinda felt caught in the middle between his loyalty to you and caring for her."

"So they took advantage of the situation and tried to explore what coulda been," Christopher surmised.

Darnell laughed again. "Man, you are intent on seeing this the way you want to, aren't you?"

"You think I want to see my brother and my wife kissing?"

"First of all, that so-called kiss lasted only a second or two. And no sooner had it happened than Byron scooted his ass out of there and came, stressing, into my apartment. Pacing and talking about how he'd fucked up."

"Then why didn't he come and tell me if he was all distraught over the shit?"

"Come on," Darnell said. "The way you were acting back then, accusing him of trying to get with your wife, if he had told you about the kiss, what would you have done?"

"I woulda beat his ass!"

"Exactly!"

Christopher looked into space, reality weighing in on him. As if reading his mind, Darnell patted him on the shoulder and walked toward the house. "Think about it, bruh."

"Where's Chris?" Andrea asked before Darnell could close the door.

"Hello to you, too, Dee," he replied dryly.

He actually had another remark in mind, but under the circumstances, he figured less sarcasm was the way to go. He pursed his lips as he looked at the two women sitting in the living room like perfect strangers. Andrea sat on the sofa, tensed, her arms folded and her legs crossed tightly. Brenda, normally the peacemaker in the bunch, lay across the love seat, watching an infomercial advertising some type of laundry detergent. Darnell recognized the commercial because he'd wrestled with buying the detergent himself.

This is ridiculous, he thought, careful not to think out loud. He knew any word he said would make matters worse, but he couldn't stand to watch two childhood friends act like this. He guessed it was true. Some wounds never healed. Here it was, fifteen years later, and that damn affair was still wreaking havoc in their lives. The last time they'd stopped speaking like this was when Andrea found out about the affair and blamed Brenda for bringing Alexis into their lives. Brenda went through hell trying to make everything right again. She had nothing to do with the situation, but you would have thought she was the one who'd been cheated on. Then, the next day, it seemed like she was the one who had done the cheating and was trying to make amends. He loved the fact that his wife cared so much, but he'd be damned if he let her begin taking on everyone else's problems again. It wasn't worth either of their sanities.

He could hear juvenile cheering coming from Latrise's room as he started trudging up the steps. *At least somebody in this house is having fun,* he thought. He took another look at his wife. The look on her face seemed different. No worry lines. No downcast eyes. She really didn't look stressed at all. She looked darn near content. Was this actually Brenda he was seeing?

"You about to get dressed?" she asked, her eyes still on the television. She reached back and rubbed her neck, then leaned her head against the back of the love seat. Not once did she look up. She didn't even cut her eyes toward her friend. It was as if she hadn't a care in the world.

"Y'all going somewhere?" Andrea mumbled, looking up at Darnell, who had stopped halfway up the stairs.

Another round of cheering came from Latrise's room, this time followed by laughter. Darnell silently thanked God the girls were oblivious to the tension building around them.

"Um, yeah," he replied. His eyes shot toward his wife, already anticipating her thoughts. He was right. The grimace she wore was unmistakable. "We're, uh, going out to eat with Jamar and Alexis."

"Oh, well, y'all have fun with that," Andrea mumbled.

"We will," Brenda snapped.

Both Andrea and Darnell turned toward her, equally shocked at the attitude emanating from Brenda's voice.

"What's wrong with you?" Andrea asked.

"Nothing," Brenda snapped, none of the vigor leaving her voice. Her eyes remained transfixed on the television.

Darnell glanced at the screen, wondering what the hell was so interesting. It seemed to be a rerun of *I Love New York*. She couldn't really be watching that. The only reality TV she watched regularly was the news. Her eyes rolled as she cut them at her friend.

"I just like the way you sat there and ignored me for the last half hour, and when you finally fixed your mouth to say something, it was directed at my husband," Brenda muttered.

"I don't think she meant anything by that," Darnell said quickly. He didn't believe the words himself, but he felt he needed to do something to quell the mood. It was about to get ugly in there.

"Then, what did she mean, Darnell?" Brenda asked.

"Ask me, Brenda," Andrea retorted, leaning forward. She eyed her friend as if preparing for an attack. "I'm sitting right here."

"I know. You've been sittin' your ass there since I walked through the door."

"Oh, so now you're cursing at me? Don't forget whose house *you're* sittin' in."

"Oh, that shit can change real quick. Just say the damn word."

More cheering. "You can't beat me, Trisey!"

Darnell quietly walked up the rest of the steps and poked his head into the girls' room.

"Hey, ladies, I'm gonna close the door so your mothers and I can talk. That okay with you?"

"Yeah," the girls said together, barely taking notice of him in the doorway.

He smiled slightly at the girls' innocence. Sometimes he wished he could go back to the days when the only important thing was getting to the next level of *Space Invaders*. He stood in the hallway and let himself chuckle at the thought before shuffling back to the battle lines that had been drawn downstairs.

Neither woman had moved from her position, but the swipes they continued to take at each other seemed to leave streaks across the walls. It always amazed him how women could cut each other so deep without ever drawing a weapon. Their stony looks were enough to cut diamonds. They were so stiff, they could put the Venus de Milo to shame. He'd heard the comments as he came downstairs, but they must have stopped when they heard him coming closer. Now, instead of angry words, there were icy stares.

Darnell rubbed the upper sides of his nose in an effort to fight off the migraine that was sure to come. This was not the way to start off a peaceful evening with family. He suddenly longed for the sailors on his base. Their issues would be a definite upgrade from what he was going through right now. He decided he would give them a call in the morning. It was time to get back home.

He stood at the bottom of the steps, wondering what to do next. He could sit next to his wife, but he didn't want it to look like they were ganging up on Andrea. And he damn sure couldn't sit next to Andrea. No way in hell he would sit on the floor. Finally, he decided to just lean against the kitchen counter. Any other move would come across as an obvious dodging technique, and that was some more drama he would much rather avoid.

"You two really need to stop all this," he said, looking back and forth at both women. "Y'all are too old for this and have been through too much."

"Tell her that!" the women exclaimed at the same time.

The situation would be funny if it weren't so sad. They were each wrong in their own way, but both had too much pride to admit it. It reminded Darnell of something his grandmother used to say: "Never point out the sty in someone else's eye without noticing the beam in your own." Suddenly, the saying made total sense.

"Look, you two need some air," Darnell said, straightening up. He walked back toward the steps. "Brenda, we need to get ready to go."

"Well, don't think I'ma be sittin' here babysittin' while you and your bitch-ass cousin talk about me all night," Andrea mumbled as Brenda rose from her seat.

Brenda had just started for the steps, but when she heard that comment, she froze in her tracks. Darnell froze in his tracks, as well, holding his breath in nervous anticipation of what would come next. This wasn't the same Brenda he knew and loved.

"Andrea," she began with all the calmness she could muster, "you have one more time to call my cousin out of her name. I don't care what's going on between you two. She's my family, and I'm not going to let you talk about her like that."

"But it's okay for her to expose some shit that wasn't even her business?" Andrea shot back, popping up from the sofa. She walked toward Brenda purposefully, her pointed finger leading the way. "It's okay for you to spread my personal shit all over New Orleans, but I don't have a right to be mad? We're talking about my damn marriage here! Your man is right here beside you, like he always is. I don't know where my husband is or if he's even coming back, because your cousin decided to open her damn mouth at the wrong time!"

"Don't be so melodramatic, Dee," Brenda replied, folding her arms. "Chris ain't going nowhere. He worked too hard to get you back to leave you over something like this."

"He wouldn't have had to get me back at all if it hadn't been for your cousin," Andrea said, rolling her neck with each word.

Brenda laughed, but it was obvious she thought nothing was funny. The noise was anything but jovial. It almost sounded evil.

"Your problems are everybody else's fault but your own, huh?" she spat. "Yes, Alexis slept with your husband. I got it. But it was your choice to kick him out, and I don't blame you. You had to do what you had to do. Still, you're the one who chose to let him stay gone as long as you did, knowing full well you wanted him back. You took it upon yourself to kiss your husband's brother. That was stupid, no matter how you try to explain it away.

"You're the one who decided to carry this hate and let it eat you up all this time. You're the one who made comment after comment about *and* to Alexis the minute she hit the city, even when you saw she was trying to make amends. You're the one who pushed the issue until she finally struck back. You couldn't leave well enough alone, could you? You couldn't find a little for-giveness in your heart for a mistake she made when she was damn near a child. You wanna blame somebody for your problems? Try looking at yourself!"

"Excuse me?" Andrea asked with her face contorted in anger.

"You heard," Brenda retorted rolling her neck right back.

Darnell wanted to pull her upstairs to get away from this madness, but he had a strong urge to watch it play out. He'd never seen his wife stand up for herself this way. He kind of liked this side of her. He often teased his wife for having a Mother Theresa complex. She had a knack for taking on other people's problems as if they were her own, which caused her undue stress. When she tried to fix things, she'd take on even more stress. It seemed that this time, she'd finally had enough.

"I think you need to calm the hell down," Andrea spat, looking at her friend in contempt. "I told you be-fore you will not stand in my house, cuttin' a damn fool. You have a problem with the way I'm handling things? Carry your ass out of here."

That was Darnell's cue to step in. This had gone way too far. Before Brenda could utter a reply, he pulled her by the arm, practically dragging her up the steps. He glanced toward the children's room, hoping they hadn't heard anything. This was no scene for a child.

The more he pulled, the harder Brenda fought to get a word in. Every time she tried to same something, Darnell would interrupt her, demanding that she come upstairs.

"You better get her out of my face!" Andrea yelled, watching them struggle.

She stomped away from the steps to a place Darnell couldn't see from his position. Yet it wasn't hard to hear how she felt. He would have to be deaf not to hear the rants coming from the living room's direction.

Finally, Brenda gave in to her husband's demands and charged up the steps toward the children's room. She beat on the door as if someone were after her. "Elizabeth! Come on and get dressed. We're going out to dinner!"

A minute passed before the door opened slowly, revealing two very disappointed girls. The images of Japanese cartoon characters danced across the television screen behind them.

"Mom, you said I could stay here while you and Daddy went out," Elizabeth whined. "Can't I please stay here?"

Brenda rolled her eyes and looked at Darnell, who leaned against the wall behind her. "Change of plans, so put some clean clothes on so we can go meet Alexis."

The little girl's eyes lit up as if a lightbulb had gone off in her head. "Can Trise go?"

Brenda pursed her lips together. There was no way in hell she would take Latrise somewhere after the way her mother had acted. Didn't Andrea tell her just a few minutes ago not to expect her to babysit?

"That's up to her momma, but I think Ms. Dee wants Trise to stay here," Brenda said carefully.

"I can ask her," Latrise said eagerly, stepping closer to Brenda.

"I don't think so," Darnell said, trying to bail his wife out of the hole she was creating. "We have some grown-up things to discuss. As a matter of fact, Lizzy, you should probably stay here, too."

Brenda's head snapped toward her husband. She glared at him. He knew what she was thinking. He hadn't tried to overrule her in front of the kids, but in

light of all the anger in the conversation that was sure
to ignite at the dinner table, the best place for two nine-
year-olds was definitely not in the middle of the inferno.

"Is it because you two were fussing downstairs?"
Elizabeth asked Brenda.

"You heard that?" Darnell asked, looking concerned.

"We both did," Latrise replied. "We couldn't hear
everything, but we heard you guys yelling and stuff."

Guilt momentarily overtook Darnell, and when he
looked over at Brenda, he could tell she felt the same
way. It was a fact of life that kids would hear their parents argue, but he hoped what they heard wouldn't be
the end of a friendship.

Brenda replaced her anger with a look of concern,
something that Darnell had grown accustomed to over
the last decade and a half. She sighed. "You two go
ahead and stay here. Finish your video games."

"We don't have to go to dinner?" Elizabeth asked
with a smile.

"No, I'll order you a pizza," Brenda told them.

The girls jumped up and down, cheering, engender-
ing in Brenda a wave of nostalgia. Slowly, she turned
and walked across the hall to their bedroom.

Darnell recognized her mood. She was missing the
times when she and Andrea couldn't stand to tear themselves away from each other. They had been friends
only since they were sixteen, but their bond had always
seemed unbreakable. They had graduated from high
school together. They had attended separate colleges but
had found a way to work their way through their toughest courses together. He remembered being astounded
when Brenda told him that Andrea had actually moved
to Virginia Beach so they could stay together. They had

laughed and cried together. Now it seemed like the open wound from a fifteen-year-old secret could be the one thing that would tear them apart.

Chapter 16

"Reggie?"

Reggie glanced over his shoulder at the sight of a moderately attractive, brown-skinned woman sporting an extremely short haircut. She wore ripped jeans and an Obama '08 T-shirt. She looked slightly familiar, but he couldn't place the face.

"Yes?"

Her smile morphed into a playful pout as she placed her hands on her hips and poked out her lip. "Don't tell me you don't remember me. Has stardom made you forget about the little people?"

His eyes darted back and forth as he searched his mental date book. He wasn't much of a player, so she couldn't be somebody he'd met on the road. Then again, those couple years before he married Nikki, when he had formed his core set of women, or his A squad, as he liked to call them, might be catching up with him.

"Boy, I really don't believe you!" the woman exclaimed, still smiling. "It's Shannon. Shannon Gold from Tulane?"

A glimmer of recognition finally made its way to Reggie's eyes. He smiled and pulled her into a hug. "Woman, what's up with you?"

"Everything is everything," she replied, laughing and returning the hug. "You living in Atlanta again? I remember you're from here."

"No, just waitin' out the hurricane," he said, leaning against a store window. His eyes landed on DeShawn, who was busy inspecting new Wii games at the Game-Stop across from them. "My man and I are heading back to the N.O. in another day or so."

Shannon followed his gaze. "That your little man?"

"Yep, that's my shadow," he replied. "What about you? You got any kids?"

"Twin girls," she said proudly. "They're twelve. Dale and I got married right after we graduated from Tulane."

"I remember Dale. He's a good dude."

"Yes, he is. He's an engineer at AGL Resources."

"Looks like you two made out pretty well. I'm happy for y'all."

"Thanks, boo. What about you? Did you and that girl Alexis ever work things out after college?"

Reggie chuckled. "It has been a long time since we talked. Lex and I never got back together when we broke up. We actually lost touch until about a year ago. She's doing pretty well for herself, though. She still lives in New Orleans and runs a pediatrics clinic."

"Wow. Who would have ever thought?" Shannon mused. "Don't tell me you've been single all these years."

"Nope," he replied and pointed at DeShawn. "I was married to his mother almost the whole time I was in the NFL. We got divorced a few months ago."

"Oh, sorry to hear that."

"Don't be. I'm not."

They laughed together and spent the next few minutes sitting on a nearby bench, catching up on old times. Besides the occasional interruption by an autograph seeker, Reggie momentarily felt like a regular guy talking with an old friend. No worries about hurricanes. No one begging him to endorse a product. No one asking for money. No arguments with the ex-wife, and no pressure to get married again.

"You know, there's a few of us here from New Orleans," Shannon said. "We get together on Sundays to watch the football games. With football season starting up again, you should drop by."

"That sounds good, Shan, but I plan to be sitting in my own crib by Sunday."

"I can understand that," she replied, smiling. "Where are you staying while you're here?"

"I'm staying with my mom. I have a house out in Lawrenceville, but I'm renting it out to some cousins until they can get on their feet."

"That's cool, but I'll bet they're not trying to get on their feet too fast."

"Why you say that?" Reggie asked, furrowing his eyebrows in confusion.

"Those places in Lawrenceville are gorgeous. You think they're trying to leave that? Ain't nothin' else gonna compare to that."

"Shiiit," Reggie remarked with a laugh. "They know better than that. I already told them that they have one year. That's long enough to find a job and put some money away."

"All right," Shannon said, patting his hand. "I hope you're right. I know I've had enough of my family tryin' to take advantage of me and Dale."

"Where is Dale, anyway?"

"Working, which is where I need to be," she said, checking her watch. She began gathering her shopping bags and stood up.

Reggie stood up with her. A glance toward Game-Stop told him that DeShawn wasn't nearly ready to go. He'd involved himself in one of the computer games on display outside the store. He and another little boy had teamed up to play some fighting game Reggie had never seen before.

"Maybe you and your son can come over for dinner tonight," Shannon suggested. "I'm sure Dale would be happy to see you."

Reggie pulled out his phone. "Sounds good. Put your number in here. I'll call and let you know."

She obliged, then looked up and smiled. "If you have a girlfriend or groupie or something here, I guess she can come, too."

Reggie laughed. "It's not like that. She's someone I evacuated with. We've been dating for a while."

"No need to explain anything to me," Shannon said, putting up her free hand in defense. She returned his phone and added, "I ain't nobody."

He chuckled. "Shut the hell up, Shannon."

"All right, well, you just let us know," she said, giving him a friendly hug. "Don't wait till the last minute, though."

"I won't," he replied, holding his hand up as if being sworn in. "Promise."

He called his son over once Shannon bade him goodbye. After a couple minutes of groaning and protesting, the boy finally obeyed.

"Daddy, can we get that game?" DeShawn asked once he'd taken Reggie's hand.

"Maybe next time, baby boy."

They walked hand in hand through the mall, headed back toward Reggie's car.

"Daddy, who was that lady you were talking to when I was playing the game?"

"That was an old friend of mine," Reggie explained. "We went to college together."

"College? Don't old people go there?"

Reggie laughed. "I guess compared to you, they're old."

"Is she gonna be your girlfriend?" DeShawn asked as they exited the mall.

"Why would you ask that?" Reggie asked, wondering what the child might have overheard. "Your daddy already has a girlfriend."

"I know. Janet's cool and all, but I figured you could have more than one girlfriend, like Marcus's dad does."

Ah, the perks of being a celebrity's son. He got to see the good and the bad. Marcus's dad, a second-string running back with the Falcons, had quite a few girlfriends. They ranged in age from eighteen to thirty, and they waited on him hand and foot. A couple of them even knew about each other, but that didn't stop them from sharing in his time. If anything, it made them work harder to compete. They seemed to be willing to do anything to win his time. He reminded Reggie of Flavor Flav without the TV show.

"I think one is enough for me," Reggie said, opening the door to his Porsche.

DeShawn hopped in the back and strapped himself in.

"You can't handle more than one woman?"

"Watch your mouth, son," Reggie admonished, staring at his son through the rearview mirror. The boy pursed his lips, showing his dad he'd gotten the message. "I don't want you growing up thinking it's okay to disrespect women. What Marcus's dad does is cool for him, but it's not the way women should be treated. I happen to enjoy being with one woman. Janet is a nice lady, and it would hurt her feelings if she knew I had another girlfriend or that you were even thinking like that."

"What if she had another boyfriend?"

Where did that come from? Had DeShawn heard something Reggie hadn't?

"Janet doesn't have another boyfriend."

"I know. I'm just saying. If she did, would it be okay for you to have another girlfriend?"

"Why are you so worried about me seeing somebody else?" Reggie asked, uncomfortable with where the conversation seemed to be heading. "You don't like Janet anymore?"

"I do. I was just asking."

"Well, don't ask. That's a grown folk's conversation."

"Okay."

The idea DeShawn had so innocently placed into Reggie's mind plagued his thoughts for the rest of the ride home. Could it be possible that Janet was seeing somebody else? He knew that lately he hadn't treated her exactly the way she wanted to be treated, but he didn't think it had come down to this. He'd have to watch his woman a little more closely. If she expected him to marry her one day, this damn sure wasn't the way to inspire him.

Jay-Z's "Gold Digger" sounded from his cell phone. He'd been meaning to change that ringtone for months. He had assigned it to Nikki's number when they separated. Nikki wasn't a gold digger. An opportunist, maybe. A bitch sometimes, definitely. Still, she was also the mother of his child and didn't deserve such titles.

"What's up, Nikki?" he greeted after pressing TALK.

"Hey, I'm not keeping you long, but I'm at the mall and wanted to get DeShawn some shoes."

"Okay, and?"

"And I wanted to confirm his shoe size. Damn!" she snapped. "Why you always gotta be so hostile toward me?"

"Guess I'm just used to it," he replied, letting himself chuckle. "He's still a four."

"Thanks."

"You still in Virginia Beach?"

"Yeah. Somebody offered to give me a ride to the mall so I could get away from that damn water for a while."

"Uh-huh." Reggie knew that *somebody* was of the male persuasion and was likely somebody with a little change in his pocket, but he didn't push the issue. It wasn't his business anymore. At least he knew his son would benefit from her good fortune.

"You know what's a coincidence?" he asked.

"What?"

"I just left the mall. Guess we're still on the same wavelength in some ways."

"I guess. You get him anything?"

"No, we were just strolling."

"Can I talk to Mommy?" DeShawn asked from the backseat.

Reggie glanced at the rearview mirror and smiled. "You wanna talk to your son?"

"Man, you know I wanna talk to my son!" Nikki snapped.

Reggie laughed again and gave DeShawn his cell phone. Whatever he thought of his former wife, he appreciated the fact that she and DeShawn had such a close relationship. It was nice hearing him laugh with her. The light moment gave him a brief respite from his brooding about Janet. His mind wasn't completely clear, but he knew there was nothing he could do about it right now. At this moment, all he had was suspicion. He'd get to the truth sooner or later.

"Daddy, your phone is beeping," DeShawn announced.

"Lemme see the phone," Reggie demanded, careful not to give him the chance to call out whatever name had appeared on the caller ID. Nikki didn't need to know all his business.

"Hold on, Mommy," DeShawn said and then handed the phone to his dad.

Reggie glanced at the number and drew his head back in surprise. "Hey, Nikki, hold on a sec."

"That's okay, Reg. Handle your business," Nikki said. "Call me later."

"I will. Talk to you later," he said. He pressed TALK to switch over to the new line. "So to what do I owe this shock and awe?"

"Just calling to say hello," Alexis replied. "You guys doing all right?"

"We're fine," Reggie replied, picking up his earpiece from the passenger seat. He placed it snugly in his ear and dropped the phone in his lap. "The worst is over now."

"Thank God for that."

"Where did you guys hide out?"

"My mom, Frank, and Roman went to Houston, but Jamar and I went to Virginia Beach of all places."

"Virginia Beach?" Reggie repeated, an image of his ex-wife appearing in his head.

What were the chances that they'd seen each other? Then again, if they had, he was sure he would have heard about it by now. Yet something else about the sound of that city bothered him, but he couldn't put his finger on it.

"Yeah," she replied. "I guess you're surprised to hear that, huh?"

"You're reading my mind, huh?"

She laughed a bit. "A little, I guess. I'm guessing you figured I would never come back here."

"Back there?"

"Come on, Reg. Are you telling me that you forgot this is where I got pregnant?"

Wow. That was why the city seemed so familiar. A million memories washed over him like a tidal wave. He would never forget the painful, tear-filled night when she told him about her secret abortion. It was the night she admitted that she'd cheated on him with a married man. It was also the night that she'd finally told him she loved him. He'd never seen her so vulnerable. Yet his pride made him break up with her, anyway.

"Hello, Reggie? You there?"

Alexis's voice, coupled with a few rapid blinks, took him out of his stupor. He hadn't even realized he'd drifted off. A quick glance in the rearview mirror confirmed that DeShawn hadn't even noticed his momentary change in demeanor. He was too busy playing with his PSP.

"I'm here," he finally told Alexis. "You just brought back some stuff I hadn't thought about in a while."

"Well, don't get it twisted," she said. "It hasn't been all that easy for me, either."

"You run into old dude?"

"Are you serious? His wife is still Brenda's best friend! I see their asses almost every day!"

"Damn. That can't be easy," he commented, coming to a stop at a red light. The white Acura next to him had Lil Wayne on blast.

"That's my song!" DeShawn exclaimed suddenly. "Lick, lick, lick . . ."

Reggie's head snapped around toward the backseat. He was horrified, yet somewhat amused, that his child was singing about a woman licking him like a lollipop.

"What?" the boy asked, noticing his dad staring at him. His head continued to bob to the beat.

Reggie didn't know whether to admonish him or congratulate him. Instead, he remained silent, shook his head as he tried to stifle a laugh, and turned back to the road just in time to see the light turn green.

"What was all that noise?" Alexis asked. "Where are you?"

"We're just driving home from hanging out," Reggie explained. "That was the car next to me blasting his music. You didn't hear Shawn in the backseat?"

She laughed a bit. "I thought that was him. Tell him I said hi."

"I will, but finish telling me about you and old dude." There was a time when he couldn't bear to hear about this part of the past, but he'd learned to live with the memories. It had taken a lot of time and soul-searching, but he and Alexis had finally learned to become friends. He was actually surprised that hearing her story didn't even bother him.

"Yeah, well, anyway, he's been kinda cool. He hasn't said much to me. His wife is a different story, though. I had to go off on her last night."

Reggie wanted to laugh. Alexis had never been one to hold her temper. "What did she do to deserve that?"

She sighed, seeming to seek the words to describe whatever had happened the night before. "That bitch. Ever since I got to town, she's been cutting her eyes at me, making sly comments, just acting like the shit with Chris happened yesterday instead of forever ago."

"Well, you can't blame her for being mad at you," he said, trying to choose his words carefully. This wasn't exactly a child's type of conversation.

"What the hell ever, Reg," Alexis shot back. "After all these years, she shoulda got over that shit. I did, and obviously Chris did, too."

"Yeah, you're right. She shoulda got over it, just like you got over things with me, huh?"

A long silence told Reggie that he'd touched a nerve. Eleven years had gone by before both Alexis and Reggie could work up the nerve to speak to each other after their painful breakup. Becoming friends hadn't been easy. A lot of bad memories came with that healing process, but with time, Alexis had learned to push them aside and concentrate on the present.

"You still there?" Reggie asked.

"Yeah, I'm here," she said. "You know that's not the same thing, Reg."

"Why not? She held a grudge against you for fifteen years, and you held one against me for eleven."

"It's just different, Reg!"

"Tell me how."

He could hear her suck her teeth and blow out some air. "Because at least I gave you a chance to make things right."

"Really, I shouldn't have had to. I was the one wronged in the situation. You were just mad because I didn't let you get away with it."

"Wow, Reggie. Is that how you really see it?"

"Just telling you how it is," he replied, pulling into his mother's driveway. The car had barely been placed in park before DeShawn jumped out and ran to the door. Reggie watched as the boy rang the doorbell and continued playing with his PSP while waiting for someone to open the door. "Not only did you mess around on me, but you got pregnant in the process. Then, on top of that, you got an abortion and tried to hide it from me. I respect that you finally admitted everything, but you can't really blame me for breaking up with you. I'm just wondering how after all those years, I wound up being the one apologizing."

"Because you broke my heart!" Alexis retorted. "You knew the type of person I was back then. It took a lot for me to admit what I did, and it took a lot for me to beg you to come back to me. You know what they say— there's a thin line between love and hate."

"So all those years you hated me because you didn't think I returned your love," he said.

His mother had opened the door for DeShawn. As the child ran in, Shirley looked quizzically toward Reggie's car. He waved and pointed at his cell phone. She nodded and closed the door.

He went on. "Now, think about it. She's your cousin's best friend. I think you told me they've been friends for years, like since you guys were kids. Then, the first chance you get, you sleep with her husband. Why do you think she's hated you all those years?"

She sighed. "I hate when you're right."

He chuckled. "You always did. One of these days, you're gonna admit I'm a wise-ass brother."

"I'm glad we're still friends."

"Yeah, me, too. Is Jamar still treatin' you right?"

"Yes," she replied, the smile apparent in her voice. "Things are good right now. He's been really supportive while we've been here."

"He'd better be. I don't wanna have to beat his ass. And I will if he ever treats you bad."

Alexis laughed. "I'll let him know you said that."

"Just tellin' the truth," he said, smiling. No matter what they'd been through, Alexis would always be special to him. It felt good having a friend who wanted nothing from him but his happiness. Someone who'd known him when he was just a young boy trying to be the man. She could be mean as hell, but she was damn good people, which was why he needed to warn her. "While we're being honest, I'd better let you know Nikki is in Virginia Beach, too."

"Yeah, I know," she replied, not sounding a bit worried. "I saw her last night."

"You cool with that?"

"Well, I wasn't at first. I was about ready to smack the shit out of her when she walked up on me last night. She happened to come around right after I went off on Andrea in the middle of a restaurant."

"You did what?" Reggie asked, leaning forward in his seat like it would allow him to hear better.

"I already told you I went off on her," she said.

"Yeah, but you didn't tell me it was in public."

"Sometimes shit happens. Anyway, Nikki and I got to talking, and she's kinda okay."

"She can be okay when she wants to be, but in your case, you might wanna watch your back. That woman is hardly your friend."

"You're starting to sound like Jamar."

"I guess this time we agree about something. Where is lover man, anyway? He know you're talking to me?"

"Of course not," Alexis said, laughing a bit. "He's in the hotel room. I'm in the hotel gym. Just finished a workout."

A quick flash of Alexis's statuesque body appeared in Reggie's head. His eyebrows sprang up in appreciation. "Still taking care of yourself, eh?"

"If I don't, who will?"

"Well, I'd better get inside," Reggie said, catching a glimpse of Janet's eyes peering through the curtains. He blew out a burst of exasperated air and shook his head. An inquisition was sure to come, and he knew she would never want to hear the truth. How would any woman take her man sitting in his car, having a private conversation with the one who got away? "You two take care of yourselves, and be safe driving back to New Orleans."

"We will. It was good talking to you."

"You too, baby girl."

Reggie smiled and leaned back in his seat after pressing END on his phone. Most men would never dream of being friends with an ex. Especially not an ex who had put him through what she had. However, it was comforting to know that they'd both grown up to where they could walk down memory lane without tripping and falling. Things hadn't turned out exactly the way he had planned between them, but he was surprisingly okay with it. Sometimes the past needed to stay in the past.

Now it was time to deal with the present. Janet and her clinginess had been on his mind all day. Deep down, he knew he wasn't being fair to her. As much of a good woman he felt that she was, he really wasn't ready to jump back into another commitment. On the other hand, he didn't want to start playing the field again. Actually, he liked being with one woman. Yet he knew he wasn't ready to go running down the aisle again. It was time to tell her the truth. She could stick with him and deal with it, or she could just move on. He was fine with whatever decision she made.

"I'ma just tell her like that," Reggie told himself as he exited the car. "At least I'm tellin' her the truth. Most brothas wouldn't even do that much."

That thought gave him the burst of courage he needed to stroll up the walkway toward his mother's house. Slowly, he raised the key toward the lock, but the door suddenly swung open. Janet faced him with a look of irritation and weariness. Reggie stared back at her, refusing to show weakness. The time had come.

Chapter 17

Janet wanted to kick herself for what she'd done. She was sure she looked like a damn fool standing at the door, staring at her boyfriend, but what else could she do? He'd been acting like a distant jackass since they'd arrived in Atlanta, and the past couple of days had been even worse. She was tired of the tension between them. How did he think it made her feel when he acted like a stranger in a house where she really was a stranger? She had no one to turn to. Who in the hell did she know in Atlanta?

To make matters worse, he had had the nerve to defend his bitch-ass ex-wife to her, like she could do no wrong. Today he had run off with his son without inviting her, talking about some damn "man time." Then, on top of it all, he'd stayed holed up in his car, having some secret conversation with Lord knows who. If this was what it was like dating a celebrity, she really didn't need the drama. She had been doing just fine before she met his ass. She had never wanted anything from him but some tickets. If he hadn't wanted anything other than some sex, he could have said that from the jump!

Reggie leaned on the doorknob and stared her down like he was tired of her shit. Well, he just didn't know that she was tired of his, too! Reggie Morgan wasn't the only man in the world. She could have her choice of plenty of men. She wasn't some broken old maid sitting on the side of the road, waiting on him to save her. If only he knew that she had turned down three men to be with his ass, and she could just as easily go back to any of them if she wanted to. Shit, she just might once this ordeal was over.

"You just gonna stand there, staring at me?" Reggie asked, his eyes straightening into slits. He pursed his lips as if anticipating her reply.

"You really don't want to know what's on my mind right now," Janet replied through clenched teeth. It took everything she had not to haul off and slap the shit out of his stoic ass.

Reggie sighed, turning his back to her and closing the door. He turned back to her and shrugged his shoulders. "Say what's on your mind, because when you finish, you're gonna hear what's on mine."

"You two need to take that out back, because we really don't want or need to hear this."

Janet and Reggie looked toward Shirley, who had just walked past with a basket of laundry. She wore a tiger-striped housecoat, which told Reggie that his mother was in for the day. Either they would go outside, or this conversation wouldn't happen. Not even retreating to the confines of his room would help. If the conversation got too heated, shouting was sure to follow. DeShawn had been through enough craziness. Besides, there was no need to disrespect his mother's house more than he already had.

"Sorry, Momma," Reggie said. "We'll take it outside."

He looked back at Janet and used his head to gesture toward the patio. Without awaiting a reply, he trudged toward the back door. This mess needed to be over. He would just break things off if she couldn't accept his offer. Yet, if she did accept the offer, it would make things easier for everyone involved. After all, they were still in his mother's house. Shirley would kick them all out if the tension got any higher.

He reached the back door and pushed it open, careful not to push too hard. He'd been after Shirley for days to get those loose hinges fixed. One day, someone would push it and the door would go flying. Maybe that would be his project tomorrow, before they hit the road this weekend.

Janet followed him outside. Reggie had been so consumed with his thoughts that he hadn't even noticed her footsteps behind him. She pulled out one of the black rattan armchairs from the matching table and slowly lowered herself onto the plush lime-green cushion. Reggie leaned against the table and studied the graceful way her legs wrapped themselves around each other. Her skin was beautiful. Coffee colored, with just the right amount of cream. His eyes traveled up her body, taking in her soft hands, sitting patiently in her lap; her breasts, which looked like they would poke right through her T-shirt; and her curly hair, which was pulled into a short, tight ponytail. However, it was her face that made him stop short. The expression of anger that she had at the front door had changed to a look of sadness mixed with exasperation. Could she be having a change of heart?

Reggie was determined not to let her sadness be his weakness. He crossed his arms and rolled his eyes, as if he was bored with the entire conversation. "Say whatcha gotta say."

Janet rolled her eyes and shook her head. Sometimes she wondered if Reggie even had a conscience. She'd read about people who possessed all the tools for a good relationship but didn't know how to use them. Could Reggie be one of those people? He said and did all the right things, but when he got into his moods, he was a totally different person. It was like all he cared about was himself.

She lifted her eyes toward him and took in his hulking frame. It had been more than a year since he'd played professional football, but besides a couple of soft spots, he had maintained his shape. His eyes seemed friendly, but his expression remained hard, as if to warn her not to get it twisted. There was no chance in hell that she would break through his walls. She cleared her throat.

"Why did you bring me here?"

"Was I supposed to leave you in New Orleans to fend for yourself?"

"No, but I could have gone to Chicago with my family."

"Did I stop you from doing that?"

"If I remember correctly, you asked me to come here. I didn't push myself on you."

Reggie nodded, then sat on a nearby chair that matched Janet's. "You didn't have to come."

She stared at him through slits for eyes as a fiery feeling bubbled in her gut. *How dare he?*

"What is your problem? Ever since we got here, you've been acting like I'm some kind of bugaboo. If you don't want me, just fuckin' say so!"

He maintained his composure, not moving from his position. His eyes remained fixed on Janet as she slowly fell apart. Didn't she realize this melodramatic show of emotion wasn't going to solve anything? Why couldn't she understand that no woman should ever have to go through this to convince a man to be with her? If a man needed this much convincing, then he really wasn't worth her time. Either that, or he might not be as into her as she was him. In Reggie's case, it was the latter. He liked Janet a lot, but he refused to be pushed into something he wasn't ready for. And she sure wasn't presenting a good case to even think of going into something deeper.

"If I didn't want you, you wouldn't be here."

Janet rolled her eyes and waved her frustrated hands in the air. "I guess that's supposed to make me feel better."

"It is what it is."

"Damn, I can't stand you sometimes."

"I'm not too crazy about you, either, right about now."

"Fuck you, Reggie," she snapped, rising suddenly from her chair. She stormed up to him and stood over him, daggers in her eyes so sharp that she could fillet him with one blink. "I don't know what's gotten into you since we got here, but you are not doing me any favors by being with me."

He looked up at her and raised his eyebrows. "First of all, you can go back over there and sit your ass down. You will not make a spectacle of yourself in my momma's house."

Janet sneered. "You weren't worried about making spectacles when you walked around the house ignoring me. You didn't care how it looked when you went to hang out today and didn't even think about inviting me."

He swallowed so hard, Janet could see his Adam's apple move. "Sit down, Janet."

She crossed her arms and stood her ground. "Explain yourself."

"I said sit down! Or would you rather my son happen to pass the window and see you makin' a fuckin' fool of yourself?"

Some of the hardness left her eyes as she nervously looked toward the window. No one stood there, but

Lord knew how she probably looked from inside the house. She sighed and returned to her seat.

"Do you want Nikki back?"

He looked at her as if a skunk had peppered the air. "Why would you ask that?"

"She's been calling here a lot lately."

"Her son is waiting out a hurricane in Atlanta while she's in Virginia Beach. What the hell is she supposed to do? Your family's been calling you to check on you. Should I trip about that?"

"No, because I didn't used to be married to the people calling me. They also speak to you when they call. They don't just demand to speak to me."

Reggie looked at her with a funny expression. "Why would they demand to speak to you if they're calling you on your cell phone? I don't answer your phone."

She bit her lip and shifted her eyes a bit. She had never told Reggie about Nikki's phone call the other day. If she said something now, she'd look like a sneaky, jealous bitch. How could she clean this up?

"I'm just saying, she never says hello to me."

"Why should she?" he asked, shrugging his shoulders. "She doesn't know you. She doesn't speak to my mother, either, because Momma doesn't like her. What does that have to do with me wanting her back, though?"

"Shouldn't she want to know who the woman is who is spending time with her son?"

"When she knows things are serious between us, I'm sure she will want to get to know you."

"Guess that will never happen," Janet mumbled, shaking her head. Her eyes began following an ant trail to avoid looking at him.

"Why do you insist on rushing this relationship?" Reggie asked, leaning forward and resting his arms on his thighs. "The ink on my divorce papers is barely dry yet, and you know how much drama I had getting my divorce. If you want this shit between us to work, you're gonna have to give me some time."

Janet leaned forward and matched his gaze. "Is that what we have between us? Shit?"

"Actually, until recently, this was one of the best relationships I'd had in a long time. No drama. No pressure. But I guess since I brought you to my momma's house, you took it to be more than what it was. I guess that was my fault."

Janet shifted in her seat and looked away, tears stinging the corners of her eyes. He had hit the nail on the goddamn head. Why else would he have brought her home with him if he didn't mean for their relationship to go to another level?

Because he was just being a nice guy, she thought. Maybe she had read too much into the gesture, but was she being that unreasonable? They'd been seeing each other exclusively for almost a year. She was at his house so much that she had her own drawer in his bedroom. She and DeShawn had grown close. Why wouldn't she think they were getting serious?

Reggie took her silence as a cue to continue. "Janet, I really like you. You are a wonderful person. I just can't give you what you want from me right now."

She turned back to him and glared at him. "So how long does it take to use my body as a goddamn playground until you figure out what you want? You fuckin' men are all the same. You want all the benefits of being in a committed relationship without putting in the work. I cook for you, listen to you go on and on about football—and I got news for you . . . I'm not that fuckin' deep into football—sex you every night, yet none of that is enough for you. Maybe if I had a big ass, big titties, and fucked around on you, you'd fall in love with me!"

Reggie sucked in a deep breath and shook his head as if she'd lost her mind. "Well, I know one thing you do have, and that's a big-ass mouth!" He stood up and walked back to the house. Before going inside, he turned back and looked at Janet, who remained in her chair, holding her face in her hands. "I'm not gonna kick your ass out tonight, but you will be on the first plane available back to New Orleans."

Janet barely had time to lift her head before a thundering slam of the door punctuated his words. What in the world had just happened? That was not how the conversation was supposed to go. Yes, she wanted to show him how pissed she was, but she wasn't supposed to lose her temper like that. They weren't supposed to break up. She wasn't supposed to hate him and hate herself even more for what she had let herself become. She was not supposed to get this stressed over a man.

Maybe this is for the best, she surmised. She should have seen it coming. A man didn't change overnight. He dropped signs and left signals throughout the relationship. It was up to the woman to pick up on those signs and signals and not allow love to throw the blinders on. *So what if he's a nice guy? Look at the track record.* What successful relationship had this man ever had? Not to say he would never have one, but he didn't know how. Did she have the patience to, as the Musiq Soulchild song went, teach him how to love?

"Hell no!" Janet said aloud, rising from the chair. She went back inside the house, mumbling, "If it's over, it's over. Let him find someone else to go through all this shit with. I have no time to be rebuilding incomplete people."

Chapter 18

Holding on to anger could be depressing. You had to keep reminding yourself that you were angry and even why you were angry. You saw the person you were mad at, and you got angry again if he or she looked a little too happy. You couldn't eat. You couldn't sleep. You couldn't even relax for thinking of what you planned to say to that person next time you came face-to-face. It could eat at every fiber of your being until it eventually drove you crazy.

Christopher was determined not to fall into that trap. The anger he felt when he found out about that kiss had the potential to eat away at him, but he refused to let it do so. Truthfully, he was more hurt than angry. Hurt because he'd gone through hell trying to get his wife back. He'd allowed her to sling her venom at him until the tears streamed down her face. She'd vowed she was a damn good woman who didn't deserve the cards she had been dealt. She was the scorned woman, and she'd played her role perfectly. He couldn't blame her. He had messed up, and he would have to pay the price.

Yet, through all of that, she'd committed the ultimate sin. She'd kissed his brother. If it wasn't all that—if it had happened only once—why couldn't they just have been honest about it? He'd had to strip down and admit to every wrong he'd ever done. Yet she'd played the perfect wife without uttering a solitary word. Byron, his best friend and brother, had played the supportive role, shunning him for messing up the best thing that had ever happened to him and encouraging him to swallow his pride to get her back. Christopher guessed his brother had forgotten to mention that he'd tongued her down in the process.

They had all made mistakes back then. They were younger then, still learning how to wade their way through life without running to Mommy and Daddy. That affair with Alexis had thrown everyone for a loop. He would have understood if they had been forthcoming, wouldn't he?

He thought back to his earlier conversation with Darnell. *I woulda beat his ass,* Christopher had told Darnell. *Exactly,* had been Darnell's reply. *Think about it, bruh.*

The more he thought about it, the more questions he had. Andrea used to say Byron was like her little brother. She had practically grilled Rayna when she first started dating Byron. The number of lectures his wife had given Byron on finding a good woman and getting his life together was endless. Christopher would secretly wonder if Andrea cared too much. Was there ever anything more to their relationship than familial love?

As he sat in the nearly empty parking lot of the *Virginian-Pilot* newspaper office, where he'd worked for nearly twenty years, he went over the past few days in his mind. Alexis. Even when she was nowhere around, she still caused him trouble. Why did she have to say anything? Everyone could have gone to the grave with that fucking secret, and he would have died a happy fool. Now the rest of his life was doomed to be plagued with unanswered questions.

His cell phone, which was sitting on the passenger seat, caught his eye. His friend Lewis suddenly came to mind. Aside from a couple of hellos when they crossed paths, they hadn't talked with each other in nearly eleven years. At one time, they were as tight as Christopher was with Byron. Yet when Sheila and Andrea drifted apart, there went their friendship. No more double dates. No more party invites. Nothing. They'd become strangers.

He had no idea what he would say, but he felt a strong urge to call Lewis. Maybe he could help; maybe he couldn't. He wondered if Lewis knew about the kiss. If Sheila knew, then chances were good that Lewis knew, too. It seemed that everyone knew about this but Christopher.

He sighed as he went through the phone's address book. There it was. After all these years, he still had it, as if deep down he'd known they would once again be friends. He pressed TALK and tapped the steering wheel while waiting for an answer.

"Chris?" Lewis answered, sounding more confused than happy.

"Yeah, bruh," he replied. "It's me."

"Damn, man, I ain't heard from you since Moses was a baby. How you doing, man?"

"Maintaining."

"You all right?"

"Not really, but I'm here."

"You don't sound too good. What's really going on?"

An uncomfortable silence went by as Christopher contemplated telling Lewis the truth. It just didn't feel right delving into his personal business with someone he hadn't spoken to in years. Instead of answering, he let his eyes fall on a couple of birds hopping around in small circles on the pavement of the parking lot.

"Chris? You still there?"

He sighed. "I'm here, man."

"You all right?"

"Hey, bro, I'm sorry I let so much time go by without keeping in touch. It's just been—"

"No need to explain, black man," Lewis interrupted. "It was just as much my fault as it was yours."

"Sheila around?" Christopher asked, his eyes still planted on the birds. He wondered what they could be looking for at this time of night.

"No, she had a meeting at the church tonight."

Christopher's shoulders jumped as he tried to hold in a laugh. It wasn't that he felt Sheila wasn't a Christian, but he found it hard to believe that she could so easily dismiss him without even trying to show some forgiveness. He hadn't been a man of God for that long, but he did learn that forgiveness was one of the hallmarks of Christianity. Then again, who was he to judge? Here he was, sitting in the middle of a parking lot, instead of talking things over with his wife at home.

"Guess who's back in town?" he blurted suddenly.

"Who?"

"Alexis."

"Alexis?" Lewis asked, sounding confused. He repeated the name again quietly, as if racking his mind for realization. "Alexis! *The* Alexis? The girl who—"

"Yeah, that's her," Christopher interrupted, not caring to hear his past transgression out loud.

"No shit. What's she doing back?"

"She's from New Orleans, remember? She and her cousin Brenda are hiding out here until Hurricane Gustav blows over."

"Oh, yeah. I've been following that on the news. Good to see that mayor is handling things better than he did during Katrina."

"Yeah," Christopher replied absently. He hadn't even thought about Hurricanes Gustav or Katrina, let alone how New Orleans was handling the disaster. He had Hurricanes Alexis, Brenda, and Andrea on his hands, and that was enough!

"You're not messing around with her again, are you?" Lewis asked cautiously.

"Hell no! I knew you were going to ask that shit."

Lewis laughed. "You can't blame me, can you?"

Christopher laughed with him. Only Byron knew better than Lewis how deeply he'd gotten involved with Alexis. He'd even entertained the thought of making their affair permanent. The sex had been just that good. So good that he had even sexed the girl while his wife slept in the next room.

It felt strange laughing about the situation now. Before tonight, he could only look back on his days with Alexis with shame. He couldn't believe the risks he'd taken to be with a woman he knew he had no future with. He still wasn't proud of his actions, but he knew he wasn't nearly the man he used to be. Yet one thing hadn't changed. He still would stop at nothing to get what he wanted. However, this time, all he wanted was his wife.

"Alexis giving you any drama?" Lewis asked.

"Actually, no. I really haven't talked much to her. She seems to have grown up a lot from back in the day."

"Is that right?"

"Yeah. She's a pediatrician now with her own practice, and she's engaged to be married."

"That's all right," Lewis commented, sounding impressed. "I think I remember her saying something about wanting to be a doctor back in the day. Glad to see she stuck with it."

"Yeah. Her fiancé seems like a good brother. He's an attorney in New Orleans. He's here, too."

"Serious? And you said Brenda's here, too? What about Darnell?"

"He's here, too. They asked about you."

"Sounds like you have a regular party going on. Maybe I can talk Sheila into coming out."

"Lewis, man, this is anything but a party," Christopher said, closing his eyes and shaking his head.

"What's up?"

Christopher, feeling more comfortable talking with his long-lost friend, blew out some air and told him the entire story. Lewis silently listened, seeming to reserve any comments until the end.

"Damn," was all he could say once Christopher had finished.

"Damn is right," Christopher agreed. "I gotta ask, though. Did you know?"

"Not at all, but think about it. You know my wife. You really think Andrea would have told her something like that?"

Christopher nodded. Sheila had a heart of gold, but she had to be one of the most opinionated people he or Andrea had ever met. Chances are if Andrea had told Sheila about the kiss, she'd still be hearing about how wrong she was.

"You talk to your brother?" Lewis asked.

"I really don't know what to say to him."

"You gotta know he hasn't been sneaking around with your wife all these years."

"How do you know? You ain't been around in the last eleven years."

"Are you serious?"

"Just bullshittin', man," Christopher said quickly, although there was a tinge of truth behind his words.

As much as he wanted to believe in his brother, he wouldn't put it past him to try something with Andrea.

Only Christopher knew that he had married Andrea so quickly to keep his brother away from her.

As if reading his mind, Lewis stated, "If you really need answers to that question, your brother is the only one you should talk to about it. He's the only one who knows what's going on in his mind."

"Yeah, but who's to say he wouldn't lie?"

"Come on, Chris! Has Byron ever lied to you before?"

"No, but he did a damn good job withholding information for the last fifteen years."

Lewis chuckled. "Same old Chris. Take your ass to your brother's house and talk to him. Don't you think he's going through the same shit you are? He mighta lost his fiancée last night."

In fact, Christopher hadn't thought of that. Aside from wondering if Byron and Andrea had some secret fling going on, he really hadn't given his brother a second thought. He felt ashamed and guilty all at once.

"Yeah, you're right, Lew," he said finally. "I knew something made me call you tonight."

"Hey, I gotta get in where I can. It might be another ten years before I hear from you again."

The men laughed together.

"I'ma make sure that doesn't happen. Tell Sheila y'all are comin' over for dinner real soon. Andrea will be happy to hear from you two."

"I'll do that, man," Lewis replied, a smile apparent in his voice. "I'll holla atcha tomorrow."

"Looking forward to it, but sit tight. I might be calling you sooner than that if things don't go right."

Chapter 19

As Jamar readied himself for dinner, he couldn't help but let his mind wander back to his earlier conversation with Alexis. With all the excitement with Brenda and Darnell's drama, he hadn't had another chance to broach the subject of Nikki being in town.

It just seemed to be too much of a coincidence that she was also riding out the storm in Virginia Beach. On top of that, he had mysteriously begun having his credit card issues as soon as they hit town. Now she was trying to be Alexis's best friend? Something was wrong with this picture.

He set out the cream-colored shirt he planned to wear with a pair of jeans, but he couldn't concentrate on making the outfit work. All he could think of was Nikki. Could she be executing some kind of revenge plan against him for causing her to lose her son? Although he didn't force her to sleep with all those men, he could easily be blamed for representing her husband against her.

Darnell's warning rang loudly in his head. If Nikki was trying to exact her revenge, she was connected enough to pull off something like credit card fraud. She had the motive and the opportunity, but did she have the nerve?

Of course she did!

Any woman who went to the lengths that she did to cheat on her husband, then have him followed when she thought he was cheating on her, and *then* visit her husband's lawyer to ask him to team up with her, could very well have the nerve to play games with a man's credit. That was one hateful bitch!

The phone rang, breaking Jamar's thoughts. It was only then that he realized he'd balled up the corner of his shirt.

"Shit!" he exclaimed softly, trying to smooth out the wrinkles. Fortunately, the garment relaxed easily. Thank goodness for good-quality clothing.

"Hello?" he heard Alexis answer from the living room, where she'd been polishing her toenails. Assuming it was Brenda, he began stripping out of his sweatpants and T-shirt so he could take a shower. "A package? Can you send it up, please?"

Jamar froze. He had forgotten he'd asked his credit card companies to overnight the fraud paperwork to the hotel. *When it rains, it pours.* How would he explain this to Alexis? There was no time to plan.

"You know anything about a package being delivered here?" Alexis asked, waddling into the bedroom.

She was already dressed in a multicolored maxi dress, Her freshly polished nails were a deep burgundy, which perfectly matched the strips of burgundy that surrounded her dress. Her hair was swept into a classy updo, with hanging strands framing her unmade-up face. Even in his panicked state, he couldn't help but appreciate the natural beauty that stood before him, if only for a second.

"Huh?" Jamar said, stalling, then jetted into the bathroom. He quickly turned on the shower.

"Are you expecting a package?" she called, sitting on the bed. She began rapidly slicing the air with her legs to help speed the drying process for her toenails.

"I don't hear you!" he shouted over the spray of water. He bent over the sink and began washing his face with Alexis's facial cleanser.

"You all right?" she asked, suddenly appearing in the doorway. "You're acting funny, just like you did earlier."

"I'm fine," he replied, drying his face. He turned off the water spraying from the sink and stuck his hand in the shower stream to test the temperature.

"You're sure not acting like it."

"I'm good."

She smiled, showing all her teeth. "You buy me a present you're trying not to tell me about?"

Jamar rolled his eyes while his back was still turned to her. It wasn't her fault that she was in this situation, but she had no idea how selfish that question sounded right now. How in the hell was he supposed to buy her anything when he couldn't even afford to buy a piece of gum? He was still wondering how he would pay for dinner tonight!

"So what did you get me?" she asked, seemingly oblivious to his mood.

"Didn't you just get a wedding dress the other day?" he asked, turning toward her and glaring in misplaced anger. "And we're going to dinner tonight. What more do you want?"

Alexis drew her head back in shock. "Excuse me, but if I remember correctly, the money for that dress came from my account. What's wrong with you?"

"I'm saying, everything's not about you all the damn time."

Her eyebrows immediately went up in offense, and her mouth dropped. Jamar held his angry gaze while mentally preparing for the Southern tongue-lashing he knew was coming, but she surprised him. Instead of unleashing her verbal tirade, she closed her mouth, backed away from the bathroom doorway, and started for the living room.

Just before walking out of the bedroom, she turned to Jamar and glared at him. He held firm, knowing his fiancée couldn't resist saying something.

Rolling her eyes at him, she said flatly, "I was just playing with your ass. I'm just going to take your funky-ass attitude as you having some shit on your mind, but don't make it a habit to be trying to talk to me any kind of way. You should know by now that I'm the wrong woman to be playing with."

"And I'm the wrong man to be playing with!" he yelled after her, although she'd already left the room.

He shook his head and stepped into the shower. He really needed to solve this mystery quickly, before he fooled around and lost his money *and* his woman. He was more than sure Nikki held the key.

He lathered up, wondering what he needed to do to put an end to this madness. He had worked too hard to build the life he'd created for himself for it to come crumbling down like this. Why did Brenda and Darnell have to interrupt him right when he had worked up the nerve to confide in Alexis? Now she was about to find out the wrong way, and there was nothing he could do but let it happen. *Maybe she won't open the package.*

Just as he was about to rinse off, the shower curtain flew back, revealing an angry half-black, half-Panamanian woman wearing a multicolored maxi dress and holding an opened brown envelope.

"Why didn't you tell me all your credit cards had been canceled?" Alexis demanded. She held the envelope up like a trophy. However, it was a trophy of failure rather than victory.

Jamar stood naked, both literally and figuratively, facing his fiancée with his mouth hanging open and soap sliding from his body. He knew he had to give her an answer, but the only thing going through his mind was how the package had gotten there so quickly. Any other time, the bellhop would have taken at least half an hour to deliver something to the room, but it was just his luck that the hotel felt like being expeditious today.

"Hellooo? I know you heard me ask you a question," she said, pushing. Her free hand instinctively rose to her hip as she awaited a response. The scowl on her face and her updo made Jamar think she looked like a dark-skinned Rosie Perez from the movie *Do the Right Thing,* but he wasn't about to be her Mookie.

"You opened my mail?" he asked, the cooling water spraying over his right shoulder.

"Jamar, don't try that 'flip the script' shit on me. Talk to me about this!"

"How about you let me get out of this shower before you cross-examine me?"

She sucked her teeth and rolled her eyes slowly while looking him up and down. "Go ahead and dry off, but when you finish, I will be waiting."

With that, she turned and walked out of the bathroom. He couldn't see where she went, but he knew she wasn't far. Alexis wasn't a woman who gave up easily. Jamar didn't surrender easily, either, but even he knew when enough was enough. He'd kept this from her long enough.

"Shit!" he mumbled as he rinsed the rest of the soap from his back.

He turned off the water, stepped out of the shower, and grabbed a towel from the rack hanging over the toilet. Slowly, he wiped off his face and neck. He had wanted to solve this problem without Alexis ever knowing what had happened. Any hopes of that happening had taken a flying leap over the balcony. And since he'd waited so long to confide in her, he might as well go hopping off that balcony with them.

Once he dried off, he wrapped the towel around his waist and trudged into the bedroom. Sure enough, his fiancée sat on the bed with her arms folded and her legs crossed. The brown envelope's contents had been spread out on the bed. Three white envelopes stared up at him, revealing the secret he'd been hiding since their arrival.

"So what's up?" Alexis asked, staring right at him. "By the way, this shirt right here is all wrong. You should put on your black button-down."

Jamar looked down at the outfit he had laid on the bed. He liked his cream shirt and decided this was a battle he wouldn't let Alexis win, but that was a fight for a different time.

He walked to the dresser and began brushing his hair. His fade was beginning to grow back in. He'd need to go find a barber tomorrow, but for now . . .

"You read the mail?" he asked, checking his face for blemishes. He caught a glimpse of her in the mirror. She still reminded him of Rosie Perez. He dared not smile, but if she shouted at him to be a man, he was afraid he'd lose it.

"Yep," she replied, her eyes boring a hole in the back of his head.

He turned around and faced her for the first time. Leaning against the dresser, he sighed and folded his arms. "Somebody's fucking with my finances."

"Excuse me? Come again," Alexis replied, her harsh expression giving way to a look of surprise.

"All my credit cards were paid off before we left New Orleans, but when I tried to pay for the room, my card got declined."

"Then how did you pay for the room?"

"I gave them another card, and it worked. But when I tried to use the same card at the club, it got declined, too."

"Why are you just telling me this!" Alexis exclaimed, rising from the bed. "How are we supposed to get home?"

"You got a job, Miss Doctor," Jamar snapped. "I'm sure you can afford to kick in a C-note or two for us to get back home."

Alexis drew her head back. "Excuse me? Did you think about that when you withheld your little news from me for the past few days? You must not have trusted me to afford *too* much."

"Come on, Alexis. When is the last time you paid for anything since we've been together?"

"That's your fault. But, news flash," she retorted, holding her hands up, "I'm not your fuckin' girlfriend. I'm not some chickenhead you're kickin' it with. I'm about to be your damn wife. You don't have to impress me with your money. I know what you have, and you should know me by now. If you can't trust me to talk to me, then who the fuck can you trust?"

"This ain't about trust, Lex. You just don't get it, do you?"

"I guess I don't. Enlighten me."

"This is about being a fuckin' man! A man takes care of his woman. If I can't afford to do that, what fuckin' good am I?"

"Jamar, don't even go there. I told you before. I know what you have, and I know what it's like to struggle. I'm the child of a single mother from the hood and a Panamanian man who died too soon. But you know what? I got through it. Just because you're going through something now doesn't mean you'll always be going through it. You're not that kind of man."

"And you're not the kind of woman to foot the bill all the damn time. Let's just put that out there."

Alexis folded her arms defiantly and looked away. "So I'm a gold digger?"

After a few moments of silence, she walked past him into the living room and sat on the couch, holding her face in her hands. Jamar angrily followed her.

"Don't put words in my mouth. I never said that. But while I'm putting shit out there, I don't want you hanging with that bitch Nikki anymore, either."

She looked up, shocked. "What the hell does Nikki have to do with this?"

"Think, Alexis!" he snapped, tapping his temple with his index finger. "I guess you think it's one big coincidence that she showed up in Virginia Beach the same time we did, huh?"

"Yes, actually, I do."

"You don't think she has anything to do with my credit cards being canceled?"

Alexis winced at him in disgust. "Come on, Jamar. When would she have had time to do that? And *how* would she have done it?"

"I don't know, but I do know there wasn't shit wrong with my cards until we got here, and she's probably still pissed about how her divorce turned out."

"Your name didn't come out of her mouth when I saw her last night. Why would she pick you to mess with?"

Jamar glared at his fiancée. Why couldn't she see something that was so obvious? And why was she defending a woman who, before last night, she couldn't stand?

"Why would she ask about me and risk exposing the shit she's doing?" he said.

Alexis smiled as she tried to hold in her laughter. "You've been a lawyer way too long. You're suspicious of everybody."

"Well, you just better hope I don't run into that bitch any time soon, because I might get disbarred behind what I do to her," he remarked, returning to the bedroom.

"Just hurry up and get dressed," she called after him. "Brenda and Darnell will be here in a few. We're not finished with this by a long shot. I'm just glad I know how you really see our relationship."

"What the hell is that supposed to mean?"

"You either think I'm tight with money or I'm a gold digger," Alexis charged. "Either way, that's some messed-up shit. You can best believe we'll be up for a good minute tonight!"

"I'm sure we will," he mumbled as he pulled on his cream shirt.

Anyone looking in from the outside would have thought the four people sitting at the dinner table at Captain George's Seafood Restaurant were blissful fools. Neither couple wanted to alert the other of the drama they'd had just minutes before, for fear of being blamed for ruining yet another evening. Instead, each painted on their happy faces, determined to make the best of an already stressful night.

Jamar and Darnell led the table in jokes, each trying to top the other with their best back-in-the-day stories. Jamar did his best to impress the table with how hard he had it back in college by describing his ten different recipes for ramen noodles.

"If that didn't work, I just called one of my girlfriends to cook for me," he added with a laugh. "One girl, Lawanda was her name, couldn't cook to save her life, but when times got hard, eating burnt chicken was a hell of a lot better than starving!"

Darnell and Brenda howled in laughter, neither one noticing Alexis's rolled eyes and strained smile. She could care less about his ex-girlfriend stories. Hell, her past would make his seem like a fairy tale. Yet she couldn't help but be bothered by the fact that he didn't mind depending on women back then, but now he acted like it hurt his manhood to depend on the woman he was about to marry. He didn't mind poisoning himself with bad food to keep from starving then, so why would he rather starve than be honest with her now?

"You were in college, so you had an excuse for being broke," Darnell said once he recovered from his laughter. "Try being a broke-ass sailor on a ship. We would dock, and all these women would be at the port, waiting on us to spend our money on them all weekend. When they found out I didn't have any funds like that, they didn't have two words for me."

"Awww, poor poo poo," Brenda cooed, squeezing his cheeks so his lips poked out. "Him didn't have no girlfriend, 'cause him was chasin' after chickenheads."

That comment finally brought a real smile to Alexis's face. As the rest of the table laughed, she marveled at how much her cousin had loosened up over the years. She used to think Brenda was too tight, always worrying about other people and never wanting to take a chance in life. It had seemed growing up that the more wild and free Alexis became, the more closed off Brenda became. It was as if Alexis's sexual escapades almost made Brenda afraid of guys. Hell, she practically had to force Brenda to talk to Darnell the night they met. Then, once they started dating, Brenda seemed to finally relax, but she became fully comfortable with Darnell only after they were engaged.

Alexis guessed it was because her cousin had finally found someone with whom she felt she could be herself. She never wanted to feel like she was being used. Brenda never had many boyfriends in school. She never thought she measured up to Andrea's beauty.

Growing up in New Orleans, Brenda was struck by the color complex that taught her that because she was darker, she wasn't as pretty as light-skinned Andrea. Their grandmother, who was as dark as Alexis, believed that their boyfriends should be light skinned so they could lighten up the family. Any dark-skinned boys who came to the house were automatically cast into the ugly bin. Once, Alexis had brought a dark-skinned boy to the house while their grandmother was visiting. She was quite cordial, as any Southern woman would be, but when she went into the back room, Alexis heard her comment to her mother, "I see that ole ugly black boy is here again."

Alexis often looked back on those days and laughed, but as she thought about it, she realized those seemingly comical beliefs might have adversely affected them both. Those beliefs had made Alexis overcompensate for her beauty, such as when she transformed herself into the campus "fun girl," while they had forced Brenda into a shell, since she felt that she would never be beautiful. She wasn't charcoal black, but her brown skin prevented her from exploring her true beauty. Although times and color beliefs had changed, sometimes minds didn't change as easily.

"Earth to Alexis. Come in, Alexis."

"Huh?" Alexis asked, realizing she'd been staring at the wall behind her cousin. She quickly covered her embarrassment by smiling and laughing a bit. "Girl, shut up."

The rest of the group laughed with her.

"I thought you had left us for a minute," Brenda said before taking a sip of her white wine.

"I'm still here. Just thinking that it's nice to finally get together again. We haven't hung out like this since we first got here."

"Yeah, when we went walking on the beach," Jamar agreed, peeling a steamed shrimp. After removing the last piece of shell, he swirled the shrimp in a small bowl of cocktail sauce and popped it into his mouth.

"Damn, that feels like ages ago," Darnell added. "Seems like there's been chaos every day since then."

"You ain't never lied," Alexis mumbled. She cut her eyes at her fiancé as she played with the last of her rice with her fork. There was still a mountain of food that she hadn't tried yet on the buffet line, but her full stomach wouldn't allow her to take another bite.

"You two okay?" Darnell asked.

"Dag, Darnell," Brenda scolded, kicking him under the table. "Mind your own business."

"Look who's talking," he replied, staring at his wife in disbelief. "Guess the pot is finally calling the kettle black."

Alexis snorted, trying to contain a laugh. "He got you there, sister-cuz."

"So, anyway," Darnell said, cutting his eyes at his wife, "what's the problem, J?"

Alexis stared at her fiancé, wondering if he would discuss his financial situation out in the open. If she knew anything about Jamar, it was his ability to hold his personal problems inside. He always had to be the strong person, the one who *solved* problems, not *had* them. *If he would take this time to be honest, it would be a mir—*

"She found out about the credit card situation," Jamar said, indicating Alexis with his thumb. "Just like I figured, she's pissed."

Had she just heard him right? Her eyes widened into manhole covers as she stared back and forth from Darnell to Jamar, and back to Darnell. "You knew about this?"

"I was there when it started," Darnell admitted, shrugging his shoulders.

"And what about you?" Alexis asked Brenda, who looked just as surprised as she did.

"Don't look at me," Brenda replied, holding her hands up in defense. "Looks like I'm the last to know on this one."

They both slowly turned their heads back to their significant others, their eyes swimming with questions. Their glares were answered with nonchalant glances.

"I don't know what you're looking at me for," Darnell said finally. "It wasn't my business to tell."

"And I already told you why I didn't tell you," Jamar added. "You need to let a man be a man, Alexis."

"Excuse you?" she shot back. All the anger she'd tried to hide earlier had come back at once. Who did he think he was, calling her out like that? "I didn't say a word. I think I did very well keeping your so-called manhood intact."

"That's the problem right there. I didn't ask you to keep shit intact. I just told you to let me handle my business."

"You must not be handling it too well if we've just about gone through our entire vacation without any money."

"You didn't suffer, did you?"

Darnell and Brenda sat silently watching the argument. Brenda wanted to jump in but didn't quite know what to say. She didn't have enough information on the situation to shed any light. She was also tired of having to be everyone's problem solver. Tonight's ordeal with Andrea had shown that her efforts were unappreciated. So, instead of going through the same thing with her favorite cousin, she just propped her chin in the palm of her hand and watched them go at it. As long as they didn't get loud, she didn't have a problem.

"You're not going to say anything?" Darnell whispered to her.

She shook her head without looking his way. It was actually almost refreshing to see somebody other than herself having issues.

"You wanna know the worst part about it, man?" Jamar asked, pulling the couple back into the conversation. He answered his own question without awaiting a reply. "She doesn't even want to admit that her so-called new friend could be involved in the shit."

"What new friend?" Brenda asked, leaning forward. She placed her elbows on the table and listened with new interest, but she would have to wait for her answer.

"Can I get you anything else?" asked the young African waiter. He stood at the middle of the table, unknowingly becoming a barrier between the two couples.

"Y'all want anything?" Brenda asked, looking around the table. Each mumbled their noes, so she looked back up at the waiter. "Can you just bring the check?"

"Sure thing," he replied with a smile. "Will this be all on one check or separate?"

The table grew silent, each person looking at the other to see who would answer the harmless, yet awkward question. Brenda opened her mouth to reply, but nothing came out. She felt for Jamar and his situation, but her family had to eat, too.

Jamar shook his head at the ridiculous moment and looked up at the waiter, who waited patiently, as if he'd seen this type of discomfort before. "Look, I'll be paying for me and my woman, and those two can handle themselves."

"Got it, brother," the waiter replied. He then smiled and cut his eyes at Alexis. "Much love to you."

"I feel you, man," Jamar said, picking up on the compliment.

Alexis, on the other hand, rolled her eyes and waited for the waiter to disappear around the corner. "Can you afford this?"

Jamar inhaled deeply and closed his eyes while exhaling through his nose. His hands slowly folded into fists. "Give it a rest, Alexis. I didn't say shit about all the fuckin' drama you caused this week, so you really need to slow your roll right now."

The collective gasp that came from Brenda and Alexis seemed to be heard around the restaurant. Brenda held her breath, praying that Alexis wouldn't go off the way she had two nights ago. She stared at her cousin, who was amazingly silent. Instead of losing her cool, she just looked away, tapping the side of her now-empty plate with her fork.

"You didn't have to go there, Jamar," Brenda whispered. "She was just trying to help."

"Well, maybe I don't need her help. Maybe she should just realize I got this."

"Maybe you should realize that you have a damn good woman who's trying to be there for you," Brenda snapped.

She felt Darnell's hand squeeze her thigh underneath the table, and she knew she needed to step back a bit. This wasn't her battle to fight. Alexis had enough fight in her to handle this herself, but why wasn't the fight coming out of Alexis? Instead of going off, she seemed to be shrinking, almost contemplating.

The waiter returned with the checks and silently set them at the edge of the table between the two couples. Brenda noticed that he wisely didn't set them in front of anyone in particular, which she thought was a good move. He was more perceptive than he looked.

Alexis reached for the check and pulled it toward her. After seeing the price, she reached into her purse and searched for her wallet.

"What the fuck are you doing?" Jamar snapped, placing his hand on top of her arm.

"What does it look like?"

"You just don't know when to say when, do you, Alexis? Did you not hear me just say that I got this?"

"Yes. I also heard you tell me earlier that I had a job and could pay for some things," Alexis retorted, snatching her arm away from Jamar's grasp.

"Do you love me, Alexis?" he asked, turning toward his fiancée.

"You know I do. If I didn't, I wouldn't be going through all this with you."

"That's true," Brenda muttered, remembering the Alexis of old. The old Alexis would have walked out on Jamar and his issues from the word *broke*.

"Shut it!" Darnell mumbled in her ear. He then turned back to Jamar and Alexis, as if watching dinner theater.

"Do you trust me?" Jamar asked Alexis, seemingly oblivious to the exchange taking place on the other side of the table.

Alexis sighed, looking him directly in his eyes. Tears of frustration stung the corners of her eyes, but she refused to cry and make a spectacle of herself. This conversation was embarrassing enough.

"Yes, I trust you, but why can't you trust me sometimes? Did you think I would leave you over this? What kind of a woman do you think I am?"

Jamar pursed his lips tightly and took her hand. "Truthfully, I didn't know what to think. You have enough going on coming back here. I just didn't want to add to that stress."

Brenda could no longer take it. "I feel like this is my fault. I'm the one who talked you two into coming here. All this stuff with Andrea wouldn't have happened if I had left well enough alone."

Alexis turned toward her cousin and shook her head. "No, what happened had to happen. That elephant has been standing in the room for years. That needed to come out."

"Besides," Jamar added, "you didn't have anything to do with somebody trying to mess up my credit."

"You mentioned earlier that you thought one of Alexis's friends had something to do with this," Darnell said. "Who were you talking about?"

Jamar turned fully toward the table and leaned in but kept Alexis's hand in his. "You two remember Lex's ex-boyfriend Reggie, right?"

Darnell and Brenda nodded, prompting Jamar to continue.

"Remember last year he went through that divorce?"

They nodded again, while Alexis just sat by silently.

"Well, Nikki—that's her name—was convinced that even though she was whoring around, Reggie was leaving her because of Alexis. She even had him followed, and she got pictures of them arguing outside of some restaurant. Ole girl came straight to my office with those pictures and damn near asked me to throw my case. She even threw it in my face that my woman was sleeping around with her husband!"

"What?" Brenda gasped. "You never told me about that, Alexis."

"That's because the shit wasn't true!" Alexis retorted. "Reggie and I were and are just friends. That bitch just couldn't take responsibility for her own actions. If Jamar wasn't the man he is, she could have wiped Reggie out and taken his son."

"Yeah, but since I got it goin' on, I saw to it that Reggie got his son, his money, and his divorce," Jamar concluded, popping his collar. "And I got my woman."

"So you think she's trying to get back at you?" Brenda asked.

"Damn good chance she is," Jamar said.

"So when did she and Alexis become friends?" Darnell asked.

"That's the trip part about it," Jamar replied. "Nikki is here!"

"Here where? In Virginia Beach?" Brenda asked. Her eyes bucked in surprise, and she grabbed Darnell's arm.

"Bingo," Jamar said, sitting back in his chair. He let go of Alexis's hand and folded his arms.

"You think she followed you two here?" Darnell asked.

"Sure in the hell do," Jamar replied, seeming to grow angrier with the thought. "I wouldn't put anything past that woman. She's shown me her track record."

"I told him that was outlandish," Alexis said. "Why would she make it her business to come talk to me if she was doing something like that? She's outrunning Gustav just like we are, so she has her own problems to worry about."

"Yeah, but she don't like you two," Brenda pointed out. "This could be the perfect time to do some dirt, while everybody's worried about what they're coming home to."

"All I know is if I get my hands on that woman, I'ma wring her conniving neck," Jamar said, rubbing his hands together so hard that Alexis could hear the friction in his skin.

She feared he meant just what he said. She would have to get to the bottom of this before he did, or something bad was sure to happen.

Chapter 20

"Byron?" Christopher called out softly, walking into his brother's apartment.

If the door being slightly ajar struck him as strange, the rest of the apartment completely threw him for a loop. A broken lamp met him at the door, followed by a trail of disarray, including books, clothing, and photos. Christopher was afraid the apartment had been broken into.

"Back here, bruh," Byron replied.

The sound of his brother's voice unnerved Christopher. It didn't contain the same swagger it usually did. He'd heard this tone only a few times in his life, and none of those occasions were good. With his spot looking the way it did, Christopher knew this night would definitely go down as one of those times.

Slowly, Christopher followed Byron's voice to the bedroom, while inspecting the damage. Somebody had done a job tonight. Spilled wine made the living room reek. Broken glasses covered the kitchen counter. Scattered papers and books lay everywhere the eye could see. What the hell? Why was the framed photo of him and Byron at Kings Dominion lying broken on the coffee table? He could hear papers shuffling. Tupac was playing softly. Yeah, something was up. Byron was playing his angry music. A thunderous boom that sounded oddly like a fist hitting a wall resonated throughout the apartment. The boom hastened

Christopher's walk to the bedroom, where he found a shirtless Byron picking up books and newspaper from around his torn-apart bed.

"What the hell happened here?"

"Fuckin' Rayna happened," Byron replied without looking up. He pulled up his sagging jeans, then dropped to his knees and used his hands to rake in all the paper that had landed under the bed.

"Cute little Rayna, the one you're about to marry?"

Byron looked up just enough to give his brother a dirty look. "That bitch ain't cute, and I damn sure ain't marrying her ass."

Christopher couldn't have heard Byron correctly. Had he really heard him say that Rayna had caused all this damage?

"Hey, man, stop for a minute," he said, sitting on the bed. He patted the spot next to him.

"Later, bruh," Byron replied, setting up the cologne bottles that had been strewn about his dresser. One of the bottles had been shattered. The cologne smell mixed with the wine aroma nearly made Christopher's stomach turn. "Don't you see my house looks like shit?"

"Nigga, sit down for a minute!"

Byron spun around and pursed his lips. The night had been bad enough so far. He really didn't need any more drama. Especially from his brother. Yet he knew Christopher wouldn't let up until he said whatever was on his mind. Dejectedly, he sat next to his brother and held his head with his hands.

"You come to finish what she started?"

"Later for that. Tell me what happened, baby boy."

Byron sighed. "I called her over to talk with her. You know, let her know I loved her and wanted to work this out. Had some wine and cheese and shit, playing jazz and whatnot. I thought I was getting through to her ass, but then I went and said it was stupid to throw away what we had over something that happened years ago. All of a sudden, she snapped, talking 'bout, 'Who you calling stupid?'"

"Damn," Christopher remarked, rubbing the back of his neck.

"Next thing you know, we're arguing about me supposedly calling her stupid. That led to me telling her that her ass wasn't perfect and she shouldn't expect me to be. That shit led to her taking a damn swing at me."

"She hit you?"

"No, she missed, but her ass kept coming. That's how a lot of the mess in the living room happened. Bruh, I came this close to beatin' that bitch's ass tonight, but I wasn't about to go to jail over no bullshit."

"Well, you know what Dad used to say," Christopher said.

"If you gotta beat her, you don't need her," Byron replied. "That's why I told her ass she had to go and she better not ever call me no more. That shit really set her off. She went through my spot like she was Gustav herself, kicking over tables and throwing shit around."

"What were you doing when all this was going on?"

"At first, I was shocked as hell. I froze. I couldn't believe the bitch was ripping up my place like that. Who woulda thought that little-ass girl had that much rage in her? By the time I came to my senses, I put her in an armlock and pushed her out. She beat on my door for a good ten minutes before the neighbor threatened to call the police on her crazy ass."

"Damn," Christopher repeated. "I sure would have never thought Rayna had that in her. She seemed so happy-go-lucky."

"I guess we never got a chance to see her mad. And I had never dumped her before. It's like she was used to sittin' in the driver's seat. When I started driving, she couldn't handle it. Her ass is just lucky she's carrying my baby, because if she wasn't, I don't know what I woulda done."

"Looks like Alexis opening her mouth helped you to dodge a serious bullet."

"Sure the hell did," Byron agreed, rising from the bed. He walked to his closet and surveyed a red splotch that streaked down the door. "Look at this shit, man."

"What is that?"

"Crazy chick threw a lit candle against the door," he replied, scraping away the wax with a piece of broken glass. "Bitch coulda burned down the whole damn complex. Thank God the flame went out."

Christopher chuckled in spite of the situation. "You sure can pick 'em."

"How was I supposed to know the bitch was crazy?"

"You were about to marry her. You mean to tell me she never showed you any indication that something wasn't right?"

Byron shook his head as he scraped the last piece of wax from the door. A stain on the door held the memory of the destroyed candle, but it was nothing a little white paint couldn't handle.

"On the real, bruh, I can't think of one thing over the past year that would make me think she was anything more than the happy-go-lucky woman that she was."

Christopher squinted at his brother, as if attempting to see through him. "Nothing?"

Byron thought back. He honestly couldn't remember a time when Rayna had ever gotten this angry. She had always seemed so carefree. They'd had some arguments, but never anything this extreme. Then again, there was the one time . . .

"You know what, bruh?"

"What's up?"

"I didn't think much of it then, but a few months ago, I ran into this chick I went to high school with. Sade."

"I remember Sade. Cute little red bone with a big booty?"

"Yeah, that's her."

"Sade," Christopher repeated, smiling. "What's she doing with herself these days? She still lookin' good?"

"Good as hell, but lemme finish tellin' my story, man," Byron admonished.

"My bad, bruh," his brother said with a laugh. "Go 'head."

"Anyway, she walked into my restaurant one day, and when I realized who she was, I gave her a hug and we started catching up on old times. I wound up sliding next to her at the bar, and we're laughin' and talkin' and having a good time. Baby boy, why did Rayna have to walk in? She gave me this look like she had caught me butt-ass naked in a hotel room."

"She didn't cause a scene, did she?"

"Actually, she was cool at first. I stood up, introduced them, and told Sade that Rayna and I were getting married. She congratulated us and asked for an invitation to the wedding."

"Okay, and then what?"

Byron stared into space, as if watching the scene from a different perspective. Even before the words came out of his mouth, he kicked himself for missing the blatant sign. "The whole time we're talking, Rayna had her arms tight around my waist. I mean, her damn arms were tighter than I normally wear my belts. When Sade left, Rayna finally let go and was cool for a minute. Then she turned around and made this crazy-ass comment."

"What she say?" Christopher asked, his eyes transfixed on his brother.

"This chick had the nerve to fix her mouth to say I had better not be cheating on her, because I'd be writing a check my dick couldn't cash."

"What the fuck?" Christopher asked, his eyes wide in amazement. "Every brother in the world knows you don't play with a man's dick."

"Who you tellin'?" Byron replied, shaking his head. "Then she turned around and said she was sorry and that she loved me. Right after, though, she slipped in that if I cheated on her, it would be the worst thing I could ever do."

"What the hell did that mean?"

"That's what I'm saying, bruh!" Byron exclaimed, turning suddenly to his brother and stretching out his arms to his sides. "I can't believe I let that shit slip! I had heard women say shit to that effect before, and it didn't mean a damn thing. I still did what the hell I wanted to do, and them bitches still begged me not to leave them. And the ones who even looked like they meant that shit got left at the damn door. I don't know what made me think Rayna was different."

"Your ass was in love this time, that's what," Christopher said after a pause that seemed to last forever. "When you're in love, you get blind to a lot of shit you wouldn't normally miss."

"I guess," Byron replied, shaking his head.

Once upon a time, Byron and his brother were the biggest players in upstate New York. Nothing had changed once he moved to Virginia Beach. He knew game. Hell, he'd invented most of it. And when a woman started showing crazy signs like his woman had done, he usually turned the other way, because no game in the world was worth putting up with a crazy-ass woman. He'd had boys whose cars had been vandalized, who'd gotten fired from their jobs, who had to take out restraining orders, all because of the wrath of an unstable woman who wasn't smart enough to realize she was being played. Who would move hell and high water to get the player to admit why he'd played her, when if she would sit down and shut the hell up long enough, she could figure out all by herself where things went wrong.

However, he had never played Rayna. She was the first woman he'd gone all in with. Before her, he would have never dreamt of commitment. He just loved being surrounded by women. He loved the chase. He loved the variety. He loved the feel of dangling strings that weren't attached to anything. He just plain loved it all.

When he met Rayna, though, her sweet disposition and take-no-shit attitude made him question everything he believed in. It wasn't a "love at first sight" moment, but he found himself excited by the prospect of being with her. Instead of leaving at the end of their dates to mount his next conquest, he found himself wanting to spend the night and take her to breakfast.

He wasn't exactly sure why she was the one. He'd met women like her before. However, he hadn't met them while he was at the crossroads of his life. She just happened to run up on him at the time when he was tired of being a player. Maybe he'd been hanging around his brother and Andrea for too long, but slowly, he'd found himself wanting the security of having one woman. A ride-or-die chick. Someone who was sure of herself and was strong enough not to take his shit. Rayna seemed to be just that woman. And now this. Damn, maybe love *had* blinded him.

Yet, he knew the worst hadn't passed. Angry or not, pissed or otherwise, Rayna and Byron still had something in common—the baby she carried. He just hoped the situation wouldn't make her do anything crazier than what she'd pulled tonight.

Chapter 21

Alone once again. Once again, alone. This was becoming an epidemic.

Andrea wandered around her dark, lonely home, wondering where she'd gone wrong. Her husband was out wandering the streets. She'd gotten into a stupid argument with her best friend. Even her own daughter was pissed at her since she didn't let her go to dinner with Brenda and Darnell. The child should be happy Andrea had let Elizabeth stay. She could have let Darnell take Elizabeth with them, and Latrise could have felt what it was like to be lonely for a while.

She lay across her bed, weary of feeling like the villain in all of this. Alexis had opened her mouth and blown out of the water a fifteen-year-old secret that wasn't even her business, and now everyone was mad at Andrea. Wasn't she the one who had been violated? Why was everyone coming down on her? Where was the justice?

One thing was for sure. She wasn't about to cry over this. In fact, she was tired of wasting energy even thinking about this madness. People seemed to forget that she had her own problems. Brenda and Alexis weren't the only people being affected by Hurricane Gustav. Andrea was also from New Orleans, and her mother and sister still lived there. They had safely evacuated to Baton Rouge with her cousins, but that wasn't the point. The point was no one had bothered to ask Andrea how her family was faring. No one had even thought about whether her own childhood home would be washed away. And now, since the city seemed to be in the clear again, it seemed that no one ever would.

Thoughts of her mother made Andrea a bit nostalgic. She glanced at her clock radio sitting on the nightstand and decided against calling to check on her mother when she saw the time was approaching eleven.

She and her mother had never had the strongest relationship, but the love had always been there. It was her mother who had made her the strong person she was today. Her mother's approach to parenting wasn't what might have seemed normal in other Southern households. Her version of a gourmet meal was taking the girls to their grandmother's house for Sunday dinner. Instead of lectures, she and the girls had discussions. Andrea had to smile at the thought of that, because those discussions did more for her development than any lecture ever could.

What killed what could have been the perfect mother-daughter relationship was the fact that her mother didn't know when to be Mom. For years, she had feared even mentioning a problem in her marriage, because she knew her mother would ask her what *she* had done wrong. It was like she always had a vote against Andrea. It was that attitude that had driven away Andrea's sister, Tina, for a long time. Things had gotten better over the years, though, and they'd all managed to grow closer, but it wasn't easy. It damn near took an intervention for the mother and daughters to come together again, but she thanked God that they finally did. These days, she and Tina spoke regularly, and they had even grown to become confidantes.

A popped lock broke the silence, sending a jolt through Andrea's body. She sat up and remained still, listening to see who had entered the house. Only one set of footsteps sounded from the stairs, so she relaxed a bit, relieved that her husband had finally come home.

"You still up?" Christopher asked, entering the bedroom and throwing his keys on the chest of drawers.

"Yeah," she replied, turning to face her husband. "You disappointed?"

"Not at all," he said, approaching the bed. Although it was dark, Andrea's night vision could make out his form walking toward her. He sat next to her and rubbed her leg. "Actually, I'm glad you're awake."

Her heart jumped with glee, but she dared not show it. "Why is that?"

Christopher remained silent for a while. Andrea could almost hear the thoughts rolling through his head. Whatever he was thinking, he didn't look happy.

"Byron and Rayna broke up tonight."

"What?" she asked, leaning toward her husband. "When? What happened?"

"Let's just say your little secret brought out a different side of her."

Christopher recounted the story as Andrea listened, covering her mouth in shock. This was the last thing she expected from Rayna. She seemed to be such a peaceful spirit. Where had this ugly side come from?

"Looks like your little friend Alexis gave the gift that keeps on giving the other night," Andrea remarked. She folded her arms and leaned back against the headboard.

"*My* little friend?" Christopher asked, drawing his head back in surprise. "What's that supposed to mean?"

"You can't tell me that you haven't thought back to the affair you two had once upon a time."

"How could I not? It happened, and there's nothing I can do to change that."

Andrea looked away, unwanted tears again threatening to break through. She was determined not to let them fall.

"Look at me, Dee."

Reluctantly, she turned back to her husband and looked at him sadly, hoping he would tell her what she wanted to hear. Yet, if what she wanted to hear wasn't the truth, she hoped he would still be honest with her. "What?"

"Just because I thought about the affair doesn't mean I'm trying to repeat it," he said, staring her in the eyes. He continued rubbing her leg, occasionally squeezing her calf. "That was a long time ago. I'm not proud of it, and I've done everything in my power to get you to forgive me for it. Did you really forgive me?" She nodded, prompting him to continue. "Baby, if you forgave me, why have you been trying to make me relive my mistake over again?"

"I'm not trying to do that."

"Bullshit, Dee. Ever since that girl stepped foot back in this city, you've been doing it. I understand, though. Had I known about your little lip-lock with Byron, I probably would have done the same thing with you. Guess that's why you held it in for so many years, huh?"

Andrea shook her head, one renegade tear leaving a trail down her cheek.

"What's going on between you and Byron?" he asked.

"Nothing."

"What *was* going on between you and my brother?"

"Chris, there was never anything between me and Byron," Andrea pleaded. She wiped away the tear and took a deep breath in an attempt to fight back more tears. "That kiss was a mistake. It never should have happened, but it came at a time when I didn't have anyone. You were gone, and Brenda and I had stopped speaking. Byron seemed to be my only friend for a while."

"You kiss all your friends?"

"Come on, Chris."

"Just answer the question."

Andrea sucked her teeth and glared at him. "No, Chris, I don't. You made your point."

"I don't think I did," he replied, taking his hand from her leg. "You didn't get caught up in a lip-lock with Sheila or Brenda, and they've been your friends for ages. If I remember correctly, you even tried dating again while we were apart, but that went nowhere. Yet you kissed Byron. That tells me that you'd thought about it before. That maybe there was an attraction between you two."

"You know what, Chris?" she started. "Yes, I was attracted to him for a moment. You had cheated on me with my best friend's cousin. That girl was almost like a little sister to me. And not only did you cheat—in my house, I might add—but you refused to talk to me for days after I caught you. Byron was the one who showed me compassion and acted like he cared. When he hugged me to comfort me, I wished it was you. After that kiss, it went no further. He went his way and I went mine, never to mention it again."

"But you did mention it, because if you didn't, no one else would have been able to bring it back up."

"Yeah, and Brenda messed up by telling Alexis."

"Do you see your responsibility in any of this?" Christopher asked, leaning toward his wife.

Andrea sighed and looked away. "I didn't mean to kiss your brother, but I assure you nothing else ever happened between us. We both love you too much to have done something like that to you, and it was that love that kept us from telling you. I figured by saying something, it would only make something out of noth-ing."

Christopher nodded. "In any other circumstance, I could accept that, but what gets me is you punished me for what I did with Alexis. Yet I wasn't the only one who was wrong. You hid your dirt, while mine got spread throughout the city."

Damn! She hated to admit it, but he had a point. After all those months of therapy, she had the chance to tell him and she chose not to. It had been eating at her for years, but she'd grown accustomed to the bite. Maybe it was a good thing the secret had finally come to light. Yet that didn't let Alexis off the hook.

"I'm sorry, Chris," she whispered. "Can't we just turn back the clock and pretend none of this ever hap-pened?"

He shook his head. "The shit's already out there. We just have to deal with it."

"You still love me?"

"Now, how you gonna ask me that?" he asked, fur-rowing his eyebrows. "Dee, I never stopped loving you. I don't like the way you handled this, but you're still my wife. I didn't work this hard getting you back just to walk back out the door."

The brightest smile Andrea had had in weeks covered her face. She leaned in and hugged him. He replied by lifting her chin and kissing her gently on the lips.

Andrea pulled back and smiled at her husband, but worry still clouded her eyes. "You think Byron and Rayna will fix things?"

Christopher shrugged, then shook his head. "That shit's over for good. You actually want them to get back together after everything that went down tonight?"

"I admit that was crazy, but they're having a baby."

"Guess they'll wind up going down as another statistic, but I highly doubt they'll get married after all this."

"Poor thing," Andrea lamented. "She's probably been hurt bad in life. Sometimes a woman can be irrational when she thinks she's being hurt all over again."

"I feel you, but you didn't see Byron's apartment. That was past irrational."

"Maybe she should get some therapy before she tries to get into another relationship."

He chuckled. "You think therapy is the answer to everything, don't you?"

"Just think about it. If she doesn't get help, then Byron's going to have to deal with baby mama drama from a woman who thinks she's been scorned. He'll never have another decent relationship."

Christopher nodded, seeming to consider his wife's point. "I hear you. But before we go solving the rest of the world's problems, let's concentrate on us tonight."

She smiled again and wrapped her arms around her husband as she pulled him on top of her. Before he could kiss her again, she drew her head back.

"What?" he asked, confused.

"Have you forgiven your brother?"

"Believe it or not, I went to his place tonight to talk this out with him, but when I saw the destruction Rayna left and the pain on his face, I had to put that shit aside," Christopher replied. "I had to think about it. I don't like what he did, and it's never going to be okay that he kissed my wife, but when I look back, he's never crossed that line again. He has never put you in a bad position or said anything out of order. So, I had to look at it as a one-time thing."

"Baby, I promise you that's all it was."

"I know. We did talk about it a little tonight, and he pretty much said the same thing you did. I just had to hear it from you, as well."

"I'm glad you two talked," Andrea said, hugging him even tighter. "I don't ever want to be the cause of breaking the bond you two have."

"You won't," he replied, kissing her again. "Enough about that. Can I make love to my wife now? We've gotta go to work in a few hours."

Andrea giggled as she pulled off her husband's shirt. Alexis might have succeeded in spreading business that wasn't hers, but she would never again kill the love the Lee family held for each other.

Chapter 22

"What's good, baby cousin?"

"Hey, Boo. What's good with you?" Nikki greeted happily.

She hadn't spoken with her favorite cousin, whose real name was Courtney Dequire, since she'd left for her modeling job three weeks ago. Only the knowledge that Boo always found a way to survive kept her from worrying herself to death over him. Besides, if something bad had happened, she would have heard the news by now.

She balanced her cell phone between her ear and shoulder as she lay on top of her bed, flipping through the newest issue of *Essence* magazine. She had planned on spending her Thursday in her room. There was nowhere to go and nothing to do, so why not spend a few hours being lazy? Especially a few hours of what she hoped would be her last day in Virginia Beach. She had to admit that the place was beautiful, but she'd had enough. It was time to get back to what was familiar, and hearing her cousin's voice really sealed the deal for her.

"Ain't shit," he replied. Even with his raspy voice, Nikki could hear that her cousin was in good spirits. "Just checkin' on you."

"Oh, I'm good," she said, sitting up and tucking her feet underneath her body. "You know a sista like me is always gonna land on her feet. Where you hidin' out?"

"Chillin' out in the ATL until Nagin lets me go back home. What about you?"

"Virginia Beach. Sand and water beat dirt and broken levees anytime."

They laughed together, the first authentic laugh Nikki had had since arriving in Virginia Beach. It felt good to have her family reach out to her, even if it was someone the likes of Boo. At first glance, no one would ever believe she had family on the wrong side of the tracks. She loved playing the regal role, as if she were above anything petty. However, her family knew differently. As comfortable as she was in stilettos and lace at the finest establishments in New Orleans, she was just as comfortable in sandals and jeans, playing dominoes at her grandparents' backyard barbecues. She could mix just as easily with the elite as she could with those who slid beneath the long arm of the law.

Boo was definitely part of the latter group. He was smarter than many people gave him credit for, partly because he preferred to use his talents illegally. He had learned from the streets how to work on computers and had used them to rob people so smoothly and methodically that many didn't realize it until it was too late. While many people in her family, including his own parents, had written him off as a lost cause, Nikki had always stayed close to him, believing he would one day change his life. She didn't expect him to get saved and become perfect—hell, she hadn't even taken that step herself and didn't plan to—but she did hope he would put his computer smarts to good use one day.

"So you're in Virginia, huh?" Boo asked. His voice was still light, but Nikki detected a calculating tone.

"Yeah. Why?"

Boo laughed a bit. "That's some shit right there."

"Boo, what the hell are you talkin' about? You know I don't like playing games."

He laughed again, even longer this time. "Shit, girl, who you foolin'? You got more games than the damn Parker Brothers."

"Whatever, Boo. Now, tell me what's so damn funny. What do you know that I need to know?"

This was what Nikki hated about her cousin. He played in riddles way too much. For most people, it was so frustrating that they didn't even bother talking to him. However, Nikki knew cutting her cousin off would be cutting off a very valuable line of communication. She'd learned long ago that Boo lived by the mantra "Knowledge is power." If he didn't know about something, it probably wasn't true.

"Cousin, you ain't gotta play games with me. You went to the Beach to get a closer look at the action, right?"

She dropped her magazine in her lap. "What action?"

"Nik, you can't tell me you don't know about the credit situation."

"Boo, stop playin'! What the fuck are you talking about?"

"You really don't know, do you?" Boo asked, some of the playfulness leaving his voice. "All these months, and you didn't have one fuckin' idea."

"An idea about what?" Now she was getting scared. What did her cousin have to do with a credit scam in Virginia Beach? And why did drama have to follow her everywhere she went? She lifted herself from the bed and began pacing back and forth, finally ending up in the living room. She flopped down on the sofa and crossed her legs Indian style.

"A few months ago, I met this li'l shorty named Tina," Boo explained. "I was gonna get with her, but the shit woulda been too easy. She had just went through a divorce and was lookin' to just give the pussy away. You know me. If it ain't a challenge, I don't need it."

"Get to the point, Boo."

"Hold on now, impatient ass."

Nikki rolled her eyes and poked out her lips in irritation. There was no use in arguing, because Courtney would do what he wanted, anyway. If he were standing in front of her right now, his neck would become accustomed to her manicured fingers.

"Anyway, I took her out a few times, and we got to talking. Come to find out, she had a sister who lives in Virginia Beach," Boo continued. He chuckled, as if he could hear Nikki's mind trying to race ahead to put together the pieces of this confusing story. "Her sister used to complain about this chick who slept with her husband years ago."

"Why she still worried about it now? Get over it," Nikki remarked, picking up the remote control. She clicked on the television and absently scanned the channels. This story was getting stupid. She'd slept with enough men to know that you couldn't change the past, so you might as well live your life. That was why she'd never apologized for the things she had done and would continue to do if the opportunity was right.

"I asked her the same thing," Boo said. "Seemed to me like they both needed to leave the past in the past. But she said her sister started trippin' again because it seemed like the chick never paid for what she did."

"What she supposed to do? Die? If she really wanted her to pay, she shoulda whupped her ass and got it over with." One thing Nikki couldn't stand was a person who carried a grudge. *This chick sounds worse than Reggie,* she thought to herself.

"I know, right? The sister wanted the chick to pay with karma, but that didn't work out too well. The girl went on to be some kinda doctor and is about to marry a lawyer."

"Shit, that sounds like somebody else I know," Nikki said, growing more interested. Boo chuckled and continued. "Apparently, Tina and her sister think the chick is still shady as hell and would run like hell if her new man turned out to not be about shit."

"So how they gonna find out if that dumb-ass theory is true?"

"By hiring a brother like me to play with the lawyer's credit and watching what happens next." He laughed again, this time louder and heartier. The longer he laughed, the angrier Nikki became.

"Boo, are you crazy? That shit ain't got nothin' to do with you!"

"Girl, whatchu talkin' 'bout? When it comes to money, it has *everything* to do with me."

"Is that what you're gonna tell the judge when your crazy ass gets arrested?" she asked, popping up from the sofa. She stormed into the bedroom and stared into the mirror. Not knowing any other way to channel her irritation, she picked up a brush and began playing with her hair.

This was not the way she wanted to start her morning. As much as she loved Boo, she could never understand why he took such risks. *He could easily be the black Bill Gates if he'd just get his head out of his—*

"So you still don't understand why I think it's interesting that you're in Virginia?" Boo asked, interrupting her thoughts.

Nikki thought for a minute but drew a blank. Who the hell would she know in Virginia Beach with that kind of drama? And if she did, why would she waste her time and money carrying herself to a city she knew nothing about just to take a closer look? *The only people I remotely know are Alexis and—*

"Boo!" she screamed, pitching the brush at the wall. Its crash echoed throughout the room, making the impact seem louder than it really was. "You tryin'a get me killed?"

"Whatchu talkin' 'bout, Nikki?"

"What the fuck do you mean, what am I talkin' about?" she yelled, making no attempt to mask her anger. "You can't possibly be that dumb! That girl and I have never got along, and by some strange coincidence, we all wound up in Virginia at the same time. You don't think I'm the first person they're gonna blame for that shit?"

"How they gonna blame you?" Boo asked, laughing. "As far as they know, that shit coulda happened because of Gustav. The same thing happened to a lot of people after Katrina."

"Stupid, Katrina was ten times worse than Gustav! Think about it. You said you been playin' with Jamar's credit for months. Now, all of a sudden, we both end up in Virginia Beach. How long you think it's gonna be until he notices what you've been doing and thinks I did it and followed his ass here?"

"Why would he think that? You don't think you're overexaggerating?"

"First of all, genius, *overexaggerating* is not a word," Nikki snapped. "Second of all, why wouldn't he think I would get back at him after how he handled my ass in divorce court? It's because of him that I lost De-Shawn. Things worked out for the best, but he doesn't know that!"

"Just so you'll know, genius, overexaggerating *is* a word. Now calm down, baby girl," Boo said, trying his best to make his raspy voice sound consoling. "Now, I'm lettin' you keep callin' me out my name because you're my favorite cousin and I know you're upset, but you need to calm the hell down. Now, listen to me."

"What the hell you got to say, Boo?" Nikki challenged, holding her head as if trying to protect it from the impending headache she was sure would come. She dropped mindlessly on her bed, preparing to tear into him again if he said the wrong thing.

"Listen to me, now!"

"I'm listening! Shit! Whatcha gotta say?" In the back of her mind, she hoped she would hear Nephew Tommy from *The Steve Harvey Morning Show* announce that she'd just been pranked, but reality told her that she'd have no such luck.

"Nik, I'm not gonna say I didn't know this dude was the one who caused you to lose Shawn," he began.

Nikki rolled her eyes and breathed in and out through her nose in a vain attempt to calm her fragile nerves. She hated thinking of herself as losing her son. What kind of mother had her child taken away from her? Admitting that Reggie had been awarded custody due to her constant cheating was like conceding that she was a bad mother, and that couldn't be any further from the truth. She might have been a terrible wife, but she was a damn good mother, and no one, not even Saint Reggie himself, could say any differently.

"You know how small New Orleans is now," Boo continued. "It's like everybody knows everybody. So, when I met Tina and she told me about that shit, I figured it was a good time to help her out, get me some ass, and help you get some catch-back, too. You can't tell me you didn't wanna beat old dude's ass after that judgment."

"Yeah, but I got over it," Nikki pleaded.

A soft beep invaded her ear. She glanced at the caller ID and ignored the call when she saw Reggie's name. She really wasn't in the mood to talk to him right now. It just wasn't a good time.

"I never woulda thought of some shit like that. If I was gonna get anybody back, it woulda been my soft-ass ex-husband," she added.

"I know what you're sayin', but it doesn't make you feel good just a little bit to know that the muthafucka is sittin' a couple miles away from you, sweatin' his ass off, and that cute-ass girl of his might be about to leave his ass?"

"She ain't that damn cute," she mumbled, ignoring another beep. Voice mail would pick up soon. "What did you do to his credit, anyway?"

"You really wanna know?"

"I asked, didn't I?"

"Baby cousin, I probably told you too much. You ain't had nothin' to do with this. I ain't tryin'a drag you down."

Nikki sucked her teeth. "Boo, you ain't gotta tell me how you did it, because frankly, I don't wanna know. But I do wanna know how bad this shit is just in case his ass comes lookin' for me."

"Probably woulda been better if you didn't know at all," he remarked with a groan. "That way, you could honestly play dumb with his ass. I thought you knew all this time."

"How was I supposed to know? I've been gone for the past three weeks, and before that, I was on the grind. The couple times we did talk, you never said a word."

"You right. My bad."

"So what did you do?"

"Let's just say the lawyer doesn't pay as much attention to his finances as he should. We been playin' in his account for months, and he didn't notice nothin' until I had the first card turned off."

"Playing how?"

"Taking out a hundred here and there, and putting it back before he could notice anything. A couple of times I took forty or fifty dollars for food. I don't think he ever noticed that, because there was never a block on his account."

"Ain't that some shit?" Nikki mumbled, shaking her head. First thing she planned to do when she got back home was pull her own credit report. If Jamar's finances could be messed with so easily, who was to say that hers couldn't be? It was a shame that most people checked their credit reports only when they needed loans and monitored their bank accounts only when they were broke and needed to cover a check. This taught her to watch her money a lot more closely. "I'ma talk with you later, Boo. Thanks for lettin' me know what's up."

"Anytime, baby cuz, but you know I thought you already knew," he replied cautiously. "You hurry up and get your ass back to New Orleans before this shit hits the fan."

Nikki shrugged. "He lives in New Orleans, too. He can try to get me here, or he can try to get me there, but one thing is for damn sure. I ain't *lettin'* him do shit to me."

"If that muthafucka tries to lay one hand on you, that's his ass. Now, get back here, where you got some backup."

"Don't worry, Boo. I'll be home tomorrow."

A frightening chill ran up Nikki's spine as she closed her cell phone. Instead of placing the phone back into her purse, she tapped her chin with it in hopes of waking up from this nightmare. She didn't mind a little drama. In fact, she thrived on it. This time was different, though. This was some serious jail time stuff. Even if she could prove she had nothing to do with it and avoided prison, who was to say she could avoid Jamar coming after her?

"No, he won't try anything," she tried to assure herself. "He loves his job too much to do anything crazy, and he would have to work too hard to prove I had anything to do with this if he tried to call the police."

She dropped the phone on the floor and rubbed her head. All she knew was she had to get out of Virginia Beach that day.

Without a second thought, she sprang from the bed and walked to the closet. Her suitcase sat just inside the door, half full of dirty clothes and underneath a curtain of dresses and outfits she'd never gotten around to wearing. She rolled her eyes, not looking forward to repacking. Why had she packed half her wardrobe for a damn photo shoot, anyway? It had worked out for the best since she was stuck waiting out Gustav, but repacking would be a monster.

She dragged the suitcase out of the closet, flung it on the bed, and then went back for her garment bag. Just as she tossed the bag on her bed, her cell phone rang again.

"This is a damn hotline today," she mumbled while bending down to pick up her phone from where she had dropped it. She hit TALK without checking the caller ID.

"Speak."

"Uh, Nikki?" asked a strange male voice.

"Who's this?"

"This is Clarke, *tesorina*. Are you okay?"

The cute term of endearment made Nikki smile despite the irritation she felt. He'd first called her that when he took her to the mall earlier that day. She hadn't wanted to seem uneducated, so she never asked him what it meant. However, she looked up the word once she got back to the hotel that night and found out that it meant "honey" or "sweetheart." Normally, she would never let any man call her baby or honey, but it had a nice sound to it when said in a different language.

"Hey, Clarke. I'm okay. Just got some stuff on my mind."

"Oh? Can I help?"

"What is it with you Italian men?" she asked, walking back into the living room. Her eyes needed a break from the mess of clothing all over her bed. She flopped on the sofa and tucked her legs underneath her behind.

"What do you mean?"

"I mean, you always wanna be the caretaker. The problem solver. Are you like that with your own women?"

"I can be no other way than what I am, *tesorina*."

The hard-hearted Nikki found herself blushing at the sound of her special nickname. "There you go sweet-talking again."

He chuckled. "I want to see you again."

She pursed her lips. There was no way in hell that could happen. She was about to get ghost the first chance she got. As good as a nice dinner and a little sex sounded, she wasn't so sure they outweighed possibly getting that crap end of some mess she had nothing to do with.

"Nikki? Are you still there?"

"Yeah, I'm here, but not for long."

"What do you mean?"

"I mean, I'm going back to New Orleans today."

"Today? So soon? Why?"

"It's time for me to go back. I can't live in this hotel forever."

"You were just going to leave without even saying good-bye?"

"I would have called," Nikki lied.

The disappointment in Clarke's voice nearly made her feel bad. Why did he have to get so sprung? All they had shared were a few drinks and a shopping spree. Besides a couple of flirtatious kisses, they hadn't come close to sleeping together. He'd never even seen the inside of her hotel room. What made her so special in his eyes? Lord knew she didn't need another softy in her life. Once was enough.

"Let me see you today, before you leave," Clarke darn near demanded. "You haven't eaten in my restaurant yet."

"Clarke, I don't have time for that. I really have to go."

"Why do I feel like you're lying to me?"

"Excuse me?" she snapped. Her wince could have melted steel. "I just met you, like, two seconds ago. I ain't got no reason to lie to you."

"You're right," he retorted, his tone matching hers. "Which is why I don't see why you choose to lie to me. If you're not interested, be a woman and say so!"

Nikki drew back her head and stared at the phone in shock. Did this guy really just come at her like that? He'd obviously been hanging out with too many black women. She almost laughed. Not because she thought he was funny, but because she'd never expected this gentle Italian to be this strong. She decided to push a little more.

"I know you're not tryin'a question my womanhood. You really got the wrong one if you think you can talk to me any kinda way. Now keep talkin' and I'ma hang up on your ass."

"What is your problem?" he asked, his voice softening a bit. "Where did all this hostility come from all of a sudden?"

That's what I thought. He ain't so bad, after all, she thought, puffing her chest in triumph. She remained silent to see where he would go next.

"Nikki?"

"I'm here," she mumbled.

He sighed, sounding defeated to Nikki's ears. She smiled at her small victory.

"You're not going to let me see you before you leave?"

"I can't. I really have to go."

Deep down, she wouldn't have minded staying another night and letting Clarke spoil her. It would have been nice to eat some Italian food. Maybe he would have even pulled a *Pretty Woman* and taken her right there in the restaurant. But even if she didn't fear the wrath of a desperate lawyer with credit problems, she couldn't stay, because of the principle of the thing. She'd just punked him for accusing her of lying. There was no way she could go back on her word now.

"Well, *tesorina,* have a safe trip back home."

"Thank you, Clarke. I will. You gonna come see me in New Orleans?"

He laughed a bit. "You'll see me sooner than you think."

She smiled devilishly and pictured the two of them hiding out at the W Hotel in New Orleans. Maybe she really would keep in touch with Clarke. Maybe not. She didn't usually keep in touch with her conquests. What happened on vacation and on business trips was not supposed to come home with her. She suddenly remembered that she needed to call Reggie. He'd called while she was on the phone with her cousin, but she'd never returned the call. It was time to get Mr. Clarke off the phone so she could let her former husband know her plans.

"What time are you leaving?" Clarke asked.

"I don't know yet. I was about to call the airline to change my ticket just before you called."

"Can I take you to the airport?"

"I'll let you know once I buy my ticket," she replied, holding back an irritated sigh. She wished he would just hang up. The man was beginning to sound a little too eager. "Look, I've got to go take care of some things before I leave."

"Okay, *tesorina*. See you soon."

The room phone rang just as she pressed END on her cell phone.

"Shit!" she exclaimed, flinging her hands in the air. "What the hell is going on today? Am I running a hot-line I don't know about?"

She stomped toward the nightstand and snatched up the receiver with such force that she knocked the rest of the phone on the floor. Ignoring the crash, she put the receiver to her ear and demanded, "Yes!"

"Ms. Morgan?" asked a female voice she wasn't familiar with.

"Yes!" she demanded again, losing none of the edge she had when she first answered.

"This is Michelle at the front desk," the lady said quickly. "There's an Alexis White here to see you."

Shit. It's starting already. Why did it seem like the entire world was out to get her all in one day? Was there a meeting the night before? Did her cousin, Clarke, Alexis, Reggie, and Jamar meet somewhere to figure out how best to bring drama to her life? And how in the hell did Alexis know where to find her, anyway?

"Ms. Morgan?"

"Yes."

"Should I send Ms. White up? I can't unless you give me permission. It's hotel policy . . ."

"Yeah, yeah, I know," Nikki groaned. "Is she by herself?"

"It appears so."

"Tell her I'll meet her at the bar in about five minutes."

Nikki picked up the phone from the floor and set it back on the nightstand. She then quietly paced the floor, wondering whether she should entertain this craziness. Why was Alexis there? Did she think they were the best of friends just because they had had one little heart-to-heart the other night? Was she there to defend her man's honor? Whatever it was, Nikki wasn't sure she was in the frame of mind to hear anything Alexis had to say.

Part of her wanted to leave Alexis hanging in that bar. What made her think she could just walk up on her like that? She was a grown-ass woman. Nobody had license to pop up on her. She'd even been known to leave people ringing her doorbell continually, never to receive an answer, because they hadn't called first.

Yet, as angry as she was, she couldn't help but be a little curious as to the reason for this little impromptu visit. If it was about the credit situation, she wondered how Alexis would approach it. Would she blurt it out or beat around the bush? No, she would most likely beat around the bush. What woman would readily broadcast her man's financial problems? That would be plain embarrassing!

"What am I worried about?" Nikki asked herself aloud. "I'm the one with the upper hand. I didn't do anything wrong. She's coming to *me* for information.

Maybe if she plays her cards right, I could be the one to help her silly ass."

That thought provided some comfort as a saccharine grin slowly overtook her face. She waltzed over to the bedroom mirror and inspected herself. Her yellow sundress hit just above mid-thigh and hugged all the right areas. She touched up her lipstick, then slid her hand around the back of her neck and flipped her hair over her right shoulder. After sitting back on the bed, she slid on her yellow sandals. Once she took a final look in the mirror, she inhaled a deep breath and headed for the door.

"Here goes nothing."

Chapter 23

"I know this girl is doing this shit on purpose," Alexis mumbled as she checked her watch for the third time. Five minutes had come and gone fifteen minutes ago. This was getting ridiculous.

Why did Nikki Morgan constantly think the world revolved around her? Here Alexis was, trying to rule out any reason to believe Nikki had anything to do with Jamar's credit nightmare, and this was the thanks she got. She guessed what everyone had said was right— Nikki was definitely not her friend.

She looked around the hotel bar and inspected her surroundings. She had to admit the place looked pretty nice. The bar was located on the twenty-first floor and offered a breathtaking view of the oceanfront. It was stocked nearly to the ceiling with various types of top-shelf vodkas, gins, and rums, and with every other spirit known to man. It was an alcoholic's paradise, but she didn't let that stop her from ordering a glass of Moscato.

Wine wasn't exactly the drink of champions after a two-mile run, but she needed a touch of liquid courage to embark on the conversation she was about to have. It was time to get to the bottom of this mystery. She wasn't sure if Nikki was the answer, but she would damn sure find out. And she needed to find out quickly, before Jamar ventured out to find her. Last night she'd stayed up for nearly an hour searching for Nikki's hotel after he had gone to sleep. No one would come out and tell her whether or not Nikki was staying here, so she had to pretend to be an acquaintance who was trying to leave her a message. At least four attendants told her that no Nicole Morgan was registered before she lucked up and got patched through. Nikki wasn't in the room at the time, but the call provided the destination she needed for her morning workout. Instead of hitting the gym, she took to the streets.

"Here you go, ma'am," the bartender said cheerfully.

She smiled a thank-you and handed him a ten.

"How much do you want back?" the bartender asked expectantly while taking the money from her hand.

"How 'bout you bring me the correct change while I think about it?" she snapped.

Instantly, the smile left his face. Eyebrows raised, he turned away from her and walked to the register. A few seconds later, a dollar and two quarters were laid in front of her.

"He coulda kept this shit," Alexis mumbled, staring down at the money. "And if his ass wasn't so mon-eygrubbin', he probably woulda got it."

She rubbed her eyes lightly and pulled at her shorts. It wasn't too long ago that she would have waved off the change from something as simple as a drink. She had probably wasted more money in her lifetime than she had saved in the bank. However, now she was planning a wedding. To a lawyer with credit problems. Problems that might not be able to get solved with a simple phone call.

Another irritated look toward the door finally brought results. The queen had finally decided to make her grand entrance. She stood at the doorway and looked around, as if waiting for Alexis to wave her over. Yet Alexis refused to give her the satisfaction. Instead, she sipped her wine and spun her stool around until her back faced the door.

"Oh, so you gonna act like you don't see me, huh?"

Alexis rolled her eyes and slowly looked up to find a vision in lemon yellow standing before her. *Doesn't this woman ever dress like a regular person?* She smirked and shook her head. "You gonna sit down or stand over me all night?"

"Well, I would, but it seems as if all the bar stools are taken," Nikki replied, looking up and down the crowded bar. Every seat was taken except an empty stool all the way at the other end of the bar, and there was no use in sitting there.

"Hey, sweetie," said an older black man sitting next to Alexis. He stood up and smiled at the two ladies. "My friend and I are just about to leave. You can take my seat."

Nikki smiled a cheese-eating grin at the man and caressed him lightly on his chubby cheek with her thumb. "That's too sweet of you. You must be a Southern man."

"Born and raised in Richmond, sweetheart," the man said, chuckling like a schoolboy.

His friend stood by, with his arms folded and wearing a smile almost as wide as the bar itself. The entire scene nearly made Alexis sick to her stomach.

"I knew it," Nikki said just as a country song blared through the speakers. The crowd, mostly older white patrons, seemed to take no notice. "Well, I appreciate the seat. Y'all enjoy the rest of your day."

"We definitely will," the man's friend said as the men walked off.

Nikki stepped onto the empty stool and crossed her legs, flashing her shiny knees. After ordering a Bay Breeze, she turned to Alexis and raised her eyebrows.

"You always get what you want, don't you?" Alexis said, leaning her elbow on the bar.

"Not all the time," she replied.

A hint of sadness crossed her eyes, but it left before Alexis could figure out what it meant. She hoped it meant Nikki was beginning to regret what she was doing to Jamar.

"So to what do I owe this unexpected and unappreciated pleasure?" Nikki asked.

"Unappreciated, huh?"

"So I guess you like people popping up on you?"

Alexis raised her eyebrows and shrugged her shoulders. She wondered how she would approach this situation. Beating around the bush wasn't the answer, and jumping straight to the point didn't seem like the best option, either. Would Nikki even tell the truth if she actually did have anything to do with it? Alexis doubted it, but she had to try.

"So what's up?" Nikki asked.

"When you headed back to New Orleans?" Alexis asked, swirling what was left of her Moscato around her glass. She stared at the golden liquid, which kind of reminded her of the tornadoes she used to make in grade school, using water, food coloring, and a two-liter soda bottle. Those were the easy days. Who knew it would turn out like this?

"I'm gettin' out of here as soon as I possibly can."

"Why's that?"

"Because I've got a home I would like to get back to!" Nikki snapped. "Now what's up with all the questions? You tryin' to get at something?"

"What's up with the attitude all of a sudden? You thought I was wrong the other night, when *I* had the attitude."

"Yeah, but I didn't walk up on you in your hotel and pull you out of the privacy of your room. And I sure as hell didn't shovel fifty questions down your throat, so what's up?" Alexis recoiled a bit. This would be harder than she had expected. Something was bothering Nikki, but she wasn't sure if she was the culprit. There was something else going on in her head. She gulped down the rest of her wine while trying to think of a different approach. Destiny's Child's old hit "Survivor" began playing.

"I thought we'd come to some kind of understanding when we talked the other night," Alexis said. She stared toward the wall behind Nikki in an effort to avoid eye contact but suddenly realized how much of a lack of confidence that showed. After clearing her throat, she lifted her eyes toward Nikki's, only to be interrupted by the bartender.

"Can I get anything else for you, ladies?" he asked, cutting his eyes at Alexis. The $1.50 remained in the same spot he'd left it, as if he was too afraid to pick it up.

Alexis shook her head. "Nothing for me."

Nikki tilted her head toward her and shot her a half smile. "You act like you're not staying long. You called me out of my room just to ask when I'm going back to New Orleans?"

She turned back to the bartender and instructed him to bring Alexis another glass of wine and to freshen up her Bay Breeze. The bartender again shot Alexis a look once Nikki handed him a twenty and told him to keep the change.

"Doesn't look like you and ole boy are gettin' along too well," Nikki observed once the bartender had walked away.

Alexis responded by lifting her eyebrows and shrugging her shoulders. "Whatever."

"Now, to comment on your statement," Nikki said after taking a long sip from her original drink. She grabbed a few mini pretzels from the snack bowl between them and popped them into her mouth. "I like you, Alexis. Not sure why, but I do. Still, whatever kind of understanding you thought we had the other night doesn't give you the right to play Sherlock Holmes on me."

"Sherlock Holmes?" Alexis tried to suppress a laugh but failed. "Whatever, Nikki. It's not that hard to find you. Your snotty ass is only going to stay in the most expensive spots. All I had to do was make a couple of phone calls."

"And what was so important that you had to make those phone calls? We ain't that close."

Alexis took a deep breath on the inside, while maintaining her confidence on the outside. Her eyes followed an attractive blonde being led to the bar stool next to Nikki. Her suitor, a brother who looked no older than twenty-five, sat her on the stool and then took his own seat. The woman set her purse in front of her and nodded at Alexis, as if acknowledging the fact that she was being watched. The bartender brought Nikki and Alexis their drinks, then turned to the interracial couple and took their orders.

Alexis waited for him to walk away before she replied, "Jamar's looking for you."

"For what? I don't owe him any money."

"Come on, Nikki. Don't play dumb. You know why."

Nikki cocked her head back in surprise and let out a soft laugh. "If I did, I would have said so by now. I have nothing to lie about."

"Since when?" Alexis mumbled, watching the blonde cut her eyes at them.

"Excuse me?"

"You heard."

Nikki leaned back and took a sip from her drink. "Alexis, where is all this hostility coming from?"

"I should be asking you that. You're the one who came down here, talking about I invaded your space."

"Yes, and you've been acting like the perfect shrinking violet all day."

Alexis sighed and rubbed her forehead. This was going about as well as any train wreck could go. "Nikki, can we just agree that we're both being bitches and move on, please? This is ridiculous."

"You're right," Nikki agreed, tracing her finger around the rim of her glass. She uncrossed her legs and then crossed them again the other way, revealing more than half her thigh. She never bothered straightening her dress. "This *is* ridiculous. How about you just come out and tell me why you popped up on me?"

"Because for some reason, I wanted to think you're not as evil as Jamar thinks you are," Alexis replied, staring Nikki in the eyes. She shot the blonde a dirty look after catching her looking toward them while pretending to look past them.

Nikki didn't flinch. "Once again, what are you talking about?"

Alexis opened her mouth but hesitated. This was one embarrassing situation. What if Nikki really didn't have anything to do with it? She'd be putting her man's business out in the street for no reason. What if Nikki *was* behind the drama, though? She wasn't going to stop just because Alexis told her to. Either way, Jamar would kill Alexis if he knew she was there.

"Come on, Alexis," Nikki chided impatiently, crossing her arms. Her foot shook incessantly. "Spit the shit out so I can get on with the rest of my day."

Alexis scowled. "You know what, Nikki? You are one heartless bitch sometimes."

Nikki smiled and held up her drink, as if to say, "Cheers." "I'm a card-carrying member. I thought you knew by now."

Alexis began to feel her blood boil. Her face turned hot as she fought to maintain her composure. She refused to make another spectacle of herself, but Nikki refused to make it easy for her. Her eyes narrowed into slits as she resisted the urge to knock Nikki's smug ass off her perch.

Nikki seemed oblivious to Alexis's internal struggle. She sipped her melting drink and slanted her head to the right. "What happened to you?"

Alexis drew her head back and scowled again. "What?"

"What happened to you?" Nikki repeated. "From what I heard, you used to be a chick who took no shit. Hell, I heard you coulda been the queen bitch around this cut."

"How—" Alexis started, but then she thought about it. The only link they had between them was Reggie, but Reggie would never call her a bitch. She guessed that maybe he'd told Nikki about the girls he'd dated in college, and she had taken it upon herself to fill in the blank with *bitch*. *This bitch is a trip.* She gulped down her wine and glared at her enemy. "You wanna know what happened to me? I grew the hell up! You really need to do the same."

"No, what you need to do is get back some of that backbone you used to have in college. Bring back that old Alexis you showed the other night, when you cursed out your girl. That bitch woulda said what she had to say twenty minutes ago."

"Maybe if you weren't a miserable woman who fucks up everything you put your hands on, you'd realize that everything doesn't revolve around being a bitch. Vindictive ass."

By this time, the blonde had leaned closer to them, while maintaining a sparse conversation with her date. Alexis shot her another look, although deep down, she knew she'd be trying to listen in, too, if she caught wind of a conversation as tense as this.

Nikki, oblivious to the eavesdropper, applauded lightly and shot Alexis a sideways grin. "I knew that bitch was in there somewhere, but I'ma tell you something. You don't know shit about me, so you need to back the hell up."

"I know you're so busy trying to make excuses for your fuckups that you're willing to ruin the life of a man who didn't do shit to you but did his damn job."

"Alexis, what the fuck are you talking about?"

"Why are you sitting there playing dumb, Nikki?" Alexis demanded, her hands stretched out to her sides. She barely missed toppling over her empty wineglass. Jamie Foxx's "Unpredictable" had just ended. The music fell silent, leaving nothing but the low rumble of the crowd and the clink of bottles tapping glasses. She leaned in closer to ensure no other ears but Nikki's heard what she had to say next. "Stop whatever game you're playing with Jamar's finances. This shit is childish and illegal."

Nikki scrunched her eyebrows and fiddled with a napkin. "Really, Alexis. What are you talking about?"

"Nikki, you're a fuckin' trip! Be real for once. I didn't wanna believe you had anything to do with this, but something in the back of my mind tells me you might. Tell me what's up."

"What's up is your ass is crazy. Of all the people on God's green earth, why in the hell would I choose you and Jamar to fuck with? You two ain't all that important to me."

The blonde's shoulders jumped like she was trying to stifle a laugh. The action wasn't missed.

Alexis leaned forward and looked past Nikki for the moment. "Excuse me. Blondie?"

The woman turned her head toward her, a look of surprise covering her charcoal-outlined eyes. "Me?"

Nikki swung her stool toward the bar to get a look at who Alexis was talking to.

"Yes, you," Alexis snapped, while Nikki looked back and forth at the two women and smiled. "How about you put your attention on your man and get the fuck out my mouth?"

The blonde lady's eyes grew wide, and her mouth dropped into an O. Her head shot toward her date and then back at Alexis.

"Is there a problem?" her date asked.

Nikki laughed so hard, she nearly fell off her chair. "Brother man, you're not gonna tell me you didn't notice your girl listening to our little talk over here. I mean, I had my back turned, but if my girl had to stop what she was saying to check your friend, the shit musta been pretty obvious."

"Whatever happened, all that hostility and language isn't called for," the man said, while rubbing his date's back, as if nursing an injury.

Nikki smiled and turned to Alexis. "He's so sweet. Taking care of his woman."

"Yeah," Alexis replied, shaking her head. She stood up. "Back in the day, he woulda been known as a superhero. Captain Save-a-Ho. Let's go find a table so this nosy bitch and her man can enjoy their day."

Nikki gasped with amusement but stood up with Alexis.

"That really wasn't necessary," the man told them. "That's why I don't mess with black women now."

All three women snapped their necks toward the man and his ill-chosen words. They looked like a synchronized swimming team.

"You know what?" Alexis retorted. "I'm not even going to argue with you. Like a black woman would even be bothered with your sell-out ass."

Before he could reply, Alexis and Nikki walked off. They found a table near the front of the restaurant and sat across from each other. Nikki smiled at Alexis and picked up the small menu sitting at the end of the table. She knew she should have left the scene, but she had to admit that she was enjoying the drama a little.

"What are you smiling at?" Alexis asked, still reeling from the confrontation at the bar.

"I guess that bitch in you didn't go too far."

"She comes out when she has to."

"Can I get you ladies anything else?"

Both women jumped and looked up at the waitress, who seemed to have appeared out of thin air. She reminded Nikki of the waitress she had had a couple of days ago. *Where do they find these fast-ass people?*

"No, we won't be long," Alexis replied with a smile.

The reply took Nikki aback because she had planned on ordering another drink. She watched longingly as the waitress walked away just as quickly as she had appeared. Alexis had stepped out on her own and had made the decision for them both. Just like Nikki was sure she was doing now. Did Jamar know his woman was there trying to fight his battles?

"You know you were wrong for calling that man Captain Save-a-Ho, right?" Nikki asked, filing her thought away for just the right moment.

"Yeah, I know. He just irked the shit out of me. Rubbing that woman's back like a baby. I know he saw how she was all up in my mouth."

"Yet and still, we as women have come way too far to keep being called hoes and other garden tools," Nikki replied, placing the menu back at the end of the table. She folded her arms. "But back to the issue at hand. If your little boyfriend has money issues, they don't have anything to do with me."

"That's really what I believed when I came over here, but there's too many coincidences happening."

"Like what? The fact that we both ended up here in Virginia Beach?"

Alexis nodded. "For starters."

"Like I said before, you and Jamar are not that important to me," Nikki said, tapping her palms on the tabletop. "I was on my way back to New Orleans from a modeling job overseas. I had a layover in D.C., but when I found out about Gustav, I figured I would drive down here and lay on the beach for a few days, until it blew over."

Alexis nodded. "You never thought about getting back at Jamar for how things went down between you and Reggie? I mean, you did try to get Jamar to throw the case in your favor, and I don't know what I would do if I lost my son."

Nikki shook her head. "Yeah, but you don't have a son, do you?"

Alexis glared at her. "You really didn't need to go there. There are some things you just need to leave alone."

"Seriously, though, I thought about getting Jamar back for all of about ten seconds. Then I realized that being a single parent would have been hard with my modeling career. I travel way too much, and he would be at Reggie's house all the time, anyway. Now, don't get me wrong. I love the shit out of DeShawn. He is my heart. But I'm smart enough to know that the boy needs his daddy, and with my schedule picking up the way it did over the past year, I have to think things worked out for the best."

Alexis gave her a sideways glance. "How do I know you're being straight with me?"

Nikki rolled her eyes in return. "I might be a bitch, but I am not a liar. That's what makes me a good bitch. Like I said, you and Jamar are not worth my freedom."

A nervous twitch invaded Alexis's right eye. Nikki seemed to be telling the truth, but it didn't make her feel better. "If it's not you, who is it?"

"You really love your boy, huh?" Nikki asked, some of the hardness leaving her face. Could it be possible that she was showing some compassion?

Alexis nodded.

"How do you know it's just not him not taking care of his business? I know you love him, but I'm sure the man's not perfect."

"No, he's not. No one is. But he did take care of his money. This was something malicious."

Nikki turned her head and looked around the bar. She couldn't imagine being in this situation. Not even her days growing up in the Lower Ninth Ward of New Orleans could prepare her for having money one day and being broke the next. At least back then, they never had money. They'd learned to survive. But how did a couple learn to survive in just a matter of days? She kind of gave Alexis some credit for riding out this situation with Jamar. Nikki wasn't sure she could do it herself. She almost wanted to tell Alexis the real truth, but there was no way she would turn over on her cousin. Alexis was okay, but she was nowhere near a friend.

What were they called? Frenemies? That sounded right. Maybe.

Nikki, get it together, girl. She tried her best to stop squirming. Keeping the upper hand in this situation was paramount. *You're sittin' up here, lookin' guilty as shit. You didn't do anything, so stop acting like it.*

"So what makes you think it's malicious?" she asked after clearing her throat. "I know a thousand brothers who would say the same thing when their women caught them slippin' with their finances. You know how many deadbeat men are out there, trying to blame the system for their problems? It's sad."

"You think I don't know that?" Alexis snapped, tapping the table with her index and middle fingers. "Why do you think I've stayed single for as long as I have? But I'm telling you that this time is not the case. If you didn't do it, somebody did, and when Jamar finds them, they'll be lucky if he just stops at beating their ass."

A chill ran up Nikki's spine, and she tried not to show it. She didn't know Jamar well, but he never did strike her as a soft brother. Besides that, he was a lawyer. Who was to say he didn't know people who could figure out that her cousin Boo was behind this? Jamar could have Boo behind bars before he could even spell *credit*.

She toyed around with incriminating Andrea's sister, but that was risky, too. What if when she was caught, the first thing she did was bring Boo's name up? Then they'd both be in jail. Not to mention she could be thrown in jail since she didn't report this whole scheme when she found out about it.

God! How the hell did I get mixed up in this? All I wanted was a drama-free vacation! So much for that! she thought.

Nikki exhaled through her nose and picked up the menu again. Maybe snacking on something could mitigate the nerves she was beginning to feel. "You really think Saint Jamar would risk his law career just to get some catch-back? It doesn't make sense to me."

Alexis shook her head and cast her eyes downward. "You can't put anything past anyone if they get desperate enough."

Ain't that the damn truth? Nikki had seen it a million times and had nearly experienced it with Reggie during their divorce. Reggie would have done anything to have DeShawn. Had he lost the case, she was sure he would have continued fighting. That woman, Tina's sister, was desperate to get revenge on Alexis, so she was willing to play patty-cake with the law to do it. *Crazy bitch. Why can't people be more like me?* Nikki wondered. *I'm like Timex. I'm a sista who can take a lickin' and keep fuckin' tickin'. Life is too short for all this revenge shit.*

Nikki rolled her eyes and let her lids flutter for a second. This conversation needed to end now, before something wrong was said. She couldn't take any more of this pity party.

"Look, Alexis," she said, preparing to rise from the table, "I don't know what to tell you. I can assure you that I don't have shit to do with this, but I can't sit here all day and help you figure it out. I'm trying to get back home."

"Yeah, all right," Alexis said, gathering her purse. She stood up and faced Nikki, who stood at least a foot taller than Alexis, making her strain her neck a bit to look Nikki in the eyes.

Nikki let out an exasperated sigh. "What's on your mind, Alexis?"

"Nothing," she replied, backing away. "This is way too much on my plate, that's all."

"That's not it," Nikki replied, narrowing her eyes into slits. She refused to break their eye contact. "You're looking at me like you're not sure if you should believe me."

Alexis shrugged. "Guilty conscience?"

Nikki stepped forward, bringing her head so close to Alexis that some might have thought they were about to kiss. "I ain't got shit to feel guilty about. You ever think the shit going on with your man might be *your* fuckin' fault?"

"Excuse me?" Alexis asked, stepping back slightly.

Nikki shook her head and waved her hand at her frenemy. Actually, the way the last few minutes had gone, they might have devolved into just plain enemies.

"Don't worry about it. I'm just saying, before you go lookin' to the world to blame for your problems, you might need to look closer to home."

With that, she stepped around Alexis, leaving her standing in the middle of the restaurant, and stormed back up to her room. It was definitely time to go. Virginia Beach had brought nothing but drama since she'd stepped foot in the city.

Chapter 24

"What the hell did she mean when she said this shit with Jamar might be my fault?" Alexis mumbled as she strolled down Atlantic Avenue and back to her hotel. "There's no way in hell this could be my fault. I don't roll like that!"

People passing must have thought the woman wandering down the street, mumbling to herself, was out of her mind, but Alexis didn't care. She had more important things on her mind. Like who was dabbling in her man's finances? Like the nagging feeling that if Nikki wasn't personally involved, she might know who was. Like would they get home before she and Andrea killed each other? Like would anyone else blame her for their problems before this vacation from hell ended?

This was the kind of drama Alexis worked hard to avoid. She chose her friends carefully and was even more careful about those whom she let closest to her. Her circle included professionals. People who brought something to the table. Those who didn't require an explanation or a payday loan when they went out.

Some would say she was a snob, or at least stuck up, but it was a title she wore proudly. It saved a lot of headaches from people thinking they could approach her any kind of way. People, clients, and acquaintances alike knew if they didn't come correct, her words would cut worse than any knife ever could.

She felt she had to be that way, because she had learned long ago that kindness too many times was taken for weakness. She'd tried shedding the armor with Tony, but that ended badly. She'd tried shedding the armor when she first opened her practice, but the patients' parents tried to take advantage and were slow to pay.

Then there were the people with whom she'd never shed the armor. People like Nikki. If Nikki even smelled weakness, she was sure to pounce. She had nearly got to her today. By making that comment about the credit situation being Alexis's fault, she'd already shown that she was a shark. Well, Alexis refused to bleed and make it easy for her to bite.

"She was probably just shooting her mouth off to get me to stop asking her questions," she mumbled just as her cell phone rang. She pulled it from her pocket, knowing exactly who it was. "Hey, baby."

"Hey, you finished with your jog yet?" Jamar asked.

"Yeah, I'm walking back now."

"You've been gone a minute. Guess you caught a second *and* a third wind, huh?"

Alexis chuckled uneasily. She had gone for a jog, but she never let Jamar know about the pit stop she planned to take at Nikki's hotel. "Yeah, well, that and sitting on the beach for a while."

"Well, when are you headed back here? Your cousin wants you to call her."

"Brenda? Why didn't she call my cell?"

"I was talking to Darnell, actually, and she yelled out to tell you to call her." They laughed together.

"That sounds like Brenda," Alexis said.

"So you on your way back, or what?"

Alexis smiled slightly. "You're talking like you miss me or something."

"I do. Now, bring your ass home," Jamar ordered. "We need to make this plan for getting back home."

"Home sounds good to me," she replied while crossing the street.

A black Accord didn't appear to be slowing down, so her walk picked up to a trot just as the car screeched to a halt. Once she reached the other side, she shot the driver a dirty look.

"Baby, let me get off this phone before one of these no-driving-ass people kills me."

Jamar chuckled. "All right. I'll see you in a few."

Alexis hit END and continued walking. Getting home sure sounded like the million-dollar answer. She missed home. She missed her family. And as the ache traveled from her feet to her shins, she realized she missed her car. She had just finished running two miles and drinking two glasses of wine. Walking was not the next logical step.

She stopped near a restaurant and leaned against a parking meter. A group of men walked past as she flexed her foot back and forth to relieve the pain. One of the men, who looked to be the youngest of the crew, looked at the distressed woman and slowed his stroll to a shuffle.

"You want me to rub those for you, baby?" he asked with a smile.

His offer was met with a set of rolling eyes. "I don't think so," she replied.

"Ohhhh!" the group exclaimed.

The man flashed them an embarrassed smile and continued walking with his friends. Alexis didn't even bother looking back at him. To her, he was just one more reason she needed to get back home. Not that New Orleans didn't have its share of losers, but at least at home she had a better chance of avoiding them.

She continued her walk. As she drew closer to her resort, Nikki and her words popped into her mind again.
Why did what she said bother Alexis so much? It was
obvious that the two women didn't like each other, and
probably never would. It was only inevitable that one
would say something to piss the other off.

Yes, but why did the words nag at her so much?
Maybe because they were still no closer to figuring out
this mess, and Nikki's words did have a kernel of possibility to them. Maybe somebody really was trying to
get to her through Jamar. Maybe someone she knew in
the past. Heck, even Tony could be a suspect. He never
mentioned how he'd found out about her engagement.
Maybe he had known for months and was trying to
throw a monkey wrench in the plan.

How could she confront him about that without
looking like an accusing crazy woman, though? She'd
already tried on that persona with Nikki. There was no
way she could accuse anyone else without solid proof.
The situation was embarrassing enough.

Jamar would kill her if he knew she'd gone and
talked to Nikki. It was bad enough that *anyone* knew,
but now that Nikki knew what was going on, it would
just make matters worse. Maybe she should have just
let the banks handle it. The real culprit would be un-
covered soon enough.

However, that thought brought no additional comfort. She still had a bad feeling that Nikki was somewhere behind the scheme. But in order to put her
suspicions to rest, she'd have to let at least one more
person know what was going on. She just hoped she
could trust him as much as she thought she could.

***

"Yeah, we had a serious houseful after Katrina," Dale said with a laugh. "A few of them flew in from Houston. Y'all remember that boy who stole the school bus and drove a bunch of folks to Houston? Some of them were my people!"

Reggie hooted in laughter. He had heard about the boy with the stolen bus. He'd even seen him interviewed on the news, but he never thought he'd meet anyone connected with the infamous trip.

"We were scared the same thing might happen with Gustav, but it looked like they all stayed in Houston this time," Dale continued. "Thank God it wasn't as bad this time."

"Yeah, you right about that," Reggie agreed. "I think I'ma hit the road tomorrow and make sure my house is in order. I'm just glad I don't have to get a new house like I did the last time."

"That's good."

Shannon walked back into the living room and took a seat next to Dale. Reggie regarded them and smiled inwardly. This was his second visit with the couple since their dinner party. He was glad to have run into his college friends. However, seeing them made him wistful about not having the happiness that they seemed to share. It seemed that they had everything he'd sought to have. Dale had married his college sweetheart, had two kids, and still managed to be successful in his career. On the other hand, Reggie had the child and the career, but he would never be with his college sweetheart. And judging from the way things were going, he'd never have a second chance at marriage.

He and Janet hadn't said two words to each other since their fight yesterday. After the fight, he took DeShawn over to Dale and Shannon's dinner party. They'd gotten back so late that Janet was already asleep. The next morning Shirley fixed everyone breakfast and was so caught up in talking about Reggie's impending trip home, she never noticed that he and Janet spoke to her but never to each other.

He hadn't taken the time to look for a plane ticket for Janet, but he would make sure to do it as soon as he got back home. There was no use prolonging the issue. He and Janet were over. It wouldn't be fair to any of them, especially DeShawn, to keep pretending. He would just have to get used to being alone for a while. It was nothing new. He'd been there before.

Only now, he was staring in the face of what he could have had. If only he were ready to take that step, he was sure Janet could give it to him. Still, you couldn't force what was not there. If she could just be patient, he was sure it would come.

"You all right?" Shannon asked, clapping her palms together. Reggie blinked a few times and turned toward her. "You look like you're lost in space."

He chuckled a bit. "I'm fine. I just got caught up thinking about something."

"Man, don't be zoning out over here," Dale said with a laugh. "I ain't seen this man since Moses was a baby, and now when we finally get to catch up, he wants to have his own party in his head. The least you coulda done was invite us."

"Man, go 'head on with that," Reggie replied, playfully waving his friend off.

Before he could say anything else, however, his cell phone rang. He picked it up from the coffee table and excused himself before answering. "What's going on, lady?" he asked, rising from the couch. He walked out to the front porch just as Dale made another comment about his "private party."

"Hey," Alexis greeted. "You busy?"

"Not if you really need to talk," he replied, sitting on the front step. "You all right? You sound like something's on your mind."

"Is it that obvious?"

"What's up?"

"I might as well get right to the point. I don't have much time."

Reggie stiffened. "This doesn't sound good. What's going on? That nigga Jamar do something to you?"

"No, no, it's nothing like that," Alexis said quickly. "Calm down, man."

"Calm down? You're the one calling me all mysterious, sounding like somebody's looking for you or something. What was I supposed to think?"

She sighed. "You're right. I'm sorry. I just need to ask you something about Nikki."

"Nikki? Did something happen between you two? I told your ass to be careful with her."

"I know," she replied, frustration in her voice. "What did you mean by that? Is she dangerous?"

"That depends on what you mean," Reggie said, leaning back. A picture of his ex-wife popped into his mind. What could be going on in Virginia Beach that would make Alexis call him like this? "She wouldn't kill anybody, but she's not one who goes down easily."

"What does that mean?"

"I'm saying, things don't just happen to Nikki. She doesn't lie down and die for anybody or anything."

"So she doesn't just drop things," Alexis surmised. "Revenge isn't far from the imagination for her."

Reggie shrugged. "She never tried to get back at me for losing DeShawn. Come to think of it, in the eleven years we were married, I don't ever remember her trying to get revenge on anybody."

"I see."

"Why do you ask? Did something happen between you two?"

"Not exactly," she said. She took another deep breath. "Do you think she would start shit with people just to be doing it?"

Reggie rolled his eyes upward and shook his head. Why couldn't she just come out with whatever she was trying to say? "Alexis, I'm spending time with some friends from college. I only interrupted our visit because I thought you had something important to say. Now, you either need to tell me what's on your mind, or let me go back inside with my people."

"Reggie, this isn't the easiest thing for me to come out and talk about."

"Then call me back when you're ready to talk about it!" he snapped. "I've got my own problems to deal with right now."

"What problems?"

"Oh, so now you care about what I'm going through?"

"What's up with the attitude all of a sudden?"

"I told you. I'm chillin' with my boy from school, and you're beatin' around the bush about something that has to do with my ex-wife. Just spit it out."

"Okay, okay," Alexis said, relenting. A few more seconds of silence came through the line. Reggie was just about to hang up when she finally spoke up. "Somebody's been playing in Jamar's credit, and I think Nikki has something to do with it."

"What!" he exclaimed, contorting his face in shock. "What would make you think Nikki would have anything to do with that?"

"You think it was just a coincidence that she showed up here the same time we did? You said yourself to be careful when you found out she was here."

"I said that because I know you two don't like each other. You two would probably get into it, curse each other out, and say some shit you don't need to be saying. The woman may not be the friendliest person in the world and may be a bit shady sometimes, but she's not a criminal."

"That's pretty much what she told me when I talked to her a while ago," Alexis mumbled.

Reggie took the phone from his ear and stared at it. Had he just heard her right? He scrunched his eyebrows in confusion as he brought the phone back to his ear. "You talked to Nikki about this?"

"Of course I did. I'm trying to get to the bottom of this."

"I understand that, but you mighta just made matters worse. You know that woman doesn't like you. And I'll bet your boy doesn't know you talked to her." Her silence confirmed his suspicions. "How do you know she won't use that shit against you? And what if she doesn't? Now you've just told your man's business to at least two people who don't have shit to do with this."

"I know what you're saying, Reggie, but that's the risk I have to take. This credit situation has taken a helluva toll on us, this so-called vacation, and our trip home."

"How bad is the situation?"

"All three of his credit cards were closed, and there's a freeze on his bank account."

"Damn," he remarked, rubbing the back of his head. "When y'all plan on going back to New Orleans? Do y'all need anything?"

"That's nice of you, Reg, but you know Jamar is not gonna take any money from you."

"I'm not giving him any money. I'm giving it to you. I can wire it to your account, and he never has to find out about it."

More silence, which meant only one thing: Alexis was considering the offer. He understood her dilemma. What man wanted to know that his woman's ex-man was supporting her financially? For that matter, what man wanted his woman trying to solve his problems? Alexis was definitely going about all of this the wrong way, but he had to hand it to her. She was down for her man. If Nikki had had that same attitude about him, they might still be together.

"Reg, how much longer you gonna be?" Shannon asked, sticking her head out the front door. "I can't listen to Dale cussing you out any longer."

Reggie laughed and turned to his college friend. "Tell him I'm coming. I had to put out a fire for Alexis."

"Alexis? That's her on the phone?" Shannon asked. She came all the way out of the house and stood over him.

"Yeah, it's her."

"Who you tellin' my business to?" Alexis asked, some of the attitude coming back to her voice.

"Girl, relax," Reggie told her. "You remember Shannon and Dale from Tulane? We went out with them a few times."

"Yeah, I remember them," she said. "That's whose house you're at? You shoulda said so!"

"You wanna say hi? I'm about to go back inside and chill with Dale."

"Yeah, sure," she replied. "And, Reg?"

"Yeah?"

"Thanks for listening to me. This credit thing hasn't been easy for us, but I appreciate you offering to help. I still have money. We'll get back home okay."

"Anytime, babe," he replied. "Here's Shannon." He stood up and handed his cell to Shannon.

"Hey, girl!" Shannon shouted in a high-pitched voice. Reggie smiled as he closed the door behind him.

Chapter 25

"All right, Shannon," Alexis said, sliding the key into the lock to her hotel suite. She walked into the living room and looked around. Jamar was nowhere to be found, but she could hear movement coming from the bedroom. "It was good catching up with you. We've gotta make sure we stay in touch."

"It was good talking with you, too, girl," Shannon replied. "Y'all get back home safely."

"We will. Talk to you later."

Alexis pushed END on her phone and walked into the bedroom. Jamar sat on the bed, folding a pair of jeans. He looked up at Alexis, rolled his eyes, and grabbed a T-shirt from the pile sitting in the middle of the bed.

"You all right?" Alexis asked, sitting next to him.

He grunted and continued folding. She scrunched her eyebrows and set her phone and wallet on the bed, next to the pile of clothes.

"What's wrong with you?"

Jamar cut his eyes at her, stood up, grabbed a suitcase from the closet, and tossed it on the bed.

"You're packing already? When you talkin' about leaving?"

He rolled his eyes upward and pursed his lips. "If you woulda bothered coming up here, instead of tellin' all my business in the middle of the hotel lobby, you'd know when we were leaving."

Had she heard him correctly? How did he know she was in the lobby? Her eyes darted back and forth in a silent panic. *Calm down, Lex. You don't know what he actually heard.* She swallowed her panic and faced the inevitable.

"What are you talking about?"

Jamar stopped packing and glared at her. "Don't play stupid with me, Alexis. You're too damn smart for that."

"I was just trying to help, Jamar," she said, holding her head in her hands.

"Yeah, well, you need to think sometimes," he said. Placing clothing into a suitcase quickly turned into violently tossing them in. He stopped when he realized what he was doing, and stormed away from the bed. He almost left the room, but instead, he leaned his forehead against the wall next to the bathroom. A frustrated punch to the wall resonated throughout the room. "You don't know who could be listening while you're reportin' my business all over the world. If I could walk up behind you and hear everything you're saying, Lord knows who else could. And to your fuckin' ex-boyfriend?"

Damn, how long was he standing behind me? Ain't no sweet-talking my way out of this one. "Look, Reggie, you were convinced that Nikki was behind this and were ready to beat her ass. I needed to find out if you were right before you got your ass arrested."

Jamar snapped his head at Alexis and punched the wall again. "First of all, I can take care of myself. I didn't come this far in my career to get pulled down by some vindictive bitch. Second of all, my fuckin' name is Jamar. Reggie is the nigga that you just told I was broke!"

Alexis gasped and turned her head in embarrassment. She hadn't even heard herself make the faux pas. Now he would think there was something going on between her and Reggie, which couldn't be any further from the truth. Still, who could blame him? *Dumb move, Alexis.*

"Do you even respect me at all?" Jamar demanded.

She maintained eye contact, refusing to lose her confidence. She might have been wrong, but he needed to know that what she did was for the right reasons. "Of course, I do."

"Obviously, you don't. I told you from the jump to let me handle this, and you insist on trying to handle my business for me. I never realized how much you run your fuckin' mouth! This is the second time this week you've shot your damn mouth off about something that's not your business!"

"Not my business?" Alexis challenged, shooting from her seat. She charged toward him in two seconds flat. "How do you figure your finances are not my business? I'm about to be your wife, so when it affects you, it affects us both! Maybe if you were a man about your shit and told me about this when it first started, it might not have gone this far."

"Oh, so I'm not a man now?"

None of the venom left his eyes. The vein between his eyes bulged so far that it nearly touched Alexis's forehead. Both of them refused to back down. Both were wrong, but both were right in their own eyes. Both were strong, refusing to show weakness.

"I hate you so much sometimes," Alexis hissed.

"I'm not your number one fan at this present moment, either," Jamar countered, matching her tone.

Alexis walked away, turning her back toward him. "You know, as long as we're putting everything out there, you might as well know I talked to Nikki this morning."

"Why doesn't that shit surprise me?"

"You're lucky I did," she replied, turning to face him. "I don't think she has anything to do with this. And for your information, that's why I called Reggie. If anyone would know if she's capable of doing something like this, he would. I needed to make sure."

Jamar scoffed, "Did you really think she would say, 'Why yes, Alexis, I've been playing with your man's money'?"

"No, but she did make a couple of comments that stuck with me."

He walked back to his suitcase and began rearranging the clothes he'd slung in there only moments ago. "What was that?"

She started to help with the clothes but stopped, not sure if she was done being angry yet. Instead, she leaned against the wall and folded her arms. "She said that she might be a bitch, but she's not a criminal."

Jamar laughed. "She said that?"

"Yep. She also said you and I aren't that important to her for her to commit credit fraud. She said she's actually happy with the way things turned out after the divorce."

His eyebrows rose, as if he were considering the information Alexis had just given him. His tongue poked against his cheek, causing a moving bump, and then he concentrated again on his suitcase. "That doesn't prove much to me. She could still be the one."

"I figured the same thing, which is why I called Reggie," she said. She swallowed, reminding herself not to mention the money offer. No need to add fuel to a smoldering fire. "He pretty much confirmed what she said. And you'll be happy to know that Reggie agrees with you that I shouldn't have talked to him or Nikki about this."

Jamar grunted again. "Guess that's one thing we have in common."

"Whatever."

He exhaled deeply as he closed his freshly packed suitcase. "Look, Alexis. I love you, but there can't be two men in this relationship. When I tell you to let me handle my business, I need you to let me do that. It's not just about protecting my ego. I refuse to be that man who lets his woman fight his battles. I have a mind. Now, let me use it."

"I hear you, but like I said the other day, let me walk with you. We're not in the Dark Ages. You don't need to leave me at home while you go hunting for food. Just like you have a mind, I have one, too."

"Then work with me. Don't sneak around me!" Jamar pleaded, holding his hands over his chest.

"You need to follow your own advice," Alexis pointed out. "You've been sneaking around me ever since you found out about this situation. Is this how it's gonna be?"

"How what's going to be?"

"Every time you get caught in an uncomfortable situation, you're going to hide things from me?"

"Are you going to sneak behind my back and try to handle my business for me when things aren't going your way?"

Once again, they were at a standoff. Who would back down? They silently walked away from each other, Alexis retreating to the living room and Jamar remaining in the bedroom. Of all the cases Jamar had won and lost in his career, his toughest opponent would be his future wife. Arguing your point was a lot easier when emotions weren't involved.

Silence became a wet blanket, forcing them to wrap themselves in tension. Alexis narrowed her eyes into slits as she watched Jamar walk back and forth in the bedroom. *Does he really think he's going to make me feel guilty? I don't think so.*

She lay on the sofa and continued watching him, but her eyes quickly averted when he walked past her into the kitchen. She listened as he opened and closed cabinets and the refrigerator, probably getting something to drink. A beer, most likely. She heard no footsteps for a while, making Alexis presume that he was standing there watching her, probably with disgust on his face. Finally, the footsteps began. Alexis peeked from the corner of her eye just in time to see Jamar return to the bedroom.

"I hate him," she mumbled quietly as her eyelids grew heavier. "Instead of condemning me, he should be thanking me."

She yawned, comforted by the feeling that she might be right in some of this mess. She needed to be right. Yes, she might have been wrong for talking to Reggie and Nikki without Jamar knowing, but she couldn't apologize for supporting her man. Isn't that what a wife was supposed to do?

The phone rang, snatching Alexis from her nap. She jumped up, momentarily forgetting where she was. A glance at the clock told her that two hours had passed since she'd lain on the sofa. As she rubbed her eyes, she could just make out Jamar's voice talking to the caller.

"She's asleep right now, but it looks like we're gonna leave tonight."

How does he know I'm ready to leave? Talking about me doing stuff on my own, and look at him.

"Yeah, I guess we can do that. You sure it's gonna be cool? We really don't need no more drama after today. . . . It's a long story."

Do what? He's just a decision-making machine right now!

Alexis presumed the caller was either Darnell or Brenda. *Oh, yeah! I was supposed to call her earlier. Foolin' around with Jamar's ass, I forgot. Speaking of calling, I haven't talked to Mommy and Frank since we got here.*

"Brenda and Andrea cool? . . . That's good."

I guess they're speaking again. I knew it wouldn't take long.

Alexis rose and trudged into the bedroom. Jamar looked up and turned back to the phone. *I guess he's still trippin'.*

"Who's on the phone?" she asked absently while walking into the bathroom. She stared into the mirror and began taming her wild hair.

"Darnell," Jamar replied. "He wants us to stop by before we get on the road tonight."

"When did we decide to leave tonight?" she asked.

"This morning, while you were out *jogging*."

She cut her eyes at him and sucked her teeth. *Damn, I hate him sometimes.*

"All right, bruh, we'll see you around nine," Jamar said into the receiver. "Lemme get some sleep, and I'll holla at you later."

Alexis felt a presence with her as she brushed her hair. Jamar stood in the doorway. She glanced at him and continued brushing.

"We're leaving tonight because the mayor has given us the go-ahead to go back home," he explained.

"Won't that same go-ahead still be open tomorrow?"

"Yes, but I wanted to devote most of tomorrow to driving and the next day to getting our house back in order," he replied. "I also need to get back to the office and check on a few things. I figured you would want to get back to check on your practice, too."

She nodded. His plan made sense. Still, she wished she could have been in on the planning process, but apparently, she was talking to Nikki when the decision had been made. Had she done what she told him she would do, which was jog and come right back, she would have been there to talk it over.

"Besides, the traffic will probably be better driving at night than in the middle of the day," Jamar continued. "With tomorrow being a workday, we're going to hit rush-hour traffic."

"True," Alexis mumbled. "I guess I'd better start packing."

"I took care of that while you were sleeping. You just need to get your beauty stuff together."

"You just took care of everything, didn't you?" Alexis commented, raising her eyebrows.

"That's what a man is supposed to do," he replied, walking out of the bathroom.

She followed him out and found him sitting on the edge of the bed. "You gonna get some sleep?"

"Yeah, in a few. You wanna order something to eat? We still have a few hours before we have to get out of here."

Alexis stood in the middle of the room and looked around. Jamar had definitely taken care of everything. There was nothing to do except shower, get some food, and maybe get some more sleep before they pulled out.

"You want a pizza or something?" she asked, fingering the phone.

"Sounds good," he replied absently.

Must be dozing off already.

Well, they didn't succeed in keeping this vacation drama free as they had planned, but they did learn a lot more about each other. Maybe if they swallowed their pride a bit, they might even venture to say that what they learned might have brought them closer together. Or torn them further apart. She'd find out soon. They had at least nineteen hours to decide.

Chapter 26

What a difference a day made.

Life in the Lee household had grown immensely lighter over the last twenty-four hours. Since Andrea had made up with both her husband and her best friend, laughter once again became a welcomed guest.

This was what made Andrea and Brenda's relationship so special. It wasn't the first time they'd stopped speaking, and it probably wouldn't be the last. Each time they renewed their friendship, though, it was like nothing had ever happened. After a long, difficult conversation, they would hug, forgive, and move on. If only every relationship could be so simple.

Andrea was sure—in fact, she'd seen them—there were relationships that had been destroyed over less than misspoken words. She'd even seen her friend Dominique stop speaking to a friend because she felt her friend hadn't acknowledged her when they saw each other in the mall. That was five years ago, and they still weren't speaking!

That would never be the case with Andrea and Brenda. They'd come too far and gone through too much to end an almost three-decade-long friendship. With so much history between them, forgiveness sometimes came easier in their friendship than it did in their marriages.

Thank God forgiveness finally came in Andrea's relationship. Seeing the damage this one had caused, she vowed never to hold another secret like this from Christopher. Well, except for the big one she shared with her sister, Tina. No one could ever know about that one. That secret coming to light could mean not only losing her marriage and her friendship, but her life and career.

Then again, she was not the one who actually went through with the scam. All she did was wonder out loud. Whoever Tina had talked to was the one who did the crime. She didn't know who he was, and she didn't want to know. In fact, the less she knew, the less she could be incriminated.

She wished she could have seen Alexis's face when she found out about Jamar's credit problem. Maybe now she would know what it was like to have problems. To have life kick her square in the ass. If things went as planned, that pretty little wedding dress would be the last expensive item she would own for a long time.

What gave Alexis the right to live such a charmed life? All through her childhood, her pretty, exotic looks got her anything she wanted. She just had to bat her eye, and boys would give her their candy, carry her books, or walk her to class. In college, every guy she dated had the potential to go far in life. Other guys wanted her, but if they didn't have a few dollars in their pockets, she wouldn't give them the time of day. Didn't they know she was nothing more than a slut? Nothing more than a little girl trying to play in a big girl's world? A child willing to break up a marriage just to get her rocks off for a few days? And just when she was about to pay for her sins, she went and had an abortion, then continued on with her charmed life like nothing had ever happened!

Oh yeah, she needed to feel hardship. She needed to know how life felt with an imperfect man. Jamar might have the looks and the career, but would she really be happy with a man who couldn't pay his bills and give her the life she felt she deserved? Andrea wished Alexis hadn't have found out about the credit situation until after she married Jamar. However, being stuck in an unfamiliar city during a major natural disaster seemed to be yielding the desired results.

The doorbell rang, reminding Andrea that she would get to look in the face of Alexis's depression one last time. That was probably her at the door, coming to say good-bye to her family. Come to think of it, that was even more evidence that Alexis was a selfish bitch. She had been there all those days and hadn't bothered once to come see her little cousin. Little Elizabeth had asked about her every day, and all she'd gotten in return were a couple of dry phone calls. And now she'd get a rushed visit before Alexis carried her tail back to New Orleans. Pitiful!

Andrea flushed the toilet and turned on the faucet to wash her hands. As the water ran, making a low rushing noise as it hit the sink, she stared into the mirror. How had she let anger bring her this low? Yet, as much as she wondered, not a drop of guilt entered her mind. If she was never sure before, she knew it now: she hated Alexis and didn't give a damn what happened to her. The treacherous bitch deserved whatever she got as a result of this manufactured situation.

A knock at the door interrupted her thoughts.

"Just a minute!" she called. She hurriedly rinsed her hands and dried them on the hand towel hanging above the sink.

"Hey, girl," Brenda said through the door. "Just wanted to let you know the pizza's here."

Andrea winced. Guessed she would have to wait a little longer for her satisfaction. "Okay, I'll be out in a minute."

"You all right in there?"

"I'm good. I'll be out in a minute," she repeated. *Dag! Why do people always ask that when a person takes longer than two minutes in the bathroom? It's like a woman can't get any privacy in her own house.*

"Well, hurry up, before the pizza gets cold!" Brenda shouted, beating on the door.

"I'm coming!" Andrea yelled back, laughing in spite of the hate that still swirled around in her chest. How could she love one person so much and hate her family member just as much?

She took one more look in the mirror and ran her fingers through her ear-length hair. She loved her short haircut, but she needed a change. Maybe she'd get some highlights that weekend.

She left the bathroom and skipped down the steps, her mouth already watering for a slice of the Hawaiian pizza she'd ordered.

"Y'all better not have touched my—"

"Hey, Andrea," Jamar greeted.

He stood over Alexis while she sat on the love seat and hugged Elizabeth. Darnell and Brenda sat across from them on the sofa, smiling like they were posing for some kind of family photo. And Christopher! You'd think he would have warned her that Alexis was there.

When did those two get here? And why are they sitting in my living room, instead of standing on the porch like they were supposed to? She walked up to Brenda and whispered just that in her friend's ear.

Brenda turned to her and pursed her lips. "Girl, it's about to rain outside. I'm not sending my child out in that kind of weather."

Alexis must have picked up on the tension. "Don't worry, Andrea. We won't be here long. We just couldn't leave without saying good-bye to my family."

Andrea nodded, but before she could say anything, Brenda broke in and told them to be safe on the road.

"We will," Jamar said. "We both got plenty of sleep and had a pizza earlier. I'll grab a Red Bull on the road if I get too tired."

Pizza? Why do we seem to like the same things? I swear, sometimes I think that woman spies on me. "When did you guys get here?" Andrea asked.

"We walked up right when the pizza guy was about to pull off," Jamar explained. He looked around the room. "You have a really nice house."

"Thank you," Andrea replied tersely, taking a seat next to Brenda. She glanced at her daughter, Latrise, who sat quietly on the floor, waiting for her friend's family reunion to end. *She is so lucky these kids are in the room,* Andrea thought. Christopher walked over and rubbed her shoulder. She knew the gesture well. It meant, "Be cool. It's going to be fine."

"Y'all got everything you need for the road?" Darnell asked cautiously.

"That's what I meant to tell you, bruh," Jamar said, turning toward his friend. "You're never gonna believe this."

"I know *I* didn't," Alexis chimed in.

"Hey, Lizzie, why don't you and Latrise run upstairs and let us talk for a minute," Brenda suggested.

"Yeah, I'll call you before we leave," Alexis assured the girl.

Without any argument or hesitation, both girls jumped up and ran upstairs. Once she was sure the kids were safely out of earshot, Brenda prompted Jamar to continue.

"It was the strangest thing," he said, looking off into space as if picturing the event. "We went to check out of the hotel. I had already paid for the room up front when my credit cards started acting up when we first got here. However, when we got ready to check out, I got another invoice for some phone calls we had made."

"Uh-oh," Darnell said.

Andrea put her head down and smirked slightly. This plan just kept getting better. She only hoped no one else would notice her private celebration.

"No, it was cool," Jamar said, holding up his hand. "I had the cash in my pocket. So, when dude asked if I wanted him to charge the calls to the same credit card, I was like, 'Hell naw!'"

The men roared in laughter. *I guess all men know what it's like to be broke at one time or another,* Andrea thought. She rose from the sofa and walked into the kitchen. She could still hear Jamar's story as she searched the cabinets for a snack.

"Only problem was, I was depending on every dollar in my pocket to get us back on the road," Jamar continued. "The money the firm broke me off with the other day wasn't gonna last forever. Hell, we'd spent half of that already."

"So what happened?" Brenda asked.

"Well, I was pissed. I was like, 'What else can happen?' I put the little bit of money I had left back in my wallet, and for some reason, my ATM card caught my attention."

Andrea stood silently in the kitchen, waiting to see what would happen next. She even slowed her chewing of the Doritos she was snacking on so she could hear better.

The doorbell rang before Jamar could continue with the story.

"I got it," Andrea announced dryly as she trudged to the door. *Let them sit like fools, acting like they're listening to the greatest story ever told. I have better things to do.* She looked through the peephole and laid eyes on her brother-in-law for the first time in days.

"Chris, Byron's here," she announced, more to interrupt the story than to share information. Then, on second thought, she realized that the faster Jamar got his little tale out, the faster he and his little hooker would be on the road.

She opened the door and almost hugged Byron out of instinct but thought better of it. Byron seemed to feel the hesitation, too.

"What's up, Dee?" he asked, stepping into the house.

The rain had started, but it stayed at a steady drizzle. Byron's jacket glistened with raindrops as he slid it off and dropped it near the door. His hands dug deeply into his oversize jean pockets. His black T-shirt seemed to just hang. He looked dejected. This was not the Byron that Andrea knew and loved.

"Not much. You all right?"

"Oh, I'm cool. Chillin'," he replied, looking into the living room. He furrowed his eyebrows when he saw Alexis and Jamar. He leaned closer to Andrea. "When did they get here?"

She pursed her lips and shook her head. "Don't even ask. They won't be here long. Join the party."

He walked into the living room and greeted everyone but didn't bother to hide his irritation at seeing Alexis. The glare in his eyes only intensified as he stared at her when he sat down. Andrea walked back into the room and leaned against the wall, continuing to snack on her chips.

"You all right, bruh?" Christopher asked.

"Not really, but I'll live," Byron replied, his eyes never leaving Alexis.

Andrea smirked again when she saw Alexis squirm. *Leave it to Byron to knock that swagger right out of her.*

"Rayna giving you problems?" Darnell asked.

Byron finally unlocked his gaze and looked around at everyone in the room. "Yeah, but it's not about me right now. Y'all were obviously in the middle of a conversation."

"Um," Jamar stammered. He rubbed Alexis's knee. "It can wait, man. In fact, we're not gonna be here that long, anyway."

"Oh, don't rush off now," Andrea said quickly. She popped a chip in her mouth to try and hide her glee. "Y'all were just about to tell us what happened with your credit situation."

Alexis turned to Andrea and tried to peel off Andrea's skin with her eyes. "Like you really care."

"I do care," Andrea protested. "We might not get along, but I don't wanna see you two hit the road tonight broke."

Byron turned to Jamar. "Y'all leavin' tonight? That shit get fixed?"

"We're good." Jamar had gone from animated to stoic in about sixty seconds. The way he held on to Alexis's leg reminded Andrea of an animal protecting its young. His eyes stayed fixed on Byron, as if awaiting any sudden moves. Did he really think Byron would put his hands on a woman?

"So the credit thing is good?" Byron asked, oblivious to the tension. It was like he didn't notice that everyone in the room was staring at him.

"Can y'all stop it, please?" Brenda demanded, holding her hands out to her sides. "Everybody's staring at each other like we're a bunch of strangers. Please don't bring that negativity back in the atmosphere."

"I knew it was only a matter of time before she said something. Still, my baby is right," Darnell agreed. "We've been good all this time, and now y'all wanna start trippin'."

"Real talk, Darnell," Byron said. "Y'all mighta been good, but because of your future cousin's mouth, I've been fightin' off a crazy bitch for the last two days."

Andrea kept her spot on the wall and just watched the show. She had already said what she had to say days ago, and had promised Christopher that she wouldn't start anything tonight. She caught a glimpse of her husband giving her the stink eye, warning her to keep her mouth shut.

"Now, Byron, I agree that things went down bad, but judging from the events of the past couple of days, I think Alexis did you a favor," Darnell said. "What would have happened if you had married her before the real Rayna came out? She just saved you thousands in wedding, divorce, and possibly hospital bills!"

Brenda and Christopher snorted, each trying to hold in their laughs. The attempted light moment only enraged Byron.

"I don't see shit funny!" he shouted, leaning forward. "In a matter of days, I lost my woman, almost lost my brother again, and my apartment still looks like fuckin' Katrina hit it! This isn't a game to me. This is my life!"

"Byron, I'm sorry that happened," Alexis said. "I didn't mean for Rayna to go off like that. I wasn't even thinking about her."

"You never mean for bad shit to happen, do you, Lexy?" Byron asked, scrunching his nose. "You fucked my brother, but you didn't mean to get pregnant. You blew back in town, but you didn't expect to bring drama. You shot your fuckin' mouth off, but you didn't expect to run my woman off!"

"Byron!" Brenda shrieked.

"Byron, first of all, you need to calm down," Jamar said, his hand now squeezing Alexis's thigh. The grip must have been painful, because Andrea could just see Alexis tap his hand. He loosened his grip and rubbed the area. "I understand you're mad, but I won't have you cursin' at my girl like that."

"Well, once *your girl* carries her ass on out of here, you won't have to worry about me talking to her *any* kinda way," Byron thundered.

Alexis stood up and gathered her purse. "Baby, let's go before I say something I don't need to say."

"Naw, Lexy," Byron chided. "You've been talkin' all this time. Say what's on your mind."

"Byron, man," Christopher whispered, "calm down. That's enough."

"Come on," Darnell coaxed, pulling Byron's arm. "Let's go outside and calm down."

Byron snatched his arm away and pointed at Alexis's nose. "If anybody's goin' outside, it's that bitch right there!"

Alexis surprisingly, at least from Andrea's point of view, kept her cool. She crossed her arms and stood her ground. *This is gettin' good,* Andrea thought. *I'm glad I invited him over here.*

"Byron, you can get your finger out of my face," she stated calmly.

"Or what?" he challenged, while Darnell and Christopher grabbed at his shoulders to keep him from walking up on the smaller woman. "What the hell you gonna do?"

Jamar grabbed his fiancée's arm and violently jerked her away from the crazed man in front of her. "She ain't gonna do shit, because I'ma kick your muthafuckin' ass myself if you get in her face again!"

"Oh, so you're Captain Save-a-Ho now?"

"Bitch-ass nigga, I will wear your ass out!" Jamar growled.

Everyone in the room begged Byron to calm down. Everyone except Andrea, that is. She'd finally stopped eating the Doritos, but she refused to get involved. Brenda was worrying enough for both of them. Instead, she stayed near the wall and tried to look worried, all the while laughing inside as she watched Christopher hold back Byron, and Darnell push back Jamar. *See what happens when you mess with the Lees?*

"You two need to quiet down," Brenda pleaded. "The girls are right upstairs. Do you want them to hear you?"

"Yeah, baby, let's just go," Alexis said, pulling Jamar by his arm toward the front door. "This shit isn't worth it. We don't ever have to see these two again in life."

"That's the smartest fuckin' statement you said in your life!" Byron snapped. He shook himself away from his brother and walked away.

"Bruh!" Jamar exclaimed, following his enemy to the dining room. "I told you before. I will not have you talkin' sideways to my woman!"

"Then get the fuck out, and I won't have to!" Byron roared. When he whipped around, his swinging arm nipped Jamar near his shoulder. "Motherfucker," he said in barely a whisper.

Jamar drew back his fist and was just about to swing, when a young, shrill voice screamed, "Stop!"

Everyone looked around at both girls, who stood on the steps with tear-streaked faces, fresh drops still streaming.

"Cousin Jamar, please don't hit him," Elizabeth pleaded, running toward the men. She wrapped her little hands around Jamar's waist and wept.

"Why are you fighting with my uncle?" Latrise asked, holding her position on the steps.

Jamar dropped his fist and looked down at Elizabeth. Andrea hoped he was embarrassed. She set down the chips on the kitchen counter and went to comfort Latrise. Christopher followed close behind.

"I told y'all to chill out with all that!" Brenda scolded, gently pulling her daughter from Jamar's waist. Darnell started to go to them, but Brenda held up her hand, as if to say, "I got this." Jamar rolled his eyes and sulked to the kitchen doorway. "Y'all satisfied now? My child doesn't need to see this."

"Neither does mine," Andrea added as she sat on the steps. "All this fighting and cursing really isn't called for."

"Well, shit, Dee, what the hell did you think would happen when you told me to come over here? Were we supposed to hold hands and sing 'Kumbaya'?" Byron muttered.

"No, but you weren't supposed to turn my house into a fuckin' war zone, either," Andrea snapped.

"Wait a minute," Christopher stated. He looked over at his wife, who was still comforting Latrise. "You told Byron to come over here?"

Andrea's eyes bucked open as she looked around nervously. "Yeah. So? Your brother's not welcome here anymore?"

"Don't play that with me, Dee. My brother is always welcome in this house, but why would you invite him over at the same time you knew Alexis would be here?" He looked up at Byron, who sat angrily at the dining room table. "And why would you come over here?"

"I'm more welcome here than that b—, uh, chick," Byron shouted. "Every time she comes to town, something pops off."

"I'm gonna need y'all to watch your language around my child," Darnell said.

"And you have one more time to call me out of my name, Byron," Alexis snapped. "Now, I already apologized to you, and if it will make you feel better, Andrea, I apologize to you, too, for everything that's happened in the past. But I can't kill myself, and I refuse to go into a depression just to appease you two. I regret what happened. Still, life goes on. And, Andrea, next time you want to fight a battle, do it yourself instead of trying to get your little brother to come after me."

Andrea breathed in deeply through her nose and exhaled through her mouth, struggling to keep her composure. Her face became so hot that Latrise began to scoot away nervously.

"Mommy?"

Andrea didn't bother replying. Instead, she just stared at Alexis, every bit of hatred she had ever felt for anyone hitting her in waves.

"Mommy!" the little girl called again, this time tapping her on the arm. The taps stung, but the bite was nothing like the pain of everything she felt when she first learned that Christopher had cheated on her. She began to feel like a piece of seaweed on a seashore. Every time she got out of the water and safely on land, the tide would come and pull her right back. She would never be able to get over this. Life just wouldn't let her.

"Dee, you all right?"

She thought that was Christopher speaking to her, but she was so transfixed on Alexis, her neck refused to turn so she could acknowledge him.

"This chick done gone crazy," she heard Alexis say. "Jamar, let's go ahead and get out of here. Brenda, I'll call you when we get there." Alexis then looked down at Elizabeth and smiled. "Can I get a hug, li'l bit?"

The girl silently got up from her mother's lap and hugged Alexis. "I'll miss you."

"I'll see you in a few days," Alexis assured her. "We'll have a girls' day out."

"Promise?"

"Of course! You know your big cousin always keeps her word."

"Pshhh," Byron mumbled. "This bitch here."

"All right," Jamar said, walking toward Byron. "I told you, and my girl told you. Now I'm 'bout to beat your ass. As much as I love my little cousin, I'm not about to let you keep disrespecting Alexis in front of these kids. How would you like it if I called your momma a bitch?"

Byron glared at him. "You best keep my mom outta this."

"Yeah, Jamar," Christopher agreed. "You're about to step over the line."

"And he didn't?" Jamar pleaded, pointing at Byron. "He's been calling my woman out of her name all night, but I'm supposed to smile and take it?"

"Just leave, and you won't have to worry about crossing any lines!" Andrea shouted, popping up from the steps. "Brenda, girl, I tried, but I can't take it anymore. Your cousin needs to get the hell out of this house before I toss her out!"

"What did my cousin do to you?" Brenda snapped. "She did what you wanted. She apologized. She's trying to respect your house. What do you want now? Blood?"

"That sounds like a good idea!" Andrea remarked, charging in the kitchen.

"What the hell are you doing?" Christopher asked, but his answer came faster than he thought it would when he saw his wife coming back toward him with a steak knife.

"Andrea, have you lost your mind?" Brenda screamed. She pushed Alexis and Jamar toward the door. "Kids, go back upstairs! Now!"

The girls started to comply, but it seemed as if a force kept them planted to the bottom step. Tears of fright streamed down both their faces.

"I told you that bitch was crazy," Alexis mumbled as turned to the door.

"Bitch? Crazy?" Andrea repeated, trying her best to get to Alexis. Christopher grabbed her and refused to let her go, but she refused to stop trying to escape his grasp. She was intent on making that woman bleed. Even the girls' screams wouldn't stop her charge. "Stay right there. I'm 'bout to show you crazy!"

"Shit!" Darnell exclaimed. "Girls, hurry up and get upstairs! Chris, get the damn knife out your wife's hand! This shit is gettin' way outta hand."

Byron jumped up and helped his brother pry the knife from Andrea's hand. Christopher finally twisted her wrist enough to get her to drop it, but not before receiving a cut across his hand.

"Shit!" he shouted, storming into the kitchen.

Byron picked up the knife and watched Christopher wash the blood from his hand, while the rest of the adults looked on in horror. Jamar tugged on Alexis to get her to leave, but she seemed transfixed by the strange, but scary scene.

"Daddy!" Latrise shouted while running back to the kitchen. The protective heart of a child. She'd seen the knife as it sliced his hand, but she wasn't prepared to see all the blood mixed with tap water in the sink. She screamed and fell on the floor, hyperventilating.

The sight of her daughter curled up on the floor and unable to talk was too much for Andrea. At this point, nothing was more important than being there for her child. She ran into the kitchen, dropped to her knees, and cradled the child's head on her lap.

"Trisey! Trisey!"

"Da, Ma, Da, Ma!" the poor girl panted.

"What's wrong with her?" Byron shouted. "What's going on?"

"Cousin Alexis, help her!" Elizabeth yelled.

"Shit! Y'all move out the way and give the girl some air!" Alexis demanded, pushing everyone out of the way. She stood over Andrea. "That means you, too, Dee."

Andrea shook her head. "I'm not leaving my child."

"Ma," Latrise panted again. "Ch-ch-ch . . ."

Alexis knelt down and looked Andrea in the eyes. "Andrea, I know you love your daughter, but you won't do her any good if you smother her like this. I am a doctor. Let me help you. You can go back to hating me later."

Andrea stared at Alexis. Should she trust her? Yet, when she looked into her daughter's glassy eyes and saw her holding her chest, she knew she had no choice. She had to trust Alexis. She backed away and laid Latrise's head gently on the floor.

"Someone grab a pillow so I can elevate her head," Alexis ordered.

Jamar disappeared into the living room and returned with a golden-yellow throw pillow, which Alexis quickly placed under Latrise's head.

Brenda, taking a cue from her cousin, quickly walked into the kitchen and began tending to Christopher. She found a dish towel and instructed him to hold it tightly on the cut to help stop the blood flow. She turned to Darnell and put him to work.

"Baby, look under the sink in the bathroom upstairs. I think I saw a first-aid kit there."

"Yeah, it's there," Christopher confirmed, wincing from the sting traveling from his hand to his wrist. "We bought it right before you came."

"I'll find it," Darnell said, heading up the steps. "You wanna come help me find it, Lizzie?"

Elizabeth looked up and nodded sadly. After taking one more look at her friend, she stood up from the floor and walked to her father's waiting hand.

"Looks like it's just superficial," Brenda told Christopher. "It should heal pretty quickly, but you might have a scar."

"I can live with that," he replied, his eyes fixed on his daughter. "She gonna be all right?"

Alexis didn't bother answering. Her attention remained focused on her patient.

"Byron, get a dish towel or something, wet it with some cold water, and give it to me," she instructed. "Not too cold, though."

Byron did what he was told, as well. Alexis applied the cool compress to the child's hot forehead and then encouraged her to breathe slowly.

"Here's the kit," Darnell announced, running down the steps. He carefully stepped around Alexis and Latrise and handed the kit to his wife. "I got Lizzie to lie down for a bit. All this was way too much for her."

"Shoot, it's too much for *me*," Brenda whispered. She then turned back to Christopher and began wrapping his hand.

"Does your chest still hurt, sweetie?" Alexis asked Latrise.

Latrise, too exhausted to speak, could only nod slowly.

"You're going be fine," Alexis told her. "You just had a little scare. You'll be back to playing your Wii. Your mom and dad are right here, and they're fine."

"What can I do?" Andrea asked, her face wet with tears and sweat.

Latrise's heavy panting had slowed, but she still didn't look good. The poor girl looked to Andrea like she had just run a marathon. Her body lay limp as her listless chest and shoulders went up and down with each breath.

"Just reassure her. Let her know everything's gonna be all right," Alexis said without looking up.

Andrea watched Alexis with a new respect as she tended to Latrise. Her careful hands and serious demeanor had turned a hyperventilating patient into a whimpering, but healthy little girl who wanted nothing but to curl up into her mother's arms.

"She's fine," Alexis told Andrea. She took away the compress and asked Byron to wet it again with slightly cooler water. He complied once again. She replaced the cloth on the girl's forehead and explained, "She just had a panic attack. All the drama tonight was bad enough, but seeing Chris bleed like that sent her over the edge. It probably didn't help much that he got cut taking that knife from you."

"I thought she was having a heart attack," Andrea said, staring into space. She looked up at her husband, who was busy flexing his fingers to keep the circulation going in his hand. The sight of the fresh bandage slapped at Andrea like a disapproving Southern grandmother. The tears came instantly. "I'm so sorry, baby. I can't believe I flipped out like that. Trying to get to her, and I managed to hurt my own family."

"Yeah, well . . . ," Alexis said, attempting to stand. She'd been kneeling so long that her thighs had locked. Jamar and Darnell grabbed each arm to assist her. "Like I said, she'll be fine. I'm guessing she's never had a panic attack before?"

"No, this is the first time," Christopher said, walking into the dining room.

He took a seat next to Byron and placed a reassuring hand on Andrea's shoulder. She leaned her head over and let her cheek touch his hand. He might be mad, but the touch told her that he wasn't leaving. She had married a stronger man than she had originally thought.

"Does she need to go to the hospital?" Christopher asked.

"No. If this is an isolated incident, there shouldn't be anything to worry about," Alexis replied. "However, I would suggest that she talk with somebody about what she experienced tonight. Bren, you might want to do the same thing for Lizzie."

"I plan on it," Brenda agreed, leaning on the kitchen counter.

"I'll think about it," Andrea said. Although she wanted her daughter to get the help she needed, she already felt embarrassed at the thought of her daughter telling some stranger that she'd seen her knife-wielding mother cut her father. *It's not about me,* she reminded herself.

"Jamar, baby, please, let's go," Alexis pleaded. "We have definitely overstayed our welcome. My job here is done."

"Alexis, wait," Andrea called. She left Latrise, who had drifted off to sleep while lying on the floor, and walked over to the couple she had once hated. "Thank you for helping my daughter. I've never seen you in action before. You really know what you're doing."

Alexis raised her eyebrows. "There's no need to thank me. Despite how we might feel about each other, I'm still a doctor. Besides, I didn't do all that much."

"Yeah, but with everybody panicking, it was good to see you work with a clear head," Christopher added.

"Yeah, um, good lookin' out," Byron stuttered.

Andrea could tell those few words took a lot out of him. Saying something nice to a woman he'd just finished cursing out wasn't something he was used to.

"I think what we're trying to say is we're sorry," Andrea said softly.

Alexis rolled her eyes slowly and shook her head. "A few minutes ago, Byron was calling me every kind of bitch known to man, and you tried to stab me. Now, when I do what I do every day, you want to kiss my ass? Y'all can keep that. I told you already. I'm a doctor, and a damn good one. You think I would let your daughter, or any child, for that matter, suffer because of how I feel about her family? Keep your apology. Let's go, Jamar."

They turned to leave, but before they could get halfway to the door, Brenda ran out of the kitchen and called out to them. "Alexis, you can't leave like this."

Alexis turned and glared at her cousin. "Brenda, please don't start with that Miss Fix-It stuff right now. She didn't accept my apology earlier, and now I'm not accepting hers. We're even."

"If that's the way you feel," Andrea mumbled, turning away from her.

Brenda emerged from the kitchen and stood in front of the crowd. She regarded them angrily, and Andrea knew a speech was sure to follow.

"Chris, why don't you take your baby to her room?" Brenda said. The statement sounded more like a demand than a suggestion, but who was he to refuse? His child was lying on the floor, after all. He gingerly picked her up and carried her upstairs.

Brenda paced the floor, mumbling to herself, as she waited for Christopher to return. She looked up and noticed that Jamar, Alexis, and Darnell were still standing there. "Find a seat."

The three scattered, reminding Andrea of her students when she was in a bad mood. Jamar and Alexis reluctantly joined Byron at the dining room table, while Andrea took the chair Christopher had once occupied. Darnell opted to lean against the wall. Andrea figured it was fair. The impending lecture wasn't directed at him, anyway.

"Brenda, sweetie, I know you mean well, but this just might be something you can't fix," Andrea said.

Brenda turned to her with her arms folded. The stern look on her face nearly made Andrea recoil. "You think that's what this is about?"

"Well, yes. That's what you do. We love you for it, but it's obvious that your cousin and I will never get along," Andrea replied.

"That's only because you refuse to see past the young girl I was back in the day," Alexis broke in. "All you see is the chick who slept with your husband when I was in college. Why can't you believe I've grown up since then?"

"I just apologized to you, didn't I?" Andrea challenged. "Okay, you're a good doctor, and you have matured a little. But do you know what it's truly like to suffer? You survived a couple of hurricanes, but you haven't truly suffered. You got pregnant by my husband, had an abortion, and just as quickly went back to school and went on with your life. You lost your fiancé. A year later, you go out and get another one. You quit your job. So what? You go and open your own practice. Another hurricane threatens the city. So what? While other folks are worried about whether they'll have a place to return to, you and your man go on vacation and go wedding dress shopping. Queen Alexis. Your charmed life continues."

"This is stupid," Alexis said, rising from the table. "Jamar, can we go now?"

"Sit, Alexis!" Brenda shouted, shocking her cousin into obedience. She turned to Andrea. "Andrea, you might see her glory, but you don't know her story."

"I know her daddy died," Andrea said, waving her hand. "She still seemed to rise from the ashes."

"Andrea, do me a favor," Alexis said. "Don't talk about my daddy. You didn't know him, and you don't know me well enough to say shit about him."

Andrea blinked and looked away. What was the big deal? Everyone knew Alexis's father died in a car crash before she was born. The sound of rapid footsteps caused her to look up just in time to see her husband coming back downstairs. *Good.* She needed him right now.

Christopher got to the bottom of the steps and looked around. Six sullen faces. He might have done better by staying upstairs and watching the girls sleep, but he was here now. He might as well stay and get it over with.

"Andrea, do you really think I've had it easy all my life?" Alexis asked.

"I just think you've never had to suffer the consequences of your actions, that's all," Andrea replied. "It's fine, though. I'm moving on from that."

"Dee, you really shouldn't assume things," Brenda said. "You've been in this world long enough to know that."

"Should we go in another room so y'all can talk?" Byron asked, fidgeting in his chair.

"No, you men all contributed in one way or another to this situation," Brenda told him. "Especially you,

Byron. What were you thinking, getting all up in my cousin's face like that? With all the family she has in this house, did you really think you would get away with that? You wouldn't have had to just worry about Jamar."

"You know what that was about," Byron replied, looking at everyone, but no one in particular. "Last week I was about to marry the mother of my unborn child. Things were cool. Now the wedding is off, my woman turned out to be crazy as shit, and I might not ever see my child."

"Did you try calling her?" Christopher asked.

"Man, I can't talk to her right now."

"Yet and still, Byron," Jamar broke in, "that didn't give you the right to get all in Alexis's face. Just like you woulda done anything for Rayna, I will do what I have to do to protect mine. I know Alexis ain't perfect, and I told her about herself when she blew your little secret up, but I accept my woman, flaws and all."

"That's some beautiful shit," Byron said, "but with all due respect, you didn't know her when she blew into town back in the day."

"And you didn't, either," Darnell said. "All you knew was this little girl messing around with your brother. Do you know how far she's come since then?"

"No, and I don't wanna know," Byron retorted. He leaned back and folded his arms.

"See, Brenda?" Alexis said. "This is the shit I'm talking about. They don't want to see me as any different. To them, I'll always be your spoiled twenty-year-old cousin." She turned to Byron and Andrea. "For your fuckin' information, my mother was a single parent who raised me. We couldn't afford little extras, like snacks and parties. I had to work for what I wanted, and when I didn't want to work anymore, yes, I did use my looks to get ahead. But you know what? I grew the hell up!

"Yes, I had an abortion in college. You know why? Because I couldn't see paying my momma back like that after all she had sacrificed for me! Chris, I know what I told you in that letter when I asked for the abortion money, but my decision was all about my momma. And, Andrea, you think I've never suffered the consequences of my actions? I can never have a fuckin' child again because of that abortion!"

Christopher stiffened. Although he knew her infertility wasn't exactly his fault, he couldn't help but feel responsible. A couple of weeks of selfish pleasure had stopped a young woman from ever having children. *Wow!* He looked down at Andrea, who looked like she was fighting a losing battle against tears that were determined to fall. He squeezed her shoulder with his good hand.

"That right there would be enough for most women to go into a depression," Brenda told Andrea, "but it just motivated Alexis to do better. That's why she became a pediatrician. And you think she only dates professional men? She only *knows* professional men. She surrounds herself with like-minded people so she's less likely to repeat the mistakes she made in her youth. And that practice? How do you turn a profit when the very people you're helping can't afford to pay? So be careful when you judge. All that glitters ain't gold."

Brenda unfolded her arms and put her hands on her hips. "Chris and Andrea, when is the last time you two went to church?"

They looked at each other and then back at Brenda. It was obvious neither of them could remember.

"That's a doggone shame, but I know why," Brenda said. "Andrea, you have let hate and anger consume you so much that you can't think of anything else. You've spent so long hating Alexis for moving on with her life. It's like you're carrying a one-hundred-forty-pound person everywhere you go—"

"Excuse me," Alexis interrupted. "I'm one-thirty-five, thank you very much!"

"Shut up, Alexis!" Brenda snapped.

A couple of people in the group snickered, making Christopher grateful for the light moment.

Brenda turned back to her friend. "That hate has drawn you further and further away from God, when you should have been drawing nearer to Him. It's a shame, because your husband is still a new babe in Christ, but your anger has stopped you both from growing. Had the cut been worse, his blood would have been on *your* hands!"

Damn, that's deep, Christopher thought. All that time, he had figured that watching Creflo Dollar on TV would be enough. It was better than having to get up and get dressed on his only day off. He'd grown accustomed to not pushing the issue when Andrea said she didn't feel like going. He should have known there was a deeper reason. She used to go to church every Sunday and Bible study on occasion. Now it was nothing.

Andrea opened her mouth but quickly shut it again. What could she say?

"Do you remember what the Bible says about forgiveness? In the eleventh chapter of Mark, Jesus teaches us that if we want our Father to forgive us, we must forgive each other. And in Luke, He talks about a woman whose sins were many, but they were forgiven because she loved much. Those who forgive little have little love.

"When you carry around this anger and hate, you are not being the woman God has created you to be.

Then you start bringing down those around you. Look around. Your husband's not going to church. Your brother-in-law is stewing in his own misery, and the strongest Christian he knows—you—hasn't given him any encouragement. You haven't even demonstrated to him the power of prayer, because you haven't even prayed yourself!"

"But don't I have a right to be mad?" Andrea challenged.

"Dee, you had a right to be mad almost twenty years ago," Brenda replied. "You even had a right to be mad when Alexis went off in the restaurant the other night. But you've got to learn to move on. You can't keep reminding yourself that you're mad, who you're mad at, and why you're mad, because that person you're expending all that energy on is living her life. You might as well go on and live yours. Besides, Ephesians four and six tell us to be angry, but do not sin. It's okay to be angry, but it's how you respond to that anger that causes sin. Look at what it's done so far."

"Wow, Brenda," Jamar said. "You're right. I was about to go back home and turn over every rock I could to find out who was dabbling in my credit. When I found them, I was gonna kill their ass." Andrea bit her lip and nervously shifted her eyes. "But you know what? I may never find out who did this. The important part is my finances got restored. If the banks know who did it, then so be it, but I'm not going to dwell on it."

"Your credit cards are working again?" Darnell asked.

"Yeah, that's what I was about to say earlier," Jamar replied. "When I had to give up those extra ends, I figured I would check my ATM card just for the hell of it. All my money was there! I started calling my credit card companies on the way here. All my credit cards had been reactivated, and the balances were the same. It was the strangest thing."

"Thank God for that!" Brenda exclaimed as everyone patted Jamar on the back. "See, y'all? That's how God works! When man says no, God says yes. He's still, and always will be, in the miracle-working business."

"I guess it was a computer glitch, after all," Darnell said, shaking Jamar's hand.

"Either that or somebody out there has some skills with a computer," Jamar replied. "Either way, I'm gonna be a whole lot more careful with my finances. This whole mess has taught me some serious lessons about watching my money. Who knows how long somebody had been messing with my accounts?"

Andrea exhaled. Maybe she was in the clear. Maybe no one would find out her role in the whole situation. She would have to call Tina later to get an update. Although she'd vowed to be honest with Christopher from now on, this would be one secret she'd have to take to the grave.

"Yeah, so that's one less thing on our minds," Alexis said. She glanced at her cousin and quickly added, "Thank God."

"Glad to hear that," Christopher said. He walked to the window and peeked through the blinds. "The rain has slacked up, but it's almost midnight. Y'all sure you still wanna get on the road tonight?"

"We'll be fine," Jamar assured him. "All this craziness tonight will give us a lot to talk about for the next few hours. Plus, we have our own issues to discuss."

Alexis looked away, an action that didn't go unnoticed by Andrea. Could there be trouble in paradise, after all? Andrea shook her head. There was no need to concern herself with that. Besides, Brenda had made a lot of sense.

"Um, Alexis," Andrea stammered. "For real, I'm sorry about the way things went down tonight. Actually, I'm sorry about a lot of things."

Alexis nodded. "I hear you. I have some apologizing to do, too."

"I mean, I don't know if we'll ever be friends, but we don't have to carry this stuff with us."

"That's what I'm saying. I don't want to carry it. I carried it for a long time, too. I really feel bad about what I caused in your marriage. I just want to move on."

Andrea wiped away a stray tear. "Me too."

"That's all I ask of you, ladies," Brenda said. "Move forward. Don't let the past determine your present. You're both better than that."

"You guys had really better get on the road," Darnell broke in. "You have a long drive ahead of you, and we have some talking here we need to do."

"You're right," Jamar said. He turned to Alexis. "You ready?"

"Yeah," she mumbled. She then looked over at Byron, who remained seated at the table. "And for what it's worth, Byron, I am sorry about how things went down between you and Rayna. I hope y'all work it out."

Byron nodded silently, but Andrea couldn't expect much else. She'd continue to pray for him, but she also had a lot of praying to do for herself. As Alexis and Jamar headed for the door, she knew she'd have a lot of cleaning to do, and she didn't just mean her home.

Chapter 27

Reggie stood in the back doorway and watched as Janet read a book while sitting at the patio table. A sad cloud remained over her head. However, her countenance showed signs of acceptance. She never fought him on the breakup, but she never asked about the ticket home he was supposed to give her. Was she willing to get back together or not?

"Feeling guilty?" Shirley asked from behind.

He shook his head. "Nothing to feel guilty about. You always told me I rushed into relationships. I'm trying not to do that this time, but she can't understand that."

"You talk to her about that?"

"I tried, but she accused me of still wanting to be with Nikki."

"Do you?"

Reggie looked back at his mother and smirked. "Ma, you know better than that. I would never go back down that road again."

Shirley exhaled, as if her son had just eased her deepest fear. She rested herself on her armchair. "I hope not. You know I never did like that girl."

He laughed. "I know."

"So whatcha gonna do about that girl out there? She seems like she really loves you. And I'm 'bout tired of you two sulking around my house. You're bringing down my high."

He laughed again. "Momma, what high are you on?"

She smiled. "High on life."

As they laughed with each other, "Gold Digger" sounded from his cell phone. He quickly hit TALK, wanting to kick himself for not changing that ringtone yet.

"What's up, Nikki?"

"Speak of the devil," Shirley muttered, then stood and walked upstairs.

"I just wanted to let you know I'm back in New Orleans," Nikki said.

"Oh yeah? When did that happen?"

"I just got here this morning. Tired of the beach. Too much drama."

Reggie chuckled. "I guess you saw Jamar and Alexis out there, huh?"

"Don't even mention those two names to me right now. I have enough problems."

"I'm kidding," he said, still smiling. "Alexis told me she talked to you."

"Yeah? Did she tell you about how she tried to accuse me of shit?"

"She did, but believe it or not, I took up for you."

"What? To what do I owe that minor miracle?"

"Nikki, we were married for more than ten years. If I know anything, I know you're not a criminal."

She grew silent for a minute.

"You still there?" Reggie asked. He pulled the phone from his ear to make sure they hadn't been disconnected.

"I'm here," she replied. Her voice had lost some of its joy. "I appreciate you taking up for me, but can you keep a secret?"

He frowned and braced himself for the worst. "Please tell me you didn't have anything to do with that."

"No, I promise I didn't," she said quickly. "But I know who did."

"Who?"

"I'd rather not say, but when he told me what he'd done, I fuckin' lost it. I told him that I would be the first person they would blame, and I was right."

"Damn. That's messed up."

"Yeah, well, he called me back late yesterday evening and told me that he called the whole thing off."

"That's good. So dude got his money back?"

"Yeah."

Reggie squinted his eyes and looked back to make sure Janet was still outside. She was. He turned back to the phone. "Why are you telling me this? You know Alexis and I are still friends."

"I don't know," Nikki said. "I guess I just needed someone to tell. Now that I know you know what happened, I figure you're the only one I can talk to about this. Since you took up for me, I'm guessing I'm not all bad in your eyes. But believe me when I say I had nothing, absolutely nothing, to do with this."

"I believe you," he replied, nodding. "Thanks for telling me. There might be hope yet for us getting along."

Nikki giggled. "Maybe. So when are you and your little girlfriend coming back?"

He looked back outside. "Maybe tomorrow. I want to be home to watch the Saints play. And I don't think Janet will be my *little girlfriend* for long."

"Why? Did something happen?"

"She just can't seem to understand that I'm not ready to run back down the aisle," he explained. "The ink isn't all that dry on our divorce papers yet."

"That's bullshit, Reg," Nikki challenged. "I know you well enough to know that you're a hopeless romantic. That kinda thinking got you in trouble with me, but it's obviously what hooked your girl."

"Still, that doesn't mean I have to marry her right now."

"I'm not saying you should, but if you like her half as much as she seems to like you, you better do what you can to keep her. Let her know you see marriage in the future, but not right now."

Could Reggie be hearing his former wife correctly? Was she actually giving him relationship advice?

"Listen to you trying to sound like Dr. Ruth or somebody."

Nikki laughed. "No, because I'm not giving you sex advice."

"Okay, you got me. Well, lemme get off this phone. I gotta pick up Shawn from his friend Marcus's house, and then we've got to get ready to get outta here tomorrow. You know Momma's cookin' big for us tonight."

"Well, take care of your business," Nikki replied. "I'll be busy cleaning out my refrigerator. It stinks like shit up in here."

They both laughed.

"Have you been watching the election coverage?" Nikki asked.

"Ain't paid much attention since Obama accepted the Democratic nomination."

"You need to start watching again. McCain picked this crazy-ass, squeaky-voiced woman to be his running mate the other day. I guess they figured since Hillary's not running, they could pick up the female vote."

"She got your vote?"

"Hell naw! Come November, I'm gonna have a fine-ass black man as a president!"

They laughed again.

Same ole Nikki. She would never change, he thought. "Girl, go finish cleaning. I'll have Shawn call you tonight."

"All right. Good talkin' with you."

"You know what, Nikki? It was good talking with you, too."

He hit END on the phone and sat down, trying to think of his game plan. There was no use throwing away his relationship, but they had to get a few things straight. As he sat and thought, Janet walked in.

She cut her eyes at him and continued walking, seemingly determined not to get into another fight. He couldn't blame her. He had been ignoring her for the past couple of days.

"Hey, Janet," he called.

When she looked his way, he patted the sofa next to him and asked her to sit down. She hesitated at first but relented. Her demeanor was stiff. With her arms folded, she sat as far away from him on the sofa as she possibly could without moving to another seat.

"Whatcha gotta say?" she asked.

He smiled sheepishly at her. "You still love me?"

Janet didn't find the gesture cute. "Don't play with me. What do you want?"

"I want you."

"You certainly don't act like it."

He sighed, dropping the cute role. It wasn't working, anyway. "Janet, I care about you, but I've been through way too much to get married right now."

"I'm not trying to marry you right now," she countered. "I just want to know that you take what we have seriously. But, instead of talking about it, you avoid me. Then, the other day, you practically kicked me out your house. How is that supposed to make me feel?"

"Yeah, that was wrong," he agreed. "Still, you can't throw your venom at me without expecting me to strike back. You're my girl, but I have feelings, too."

Janet nodded, considering Reggie's words. He wondered if he was getting through to her. She then looked at him, locking in his dark brown eyes. "Do you love me?"

He sighed. He knew that question was coming, but was he ready to answer it?

Janet shook her head and got up. "I didn't think so."

"Wait!" he exclaimed, grabbing her hand. He pulled her back toward him and coaxed her to sit on his lap. "Janet, I do love you. You make me feel better than I've felt in a long time. But can we love each other without rushing down the aisle?"

"Reggie, I have an aunt who's been in a relationship with a man for sixteen years, and he's no closer to marrying her now than he was when he met her. Whenever she brings up the subject, he starts talking about something else, or he starts an argument and the subject gets dropped. They have kids and everything. I don't want that to happen to me."

"That's not going to happen to you," Reggie assured her. "Rushing into marriage isn't going to make either of us happy, though. If you wait until we're both ready, until DeShawn gets more used to having you around, until I get used to having Nikki out of my life, then maybe we can look at that. Unfortunately, you caught me at the wrong time, but I'm not running."

She smiled. "I know. That's why I want to be with you."

"I want to be with you, too, but we'll be a lot happier and a lot stronger if we're patient. Can you do that for me?"

She nodded. He hugged her. They kissed.

"I'm glad you two settled your differences," Shirley announced, coming down the steps. "I was just telling Reggie y'all little attitudes were workin' my last nerve."

They laughed.

"Don't worry, Ma," Reggie said. Janet stood up and allowed him to stand. "We won't mess up your high again."

"Good. Now, go get your son so we can eat."

Epilogue

The night of November 4, 2008, found everyone glued to the television at the White household. No matter the result, this election would make history. Either the United States would have its first African American president, or it would have its first female vice president. Alexis prayed it would be the former.

Senator Barack Obama held a sizable lead, carrying states that only four years earlier were loyal to the Republican Party. Even Florida, the incumbent president's brother's state, had changed party ties and had voted for Obama. It was a sure thing that the nation would elect its first African American president.

Yet that didn't stop Mary White from worrying. She remembered Jessie Jackson's failed attempt at becoming president in 1984, and she even remembered Shirley Chisholm's uneventful run in 1972. Had the country really come far enough to consider having a black president?

Maybe it had. Obama led the polls with women voters, with men, and with nearly every age group. Yet he didn't carry their state of Louisiana, which disappointed Jamar.

"As much as we've been through as a state, why would our folks continue to vote Republican?" he ranted. "Our folks had better wake up!"

Darnell agreed. Although most military personnel traditionally voted Republican, he felt that it was a Republican president with a personal score to settle that had gotten the nation stuck in two major wars. Many of his friends in all four of the major services had been killed in Iraq and Afghanistan, so even if Porky Pig were running on a platform of pulling the troops out of combat, he was going to vote for him. He just thanked God that the man vowing to pull them out was an intelligent, articulate black man.

The results were in.

"It's official, ladies and gentlemen," announced the reporter. "With three hundred and sixty-five electoral votes, Senator Barack Obama has been elected the forty-fourth president of the United States."

Everyone stood and cheered. Mary cried, repeating "Thank God" over and over.

Frank stood in a trance. "I never thought I would live to see the day," he said. A tear traced the contour of his right cheek. "My God."

"Roman, how does it feel to watch history?" Alexis asked her brother.

"That's what's up," he said nonchalantly. "I knew the brother would win."

"You just don't understand what this means," Jamar told him. "This country has changed. Black people didn't do this by ourselves. White folks had to vote for him in order for him to get in."

"That's true," Darnell agreed. "We only make up about twenty-something percent of this country. Even if every black person in America had voted for him, he wouldn't have gotten in without the white vote. That's truly change you can believe in."

"Listen to y'all," Roman said with a laugh. "Y'all already got brainwashed by that 'change' platform. I'll believe in the change when I start seeing it."

"It's not gonna happen right away," Alexis told him, "but it's gonna happen. He has a strong First Lady behind him to make it happen, too."

"And a crazy-ass vice president," Jamar added.

Everyone laughed, but the gravity of the event was missed by no one. Alexis walked over and hugged her mother and her stepfather at the same time. She knew they had just seen what many thought was impossible. For them, Dr. King's dream had come true. Medgar Evers hadn't died for nothing. The children who were beaten and jailed in the sixties, Frank being one of them, hadn't come forward in vain.

"What a way to end the year," Brenda commented as she hugged her husband. When her cell phone vibrated in her pocket, she happily pulled it out and hit TALK. "Obama headquarters!"

"Did you see it?" Andrea yelled into the phone. "We have a black president!"

"Yes!" Brenda shouted back. She could hear Christopher and Byron celebrating in the background. "You guys sound like you're having a blast."

"We are. Even Rayna's over here celebrating."

"Rayna?" Brenda asked, her eyes wide. "They got back together?"

"No, but she was by herself, so Byron told her to come over," Andrea explained. "She's starting to show big-time now, so they're trying to get along for the baby's sake."

"Well, that's good. What about Obama, though? Girl, this is the proudest day in my life!"

"Church is gonna be good Sunday!" Andrea said. "Pastor was just saying Sunday that we all needed to get out and vote. It was too important not to."

"He was right about that," Brenda agreed. "Girl, lemme go so I can hear our new president's speech."

"Okay, tell Jamar and Alexis we said hi."

As soon as Brenda hung up, Alexis's phone rang. "Hello?"

"Congratulations on having a black president," Reggie announced.

Alexis laughed. "We are partying big over here."

"I can imagine. Janet, DeShawn, and I are at my boy Levi's house. I'll bet nobody's having an election party like this one. Drinks are flowing over here. Levi created one called the Barack Special. These fools even started playing the 'Cupid Shuffle' when they announced the results!"

Alexis laughed so hard, she nearly dropped the phone. "You football players sure know how to party."

"It's going to be a good year," Reggie said. "Got a black president, I started my commentator job, Shawn's doing good in school, and Nikki and I are actually getting along. Don't say anything, but if things keep going like this, I might ask Janet to marry me next year."

"That's good," Alexis replied. "Jamar and I are just about done with the wedding plans. We're still set for March."

"Am I invited?"

"Lemme see." She placed the phone on her shoulder and turned to Jamar, who was in the kitchen, fixing a drink. "Jamar, Reggie wants to know if he's invited to the wedding."

"Yeah, as long as that ni—uh, brother, doesn't try to steal my woman again."

Alexis smiled and turned back to the phone. "He said, 'Of course you're invited.'"

Everyone burst out laughing, including Reggie. "I heard what he said, but tell him that he ain't got nothing to worry about. I got what I want right here."

She laughed again and bid him good-bye. Then she looked around the room at her family. She didn't have everything she wanted, but she thanked God that she had everything she needed.

It was funny. She had never wanted to go back to Virginia Beach, but something valuable had come of it. By visiting her past, she had improved her future. She and Andrea had finally made peace, and Byron had agreed to leave the past in the past and move forward.

Since their return from Virginia Beach, she and Jamar had grown closer. Their conversation in the car on the way home had gotten tense at times. Still, it helped them to understand each other. They now knew how to approach each other, and to leave one another alone when one of them needed space.

They had even begun going to church with Jamar's parents. They hadn't become hard-core Christians yet, but a relationship with God was definitely forming.

She'd also learned to appreciate her infertility. She couldn't have children, but look at the countless children who depended on her each day. Her own little cousin Elizabeth thought the world of her. That was what really mattered. What you had, not what you wished you had.

"You know what?" Mary said finally. "Let's start planning Thanksgiving. After that hurricane and this election, we have a lot to be thankful for."

Alexis smiled. It was like her mother had read her mind. "That's true, more than you know, Momma."

RHONDA M. LAWSON

Rhonda M. Lawson is the award-winning author of *Cheatin' in the Next Room, A Dead Rose* and, most recently, *Putting It Back Together*. She is also an army journalist, garnering various journalism awards, including the 1997 Training and Doctrine Command Journalist of the Year. She is a sergeant first class stationed at Fort Stewart, Georgia, where she works in Army Public Affairs, and she just recently returned from Iraq, where she was deployed in support of Operation New Dawn. Perhaps even more impressive than her seventeen-year career as a soldier is the proud role she plays as a single mother of a young daughter.

Without any thoughts of publication, Rhonda began writing when she was twelve. "I just knew I loved to write," she says. "Today I still write purely for the love of it." Unlike some authors, who emphasize entertainment over content, she readily acknowledges that she has something to say and is doing so via her writing: "I want to touch people with my stories. All my books are entertaining but have a message." That message has not been lost on Rhonda's readers, who write to her about how they identify with her characters and their situations. "This is why I write," Rhonda says. "And this is why I say I write *real* fiction for *real* people."

Rhonda's journalism career began at Loyola University in her native New Orleans, Louisiana, where she served a short stint on the campus newspaper. When she left college and joined the army in 1994, she continued her journalism career. Her first duty station was Fort Knox, Kentucky, where she edited all sections of *Inside the Turret,* the post newspaper. During this tour, she earned awards for both her commentary and feature writing.

In 1997 she moved to Fort Story, Virginia, and served as Fort Story bureau chief for the *Fort Eustis Wheel* newspaper. Named Journalist of the Year and Noncommissioned Officer of the Quarter, she began pursuing her first love, fiction, and started working on her first full-length novel, *Cheatin' in the Next Room*. Rhonda's career as a soldier-journalist has taken her to various parts of the world, including Japan, Hawaii, Korea, Afghanistan, and Egypt. Her work has appeared stateside in various army and civilian publications, including *Soldiers* magazine, the *Seattle Times*, and the *Army Times*.

An active member of Zeta Phi Beta Sorority, Inc.–Chi Pi Zeta Chapter, Rhonda holds a bachelor of arts degree in communication studies from the University of Maryland University College and a master's in human relations from the University of Oklahoma. She is also a member of the Divine Literary Tour, an organization made up of authors who are members of African American fraternities and sororities, and the U.S. Army's Sergeant Audie Murphy Club. She has contributed to seven different anthologies: *Second Chances, Crimes of*

About The Author

Passion, Gumbo for the Soul, The Heart of Our Community, Surfacing, Heart of a Military Woman, and the recently released *The Color of Strength: Embracing the Passion of Our Culture.*

Notes

Notes

Notes

ORDER FORM
URBAN BOOKS, LLC
78 E. Industry Ct
Deer Park, NY 11729

Name: (please print): _____

Address: _____

City/State: _____

Zip: _____

QTY	TITLES	PRICE
	16 On The Block	$14.95
	A Girl From Flint	$14.95
	A Pimp's Life	$14.95
	Baltimore Chronicles	$14.95
	Baltimore Chronicles 2	$14.95
	Betrayal	$14.95
	Black Diamond	$14.95
	Black Diamond 2	$14.95
	Black Friday	$14.95
	Both Sides Of The Fence	$14.95
	Both Sides Of The Fence 2	$14.95
	California Connection	$14.95

Shipping and handling-add $3.50 for 1st book, then $1.75 for each additional book.

Please send a check payable to:

Urban Books, LLC

Please allow 4-6 weeks for delivery

ORDER FORM
URBAN BOOKS, LLC
78 E. Industry Ct
Deer Park, NY 11729

Name:(please print):_____

Address: _____

City/State: _____

Zip: _____

QTY	TITLES	PRICE
	California Connection 2	$14.95
	Cheesecake And Teardrops	$14.95
	Congratulations	$14.95
	Crazy In Love	$14.95
	Cyber Case	$14.95
	Denim Diaries	$14.95
	Diary Of A Mad First Lady	$14.95
	Diary Of A Stalker	$14.95
	Diary Of A Street Diva	$14.95
	Diary Of A Young Girl	$14.95
	Dirty Money	$14.95
	Dirty To The Grave	$14.95

Shipping and handling-add $3.50 for 1st book, then $1.75 for each additional book.

Please send a check payable to:
   Urban Books, LLC
Please allow 4-6 weeks for delivery

ORDER FORM
URBAN BOOKS, LLC
78 E. Industry Ct
Deer Park, NY 11729

Name:(please print):_____

Address: _____

City/State: _____

Zip: _____

QTY	TITLES	PRICE
	Gunz And Roses	$14.95
	Happily Ever Now	$14.95
	Hell Has No Fury	$14.95
	Hush	$14.95
	If It Isn't love	$14.95
	Kiss Kiss Bang Bang	$14.95
	Last Breath	$14.95
	Little Black Girl Lost	$14.95
	Little Black Girl Lost 2	$14.95
	Little Black Girl Lost 3	$14.95
	Little Black Girl Lost 4	$14.95
	Little Black Girl Lost 5	$14.95

Shipping and handling-add $3.50 for 1st book, then $1.75 for each additional book.
Please send a check payable to:
Urban Books, LLC
Please allow 4-6 weeks for delivery

ORDER FORM
URBAN BOOKS, LLC
78 E. Industry Ct
Deer Park, NY 11729

Name: (please print):_____

Address: _____

City/State: _____

Zip: _____

QTY	TITLES	PRICE
	Loving Dasia	$14.95
	Material Girl	$14.95
	Moth To A Flame	$14.95
	Mr. High Maintenance	$14.95
	My Little Secret	$14.95
	Naughty	$14.95
	Naughty 2	$14.95
	Naughty 3	$14.95
	Queen Bee	$14.95
	Say It Ain't So	$14.95
	Snapped	$14.95
	Snow White	$14.95

Shipping and handling-add $3.50 for 1st book, then $1.75 for each additional book.
Please send a check payable to:
Urban Books, LLC
Please allow 4-6 weeks for delivery

ORDER FORM
URBAN BOOKS, LLC
78 E. Industry Ct
Deer Park, NY 11729

Name:(please print):_____

Address: _____

City/State: _____

Zip: _____

QTY	TITLES	PRICE
	Spoil Rotten	$14.95
	Supreme Clientele	$14.95
	The Cartel	$14.95
	The Cartel 2	$14.95
	The Cartel 3	$14.95
	The Dopefiend	$14.95
	The Dopeman Wife	$14.95
	The Prada Plan	$14.95
	The Prada Plan 2	$14.95
	Where There Is Smoke	$14.95
	Where There Is Smoke 2	$14.95

Shipping and handling-add $3.50 for 1st book, then $1.75 for each additional book.

Please send a check payable to:

Urban Books, LLC

Please allow 4-6 weeks for delivery